A SONG FOR A NEW DAY

"A lively and hopeful look at how community and music and life go on even in the middle of dark days and malevolent corporate shenanigans."

Kelly Link, Pulitzer Prize finalist and author of *Get In Trouble*

"Pinsker has written a wonderful epic about music, community, and rediscovering the things that make us human. Pinsker has an amazing ear for dialogue, a brilliant knack for describing music, and most importantly a profound awareness of silence, in both its positive and negative aspects."

Charlie Jane Anders, bestselling and award-winning author of *All the Birds in the Sky* and *The City in the Middle of the Night*

"Pinsker has one of the strongest voices for character in fiction today; everything her characters do is compelling. When I put the book down, I actually suffered from FOMO because I felt like the characters were continuing on their stories without me."

Mur Lafferty, author of *Six Wakes*

"Sarah Pinsker plays genre like a favorite guitar, and I am in awe of her talents. How can a writer so new be so central, so necessary?"

Andy Duncan, author of *An Agent of Utopia*

"*A Song for a New Day* is a compulsively readable story about music, freedom, taking chances, and living with your past. I meant to read it slowly, savoring Pinsker's near-future world-building and her perfect descriptions of performance, but I ended up gulping it down, so eager to see what happens."
Kij Johnson, author of *The Dream-Quest of Vellitt Boe*

"A full-throated call to arms in the service of music, creation, and shared experience, *A Song for a New Day* resists both extremes and easy tropes, offering hope in the face of catastrophe through the engrossing stories of characters you'll want to spend more time with. Pinsker gives us a future rooted in fully-drawn, believable characters and sensory, unflinching descriptions."
Malka Older, author of *Infomocracy*

"Let freedom ring in the growl of an angry guitar chord! Sarah Pinsker's *A Song for a New Day* is an absorbing tale of a quiet, all-too-believable American dystopia in which a passion for music becomes the secretive, surprising seed of rebellion."
Linda Nagata, Nebula Award–winning author of *The Last Good Man*

"At last, the answer to the question science fiction fans have been asking: YES, Sarah Pinsker can write a novel with all the energy and heart and wonderful wackiness that characterize her magnificent short stories. *A Song for a New Day* is a must-read from a new voice you won't forget."
Sam J. Miller, author of *Blackfish City*

"Woven through Pinsker's meticulously crafted future of technology-enabled isolation and corporate-consumerist powerlessness is a stirring anthem against the politics of fear. A dazzling tale told in multiple voices, with not a single note out of place. This is the lyrical protest song that we have always needed, perhaps more so now than ever."

Ken Liu, author of *The Grace of Kings*

"[A]n unsparing vision of a near-future world only a few degrees removed from our own, but has the nerve and audacity to leaven the darkness with hope. A powerful novel whose unforgettable characters channel humanity's true superpowers: art and the act of creation."

Elizabeth Hand, author of *Curious Toy* and *Generation Loss*

A SONG FOR A NEW DAY

SARAH PINSKER

An Ad Astra Book

First published in 2019 by Berkley, an imprint of Penguin Random House
First published in the UK in 2020 by Ad Astra, an imprint of Head of Zeus Ltd

1 3 5 7 9 8 6 4 2

ISBN (HB): 9781800243835
ISBN (XTPB): 9781800243842
ISBN (E): 9781800243866

Title page art: Music sound waves by Shutterstock/Liubou Yasiukovich
Book design by Elke Sigal

Printed and bound by CPI Group (UK) Ltd, Croydon, CR0 4YY

For everyone who plays music live and everyone who listens

And for Zu, who inspires all my songs

PART ONE

1

LUCE

172 Ways

There were, to my knowledge, one hundred and seventy-two ways to wreck a hotel room. We had brainstormed them all in the van over the last eight months on the road. As a game, I'd thought: 61, turn all the furniture upside down; 83, release a pack of feral cats; 92, fill all the drawers with beer, or, 93, marbles; 114, line the floor with soapy plastic and turn it into a slip 'n' slide; etc., etc.

In my absence, my band had come up with the one hundred and seventy-third, and had for the first time added in a test run. I was not proud.

What would Gemma do if she were here? I stepped all the way into their room instead of gawking from the hallway and closed the door before any hotel employees could walk past, pressing the button to illuminate the DO NOT DISTURB sign for good measure. "Dammit, guys. This is a nice hotel. What the hell did you do?"

"We found some paint." Hewitt's breath smelled like a distillery's dumpster. He lingered beside me in the vestibule.

"You're a master of understatement."

All their bags and instruments were crammed into the closet by the entrance. The room itself was painted a garish neon pink, which it definitely hadn't been when I'd left that morning. Not only the walls, either: the headboards, the nightstand, the dresser. The spatter on the carpet suggested somebody had knifed a Muppet and let it crawl away to die. For all the paint, Hewitt's breath was still the overwhelming odor.

"Even the TV?" I asked. "Really?"

The television, frame and screen. Cable news blared behind a drippy film of pink, discussing the new highway only for self-driving cars. We'd be avoiding that one.

JD lounged on the far bed, holding a glass of something caramel colored. His shoes were pink. The bedspread, the site of another Muppet murder.

"We considered doing an accent wall." He waved his glass at the wall behind the headboard.

April sat on the desk, sticks in hand, drumming a soundless tattoo in the air. "How was your day?" she asked, as if nothing was wrong.

"Excuse me a second." I ducked into the hall and fumbled for the keycard to the room I shared with April. Our room was quiet and empty and, most importantly, not pink. I leaned my guitar bag in a corner and let out a breath I hadn't known I was holding, then lay back on the bed and dialed Gemma.

"We're not supposed to be out here alone," I said when she picked up. "When are you coming back?"

She sighed. "Hi, Luce. My brother is fine, thanks for asking. The bullet went straight through him without hitting any organs."

"I heard! I'm glad he's okay! I'm sorry, I should have asked first. But do you think you're coming back soon?"

"No, I really don't. What's the matter? Do you need something?"

"A tour manager. A babysitter for these giant children you ditched me with, so I can concentrate on music instead of being the adult in the room when I'm younger than all of them. Never mind. I shouldn't have called, and I'm sorry I bothered you. I hope your brother gets well soon."

I disconnected. We should have been able to handle a few weeks on the road without a tour manager. Lots of bands did fine without one, but those were probably real bands, where everyone had a vested interest; I'd played solo until the label hired these so-called professionals to back me on tour.

Hewitt let me in again when I knocked. Inside the fridge, two large bottles had been crammed in sideways, gin and tequila. The painted minifridge left my fingertips pink and tacky. My prints made me complicit, I supposed. I pulled out the tequila and took a long slug straight from the bottle. Cheap, astringent stuff. No wonder they were chilling it. The armchair under the window was paint free, so I made my way to it with the tequila, trying not to touch anything else.

"Well, April," I began, answering her question as if I hadn't left, "since you asked, my day started at five this morning, with stops at two different TV morning shows. Then I did a radio call-in show. Then I spent two hours on the phone in a station parking lot arguing with the label about why we still don't have our new T-shirts. Then I did a couple of acoustic songs for a local music podcast, ate a highly mediocre burrito, and came back here to find you've been far more productive than me. I mean, why did I waste all that time promoting our show tomorrow night when I could have been helping you redecorate?"

They were all glare resistant; not even April had the decency to look uneasy. They knew I had the power to fire them if I wanted, but I wouldn't. We got along too well onstage.

It wasn't in me to maintain stern disinterest. "So where did you get the paint?"

April grinned. "We looked up where the nearest liquor store was, right? We had to run across the highway to get there, and there were, like, six lanes, and it was a little, uh, harrowing. So on the way back, we tried to find a better place to cross, like maybe there was a crosswalk somewhere, and then we passed this Superwally Daycare that had a room being redone and it was completely deserted, right? But the door was open, I guess to air it out."

A groan escaped me, and I took another chug of tequila. "You stole from a daycare?"

"A *Superwally* Daycare," said JD. "They won't be going broke on our account, I promise you. Anyway, we also went back out again to the actual Superwally and spent some money there that we wouldn't have spent otherwise, so it cancels out."

I was almost afraid to ask. "What else did you buy?"

"That's the best part." Hewitt flipped the light switch.

The room lit up. The pink television and the wall behind the headboard had been painted over with an alien-green glow-in-the-dark wash only visible with the lights off. On the wall backing the bathroom, our band logo: a sparking cannon. April's drumsticks glowed, too; if only they'd stuck to painting things they owned.

"I hope one of you pulled a Cheshire Cat, because I need somebody to punch in the teeth."

JD's voice came from beside me. "Like I said: we considered an accent wall, but then we decided against it."

I put the bottle to my mouth to keep myself from saying something I'd regret later. Dozed off for a second in the chair, then started awake when the lights came back on. April had disappeared, probably back to our room; JD was asleep on his bed; Hewitt was singing to himself in the bathroom. I might have rested my eyes for longer than I thought.

The tequila walloped me as I lurched to my feet. I tried to channel Gemma, our absent tour manager. She'd gone home three weeks before, after her brother was shot eating lunch at a mall. The label hadn't wanted us to keep touring without her, but I had promised we'd be fine. I shouldn't have called her earlier; this wasn't her fault. Anyway, even if she'd been here today, she'd have been driving with me, managing the promotional appearances so I could play the pure artist. The band would still have been left to their devices, though they'd probably have thought twice about pulling a stunt like this with her around to ream them out.

What would Gemma say? I channeled her to mutter, "If and when the hotel bills us for damages, it's coming out of your salaries. You shouldn't need a babysitter when I leave you alone for one single day. I'm supposed to be the artist here. If anybody is entitled to pull shit, it's me. You're supposed to be the professionals, dammit."

Neither of them responded, if they even heard. That was as far as I needed to take playing grown-up. It was the label's fault they hadn't sent a new tour manager, and the label's fault the band got stuck at a suburban hotel all day while I left with the van to do promotional work solo. My jealousy that they kept bonding and I kept getting left out was best tamped down.

I took their tequila with me and went next door. April lay on the far bed, her back to me, though I had a feeling she was pretending to sleep. The bed looked tempting, but my face broke out if I didn't scrub off my makeup, and I reeked of the podcaster's unfiltered cigarettes. I kicked my smoky clothes to the corner and stepped into the shower. Closed my eyes and let the water hit me. Shampooed my hair, eyes still closed.

I didn't immediately recognize the next sound. Like a school bell, except it kept on signaling. My hazy brain took more than a few seconds to declare it a fire alarm.

"Shit," April said, loud enough for me to hear over the shower. "What is that?"

I shut off the water and regretfully pulled my smoky clothes back onto my wet self. Ditched the underwear, stuffed the bra under my arm. Shoved my feet into my boots, sans socks. "Fire alarm. Though if those yahoos in the next room turn out to be the cause, we're leaving them here and moving on as a duo."

My backpack still lay at the foot of the bed. Wallet, phone, van keys, laptop, tour bible were all in there. I dropped the smoky bra into it, then slung backpack and guitar bag over my right shoulder. If we were talking real fire, those were the possessions I meant to keep.

April trailed me down the hallway, where a flashing light joined the clanging bell. We ran into the guys in the stairwell. JD was naked except for his boxer shorts, gig bag, and tattoos. Hewitt wore the hotel bathrobe, covered in paint; he hadn't grabbed his guitars.

One look told me neither of them had pulled the alarm. Other people joined us on the stairs, hurried but not panicked. They gave the guys a wide berth.

The stairs spilled us out into a side parking lot. A crowd already milled on the asphalt, watching the building. A few people sat in their cars, a better idea. A gust of cold wind hit me as I hit the pavement, plastering my wet clothes to my body.

"Get in the van," JD said. "Can't let our singer get sick running around with soapy hair."

"Says the bassist in boxers."

He shrugged, though goose bumps had risen on his arms and legs.

He, April, and I walked past the crowd to where I had parked the van in the brightest spot available when I got back an hour ago—had it only been an hour ago? I fumbled for the keys in my bag, and we piled in.

"Where'd Hewitt go?" I asked, turning on the van and cranking the heat. My suitcase was still in the room, along with any warm clothes I had with me.

"He hung back to figure out what was going on," JD said.

"So it wasn't you guys?"

"Ha-ha. You think we'd pull a stunt like that?"

"You do remember that an hour ago you were showing me a DIY hotel paint job, right?"

"That's different. It didn't hurt anybody. I'd never."

I could have pointed out they'd cause problems for whoever was responsible for cleaning their room after we checked out, or that they might hurt my relationship with the label. But I knew what he meant. Leave these guys too long and they'd get into some stupid human tricks, but they wouldn't have risked panicking sleeping kids. They wouldn't have wanted somebody tripping and falling down the stairs because of a prank. I was pretty sure. I'd only been playing with them for eight months now, but I thought I knew them at least that well.

The back door slid open and Hewitt climbed into the third row. "It's not a fire. Bomb threat."

JD frowned. "Maybe we should get out of here."

"We can't go," I said, giving him a look. "Most of our stuff is still upstairs. Besides, if it's a bomb threat, it'll look bad for us to leave, considering everyone in that stairwell was already giving you guys the side-eye."

JD wasn't calmed. "Shouldn't they be moving people farther from the building if they think there's a bomb? Or going through it with robots or dogs or something?"

Hewitt nodded. "They're waiting for a bomb team."

"Are bomb-sniffing dogs a thing?" April asked. "I thought they were just for drugs."

"There are definitely bomb-sniffing dogs," said JD. "Also bomb-sniffing bees and bomb-sniffing rats, but I think those are used in combat zones, not hotels."

A thought nagged at me. "Wait. Where are the fire trucks? Or the police? I thought I heard sirens, but they aren't here."

Hewitt shrugged. "Busy night, I guess."

We watched for a while. I guessed the people still standing in the parking lot hadn't thought to bring their keys out. A few parents juggled children from hip to hip. I leaned my head against the window and closed my eyes. The others did the same, except JD. He sat tapping a foot against the frame, hard enough to make the whole van shake.

"Will you stop?" April tossed an empty soda can at him. "Try to get some sleep."

That wasn't going to happen. I nudged him. "Grab your bass."

He cocked an eyebrow at me. "What?"

"Your bass. Come on."

I climbed into the backseat and returned a moment later with my little practice amp, the one I'd bought with babysitting money when I was fifteen, along with my crappy first guitar. It wasn't the best-sounding amp, but it would do for my purpose. About fifty cold, scared-looking people still stood in the parking lot, the ones who hadn't grabbed their keys or their wallets, who couldn't escape to their cars. If they were stuck, the least we could do was distract them for a little while.

JD found an outlet on the cement island by the parking lot's gate, and we both jacked our guitars. A couple of people reoriented themselves to watch us instead of the hotel.

"What are we playing?" JD asked.

"You pick," I said. "Something cheerful. Something that'll work even if they can't hear the vocals. 'Almost Home,' maybe?"

He didn't answer, but instead started playing the opening bass line. I followed with my guitar part, and then started to sing as loud as I could without straining my voice. I hadn't noticed April following us, but when the second verse started, a scratchy beat locked in with JD, and I glanced behind me to see she was playing a pizza box.

The parents brought their kids over—I imagined them grateful for any diversion at that point—and then others followed. The hotel must have appreciated the distraction, too, since they didn't stop us. The police might have taken issue with a two a.m. concert, but they still hadn't arrived.

We had the crowd now. When we played "Blood and Diamonds," a teenager said, "Mom! They're from SuperStream! They're famous!" My surge of pride accompanying that statement had gotten more familiar, but I still wasn't used to it. I'd never expected anyone to know my songs.

Hewitt had discarded the bathrobe somewhere. I made a mental note to make sure he found it again so we didn't get stuck paying, then remembered it was covered in paint, so we probably owned it now in any case. He danced in front of us wearing a kilt and a band sweatshirt. At least that way the crowd knew who was playing for them. If I were a better shill—if I didn't feel self-conscious doing it—I would have told them about our show the next night at the Peach.

We played eight songs before a haggard-looking hotel manager made his way to us. His upside-down name tag read "Efram Dawkins," and his hair was flat on one side. I wondered where he'd been sleeping.

"I'm sorry," he said.

"It's okay, not a problem, we'll stop." I raised a hand in appeasement.

"No, it's not that. I mean, you probably should stop, but not because there's any problem with the music. I appreciate that you've kept people entertained. But—the police aren't coming. Not before morning."

I laid my hand across my guitar strings. "False alarm? We can go back in?"

"Well, you see, we can't let people back in after a bomb threat without the police clearing the hotel, but the police aren't coming, so we can't let anyone back in at all." The manager massaged the back of his neck with his hand. "Company policy."

A woman who had been dancing with her kid a moment before turned on the guy. "Wait, so you won't let us go back to our rooms to sleep or to get our keys? What are we supposed to do?"

Dawkins shook his head. "I don't know. I'm just telling you what the police said."

"Fine, then you're going to give us a ride to another hotel from your chain, and put us up there, right?"

"I'd love to, but . . ." He paused, glancing around like he hoped someone might bail him out and finish his sentence. Nobody came to his rescue. "I'd love to, but every single hotel in the area received the same threat."

"Every hotel in the chain?"

"No. Every hotel."

"Surely not all the threats are credible?"

Dawkins shrugged. "The police seem to think they're all credible, or they can't tell which are credible and which aren't."

I looked at all the exhausted faces. A minute before they'd been dancing, cheering. Now they looked like two a.m. again.

"This is ridiculous," said a man in saggy white briefs, clutching an attaché case in front of him. "I wouldn't travel anymore at all if I didn't have to. In the last month I've been through three airport evacuations and one 'shelter-in-place' at a restaurant."

An elderly woman spoke. "We must be reasonably safe, or they'd have somebody here. A squad car, a fire chief, a dog. Somebody. They must have some kind of triage going to prioritize."

Dawkins shrugged again.

"Okay, look," I tried. "What about mitigating the risk? Letting one person in at a time to at least get their keys or wallets?"

"I'd love to, but what if there is a bomb? What if it goes off while even one person is in there? Or what if one of you set it? I can't let you do that."

Now my making-the-best-of-it crowd from a few minutes before all eyed each other like there was a killer in our midst. A little boy started crying. "Look," said a father with a sleeping toddler draped over his shoulder. "We need someplace to go."

April stood up from the curb. "Um, I have an idea. A place, you know?"

She wasn't much for public speaking. When the hotel guests all turned her way, she raised her pizza box as a shield. "There's an unlocked Superwally Daycare down the road." She pointed. "They were repainting the playroom in the front, but the paint was low-odor and there's a whole napping room in the back with mats. You have to cross the road, but there aren't too many cars out anymore, right? It's walkable."

April and Hewitt led the group over, while Dawkins made phone calls to the local police to make sure nobody got arrested for trespassing. That left JD and me standing in an empty hotel parking lot.

He sighed. "Wanna play a little more?"

"Might as well."

I'd quit singing an hour before to save my voice, but JD and I were still playing at four a.m. when April and Hewitt made it back.

"Don't you two ever get tired?" Hewitt asked, collapsing onto the grass.

I held out my hand. "My calluses have calluses. Anyway, I'm not awake. I'm dreaming this."

"I'd appreciate if you woke up, then. This is ridiculous."

I'd been running on adrenaline, but now that everyone was gone, exhaustion washed over me. We unplugged the guitars and dragged ourselves back over to the van. I settled into the crumb-covered middle bench, where I could at least get horizontal even if I couldn't stretch out.

"So, where to?" JD asked from the driver's seat.

April, from the bench in front of mine, said, "You're still too drunk to drive. I think we all are."

"I know I am." Hewitt hoisted the gin bottle. "I've been topping up."

"Anyway," I said. "There's no place to go. We've got a show here tomorrow, which is today, so there's no point in driving anyplace else."

"We could go to the next town to sleep."

Hewitt shook his head. "If they evacuated all the hotels in town, every single person who managed to walk out with a car key in their hand when the alarm went off has been asleep in a hotel room in the next town for an hour now. Every town in every direction."

"Night in the van it is." I closed my eyes. "Still more comfortable than my first place in New York. Bigger, too."

"Whoa," said April. "Did she just share a personal detail? She has a past?"

My eyes were still closed so I didn't know if she saw me stick out my tongue at her. "What are you talking about?"

"You're not the most forthcoming person. We've been in this van for eight months and we barely know anything about you."

"There's nothing to tell."

"That's why we've invented an origin story for you from the two things we know—three now—you taught yourself to play guitar in high school, and you're, like, the last person in the world to get a label deal from busking on the street. That's it. That's all we've got, other than this new tidbit, so we've made up the rest. Your parents are werewolves, but you didn't get the gene."

The others chimed in, alternating with each other. "You traded your family cow for a magic guitar." "You sold your soul at a crosswalk for the ability to play." "You turned down a life of riches for a chance to play in a band." "You're from Antarctica, which is why you turn the AC up so high when you're driving, to feel like home."

They were joking, but I caught something serious behind it. A challenge to let them in. But what to say? What difference did it make that I'd run away at fifteen rather than tell my frum parents and six siblings I was queer? That I didn't have that word yet, or any other, only the conviction it wasn't safe to say the words I didn't have? Or how just before, little Chava Leah Kanner had wandered into a street fair and heard an electric guitar for the first time? That I'd looked at the guitarist and thought, That's *me*, without any road map for the journey, and everything afterward had been an attempt to reconcile who I'd thought I was supposed to be with who I really was? How when I left Brooklyn for my one off-the-path aunt's apartment in Washington Heights, after months of planning, that first subway ride was a thousand times as long as any drive I'd made since? How I'd only been told of that aunt's existence by someone from an organization that helped people leave the community, and knew I'd be erased from the family in the same way? I couldn't articulate any of that to these people, even after eight months in a van together. Maybe someday, when I trusted they wouldn't joke about it.

"Your version is way more exciting than the truth, I promise. Like I said, there's nothing to tell."

"Sure," April said. "Just because it's not exciting doesn't mean we don't want to hear it."

She sounded more annoyed than I thought she had the right to be, so I tried to salvage the situation. "But how did you guess about the family cow? I never mentioned Bossie before."

"I knew it!" JD's voice held sarcasm and triumph. "There's always a cow."

The voices quieted, and I knew they were waiting for me to add something real, but I didn't, and the silence stretched until JD's breathing changed and April started to snore.

"Hey," Hewitt whispered as I started to drift. "Luce, are you still awake?"

"Awake enough. What?"

"Percentage impressed versus percentage dismayed?"

"Sorry?" I asked.

"The hotel room."

"Ten percent impressed."

"Only ten? C'mon. It was awesome."

He couldn't see my smile. "Fine. Fifty percent impressed. You get points for creativity. The glo-paint was a nice touch."

If anyone stayed awake after that, I wasn't awake to notice.

2

ROSEMARY

Another Happy Superwally Employee

Listen.

Learn.

Communicate.

Our goals are speed and efficiency.

Hang on! Don't hang up!

You are valued but replaceable.

The last poster was Rosemary's least favorite among the six mandatory inspirational posters adorning her workspace walls. The company sent new ones every three months, along with suggestions for their arrangement. Rosemary dutifully hung them, dutifully snapped daily photos of herself in her work environment to send along to headquarters. Her morning photo had even made the company website once, under the caption "Another Happy Superwally Employee."

She wasn't a happy employee. Not a sad or disgruntled one,

either, just indifferent. Every morning she woke, ate breakfast with her parents, and went back to her bedroom, where she'd transformed her childhood desk into a Superwally Vendor Service Center. Beyond the workstation, out of the company camera's view, were posters of the Iris Branches Band and Brain in a Jar and Whileaway; even though she'd bought them from Superwally, with her employee discount, they still weren't part of an approved workplace environment. She used them to remind herself that she didn't belong to Superwally: if she was valued but replaceable, so was her employer. In theory, anyway. She'd never had any other job.

At 8:29 she turned off the music player on her ancient Superwally Basic Hoodie, the school-issued one she'd had since seventh grade, placing it on the charging pad by her bed. She slipped her work Hoodie over her head and adjusted her mic.

"Welcome, Rosemary! Have a productive day!" flashed in her vision. She waved it away.

The first call, somewhere between 8:30 and 8:35 every morning, was always a test call from Quality Control. She knew that even though they never identified themselves as such.

Her earpiece chimed at 8:32. She answered on the second chime, optimal. A message praising her quick action flashed in the corner of her vision, and the hoodspace resolved into a room with a small, uncluttered wooden desk and dusky blue walls designed to project calm.

"Good morning. You've reached Vendor Services. I'm Rosemary."

"Good morning." An avatar of a gray-bearded Sikh man materialized in the virtual chair opposite her. "I was wondering if you'd help me with a problem I'm having."

She didn't bother skimming his culture and gender specs like she would for a real customer. "Sure, Jeremy, how may I help you?"

The man tensed, went still. "Can't you even pretend you don't know this is me? We're recorded. We get evaluated."

Rosemary sighed. "Sorry. Right. Stick to the script. . . . What can I help you with today? You are a valued vendor in the Superwally family and I'm sure I can find a solution for you quickly and efficiently."

"Thank you. Our fulfillment interface is throwing a glitch. I can't see which items you need us to replenish in your Tucson warehouse."

"Certainly, valued customer. If you give me your vendor ID number, I'm sure we can sort this out."

Jeremy, wearing the day's bogus vendor avatar, gave her the day's bogus vendor ID number and sat watching as she solved the day's bogus issue. This wasn't a hard one at all, but she resisted the urge to tell him to throw something more difficult at her. Somebody would, sometime during the day, she hoped. Those problems were all that made the job interesting.

She pictured Jeremy sitting in his own home vendor service center, somewhere in—where had he said that one time? His workspace walls no doubt looked the same as hers, but maybe he kept his own posters out beyond the camera's range, too. She wondered, not for the first time, if he also still lived with his parents. She thought he might be around her own age, twenty-four, but he could as easily have been thirty or forty.

His avatars didn't give any clue, since Quality Control were allowed to vary their looks day to day. Everyone else's avs were set to age thirty-three, an age the company had at some point determined to project the right mix of experience and youthful enthusiasm. The most she had ever gotten from Jeremy, in all his early morning test calls, was his name and that he lived someplace starting with a *V*. Virginia, she thought. Or Vermont. Neither of those data points was necessarily true, either, but it was more than she knew about any of her other coworkers. The rest existed as a long list of employee performance ratings to compete against.

She took seventy-two seconds to solve the morning's problem, and another "Timely service!" message rewarded her efficiency. Once Jeremy had gone, she flipped to clearview, straightened her desk, and waited for her first real customer. It didn't take long. At 8:47, the earpiece chimed again. She forced a smile and answered.

"Good morning. You've reached Vendor Services. My name is Rosemary. How may I help you?" *Good job! Your customer can hear your smile!* scrolled at the corner of her eye. She waved away the bonus point.

"We've got a massive problem this morning." The voice came first, then an avatar of a tall young Korean man appeared beside her virtual wooden desk. It was a high-end av, fine enough to show her the tension behind his expression.

"I'm sure I can find a solution quickly and efficiently. May I have your vendor ID number?" Her words, from her avatar's mouth. Per company policy, her avatar wore her photographic likeness, but aged up to thirty-three, with neater hair and makeup. She was glad they didn't care whether she wore makeup in real life, even if they did insist she get dressed in the company uniform every day. They spun that as "look your best to work your best," but she knew about the tech woven into the fabric, the better to quantify you with, my dear.

He rattled off his vendor ID, one she didn't recognize. Rosemary entered it, trying to conceal her excitement at the company name that popped up. "Can you confirm your vendor name?"

"StageHoloLive or StageHolo. I don't know if we're in there as a subsidiary or our own entity."

"Your own entity," Rosemary confirmed.

She had been at Superwally six years now, but had never gotten a call from StageHoloLive. It had never even dawned on her that they were Superwally vendors. Of course they were. Where else would you buy your StageHolo projector or SHL-enhanced Hoodie? Who'd fulfill orders for physical souvenirs of their shows? And for that matter, whose lines did they use when they streamed one or another of their services—SHL or SportHolo or TVHolo—into every home and Hoodie in the country?

Almost every home, anyway. Her family didn't even have the

basic StageHolo living room box that played TV and movies, let alone the add-on subscriptions or immersive live experiences. It was mostly a money thing, partly some Luddite parent principle. They would have tossed her old school Hoodie, too, if she hadn't insisted she still needed it. It couldn't handle much of anything, but it let her pretend she hadn't been left totally behind.

"How can I help you?" As she asked, she repeated the vendor number to herself, so she'd recognize it faster in the future. It was palindromic, an easy number to memorize.

"We've got a big show tonight, and the site is telling anyone who tries to register at the day-of price point that ticket sales are closed. It was fine yesterday."

So Superwally ran their registration sites, too. That made sense. Otherwise they'd have created a competitor by now to drive StageHolo out of business.

"Let me get right on that for you." Rosemary pictured the code before she looked at it. It was easier when she imagined it as it should be before scoping out the real thing. When she opened her eyes to the visual representation, she spotted the problem. It took only a few keystrokes to fix. She puttered for a moment longer before closing out, so it wouldn't look as easy as it had been. Don't make the customer feel stupid, or like they could have solved it themselves.

"Got it," she said. "It'll work fine now. Do you want to test it from your end before I disconnect?"

"That'd be great. Hang on." The av went still, then reanimated with visible relief. "Yep. You fixed it."

Rosemary glanced at her timer. If she ended the call now she'd get another bonus point for efficient solving, but something nagged at her. "It's not my place to ask, but I'm guessing this isn't the first time this has happened?"

"No, actually. I've called twice in the last month. Why do you ask?"

"I fixed it for this particular show, but I think there's a bug in how the system is coding dates across your entire site. It'll probably keep happening."

"Interesting. Could you, uh, stop it from happening?"

"I can, if you'd like."

"Of course. That's why I called."

"Well, you called about the specific issue, which I just fixed. We're supposed to fix the problem at hand, 'quickly and efficiently.' Which I did, but the more efficient solution is to make it so you don't have to call back when it happens again in a week."

"Great. Do that, please."

Rosemary grinned for real this time. The repair took fifty-eight seconds; she didn't wait for the optimal time. "Can I help with anything else for StageHoloLive?"

"No, but listen. You were so quick, and I appreciate that you took the initiative to fix the problem behind the problem. Can I send you a code to attend tonight's show for free?"

"I'm sorry. I can't accept gifts from vendors. It's against company policy." That saved her from mentioning how the only Hoodies in her household were this work-dedicated one, which she was prohibited from using for entertainment, and the Basic the school system had subsidized when she was thirteen and school had gone virtual, which was still good enough to listen to music and hang out with her friends, but too archaic to handle SHL technology.

"Gotcha. Oh, well. I don't want to get you in trouble, but can I get your employee ID number? Or a direct line to contact you? You're my new hero. I'd like to be able to contact you again, and maybe send a compliment to your supervisor."

She didn't see any harm in that; she already had a few vendors who contacted her directly. She passed her ID number.

"Thanks, Rosemary. Have a wonderful day."

"You, too. Thank you for being a loyal customer."

The call disconnected. Rosemary glanced at her reward center. She had lost her bonus point for problem-solving efficiency—the call had gone two minutes over optimum—but got another one for refusing a gift. She was 157 points away from a merit raise. Maybe she'd use it to buy an SHL-compatible Hoodie, even if it pissed off her parents.

The remaining shift-hours passed in a series of mostly easy fixes and a couple of trickier ones. Rosemary appreciated the tricky ones, even if the system didn't adjust to give credit for dealing with more complex problems. She imagined there were other people in her position who found ways to shunt off those issues, to go for time points rather than completion points; she occasionally got calls that had been bumped from other vendor services staff. She'd never met or talked with any of them, so she could only guess some note in the system marked her.

If her parents were correct, sooner or later it would cost her a raise. The company would keep her where she was, solving everyone's problems, but not solving them quickly or efficiently or whatever the other inspirational posters of the month demanded. At lunch she ate her yogurt with speed and efficiency. She solved issues as quickly as possible, but some couldn't be solved any faster.

Just before she took her Hoodie off for the evening, one more message chimed. Annoyance surged through her. She was obligated to take it, even two minutes before quitting time, but she didn't get overtime without prior approval and she'd get dinged if she ignored it.

She tapped the message envelope and found an optional overtime assignment. StageHoloLive had put through a formal request for her to observe that evening's show to make sure there were no technical glitches from the Superwally end. Observe the show itself, but with access to the code if she was needed. She read it twice to make sure they were serious.

"I'd be happy to, but my hood isn't SHL-enabled. I'll see if I can borrow one in time, but it's unlikely," she wrote back. "I apologize for not being able to fulfill this assignment."

The system passed her message along to whomever had sent it. She changed out of her work uniform; they weren't supposed to track her after she clocked out, but she didn't trust them not to.

Walking from her bedroom/workspace into the kitchen was a walk back into reality. Enclosed in her Hoodie all day she sometimes came to believe there were no real people, just voices and messages and lines of code and avatars spread out across the world. Faces that needed help from her in order to feed themselves data and packages and money. Then she stepped into the warm kitchen and was reminded humans existed, real flesh-and-blood people, and they didn't all need something from her.

"What can I do?" she asked, stretching one arm against the doorframe, then the other.

Her mother was chopping carrots for soup, her crutches leaning against the counter beside her. She hadn't bothered with her prosthetic today. "If you take over on the vegetables, I'll do the chicken."

Rosemary took the proffered knife, popping a carrot piece into her mouth, then spitting it out again. The handsome carrots Superwally droned in never tasted as sweet as the stumpy and gnarled red-cored Chantenay they grew in their garden, but those had all been harvested months ago. Her mother gave her a look, and she ate the bland piece rather than waste it.

"Hey, Ma, do you know anyone nearby with a StageHoloLive hood? Near enough for me to get it in the next hour?"

"Why?"

"I've got a chance to go to a free concert. I thought it might be interesting."

"That's not 'going to a concert.' Trust me, it's a slippery slope. The hood is cheap, and maybe the show itself isn't too pricy, but then they make you pay for more and more inside the experience, and it's too easy just to say yes and transfer money. It's a system designed to make you spend and spend—"

She heard the frown in her mother's voice without seeing her face. "I know, I know. But they're covering me. I'm curious about the full experience. Just once. I'd get paid overtime, too."

The overtime made a little difference. "I didn't realize it was for work. Maybe Tina Simmons? She practically lives inside that corporate playground."

Rosemary didn't bother to check; her mother hadn't noticed she'd been avoiding Tina for years. She wracked her brain for others among their closest neighbors, but nobody came to mind whom she'd be comfortable asking. The more she considered it, nearby was only the first problem. Her mother was right that Tina spent all her time in hoodspace, like everyone else but Rosemary; asking to borrow something most people put on when they woke and took off when they went to bed was the second problem. It wasn't going to happen.

She cut the remaining carrots, moved on to celery and onions. She was setting the table for dinner when the proximity alarm on the front door beeped. Her mother washed her hands, wiped them on her jeans, and pulled her phone from her pocket to check the security camera feed. "Package drone. Are you expecting anything?"

Rosemary shook her head. "I'll go see what it is."

She unlocked the door. The package was small and light. It was addressed to her employee ID number, not her personal ID. Inside nestled a brand-new, top-of-the-line, honest-to-goodness name-brand Hoodie™, along with all accessories. She turned it over in her hands, amazed at how little the new model weighed. No wonder people never took them off.

The packing slip had a sentence in the notes section saying, "Thank you for supporting our concert this evening." She ran back to her room and pulled her work hood back up to check if the assignment was still available to her. It was.

"I will be able to assist," she said, happy that the interface wouldn't convey her excitement.

3

LUCE

The Peach

The morning sun pried my eyelids open far too early. Hewitt slept in the passenger seat, wrapped in the pink bathrobe, T-shirt over his face. JD dozed against the steering wheel. April had taken the far back row, behind me. She was already awake. "Good, you're up. I needed to show this to somebody."

She passed me her tablet. I rubbed sleep from my eyes with my still-smoky sleeve, wincing at the odor. Focused on the tablet. Looked up. "Every hotel?"

"Every hotel."

"The whole city?"

"The whole state."

I closed my eyes again. "And no bombs were found?"

"No. Not yet. The bomb squads haven't gotten to half yet."

"And they're planning on getting to all? They haven't caught someone or found something to make them think it was a hoax?"

"Are you going to read the article or not?"

"No." I handed her back her tablet. "It stresses me out. It's some terrible hoax. I need sleep. We all need sleep, and then we need to get ready for the show tonight."

April and JD and I spent part of our per diem on breakfast at a diner near the hotel while Hewitt dozed in the van. The diner was packed with groggy people, some of whom I recognized from the parking lot. I dumped sugar in the weak, acidic coffee until it approximated something drinkable.

We had a noon radio spot scheduled, but we still weren't allowed back in the hotel room, and I still stank like the podcaster's ashtray. I scrubbed myself as clean as possible with paper towels in the diner bathroom, and tried to scrape the caked shampoo out of my hair, but it didn't fix my clothing.

"It's radio, Luce," JD said when I returned to the table. "Nobody can see that you smell."

He ducked the yellow sweetener packet I chucked at him.

I hated shopping at Superwally, resented the way they underpriced local businesses to close them, then automated the checkouts and fired cashiers, but it seemed the best option given the circumstances, so I ran across the parking lot to buy clean jeans and a tank top, hoping Hewitt would do the same when he woke. I couldn't say that, though. The one other time I had tried to suggest he change clothes for a show, he had shown up wearing a wrestling thong.

Why did he have a wrestling thong with him? We made guesses among ourselves, but refused to ask him directly; better to look unimpressed, so as not to encourage him. He couldn't surprise us with anything from his bag today, but if I asked him to buy something to replace the bathrobe he'd probably arrive in a union suit and bunny slippers.

When we got back to the van, I was relieved to see he'd found jeans somewhere, which he wore with the band-logo shirt he had liberated the night before. We didn't have his guitars, anyway, so he could have sat the radio promo out, but I appreciated the effort.

The radio show was business as usual. Guitar, bass, an overturned plastic garbage can for a drum, all within a space the size of a port-a-potty. There was an old Disappear Fear song with a line about negotiating the angles of guitar necks in radio studios, which always came to my mind as we tried not to put each other's eyes out.

"Is 'Blood and Diamonds' autobiographical?" the DJ asked after we played it.

"No." Served him right for asking a yes/no question, anyhow. Everybody knew you asked open-ended questions if you wanted open-ended answers. If he had asked "What inspired that song?" I might've given him something. As it was, April and JD exchanged a smirking glance, and I realized I'd shut down another personal question, like they'd said the night before. It wasn't that I set out to tell nothing; I didn't see how it mattered.

The DJ realized his own mistake—shrugged at me in apology—and moved on. We answered questions about that night's show, the tour in general, the album, the hit song, and even managed to turn the hotel scare into a more lighthearted anecdote. We gave away some tickets to a few lucky listeners. Watched in amazement, not for the first time, as actual callers lit up actual phone lines to get the tickets. The DJ passed me his tablet to show that people were responding on social media as well.

I still hadn't gotten used to being in demand. After seven months of slogging, we had played seventeen sold-out or near-sold-out shows in the last twenty-two nights. It had all happened so fast. One video in the right place at the right time, a feature on SuperStream, and all of a sudden we had been bumped from opening act to feature. "Blood and Diamonds" wasn't even my best song. It was easy to believe in the mundane details of promotion and driving and lousy food and scuzzy club bathrooms and time onstage, but the idea that people were listening was still beyond my comprehension.

They let us back into the hotel at two in the afternoon, just before I transitioned from panic to high panic. April had already started searching online for a local store where we'd be able to buy or rent Hewitt a new guitar, and I was trying not to think about having to go back out to Superwally to find makeup and something appropriate to wear onstage. Nobody from the hotel mentioned the pink room, which made me think either the bomb squad never got to our rooms or they had orders to ignore anything other than what they were looking for. Made sense. Nobody wanted to walk through hotel rooms that weren't expecting visitors.

"Maybe we should take everything with us in case it happens again." April flopped onto her bed and closed her eyes. She had a habit of taking her clothes out of her bag and putting them in the dresser and closet, even when we were only in town for a night. Said it made her feel less vagrant.

"That can't happen twice in a row. Can it?" I pawed through my own chaotic bag of stage clothes, looking for what I wanted to wear. There weren't many options. I'd spent Monday, our usual laundromat day, doing the promo for tonight's show, and the band had spent it redecorating. The plan had been to make up for it today, but we hadn't anticipated getting locked out of the hotel.

April started snoring gently, and a nap struck me as appealing. I set an alarm on my phone and closed my eyes. Woke what seemed like two seconds later to my phone's chime. April was drying her hair. I never figured out how she managed to wake herself without alarms, no matter how little sleep we'd gotten. I followed her lead with a blissful, uninterrupted shower.

I debated taking everything with me, decided against it, then for it, then against it again. What were the odds that someone might pull the same hideous stunt two nights in a row? I packed my gig stuff into my backpack and left the larger bag, just to make a point.

The guys met us in the parking lot. I handed Hewitt my tour bible, and he read the address to the van's GPS to route us. The guys had laughed at my insistence on a hard copy of our itinerary for the first few days of the tour, until the afternoon the phones had crashed but I still knew where we were going. We stopped to buy an actual atlas that day. "Haven't sold one of those in a while now," the convenience store clerk said. Nobody had mocked my book since then, and I loved making notes in the margins of the atlas. A childhood spent in the confines of a single neighborhood had left me a fan of maps and all they could tell.

We drove through a cute little business district full of boutiques and restaurants, before turning off the wide street and onto a narrow one.

"Stop the van." I was already opening the door. "Stop, stop, stop."

Hewitt slammed on the brakes, and I jumped out. The Peach, our destination, had an old-fashioned marquee out front. An old-fashioned marquee with my name on it. TONIGHT: LUCE CANNON. I had seen my name on chalkboards and posters, but never on a marquee before.

A year before, when things had started moving for me, I'd made a list of all the things I wanted to accomplish in my music career. Two lists, actually: one of things within my control, and one of things outside my control. On the first list, I had line items like "learn how to play better lead guitar." On the second, the more pie-in-the-sky stuff: clubs and theaters I wanted to headline, people I wanted to share a stage with. I had never even thought to put "my name on a marquee." The first chance I had to open my journal, I'd write it down for the thrill of crossing it off.

"How cool is that?" I asked nobody in particular, pulling out my phone to snap a quick picture.

A car honked behind our van, and I waved the band on. "I'll meet you inside."

Hewitt had my tour bible, which meant he'd seen the note about the loading dock behind the club. This gave me another few minutes to admire my name in lights.

A woman walked by on the opposite side of the road with a German shepherd, heading into a park.

I pointed at the sign. "That's my name!"

She smiled and gave me a thumbs-up.

The theater looked like it had been a cinema once upon a time. The label's PR team had sent posters, and one was displayed in a fancy bulb-framed display beside the old-fashioned ticket booth. I tried three locked doors before I found one that opened into a rotunda-style lobby with a bar. A guy in a black T-shirt with a giant peach on the back was stocking a beer cooler. He looked up when I entered.

"I'm in the band," I said before he asked. "Is the loading dock open, do you know?"

He nodded, and I stepped into the theater.

No wonder they had been pushing me to do promotionals in this town. We'd mostly been playing midsized rock clubs, but this was an honest-to-goodness theater, with chairs and a balcony and everything. A theater we were headlining. I was headlining. On a Tuesday, granted, but still a step up.

I walked down the aisle. The house lights were on, displaying all the details: the art deco wall sconces, the carved proscenium. April staggered onto the stage from the wings with her giant bag of drum hardware, always the last thing loaded and the first thing unloaded, as tall as she was, and twice as heavy. Behind her came the other guys, with her throne, her cymbal bags, her bass drum. Everyone helped with everything, but April always grabbed the big bag herself as a point of pride.

I made my way out to the van. Gemma had said early on that I didn't have to help unload. "Play diva if you want. We're on your payroll."

Maybe I'd have been able to get used to it, but it felt like a weird separation between me and the people I played with, even if they were hired guns. I wanted to be part of the group, but situations kept conspiring to set me apart: the solo promotion spots, their painting expedition. My own unwillingness to share much of myself. The least I could do was carry my own gear and help with theirs.

After Gemma left, I was glad I'd already gotten them used to me stepping in alongside, so it wasn't some weird change in procedure. I might claim some point of "That's my name up there" privilege every once in a while, but I didn't actually know how to play diva, when it came down to it.

We got everything unloaded, and started on setup. Another Peach-shirted employee joined us onstage after April had assembled her kit. He started pulling drum mics and stands from an alcove and fussing with their placement.

"Hi—I'm Luce," I said when he paused for a moment. Step one: always be nice to the people responsible for making you sound good.

"Eric Silva. Call me Silva. I'm looking forward to this. We've been playing your stuff in the house mix for the last few weeks, and I really like your sound."

Points in his favor. I could often tell how the show was going to go by the sound person's attitude. The ones who didn't want us to be there, maybe preferred another genre or didn't go for chick singers, didn't introduce themselves by name. When I introduced myself, they'd grunt or nod or go about their business. Those guys directed all their questions to JD or Hewitt, and talked down to April and me, or didn't talk to us at all. I'd learned the introduction served as an easy test.

Somebody in the booth was cycling through various gels and positions for the lights, throwing rainbows and occasionally blinding us. Silva orbited the band as we set up, placing mics and shifting monitor angles. He didn't ask us any questions about the makeup of our band, or where we wanted the monitors, and I realized he'd actually studied our tech rider, something that put this place in the top one percent of venues as far as I was concerned. When somebody met us on the stage with all our needs and preferences attended to, I got the feeling the show would be a good one.

The soundcheck went well. The theater had the nicest sound system we'd run into on this tour, and Silva gave us the exact monitor mixes we wanted. The room sounded like a cathedral, full and warm; it would sound even better filled with people. After Silva had all the levels set, we asked him if we had a few minutes to work on a new song I had written over the weekend.

"Be my guest," he said. "You've got two hours before the doors open and dinner's on its way to the green room. Come find me if you need me."

I had gone through a fallow period at the tour's start where I couldn't figure out the rhythm of things. We were driving to the next town after each show, checking into hotels in the middle of the night, sleeping a few hours before I had to start the promotional cycle; everyone else got to sleep a few extra hours while Gemma dragged me to morning shows. I was haggard, getting myself wired for shows on caffeine alone, eating crap.

After three weeks, I begged Gemma for a change, and we settled into a new schedule. When possible, we started sleeping in the town we had played, so I could get a solid night's sleep. Wake up, try to get to the hotel gym, drive, soundcheck, play, sleep. It didn't work if we had to be at a radio show six hours away by eight a.m., but the PR people got some promos rescheduled for lunch shows instead of morning, and worked it out that I called in for others.

The previous Saturday, in the hours between soundcheck and show, I'd sat down to write for the first time in the entire tour. An idea had wormed its way into my head while I drove. I got most of my ideas behind the wheel; something about the rhythm of the road lent my mind permission to wander.

The seed had been a piece of graffiti I'd spotted along the way. DON'T EVEN THINK ABOUT IT, the sign read, scrawled on the WELCOME sign below the town's name, the mayor's name, and the population. Don't even think about what? I wondered, and from there the song came, a punchy little meditation on insularity and fear. I had written it out for the guys in the van on Sunday morning, and we had tried an arrangement at that day's soundcheck that made me happy.

Two days later, it sounded a little less ready than it had on Sunday, when the newness had obscured the roughness. This far into the tour, I had mostly outgrown my hesitance over telling the band what to do. At the beginning, I'd been reluctant to tell them when I thought something wasn't working.

"Let us know," April had told me, when she noticed. "We're here to make you sound good."

"But you're all more experienced. You're amazing musicians. Maybe I'm wrong?"

"They're your songs, right? We can make suggestions, but you get final say. We'd all rather sound good, at day's end, right? We'll sound better if you're happy."

I'd worked on it over the following months. Developed the nerve to say when I thought someone was out of tune, or a drum fill was too distracting.

"JD, why don't you and April both wait to come in on the second verse?" I asked now. "The beginning needs a little room to breathe."

We tried it the new way. I made another tweak, a change from one chord to its relative minor. It brought a dark nuance the song needed.

"I think that's it," I declared after the fourth time through. The lyrics still weren't quite right, but nothing was set in stone until we recorded it.

"Thank goodness," said Hewitt. "I'm hungry enough to eat my own arm."

"Not our fault you don't bother to eat breakfast," said April. "It sounds good, Luce."

I flashed her a grin. "Do you guys think we can squeeze it into the set list for tonight?"

"If you think we can get through it without messing up." JD leaned his bass against his amp and flipped the standby switch.

"Do you mind if I play a little more?" I asked into the mic.

"Go ahead. Opening band hasn't shown yet." Silva's disembodied voice came back to me through my monitor. "Do you need me to stay up here?"

"No, thanks. Everything sounds perfect."

I lingered for a few minutes after everyone left to find dinner. Not because I had anything left to do, but I wanted a moment alone on this beautiful stage. The house lights were on again, and I looked out on a sea of empty seats, two long aisles, an elegant balcony level. I played a cover I used to play on the street, digging how my voice sounded rich and strong, my guitar muscular. It expanded to fill the space, like a liquid or a gas, pushing into the farthest corners. I belonged here.

My phone buzzed, a text from April. Check out this green room.

The second I walked in, I knew why she had messaged me. It was bigger than any other green room we'd crammed into on this tour. The couches were worn but didn't look like the biohazard sites we often found backstage. A mirrored vanity table sat in the corner, promising movie-star glamour. The walls were plastered with band stickers and black-and-white 8 x 10 photos, new and old.

"That's not intimidating at all." Hewitt pointed to a signed photo of Johnny Cash. He was kidding. I'd never seen him daunted by any room or any situation. He was a lead guitarist through and through, full of lead guitarist confidence.

"Is that a bathroom? We get our own bathroom?" I asked. In most clubs we had to share a green room with one to three other bands, so there was no place to change except the public bathroom, standard model: two stalls—one clogged, one dubious, no toilet paper; more graffiti than wall; cracked mirror for putting on makeup; and no surface that looked safe to touch without a glove. This one sparkled with cleanliness, even if it was still too small to change in easily.

"Eat something." Every once in a while, April tried to step into Gemma's managerial shoes for a minute. Not long enough to, say, choose not to paint the hotel room pink, but at least long enough to make sure I considered dinner.

I looked over the spread. They'd followed our full rider; lots of places ignored what we asked for and served us pizza and M&M's, or handed us money and told us to buy dinner. I didn't mind the buy-dinner option—that was when we got a chance to find local restaurants, see a little of a new city.

After that lousy night, the side table holding an electric kettle, throat-health tea, and honey and lemons looked enticing to me. Other teas and coffee for everyone else, since they all agreed that throat tea tasted like rotting licorice. Veggies and hummus, cold cuts, cheese for the nonsingers in our midst. I made myself a plate, started a tea steeping, put a chipped saucer over it to concentrate it, and settled on a couch to eat.

"The show is sold out," April said. "I talked to the lighting tech outside. The venue's super happy."

"Awesome."

"If it goes well, maybe the label will book the whole next leg of the tour in theaters like this. I could get used to that. If we don't all get fired for painting the hotel room."

That was probably as close to an apology as I'd get.

Somebody knocked on the door, sharp and urgent.

"It sounds great out—" I started to say when Silva walked in, but the sentence died halfway through. He looked distraught.

He waved his phone at us. "Have you seen?"

None of us had looked at any news sites since we'd gotten to the club.

"Is it the hotels again?" asked JD.

Silva shook his head. Didn't offer any more.

"Oh, God." We all turned in April's direction. She had her tablet out and her face had gone pale.

She turned the tablet to face us.

4

ROSEMARY

The Crash

Rosemary spawned in a parking lot.

The Bloom Bar's exterior carried a strange air of both "Welcome" and "Get lost." Daisies and black-eyed Susans overflowed from beds on either side of the door and beneath the long dark windows. The outer walls were yellow stucco, and both *o*'s of "Bloom" had been transformed into smiling flowers. The friendliness ended there.

A sign over the parking lot proclaimed PATENT MEDICI E TON TE! SHL! A dry-erase board by the door said the same thing, but without letters missing. Rosemary wondered why a virtual environment pretended to run out of letters for their sign; she guessed it added authenticity. For that matter, the entire parking lot was unnecessary; just another place for people with money to show off their gas-powered sports cars and unicorn-drawn pumpkins and whatever other virtual extravagances high-end hoodspace offered. Not that she'd ever been in any hoodspace this well-developed before.

An av perched on a stool between two doors: at least ten feet tall, sized well past human. No, not an avatar, a nonplayer bot. Rosemary wasn't sure if he was security or a ticket taker or both. A scanner sparkled on the wall beside him.

"Are you here for the show or the bar?" The bot's tone was bored.

"The show?"

He nodded as if she had given the answer he expected, which she probably had; she couldn't imagine that people paid for the privilege of hanging out in a virtual bar if they weren't going to the show. Then again, there was a dragon tethered in the parking lot. People paid for all kinds of strange privileges.

He looked at her as if she had missed something. "Thirty dollars if you didn't prepurchase," he said, and she guessed he was repeating it.

"I have a code? To get in free?" Apparently her nerves turned statements into questions.

"I'm working for SHL," she said, attempting a sentence.

"Paste your code here."

She opened her bag of holding and snagged the invitation, dropping it in front of his scanner.

The bot waved her past. "Door on the right."

She guessed the left door was where the regulars went, whoever came here for the bar instead of the show. This bar probably existed in the SHL virtual landscape even when shows weren't going on, for subscription holders' benefit.

The ceiling dropped low as she entered, less than a foot over Rosemary's head, the passage narrow and dark. She made it ten more feet before she encountered another person on another stool, this one a tiny blonde woman.

"ID," said the woman. Av or bot?

Rosemary fumbled for her bag of holding again, managing to open two other apps and a screenshot camera before she flashed her digital ID. "Sorry, new Hoodie."

The woman was unimpressed. "Bag."

Nobody here spoke in anything more than one-syllable words. Rosemary opened access to her bag and waited while the woman searched it. "It's my wallet and camera and workstation. I wasn't sure what I was supposed to bring, you know?"

The woman gave her a strange look, enough to tell Rosemary she was an av, not a bot.

"I'm sorry," said Rosemary. "I know I'm talking a lot. It's my first time here. First time at an SHL show, too. In case you couldn't tell."

The woman handed her bag access back. There didn't seem to be any point to the security rituals; maybe they added authenticity for those who remembered real places like this. Or maybe they were meant to dissuade people who brought virtual guns to virtual bars.

As she moved past, the woman spoke. "You can only use your camera app for the first two minutes of the show. The first two minutes use a different format, so people can take pictures with the band if they want and tell people they were here. After that, don't bother. The rest don't photograph well. If you keep trying, people will know you're new. Also, don't go in the bathroom unless you're looking for drugs or sex."

Rosemary flashed a grateful smile. "Thanks!" She wasn't sure why anyone wanted to photograph a holo, or why a virtual club needed a bathroom, but she filed the information away. She blew her next moment of cool by pushing on a pull door.

After passing Door Entry 101, she found herself in a room so dim she had no sense of the space's size. It felt limitless. She'd seen the building from the outside, but the outer dimensions didn't correspond to anything inside. This was SHL's world.

SHL's world. Her eyes adjusted. The club was as large as any room she'd ever been in, but blander, like it hadn't yet been mapped over with any personality or style. No, on closer look, it was more than the black box it had at first appeared to be. There were layers, textures. Black paint on black walls, black tape on black paint on black walls, strata of stickers upon stickers upon stickers on black walls, some with embedded links. The illusion of metal struts and lighting scaffolds, far above their heads, and of grime on the scuffed cement floor.

Staring at the Bloom Bar logo on the wall revealed a text scroll explaining how this was an amalgamation of several venues from Before, not a re-creation of any one in particular. There were also options for a list of bands that had played here in the past, and the full upcoming music calendar. She blinked it all away.

The first person who crossed her sight line looked like a lion, and for a panicked moment Rosemary wondered if cat avatars had come back into style while she wasn't paying attention. They had been all the rage among those who could afford them when she was in high school, but after schools and Superwally workplace policies banned them, the fad petered out. On second glance, this was a man's avatar with a big teased halo of blond hair. She scanned the room to see if that hairstyle was a popular one, but there weren't any others like him.

All the seats at the bar down the long side of the room were taken. She studied the people on the stools, trying to pick up what to say. She'd only been in a bar one time before, for her twenty-first birthday, when her school friends had made her meet them for drinks. Real cocktails, which droned to her doorstep in mason jars nestled in protective packaging. The bar itself had been flat and boring, a generic Irish bar with outdated graphics and a glitchy interface made worse by her Basic Hoodie. She'd never cared to repeat the experience; she preferred chatting with friends in a game or somewhere else where they had something to do while they talked. Her friend Donna had said the bar had history, like history was a selling point. The highlight had been the jar of vodka-spiked basil lemonade.

She watched people at the bar order wine by the glass, bottled beer, cocktails in tumblers. Somebody walked away, and she pushed in to grab his stool. Rested her elbows on the bar, careful not to let her hands touch it. It was virtual, but it still looked sticky. The bar itself held a shimmering menu that appeared when she was right on top of it, advertising a variety of drinks and legal drugs, with two prices beside each, real and virtual. When the bartender finally noticed her, she ordered a birch beer.

"Real or virtual?"

She was on the clock, and it took an hour for drones to get to her house, anyway. "Vee."

"VCash or Superwally credit?"

"Superwally!" She hadn't even thought that was an option. Excellent. The drink could be debited straight from her store credit account. The bartender pulled out a handheld and she passed her account number. He grunted and turned his back to make her drink. He'd have to hold the glass, and scoop the ice, but the birch beer came out of a bottle. She wasn't really drinking it, she reminded herself. Any germs were virtual ones, too.

"If you use Superwally there's no way to tip him. He only takes VCash tips," whispered the person to Rosemary's right. She turned. A black woman with a cloud of natural hair raised a phone in her direction and wagged it. "If you're planning on having a second drink or coming back here again, throw a dollar or two in cash on the counter. He keeps track of who stiffs him."

She hadn't even considered anybody would need to be tipped.

"Thank you," Rosemary whispered back, reaching for her wallet. When she looked over at the woman again, she was amazed to see that the avatar's face was covered with pox scars. Even at Superwally, where avs were supposed to be photorealistic, she'd never seen one with scars. She hadn't even considered that it was possible, though if you could have a cat head, of course you could have scars if you wanted. Her hand went to her stomach, where her own scars were worst.

She hadn't meant to stare, but now the woman was watching her, and she felt obligated to make more conversation. "Are you a big fan of the band?"

"I don't care who plays. This place reminds me of a club I used to hang out in. How about you?"

Rosemary shrugged. "I like their music, but this is my first time seeing them. My first time seeing any band, actually."

The av brightened with enthusiasm. "In that case, you should go get closer."

"Closer?"

"Trust me." She pointed toward the room's center. A loose circle of people had formed around the stage area. "If this were my first show, I'd be over there."

The bartender handed Rosemary her drink in a red plastic cup. She made sure he saw his tip, then went in search of a good place to stand. The projectors—projections of projectors, really—moved in a circle above a clear area ringed with angled speakers. She guessed that meant the band holo appeared in the center. She situated herself behind the largest group, under the assumption they knew what they were doing.

This was the most people Rosemary had seen in one place since she was a kid, even in hoodspace. More than any of her classes, or any party she'd ever been to, though in truth she preferred smaller gatherings. She wondered if it was an unlimited space, or if there were multiple iterations of this same bar, or if it was coded to allow overlay. She could look, but she didn't want to know. The thought of someone else standing in the same spot as her, even virtually, made her shudder.

The room buzzed with voices, a baseline noise. Snippets of conversation drifted her way. Discussions of bands they'd seen, bands they wanted to see, bands they wished they had seen. The weather where they were. She concentrated on their clothes, on what people put on their avatars in this place. She'd used her work avatar, with her work avatar's uniform, a polo shirt and slacks. She hadn't been sure if she was allowed to change into more casual clothes, given that she was here on assignment. Her real body wore her uniform as well, of course. A majority of the crowd wore T-shirts for Patent Medicine, or else for other SHL bands. One man had dressed all in feathers, another person in tight leather pants and a skin that she was fairly sure she recognized as a celebrity from her parents' generation. She filed the information away for the future, if she ever got to do this again. Even if they didn't ask her for the fancy Hoodie back, she couldn't afford a subscription, so it was a moot point.

The dim overhead lights got even dimmer. The crowd cheered.

Who were they cheering? It wasn't like the band could hear them. Rosemary hesitated, then joined in. It felt good to add her voice to a group. She'd never done that before. It left a pleasant vibration inside her; she'd done it in real-space as well. She imagined what it must have been like in the old days, when entire stadiums cheered together.

The rig overhead whirred to life. Rosemary glanced up, and was rewarded with a blinding flash. She looked back to where ghost gear now rested in what had been the empty space. A drum kit at the center, a couple of large amplifiers, three microphone stands. A rack full of ghost guitars. Somebody near the stage reached a hand out and chopped through a guitar neck. He disappeared a second later; there were penalties for disturbing the illusion.

The lights flickered, and a moment later musicians stood holding the instruments. The effect was eerie. The original empty stage must have been a recording, because there wasn't even a second's pause before they hit a chord. Out of nothing, music: three voices and two guitars. They held the note for ten seconds, then drums rolled over it.

Rosemary had been to a wave pool once when she was five, at a run-down amusement park, in the Before. She had waded out into the water holding her father's hand. The pool was crowded and flat, full of people lounging in tubes in the lull between wave sets. She spotted something on the bottom, a nickel or a quarter, shining just beyond her reach, and released her father's hand to grab it. That was when the first wave hit, knocking her back toward the shallows. She surfaced lost and sputtering and terrified, but strangely exhilarated.

The music hit Rosemary like a wave, knocking her breath from her. Louder than anything she had ever heard, filling every corner of her. One chord, and she was full. Don't stop, Rosemary thought. Don't ever stop.

The song shifted, and she recognized it now. It was one of the songs she had checked out this evening before the show, but altered. The intro in the recorded version had been tamed, tempered. She had thought it was okay, nothing special. She hadn't realized music could reach inside you.

She pushed closer. Camera flashes went off throughout the room. The bag checker outside had said pictures were possible for the first two minutes, but she couldn't tear her attention away from the band long enough even to blink a screenshot. What would it have captured anyway? Ghostly faces, a tinny recording. Nothing like the magnet in her gut drawing her toward the stage.

The holo quality changed, the second-minute change the girl had mentioned, a momentary shimmer. Rosemary pressed her avatar up against the people in front of her, the closest she had been to strangers in her adult life. The Hoodie gave a warning jolt, but the other people didn't notice, or if they noticed, they didn't care. A gap opened between two men in front and she pushed through, hoping there wasn't etiquette against it. The space expanded before her, a highlighted path leading her to a better spot.

She found herself in the front row and right of center, gazing up at the bassist, a tall, lean, shaven-headed woman with skin so brown the hologram pushed it into purple. She wore jeans and a sleeveless T-shirt, showing off amazing biceps, and she was barefoot. She had a bruise under her left big toenail, which made her more real. Rosemary fought the urge to touch her; God, she fell in love easily, not that it ever led anywhere.

Rosemary had always liked music, even if she didn't know much about it. She'd listen if somebody told her to listen to something, bought songs and posters of artists she enjoyed, but she had never gone out seeking anything. She didn't know what was cool and what wasn't. She'd played this song, "The Crash," after the Hoodie arrived this evening, and had thought it was decent. Nothing like how it sounded now. Nothing had ever satisfied her the way writing code did, but now she was the code, and she was being overwritten.

"The Crash" ended. Rosemary felt its absence as a physical loss. She placed her drink by her feet to clap, and a second later it disappeared. The lead singer stepped back to the mic. He shielded his eyes and peered out as if he saw them. The people in front of him hollered for attention he couldn't give them.

"Good to see you all. Good to be here at the Bloom Bar." His lips shimmered as he said the words "Bloom Bar," as if they had been inserted separately. A lock of hair fell in his eyes and he brushed it aside. "We're going to go ahead and play some songs for you, yeah?"

The bassist opened her eyes for the first time. Something caught her attention, something in whatever place she was actually in. She glanced down, shook her head, then looked straight at Rosemary and winked. It was the sexiest wink Rosemary had ever seen. She knew it hadn't been meant for her, but it might as well have been. She took a step forward before reminding herself she was an avatar looking at an avatar of someone standing in a warehouse somewhere—where?—a hundred or a thousand or three thousand miles away. Someone who had just winked at someone else.

Rosemary refocused on the singer. Something shimmered above his head, and when she examined the link she found a menu of optional enhancements and accessibility options. Subtitles, translation subtitles, vibration boost, visual description tags. Nothing she needed, but cool to know it was there.

The next song began with a bass pulse. The bassist closed her eyes again, and Rosemary stepped back, trying to regain her composure. She examined the stage. From here she could read the song titles on the set list at the bassist's feet, though she didn't recognize any of them after "The Crash." Ghost sweat rolled off the drummer's face, and he wiped it with a ghost forearm.

What would it be like to have a subscription and relive these shows anytime she wanted? To capture this band and have them to herself? Go to more shows? Not for the first time, she wished she could do this every night. If SportHolo and TVHolo were this real, too, that explained why her friends always looked at her with such pity when she said her family didn't go in for any of it. She'd been missing out on so much.

"Encores are awkward in this situation," the lead singer said after the twelfth song. "So we're all going to pretend that was our last song, and we left the stage, and you stomped and cheered until we came out to play one more. We'll play one more and then we're going to go for real. Thanks for listening."

Don't go, Rosemary wanted to say. Keep playing. It didn't matter that she didn't know the songs. The music had stirred something inside her.

The real last song ended with a long cymbal splash and four cha-chunks of the guitars, which also wasn't the ending on any music she'd ever heard before. It had to be rehearsed, but it felt a little wild at the same time, a loose possibility that things might not work out as planned. The band members grinned at each other on the third cha-chunk, and the bassist raised one lovely eyebrow as she watched the drummer. The last note hung in the air, the singer gave a final salute, and then the band blinked from existence. They were there and then gone, like magic, leaving a three-dimensional StageHoloLive logo floating in the place where they had stood.

It was followed by a voice saying, "Patent Medicine merchandise is for sale here, as well as at Superwally and StageHoloLive. Purchase now to wear instantly inside, or have the real thing droned to you by the time you get home."

A recording filled the room, flat in comparison with what had been there a moment before. The lights came on. The room was much smaller than it had seemed in the dark, or maybe that was an illusion, too. The ceiling lower, the walls closer, the floor scuffed and littered with plastic cups, which winked away a moment later.

Most of the audience had already headed for the exit or blinked out from where they stood, but a few people still lingered by the bar, or stood blank and absent, probably buying Patent Medicine merchandise. A couple of T-shirts changed before her eyes. Rosemary understood the appeal. If there were a way to capture that first moment, when the band had played the chord that had crashed into her, she'd buy it. A T-shirt wouldn't do that. Maybe, maybe a live recording. If not, she'd have to find a way to see them again.

She could have pulled off the Hoodie and disappeared from the room, but she wanted the full experience. Her ears rang as she walked out. There was a muffled quality to everything, like she had cotton wrapped around her. She stayed in the silent hood even after she had turned off the visual; she didn't want to lose the feeling she had walked out with.

In her dream world, a job offer from StageHoloLive would be waiting when Rosemary checked her messages again, along with a drone delivery of a concert souvenir—a T-shirt, maybe, or a poster to add to her bedroom collection—and a free SHL subscription. Or any of the above. She wasn't greedy.

It wasn't until a message chimed in her work Hoodie that she remembered she'd ostensibly been there on business.

"Thank you for your help," the message read.

She hadn't done anything, though she would have. She had to word this carefully, so her own bosses didn't think she had charged fraudulent overtime, or used their time to pursue something else. In the end she decided on, "I was happy to do it. It was useful for my professional development to experience how the StageHoloLive system works firsthand. Please let me know if I can be of any assistance in the future."

She took off her work rig and replaced it with her fraying Basic. Lay back on her bed, turned on audio of "The Crash" again, closed her eyes. It wasn't as good as the live version.

5

LUCE

The Last Power Chord

A baseball stadium, or what was left. Smoking wreckage gaped where the stands behind home plate had been.

"Were there people there?" I asked, as if they knew more. I glanced at the clock on the wall. Six p.m. "It couldn't have been full yet."

"West coast," Silva said. "Seventh inning, first matinee of the season. The stands were packed."

"Oh, God," April repeated.

A number scrolled past, an estimated casualty count, but my brain made no sense of it.

"Do they know what happened?" Hewitt asked.

"Bomb." I pointed at the screen.

"That's not all," said Silva. "There've been bomb threats tonight at three other baseball stadiums, two airports, an arena concert, a convention, and a whole bunch of malls. All over the country. The president made a statement a few minutes ago, asking people to stay home tonight if possible and cancel public gatherings."

"Isn't this when they usually tell people to go about their business, and not to let terrorists terrorize?" My voice pitched itself an octave higher than usual. The picture on the screen moved closer. Rubble, smoke, a tiny shoe. I looked away.

"That's what they say when they think the threat is gone." JD shook his head. "They say that after."

I couldn't wrap my head around it. "But this place wasn't threatened? We're still playing?"

Silva shrugged. "Nobody from the office has said anything yet."

I pulled out my phone, muted since before soundcheck. I had a dozen messages and missed calls, mostly from the label. An email, also from the label, saying they'd been trying to call.

My phone buzzed in my hand. Margo at the label, texting. Cancel your show tonite. Tell me u got this.

Silva's phone chimed as well. He looked down, then back at me. "The production company wants to know if you're playing. They say it's up to you."

I glanced at the clock again. "If doors open at seven, people are probably already on their way here."

"We'll do refunds, or promise tickets to another show. If they're listening to the news, they'll have turned back by now."

I wandered over to where I'd left my tea. Condensation beaded on the underside of the saucer I'd used to cover it, and dripped when I lifted it. The tea was even more bitter than usual when I sipped; I'd forgotten to stir in honey. I added some, watched it stick to my spoon, then grudgingly dissolve, like it was trying to hold on to its shape.

I wished Gemma was still with us to make the decision. She worked for the label, so she would have followed their instructions. They'd never ask us to cancel if they didn't think we had to; they were all about pushing through and playing, regardless of weather or health or whatever else had been thrown in our way. For them to tell us to cancel, it must be serious. They had insurance. As Silva said, the theater would give refunds or reschedule us or give tickets to another show. We'd have a chance to play here again, on a less somber night, to a fuller house. There'd be other, safer opportunities. If we played, it might be for nobody at all, or for ten people who felt awkward in a giant empty theater.

Or it might be for ten people who needed a lift tonight, who wanted music to make them forget the news, or make sense of it. Maybe there were people who wanted to defy the "Please stay home" order, to show they weren't going to let anyone make them afraid. How could we deny that, when we had the power to give it? No answer seemed the right one.

"Don't look at me," Hewitt said when I turned in his direction. "You're the boss."

April and JD shook their heads as well, telling me it was my decision. I had no logic in me; the only picture in my head was that one tiny shoe in the rubble. What was I supposed to do with that image? I couldn't weep over a number, but I could weep over a shoe if I let myself. A shoe could wash me away if I didn't have something else to do, something else to think about.

I wanted to play, but I didn't want to force them. "Somebody say something. You've never held back opinions before."

JD studied the posters on the walls. "Who are we to keep the staff here if they want to get home to their families? Or to put them at risk if there's a legitimate threat? Let's call it off."

"I think enough of them would be willing to stay," Silva said. "And I've been here all day. I don't think there's a big risk."

"We walked right in," April pointed out.

"Nobody else did."

"Would your bosses be pissed off if you paid to keep staff here and nobody came? Nobody bought drinks?" Hewitt had been a bartender.

Silva scratched his head. "I think it'd be okay. The thing is, if we hold the show, I'm not sure the people who stayed home as instructed would get their refunds. I guess we can work something out, under the circumstances. I suppose people are as safe here as anywhere."

"Was that an opinion? Do you want us to play?" I tried to read him, but gave up. "I don't know you well enough to tell."

"Not an opinion. Sorry. This is all you."

I tried another tack. "How many staff do you need to keep

here to hold the show, knowing a lot of ticket holders won't show? Could you let the ones who are scared to stay go home?"

He thought a moment. "We wouldn't want to lessen security. Other than that, we can get by with one person at the box office, one bartender. If you don't mind the lights and monitors staying static, I can let most of my crew go home."

"So you'd be willing to stay yourself?"

"I'm here. I'd stay. And since it sounds like you're leaning that way, I'll say I always prefer having a show to explaining to a bunch of angry people that they shouldn't have come."

"Okay. We'll play. I want to play." Saying it made it even more true. I surveyed my bandmates for affirmation I'd made the right choice. April gave me a thumbs-up. Hewitt grinned.

Silva pulled a walkie-talkie from his belt and asked his staff to meet him in the lobby. I glanced at my silent phone. A repeat message from Margo, and two more missed calls. I turned it off. Sipped my tea again. Still bitter, but bearable with honey.

JD grabbed my arm. "Hey, Luce, can we talk for a sec?"

"Sure. Oh, do you mean in private?" Privacy wasn't usually a consideration in this band; we'd given it up months ago. The others had settled on the couch and looked immovable. I motioned toward the bathroom. "Step into my office."

The space wasn't made for two people. He sat on the closed toilet, and I leaned against the sink.

"I'm trying to stay on board," he said without preamble, "but I don't know if I can do it."

"What? Why didn't you say that a minute ago?"

"I didn't expect everyone else to agree to do it. I didn't want to be the bad guy."

"There are no bad guys here. I wanted opinions and nobody gave any."

"I did. I thought someone else would agree with me. It's not safe to play and I don't want to be here. I have a family."

"We all have families."

"Yeah, but I actually like mine. I want to see them again."

I ignored the dig, built on more made-up stories. "Nobody's going to do anything. We're not famous. We're at a not-so-famous theater in a random town."

"You say that, but somebody called in bomb threats to the hotels here last night."

"The whole state got bomb threats, not bombs."

"And today there were actual bombs. I thought you said there wouldn't be any hard feelings if we didn't want to play."

"That was ten minutes ago, before everybody agreed."

He shrugged. "I can't do it. I'm sorry. I can't play."

"We can't do the show without bass."

"I'm so sorry, Luce. I'll go back to the hotel, or sleep in the van, or clear out entirely if you want me to."

I couldn't think of anything else to say to convince him. Hewitt and April looked at me when I stepped out, and I shook my head. Why had he spoken to me in private, anyhow? It wasn't like they wouldn't find out a minute later. He couldn't sit in the bathroom forever. Wouldn't want to, if he was that scared.

I went to find Silva, to tell him we wouldn't be playing after all. Out in the lobby, a woman was unpacking our merchandise. We carried some with us, but since Gemma had gone home, the label had been shipping the bulk of it to venues—everything except the new T-shirts that had disappeared into the shipping ether—and hiring local fans to run the booth.

"Hi, I'm Luce."

"Alaia Park." She jotted a number on the side of a box, looked up, and smiled. She was older than me, maybe midthirties, with jet-black hair framing her face. When she spoke, she tucked one lock behind her ear. "I expected you to be taller than me."

"The video was filmed from a low angle. I get that a lot. Did Silva already talk to you? You were okay with being here tonight?" I asked her. I'd already shifted into past tense, resigned to the decision JD had made for us.

"Are you kidding? I've been waiting for this for weeks. I love your music."

"You're not scared?"

She bit her lip. "I'm a little scared, but I'm also scared some semi driver will fall asleep and cross the median while I'm driving home, or somebody will ignore a stop sign when I cross the street, or I'll step on a snake while walking my dog, or I'll catch some terrible virus from a public bathroom. All of which seem more likely than somebody attacking this place tonight."

I signed a poster for her: "To Alaia, who is brave." She let her fingers brush mine when I handed it back to her.

I found the narrow stairway to the sound booth.

Silva tucked a bookmark into the paperback he was reading and folded his arms over it.

"Better futures?" I asked, pointing to the rocket ship on the cover.

"Different futures, I guess. The staff all want to stay, except for one bartender. I won't need them all, but I didn't want them to lose a night's pay if they were willing."

"You're going to have to disappoint them after all. My bassist is bailing."

"What? I thought they were down to play."

"I thought so, too, but he waited until you left the room to express his concerns."

"Huh."

"I'm sorry."

"Me, too. Damn."

"I'll leave you to talk to your staff again, I guess." I turned to leave.

"There's one other option," he said.

"What's that?"

He gave a half smile. "I play bass."

He must not have had trouble reading the skepticism in my look. "I can do it," he went on. "I've been playing bass longer than

I've been running sound, by a long shot. And your songs are pretty straightforward—no offense meant. I've been playing you in the house for a week now, so I'm familiar with the stuff you've recorded, and if you give me a cheat sheet of keys and changes I'll be good to go."

"Who'd run sound?"

"The lighting tech can do both. She's more than good enough."

I gave him another look. The offer was sincere. "I guess we've got nothing to lose, since we're not thinking anyone's going to show up anyway. Welcome to the band, I guess."

He grinned. "I was hoping you'd say yes."

We waited to see how many actually came out of the two thousand ticket holders. The local opening band never arrived; neither did the DJ whose show we had played earlier in the day, who was supposed to introduce us.

I stood in the wing, behind the curtain, and watched people file in. Tried to interpret their expressions, figure out why they had showed up. The theater had assigned seating, so some sat too far for me to read their faces, but body language had a longer wavelength: grim, weary, wary. A couple near the front laughed and joked with exaggerated movement, trying too hard. The rest were quiet, far quieter than usual. Most nights, canned music filled in the wait time, but what to play on a night like this? Any choice was a statement, to be judged too upbeat, too downbeat, too heavy, too disrespectful. None of those options were right when there was a tiny shoe in rubble three thousand miles away.

The house lights were off, so I had no idea of the size of the audience, though I knew from their movement in the dimness there were at least a few people out there. I wasn't sure if I'd have made the same decision in their shoes, to risk being out in public.

Except I had; I kept forgetting. Some part of me kept fooling the rest of me into thinking I hadn't had a choice. Music wasn't a choice as far as I was concerned, even if I hadn't managed to say as much to my band. Playing music was the fire that kept the monsters at bay. Nothing could touch me in the middle of a song.

The audience had a choice; they had come. Checking their phones, murmuring numbers and updates to each other, shaking their heads, but present. Maybe they wanted my guitar to keep them safe, too.

April walked up behind me.

"What if they don't like us?" I whispered.

"They like us, or they wouldn't be here," she whispered back.

Hewitt appeared from the wing, looking grim. "They've grounded all planes. Schools are canceled tomorrow."

"Damn," I said.

He waved his guitar at me. "I'm going to go out and tune one more time for both of us. When we're ready, you're going to come out there and start playing, and we're going to make people forget what's outside this room for a little while."

I peeked out from behind the curtain again, then nodded. I still hadn't thought of anything worth saying. No words could be more appropriate than the four bars of guitar noise starting "Block Letters."

Hewitt tuned my guitar one more time, then his. The others took their positions, Silva the soundman standing in JD's spot. The room was eerily quiet. Normally there'd be cheers, clapping. I panicked. We should have had someone introduce us. I should have come up with something to say. I had no idea what they wanted from me.

My band looked in my direction. Waiting, watching as I stood paralyzed. As the numbers from the news hit me, a wave of numbers that were also names, names I didn't know, people. People who had gone out to a baseball matinee and hadn't come home. In all the fussing over whether to play or not to play, I had locked that image away from myself. Had these people done the same? Numbly gotten in cars, driven to our show because it was what they were supposed to do tonight? Or did they want more from me?

I took a step out onto the stage. It was dark, except for a spotlight where I was supposed to be.

"You got this, Luce," April whispered. I walked past her, to where my guitar and my spotlight waited. I put my hand to my brow to shade my eyes, strained to see the people scattered among the empty seats. They sat quiet, waiting. Waiting for me.

I stepped to the mic. "Come closer. There are plenty of empty seats up front." Then, "Please."

Nobody moved for a moment, and then one person in the back stood. Her chair closed with a creak behind her. It was so quiet every step echoed as she walked to the third row and chose a new seat. Another pause, then others began to move, as if she had given them permission. I strapped on my guitar while they rearranged themselves.

When the shuffling and creaking stopped, April counted us off. I hit my distortion pedal and played. Four bars of noise scaffolded on the solid frame of an A chord and its cousins, all of us building onto it with muscle and bone and blood. I almost forgot to come in with the vocal, the guitar felt so good in my hands.

With the song came the realization. The audience wasn't here for mourning; they had come for elegy. That was within our power.

We had chosen our set carefully. No "Timebomb," no "End Days." Tried to keep to the upbeat stuff, other than "Blood and Diamonds," which was uptempo but dark, and which they'd expect no matter what. Really, it didn't matter what we played. Silva locked in with April as if they had been playing together for all the months JD had been with us. We butchered "Don't Even Think About It," the new song, but it was Hewitt who forgot the change we'd made at soundcheck. It came around by the end, though. What mattered was that we were there and they were there, a conspiracy against despair.

The ovation surprised me. I toweled my neck, turned to the band. "Do you guys mind if I do one alone?"

"It's your show," Hewitt said.

"Thanks—can I use your acoustic?"

He passed it over. I put my own guitar back on its stand.

"Can you bring the house lights up, please?" I asked into the mic.

We saw them for the first time for real. Maybe fifty people out of two thousand seats, all crowded to the front.

"If you get the gist and want to sing along, feel free." My lone voice felt enormous in the silent room. I hadn't played this cover in years, but it was the kind that came to my mind on a night like this. A few voices joined in, then more. When the song ended, I gave a little salute and hopped off the front of the stage.

"That's it," I said. The house lights rose, again without music. Hewitt came to take his guitar from me.

"Go on," he said. "I'll pack up."

I spent the next thirty minutes chatting with the people who'd come. Sold some T-shirts, signed some records, but mostly hung around and talked. Everyone was reluctant to step back into the ugly world outside.

"Thank you for playing. I couldn't sit at home alone tonight," one woman said.

"I drove an hour to get here," said another. "I'm glad I did."

More so than usual, they all wanted a piece of me, a moment. I tried to give the time they needed. One after another, they each gave their variation on that story, and then wandered out into the night.

One thousand, three hundred, and twenty-three people died in the stadium bombs. Five more—all janitorial employees—died in another bomb in a shuttered mall while we were onstage.

A couple of years later, a journalist worked out that our show was the last large concert. They had to stretch the definition of large to make it work, but I guess they went on the theater's size, and the fact that all the stadiums and arenas and concert halls went dark that night for good.

The journalist didn't know it, and I didn't bother to say, but I think we probably had the last two shows, if you wanted to count the dance party in the hotel parking lot in the early hours of that day. I tended to always think of the one whenever I thought of the other. Making music in the darkness, then music against the darkness. The decision to play for the people who chose to go out instead of hiding in their homes. They'd have years and years for that.

All that came later.

That night, after the audience straggled out, after Alaia boxed up and counted our remaining merchandise, after her hand lingered against mine again far longer than necessary for passing a pen from one person to another, she and I stole a moment in the dark balcony. Hewitt called for me once from the bottom of the stairwell, and we giggled and shushed each other to keep from giving ourselves away. We leaned into each other, me and the woman who mistakenly thought I was the brave one. She wanted me, and I wanted someone to coax me from my head for a few minutes. Maybe that was what she'd come looking for, too; we didn't talk.

I don't know how JD got back to the hotel, but all his stuff was gone from the room he and Hewitt had shared. The DO NOT DISTURB sign was still illuminated, the pink room still a problem we'd have to deal with later.

"Do you want me to take JD's bed so you can have a room to yourself?" April asked, reaching into the painted fridge.

"No," I said. "But I'd love a few minutes alone."

"You got it, boss."

On the way out, I snagged the can of glo-paint. Back in our room, I propped my guitar in the corner and grabbed a needle from the emergency sewing kit I kept in my bag. Pushed aside the dresser, dipped the needle in the remaining paint.

Where nobody was likely to ever see it, I wrote the lyrics to a song I wasn't yet prepared to put to music: a song that had come to me on the silent drive back to the hotel from the show, jumbled and half-formed. Some songs stayed that way forever, ragged and ruptured and far from reach; those ones I'd rehearse and put aside, start again and put aside, saying it's not ready yet, but someday. I locked this one into order, painstakingly, letter by letter.

The dresser was back in place by the time April slipped into the room. I had the lights off, my guitar in hand, and I was listening to the tiny words that glowed behind the dresser, waiting for them to tell me what form they wanted to take. There were, to my knowledge, one hundred and seventy-three ways to wreck a hotel room. The one hundred and seventy-fourth was a slow, small form of destruction: tiny words, tiny fears, tiny hopes, etched in a place they might never be found.

6

ROSEMARY

Career Opportunities

She'd never had any plan to leave Superwally, so Rosemary couldn't say why she started poking around StageHoloLive's job listings, only that she was curious. The position that initially caught her eye was "upload supervisor," which involved being online at home to make sure there were no glitches in getting performances to the people who had paid for them. She was qualified; she had six years' experience at Superwally, including working out that bug before one of SHL's own concerts.

She debated expanding her one concert experience into talk of a lifetime's love for SHL, but they probably had ways to check. Cross-reference her address and they'd know she didn't have a home box, much less an SHL-enabled Hoodie. Cross-reference her credit account and they'd see the one drink at the one concert. She settled on mentioning how wonderful that Patent Medicine show had been, leaving out that it was her only one.

As she went over the job description one last time, she noticed a listing for an "artist recruiter." It paid the same, but included travel and expenses. What kind of job required travel? Plumbers and construction workers and blacksmiths drove around the area, but they made it home every night. This position didn't require experience; just enthusiasm, love of music, people skills, and a willingness to travel. She had enthusiasm, she loved music, and she could point to her vendor services record as proof of her people skills. She *was* willing to travel, even if she'd never done it before. She checked the boxes to apply for both positions.

The skills assessment and psychological section were easy enough. Then there was a fun little field test, where they posted a series of live videos with all information stripped from them, and she had to decide whether to pass on each act or make an offer. Five in total.

She didn't know anything about the music business, so she approached the problem in the same way she approached code, envisioning a perfect combination of catchy music and visual style first, using Patent Medicine's show as a guide, and then looking at the examples to see where they deviated. There wasn't such a thing as perfect in this case; music wasn't code, and musicians didn't snap to her rulers. Still, she disqualified one video because the act lacked energy, and another because they came across unfocused. She "signed" one band of the five. Nobody had messaged her to ask for the SHL Hoodie back, so she used that for the remote interview, rather than risk using her work rig or the glitchy old Basic model.

She was surprised when the offer came through for the recruiter job instead of the upload supervisor position. She closed and reopened the message, making sure she hadn't misread it. "Uniquely qualified," they said. She went back and reread her application to make sure she hadn't promised anything she'd be unable to deliver, but she'd made no rash declarations. She hadn't even exaggerated much. Her enthusiasm must have shown through, or maybe her dedication to her current position. Or maybe they saw her as a blank slate. Moldable.

Leaving Superwally was trickier. For starters, she had no idea how to do it. For all their "You are valued but replaceable" posters, they didn't leave any instructions for severing ties with the company. Maybe that was deliberate. In the end, she waited for Jeremy's morning call.

"You're doing what?" he asked. He was a young Igbo man today, wearing a mix of traditional and modern clothes. The Superwally avatars weren't fancy enough to show much emotion, but his made a good stab at surprise.

"Quitting. How do I quit?"

"Why would you quit? You have six years' seniority. You're good at your job."

"I found a better job. I hope. A different one, anyway."

"Nobody quits, Rosemary. There are no better jobs."

"You mean no better jobs for people like me?" That was what she'd been told since high school. She hadn't been able to afford the online certification courses she needed for higher-end jobs, and her parents' credit hadn't been good enough for loans. She spent all of high school preparing for Superwally customer service. Leaving was unthinkable.

"For people like us."

"I am. I'm leaving. I'm leaving Superwally." She psyched herself up in the saying. It was as much for her benefit as Jeremy's.

He sighed. "I'm sorry to lose you. You've been reliable."

He gave her instructions for contacting a mysterious Talent Management hotline. She repeated the whole conversation, almost verbatim, with a generic gray-blonde white woman avatar exuding generic concern. It wasn't that anyone was worried they couldn't replace her. It was touching; they genuinely didn't believe there were other jobs out there. She appreciated the concern. It embroidered her own terror nicely.

What was she doing? She had a real job, a good one, one she performed well. She was leaving it because she had been struck by lightning, had gone crazy, had some idea she could do something else.

"Superwally is reliable work. What if this new company goes out of business? Where will you be then?" her father asked when she told him. He asked all the questions that swirled in her head, as if they were leaking out.

She held a panel for him at the windmill's base while he fiddled inside it. They wore thick winter work gloves, which made the adjustments cumbersome and slow. "They're not new. They've been around for a bunch of years and they're in eighty percent of American homes." Answering felt good. It built her own confidence in her decision.

"What if Superwally decides to go into the concert business? They're in even more homes."

"If we—they—wanted that they'd have done it already. It's some kind of partnership, with Superwally as the conduit."

"And tell me again why you have to go there in person?"

She hadn't yet mentioned that her job would involve more travel after this trip. Baby steps. "It's a training program. They want us to see how they make the magic happen, so we can fix it when it goes wrong."

"Wrong magic?"

"Wrong metaphor, I guess, but you know what I mean. And how cool is it that I get to go someplace?" Her father looked hurt, and she scrambled to appease him. "Not that I ever felt like I needed to go anyplace before, but I've been doing the same job for six years. I think I'm allowed to want to change it up a little, aren't I?"

He scratched his winter beard. "I want you to be safe."

"And happy?"

"And happy, but mostly safe."

"I'm old enough to take care of myself. You lived in a city a thousand miles from your parents by the time you were my age."

"That was a different time . . ."

She knew the speech by heart. " 'That was a different time, and this was a different country. The best thing we can do now is take care of each other and stay in the safest place we can, and make ourselves as self-sufficient as possible.' " She paused. "But Dad, you've been saying that my whole life. You've made this a great place to grow up, but if you don't want me in a hood twenty-four/seven *and* you don't want me to go anywhere, then I'm trapped with Superwally forever. I'm not going to do anything dangerous. I just want to know what else is out there."

He held out his hands, and they fit the panel back into place. The more he argued, the more convinced she was she needed to try this.

7

LUCE

Something's Gotta Change

A hotel in Pennsylvania found another bomb before it detonated. A gunman had shot up a bus station in Mississippi and barricaded himself in. That was the news we woke to the following morning: a study in random lone wolf horror, with nobody sure if it was actually random lone wolves or not, and the same ominous requests from the government to get home, and stay home. Whatever they knew, they weren't telling.

"The tour is over," Margo at the label repeated over the phone. "All the venues are dark. Go home."

Home. I didn't have one. I'd sublet my rented room in Queens a year before, to a guy who had taken over the lease when I didn't come back. He had offered to give my bed back if I came knocking, but I didn't have any particular ties to the furniture, and my few personal belongings traveled with me.

I sent messages to friends in a few cities I thought I could survive lying low in, and was rewarded with an offer of a situation similar to the one I'd left: a furnished sublet in a Baltimore artists' collective. The occupant was also a touring musician, currently on an extended gig in Europe.

What about a European tour? I texted Margo.

Months to arrange. Visas, instruments, etc. We'll see, she wrote back.

April and Hewitt tried to book flights home, to New York and L.A. respectively, but the planes were grounded. Hewitt ended up squeezing into a rental car with two businesswomen who were also trying to get west, and April bought a one a.m. bus ticket, the only one available.

The van felt empty, quiet, even with music playing. Loosed from the magnetic pull of the next show, the next stopover, the potential of any nextness at all, the road dulled and flattened. I was the losing team slinking home, except my destination wasn't even home. I dumped my meager belongings at the new place, turned in the rental van with a wistful pat, and resigned myself to a stay of unknown duration in someone else's bed in someone else's room in someone else's house in someone else's city.

I had no idea what to do with myself. I woke around noon every day. Checked the news before leaving bed, to see if the curfew had been lifted; it hadn't. People protested here and there, on principle, but the protests were halfhearted. The frequency of the attacks and the randomness of the ongoing threats had left people genuinely scared.

I'd pad downstairs in pajama bottoms and an old T-shirt, not even bothering to get dressed. There were four roommates: a sculptor, a nurse, a filmmaker, and a burlesque performer. The filmmaker, Jaspreet, was a teacher by day, but the rest of us kept odd hours. We mostly ran into each other in the kitchen: someone on coffee, someone else eating breakfast, another lunch.

"We should be getting back to normal," one would say. "Before we forget what normal is."

"We have to find a new normal," said another. I knew all their names by then, but it didn't really matter who said what. It was the same conversation, over and over.

Then somebody would point out some aspect that was

improving—schools reopening, say—and we'd all pretend to be cheered. I'd fill a bowl with cereal and slink back upstairs. It wasn't that I disliked their company; it just wasn't what I was looking for.

I'd call Margo at some point in the afternoon. "Have you heard anything today?"

She'd assure me that she'd let me know if she had, and I didn't need to call daily. She didn't understand that I did. I needed her to tell me to head back out on tour. I thought of Alaia and the staff at the Peach, and at all the other places we'd played. They all got paid hourly. How many people were going to struggle to pay their bills next month if the clubs stayed closed? Clubs, theaters, cinemas, stadiums, malls. Even a day could be devastating for an hourly worker. I remembered what that was like.

I'd never done so much nothing before. High school had been a blur of new experiences once I relocated myself to my aunt's couch uptown: jeans, guitars, music, girls, the entire glorious city I'd missed out on. When I graduated, booking and playing and promoting for myself were three full-time jobs, even while I held a fourth to pay my rent. Touring and promotion kept me busy once I got on the road; writing and recording and rehearsing kept me busy the rest of the time. Downtime was new territory.

Telling myself to write didn't work, either. The song I'd written on the hotel wall had hidden itself from me. The lyrics still glowed in my head when I closed my eyes, but it didn't feel right putting them to music. I lay on my bed and did nothing, a pointed nothing, an arpeggiated chord of a nothing, strung out over the afternoon.

April called once to ask me the same question I asked Margo; I gave Margo's answer.

"You're a mess." April's hands tapped a beat into her kitchen counter.

I turned off my camera, though she'd already seen me. "How are you *not* a mess? Where are you, anyway?"

"Home." She looked unperturbed. "New York is always New York."

My heart lifted. "Do you mean clubs there are open?"

"No. The clubs and museums are still closed, and there aren't many tourists, but that makes it nicer. I've found enough session work to pay rent. Everybody's recording since they can't play out. What are you doing? You look like shit. When was the last time you washed your hair?"

I couldn't remember. "I'm not doing much. Our stuff has been selling well online since people got stuck inside. SuperStream royalties are decent. It's paying the bills."

"Silver lining, I guess. You can come visit if you want."

It took me another month to convince myself to take her up on that offer. Schools reopened, then a scattering of other places: local stores, a movie theater here or there. More threats rolled in behind. Major League Baseball discussed kicking off an abbreviated season, then called it off. A museum opened for a day, then closed again.

"If this were a war zone, people would go about their business." My sculptor-roommate was Syrian, and knew war zones. "People here fool themselves into thinking they're safe, and they can't take it when that illusion gets shattered."

I nodded, retreated to my room again, called Margo. "There's got to be someplace to play."

"Not enough to build a tour on, Luce," Margo said. "Hang in there. We're waiting to hear about summer festivals. If those are a no-go, we can start looking for small clubs again, maybe."

I called April. "Waiting is killing me. Are you still telling me there's not a single club open in New York?"

"That was last month. Now there are some spots booking shows under the radar."

She tossed venue names at me. One was a hole-in-the-wall I'd played as a teenager. I called and convinced them to let me do a show under a different name, no publicity; nothing that would draw attention while they were supposed to be closed at night.

I took an interstate bus up to the city. I'd expected people to be warier, but we stood in line and chatted as if the social contract was still being followed by all parties. Everyone angled for a window seat; I earned a few dirty looks when I leaned my guitar into the window and sat beside it on the aisle, but I waved a second ticket at them. "She paid, too."

The road looked the same as when I'd left it, if a little emptier. The bus spit me out at six p.m. in midtown and I wasn't due until eight, so I walked the forty blocks down to the bar, stopping on the way for a hot dog and pretzel from a vendor. New York looked the same but emptier. Mine and not mine.

Mine: the street corners where I'd played at eighteen; the clubs that hadn't blinked an eye as long as I walked in with a guitar; the bands that saw me sitting hungry in a corner during their soundchecks and shared their fries and let me open for them.

Not mine: the combination of the resolute "We are New York" bustle and emptier-than-usual streets. The feeling that behind the bustle, even New York was afraid.

I wondered if my parents had noticed any of the upheaval. They and all my siblings were over the bridge in Brooklyn, where they might as well have been on another continent, living as if a wall separated them from the rest of the city, with their own wonderful social structures that I guessed were impervious to the closures hitting the outside world. Once in a while I'd tried calling a sibling to invite them to a New York show, but I never expected them to come, and they never did.

April was already at the Carryback when I arrived, nursing what looked like a hot toddy. I almost hugged her after so many months living with strangers, but I held back. She looked more tired than I'd expected.

"I'm sorry you can't play with me here. No-drums policies are stupid."

She shrugged. "No worries. This place is pretty small for a full band."

"I remember."

"I forgot you'd played here before. They still have the same house amp, but half the knobs are broken off and it sounds like crap. Anyway, I borrowed a better one for you."

"You're the best," I said. "Can I pay for your drink?"

"I already paid for this one, but you can buy me another." She raised her empty mug.

I paid for another toddy for her and a Casa Dragones for myself, and we stepped past a thick curtain into the back room, April dragging a small road case behind her. The venue space was tinier than I remembered. Six barstools stood under a ledge on the far wall, and there was room for another fifteen or twenty people to stand, if they didn't mind getting cozy. A small soundboard ate into the raised staged area, which was barely large enough for two people with guitars. Definitely not a drum kit. "You could have played bongos, I guess."

"Bite your tongue," she said. "Anyway, I feel cruddy tonight. Just as well you fly solo."

"That explains the cold-weather drinks. Hung over?"

"I shouldn't be. I dunno." She hoisted her small case onto the stage, pushing aside the house amp. The house amp's grille cloth had torn down the middle like an autopsy, exposing twin speakers underneath. The treble, volume, and overdrive knobs were missing; pliers rested on the cabinet for anyone who wanted to make adjustments.

"Ouch." I tried turning a knobless knob. "That has definitely seen better days."

"Right? You'll like this better. My friend Nico made it. It's good for small spaces."

I unclasped the case April had brought, and removed the top to reveal the amp inside.

"Whoa. That's beautiful." The cabinet had an art deco look, stylish and sleek. No branding on the front, but a little brass plaque on the back read "Nico Lectrics, B'klyn." I plugged the amp into the surge protector and my guitar into the amp. Turned my back on April to fiddle with the settings and play a bit. It had a wicked clean crunch, and I found a tonal sweet spot before I raised the volume to five.

"It sounds gorgeous," I said to April. She leaned against the wall, looking a little worse for wear. "I don't suppose he'd sell it?"

She shook her head. "One of a kind. I told him you had the money to pay for it if you fucked it up. I'm pretty sure that's true, but don't."

I played a while longer, then glanced at my watch. Eight o'clock. "What time do the doors open? Shouldn't the sound person be here already?"

"Not if you haven't paid one, sweetie," someone said, stepping through the curtain. "And hopefully you're not expecting to get paid, either."

The man speaking might have been an old forty or a young sixty, with an unfiltered-cigarette voice. He leaned a battered guitar case against the stage; the case was mostly duct tape. I wasn't sure how much protection it actually gave the instrument inside.

I smiled my fakest smile. "If I needed money, sweetie, I wouldn't be playing here. Thanks for letting me know about the sound, though. Not a problem. Are you on the bill tonight?"

He nodded. I couldn't tell if he had caught the chastisement. "The owner shows up with the set times at some point. I'll run sound for you for twenty bucks if you want."

"I can take care of myself, thanks. If you want, I'll run sound for you for fifty." I dropped the smile.

April stifled a laugh, then a cough. The guy stared at me for a minute, then moved on to ignoring me, which I could already tell I'd prefer to anything he said. Even if I'd needed his help, which I didn't, I knew his type. It had been a while since I'd had to deal with an asshole of this particular variety; I'd gotten spoiled.

The bartender pushed through the curtain, waving a slip of paper and looking harried. "Hey, y'all, Shaun's sick, so he's not coming in. He said these are the set times, but if you don't like the order, you can switch. It's just you."

The other musician walked over to grab the paper from her hand.

"You're here because you want to play," April whispered. "Don't let him ruin your night."

She was right; he had already crept into my mood. An evening of like-minded musicians pushing back against ridiculous times would have been nice, but this wasn't going to be that, and that hadn't been my purpose in coming. I needed to play. I said a silent prayer to have even one person show up; playing for April and this dude wouldn't be the same.

"Ladies first." The other musician held up the scrap. Two forty-minute sets, me and then him, starting at nine thirty. I realized we hadn't even introduced ourselves. The paper had his name as Tanner Watkiss.

"Molly Fowler?" He squinted at the page. "I haven't heard of you. Where else do you play?"

I hadn't even remembered the name I'd chosen when the owner had suggested a pseudonym. I shrugged. "This is my first show. It's probably better that I'm opening for you."

Watkiss gave me a suspicious look, and I tried to mold my face into some semblance of innocent and sincere.

Messing with his head distracted from the empty room, in any case. So did finishing my self-soundcheck. I pulled my own microphone from my backpack to replace the club's battered SM58. It was possible to adjust the PA faders from the stage if I didn't mind working upside down, which I didn't. Watkiss judged in silence from the center of the room. April sat on a stool against the back wall, holding her drink to her face to inhale the dissipating steam. Normally I'd have asked her if I'd gotten the balance right, but I didn't want to leave an opening for Watkiss's opinion, so I decided to trust my own judgment. When I was satisfied, I leaned my guitar against the amp and went to sit with April.

"Sound okay?" I asked.

She opened her eyes. "I'd be lying if I said I'd been listening. Sorry, Luce. I feel like crap."

"No worries. Sorry you're sick. Do you need to go?"

"Nah. I'll sit here and hold up the wall 'til you're done."

To my relief, four people walked in as I finished writing my set list. Prayers answered: an audience, albeit a small one. I knew they hadn't come for me, since "Molly Fowler" didn't exist. That meant either they were Tanner Watkiss fans or they'd come to hear new music. I spotted Watkiss giving them the same once-over, and settled on the latter. Excellent.

By nine thirty, five more people had wandered in. It didn't take much to make this room look full. I stepped onto the tiny stage, tuned one more time, then flipped the little amp on and stepped to the mic. The small crowd kept chatting among themselves.

For one moment, staring out at eleven people from a stage the size of a shower stall, nerves gripped me. I shook it off. Ridiculous. I'd played for thousands without a second thought. Why did eleven hit me this way? Because I had to win these people over from scratch. It had been a while since I'd done it, but it wasn't like I'd never been in that position before.

"Hi, I'm—" I paused to remember the pseudonym, but it was gone. It didn't matter, anyhow. "—I'm gonna play a few songs for you. Thanks for coming."

The set I'd written skipped the songs that had hit it big on SuperStream. I lit into "Lost and Found," urgent, upbeat, an opener designed to silence anybody who thought they'd talk through my set. It worked. I shifted my gaze, stopping short of eye contact to avoid making anyone uncomfortable in a room this small, inviting them into the song but not putting them on the spot.

The speakers let out a squeal and broke the spell I was trying to cast. In between lines I glanced over at the PA: Watkiss was playing with the equalizer levels I'd set. I glared at him, but he didn't look up. I knew his type; he'd never stop fiddling. He stared at the knobs as he twisted them, like perfection was just out of reach.

I brought the song to its end, then turned to him. Silent stares weren't going to do it. "Dude, step away from the mixing board before I break my guitar over your head."

A few laughs from the audience. At least they understood I wasn't the problem. When I had the levels back where I wanted them, I turned to the mic. Smiled. Pretended the first song hadn't happened. "Hi! I'm gonna play a few songs for you. Thanks for coming." Another laugh. They were on my side.

The set went fine after that. The audience was there because they wanted to hear something new, or maybe because they wanted to pretend things were normal for a minute.

I was there because I needed the energy I could only get from this connection: the elusive collision of a song, a performance, a moment; the agreement that I would try to reach them, and they'd open themselves to being reached. The last few horrible months fell away for the duration of nine songs. Nine songs to stave off whatever was going on outside. I'd thought I needed to be on tour, but it wasn't the road I was missing. It was this, in whatever room I could find this, big or small.

I didn't want it to end. I had enough songs to play another hour, but this wasn't my room. I finished my last song and walked off to solid applause. Waited a moment to show the set was really over, then stepped back up to grab my guitar, mic, and amp. No way was I sharing my gear with that dude.

"Good set, sweetie," Watkiss said. "You could probably make a go of it if the world wasn't going to shit."

"Apology accepted." He looked like he had more to say, but I turned my back on him.

A couple of people stepped over to make conversation. "Do you have anything I can buy?" asked one of the women who had walked in first. Her tank top showed off amazing shoulders. I'd kill for shoulders like that, though working out or swimming to get them made more sense than killing.

"Or SuperStream?" one of her friends asked.

I almost said no, then realized the pseudonym's purpose had been to keep from bringing too many people into the room; it didn't matter now that the show had ended. "Yeah, but it's under another name."

Most of them looked blank at my name, but one opened his eyes wider. "Oh, man. You've got that song. I know that song."

He sang the chorus of "Blood and Diamonds" and the others nodded in recognition.

"What are you doing in this dump?" his friend in thick-rimmed glasses asked.

"It's the only place open," another answered before I could.

"She could be playing StageHolo to way more people."

I looked at the guy with the glasses. "What's Stage Hollow?"

"It's a new company. I've got a friend who works there. It's going to take off huge any day now."

I made a mental note to look into it.

"I'm glad you're here, anyway," declared the guy who'd recognized me. "I didn't care who played tonight, but I'm glad it was you."

"Can I buy you a drink?" asked the woman with the delicious shoulders.

Come-on, or friendly offer? She put her hand on my arm. A strong hand, with exactly the right weight behind the gesture. Definitely hitting on me.

"I'd love nothing more, but my friend over there"—I nodded my head toward April—"needs help getting home."

She looked at April and withdrew the touch. "Uh, yeah. She doesn't look so hot. Rain check."

Tanner Watkiss started to play, and the group that had chatted with me reoriented themselves toward the stage. I'd hoped he would be an awful performer, but he was disappointingly adequate. He'd bypassed the amp and plugged his Gibson Hummingbird into the PA. He had a solid fingerpicking style, and his singing voice had craggy charm. The song wasn't memorable, but he played it well.

Politeness dictated that I stay for his set since he'd stayed for mine. On the other hand, April looked worse by the second. I turned my back on Watkiss.

"Let me help you get back to your place," I told April.

She opened her eyes. "Yeah, okay."

The fact that she didn't even try to protest told me it was the right move. I didn't have to wait to get paid since there wasn't going to be any money. I slung my gig bag and knapsack over my right shoulder. The amp's road case, blessedly, had wheels and a collapsing handle.

"Can you walk?" I asked.

April nodded. As she slid off her stool I doubted it, but she made it to her feet. I let her lead the way so I could keep an eye on her. She traced the wall with her hand as she walked.

It was only eleven p.m., and the weather was on our side. The Hack I'd called arrived before we even made it to the door. April slid into the backseat, but didn't shift over. I piled my gear into the trunk and walked around the other side. "Are you sure you don't want to go to a hospital?"

She shook her head. "No hospital. I let my insurance lapse. Stupid, I know. I'll be fine. I'll sleep it off."

I put a hand on her forehead. "You're burning up."

"A cold. I'll be fine."

I knew she wasn't fine just from the fact that her hands were still. I thought back through the entire evening, but couldn't remember her hands drumming at all.

We rode to Harlem in silence. I carried the gear to her third-floor walk-up, then came down to help her with the stairs; she'd only managed the first four steps. I put her in bed in her clothes. In the kitchen, I pulled a glass off the drying rack and filled it with water. It was a mystery to me whose stuff was whose in the bathroom, but I grabbed a bottle of Tylenol and another of store-brand cold medicine for her to choose between. I didn't know what else to do for her. Didn't know where she'd intended for me to sleep, either: the living room had a curtain pulled across the entrance and was clearly now somebody's bedroom. I opened her closet and rummaged until I found her sleeping bag and laid it out on her floor.

April moaned and tossed, obviously exhausted but not sleeping. I felt helpless. She needed a doctor, but I couldn't make her go. I sanitized the bathroom and kitchen sinks and all the doorknobs, scrubbed my hands raw with soap and hot water, and managed to fall into a half sleep until one of her roommates walked in around four. I got up to talk to them, but the other bedroom door closed before I got there, and nobody answered when I knocked. Back to the sleeping bag.

"Go home," April whispered not long after the sun rose. "I'll be fine."

"Like hell. I'm not leaving until you go to a doctor or one of your roommates says they'll keep an eye on you."

"Don't count on that. They're assholes."

"How about a clinic, at least? Finite cost. I'll pay if you don't have the cash." I knew I shouldn't have said that the second it was out of my mouth.

"Go home, Luce. I'll go to a clinic later if I'm not feeling better. I promise."

I'd stepped over a line. We weren't really friends. I'd been her employer, sort of. We'd been in a band, sort of. Her pride was never going to let me help more than I'd helped already. I went online to switch my tickets to an earlier bus.

"Feel better. Thanks for the gig and the awesome amp and the place to stay . . ." My voice trailed off.

She propped herself on one elbow. "The amp? It made it back here, right?"

I pointed to the corner, and she leaned back again. "Thanks."

"You're sure I can't do anything else?"

She waved me away. I would have preferred to tell a roommate how sick she was, but I didn't see anyone, and she had said they were assholes. I showed myself out.

I bought a coffee and a sourdough bagel on the way to the subway, both of which I regretted when I realized it was rush hour. Even with all the closings, rush hour in New York still strained the system. I had to swing my guitar off my back and hold it in front of me to protect it, while the other elbow hooked the pole, keeping my coffee from my face. I distracted myself by people-watching, but even that was less fun than usual with the bad night's sleep setting in. It might have been my imagination, but everyone looked drawn, lessened. By the time I got off the train, my coffee had gone cold. I tossed it in the nearest wastebasket.

The morning bus back to Baltimore wasn't as crowded as the one I'd taken the day before. Nobody fussed over the guitar's seat, and there were enough windows for everyone. I took a seat on the top level to see Manhattan as we drove away; New York always looked majestic from New Jersey. After the island's southern tip dipped from view, I turned my attention to the thought I'd been avoiding.

What to do next? I'd hoped playing a show would buoy me, but a single show's high faded too fast. It had been a temporary distraction at best. I needed something real and lasting, and nothing I thought of fit the bill.

What was the new site the guy with the glasses had mentioned after my set? At least researching and setting myself up on a new platform might eat some time and make me feel productive. He'd called it Super Hollow. No. Stage Hollow? I searched on my phone until I found it: StageHolo. Not the catchiest brand name.

The bus braked hard and I braced against the seat in front of me, arm across my guitar to keep it from shifting. I looked out on a sea of brake lights. A little odd heading away from the city at this time of morning.

I turned back to the StageHolo site. It looked like they were offering private shows through proprietary hardware, at a fee. "No parking, no puking. Like a live show, but better." Their taglines needed work, and they didn't seem to have an artist sign-up link. It looked a little rough.

The bus still hadn't moved. I stood to look through the front window. Others did the same.

"Can you see what's the delay?" I asked a man who looked like he'd been paying attention.

"Nah. An ambulance pulled up on the other side of the highway, way in front. I think they tried to get through on this side but the shoulder was too narrow."

I went back to my seat to wait. Another twenty minutes passed. The bus lurched forward, and eventually passed a tow truck trying to extricate a car from the guardrail. Once we got past, the highway emptied out again, as if there'd never been a problem.

We made it as far as the Thomas Edison rest stop. This was supposed to be an express from New York to Baltimore, but the loudspeaker crackled and the driver announced, "We're making a quick stop to disembark a sick passenger. Stay on the bus and we'll be back on our way momentarily."

The doors were on the opposite side from where I was sitting, so I had to crane my neck to see. An ambulance waited for us at the rest stop, and we all watched as a passenger I didn't remember from the line made his way to it with the help of two paramedics. There hadn't been much noise from downstairs; I assumed if something dramatic had happened, we would have heard it upstairs.

I checked the time. Eleven a.m. already. Late enough to text April without feeling too guilty if I woke her.

How u doing? I wrote. No response.

The bus started again. The rest of the ride was uneventful. I texted April a couple more times then gave up, hoping she was sleeping it off. If she didn't answer, I didn't have any other way of reaching her.

Trudging from the bus back to the house reinforced the letdown. A single show was not a tour. It wasn't even enough of a rush to get me through a day. I let myself in to the house I lived in, a house that still didn't feel like a home. Not that there was anything homey about a tour's worth of hotel rooms, but at least that carried some payoff. Home was the road, the gig, the music.

There was nobody in the living room. Nobody in the kitchen. A cat I'd never seen before mewled a greeting, but when I stooped to pet it my gig bag swung off my shoulder and it skittered away. Back in my room, I leaned the guitar against a wall and collapsed on the bed in an exact replay of every day previous to the day before. Playing a single show hadn't changed anything, and I still didn't know what would.

8

ROSEMARY

Little Boxes

The farm truck hadn't been allowed on highways since the phase-out, so Rosemary had to hire a single-cell cab to drive her to the StageHoloLive orientation. She'd never been in a single-cell before. A nice bench seat to herself, and if she kept her hands in her lap she didn't have to contemplate the other people who'd sat here and touched the surfaces. She didn't have to touch anything other than her own phone and the door handles, and there was no driver to force awkward conversation, the way they did in her parents' old shows.

She was glad she hadn't driven the farm truck; she'd be stuck watching the road ahead and listening to the misfiring engine, which roared too loud for her to bother with music. In the truck she'd be stuck on the rutted county roads, since Rattlebang wasn't allowed on this smooth new automated highway. This way she got to look out the windows at everything she'd missed for the last dozen years stuck in Jory. Not that she could see much from the highway, but she caught glimpses: shopping centers turned detention centers turned Superwally distribution centers; barns with winter-bare oaks thrusting through caved-in roofs; the skeletal spines of roller coasters in an abandoned amusement park; a motel captured in time; a cinema, where total strangers used to gather in large groups to watch movies. Everywhere, the ghosts of a past she was old enough to remember, barely, but not to remember well. Her parents' world, not hers.

Her own world overlay theirs. The silent-running cab meant she could listen to Whileaway songs as she rode, the perfect soundtrack. She kept her new Hoodie in mapview, generated highways painted onto blacktop, landmark identifiers whizzing by in the periphery. Ads for the latest Patent Medicine song and Nightlights birch beer hovered in the cumulus clouds. Migrating flocks, flying north, tagged on the wing with the BirdGoggles app. Here and there, a walled compound, the houses of those who had fled the city with more money than her family, or a trailer enclave, for those with less.

She didn't resent the tiny safe place they had built for her. She'd had friends, even if they were online. There was always enough to do to keep her from getting bored, except for at work, which was expected. If she took this one opportunity to see what went on outside of her Hoodie, her house, Jory, then she could say she'd done it. Done something, even if it led right back to her room.

Her stomach tied itself in knots as the single-cell exited the highway and navigated a series of quick turns to arrive at a ten-foot security gate. NO UNAUTHORIZED VEHICLES read one sign on the gate, alongside NO UNAUTHORIZED VISITORS. A bored-looking white guard at the gate inspected her ID through a clearviewed Hoodie. "You're on the list," he said after a moment. "But the vehicle isn't. I can get them to send a car up here for you, but if you're able to walk, it'll be less hassle."

"I can walk." No point in making trouble. The single-cell puttered off toward its next customer as soon as she'd lifted her bag from the trunk and released it. No turning back.

She wanted to ask where she was supposed to go, but she didn't want to be a bother. Anyway, there was only one road, wide and tree-lined. The ancient suitcase she'd borrowed from her mother had one cracked wheel and pulled to the right as she walked. Too early for budding back home, here trees bloomed pink and white, big puffballs she didn't recognize. It must have rained recently, because the ground was carpeted with more blooms, making it that much harder to pull the suitcase, even if it did serve as a delightful welcome mat rolled out just for her.

After a ten-minute walk, an enormous building loomed into view. Bigger than the abandoned high school in town, bigger than the Superwally Fulfillment Center between Jory and Belgicus. There was a giant door and a human-sized door, so she picked the human side.

A man about her age smiled at her from across a reception desk, and she realized with a shock that she couldn't identify his features. Online she knew the shorthand that told you an avatar's ethnicity, or where to check if you didn't know. It was considered appropriation to wear an avatar of a culture that wasn't yours, unless you were Quality Control, and even they only did it for a minute. She wasn't sure how to categorize his ethnicity at all, and her assumption of male pronouns might be wrong, too. Nor was she sure why it mattered, or if it mattered. Maybe she cared because she liked the idea of being from somewhere, even far back in family history, since she wasn't from anywhere special. Maybe she was used to inhabiting spaces where people had ways of telling you how they wanted to be perceived. All those thoughts ran through her head in the time it took him to say, "Welcome to the StageHolo family, Rosemary," in a Texan accent.

StageHoloLive had the same Talent Management hoops to jump through as Superwally; they called it People Operations here, perhaps to distinguish from the actual talent onstage, and after letting her drop her bags in the dormitory room, they ran her through all the paperwork required to get paid and stay employed. She waited for the part where they'd start listing workplace restrictions, but they didn't seem to care. They didn't require inspirational posters, or put any demands on her workspace at all. She also wouldn't be doing much work from home, though they didn't say what that meant. Those were the pleasant surprises.

Her private room was a pleasant surprise, too, with its own tiny bathroom and meals delivered to the door during her stay; she hadn't realized how apprehensive she'd been about sharing space until she walked through the dormitory area. The macaroni and cheese she ordered had different spices from those she was used to—onions, and paprika—but it was still a relief not to have to eat in a cafeteria. She'd seen cafeterias in her parents' old movies, and they always looked chaotic and dirty to her.

It turned out the main reason they brought new employees in to the compound, other than the paperwork, was to show them how the actual concerts were recorded. It made sense. Some new hires would be working on the broadcasts, as stagehands or technicians. Others supported the talent: makeup, wardrobe, artist liaison. There were eight altogether in her training group, all around her age or younger, but Rosemary was the only new hire going out to work "in the field," whatever that meant.

The second day started with a tour. Her training group all eyed each other, assessing, leaving as much space as possible between their bodies in the small classroom. Rosemary had agonized over what to wear to an in-person training, settling on something not too unlike her Superwally uniform. The others were a little more casual, in jeans or tights and unbranded long-sleeved T-shirts. They all looked scruffy in comparison to the avatars she was used to interacting with. Their colors were off, their hair frizzed. A couple had pox scars on their cheeks or arms. She'd been lucky enough to get through the outbreak with scars only on her torso, hidden beneath her clothes.

"Ah, you're all here! Welcome!" The new woman in the room had a military bearing, ramrod spine, and a geometric twist piled on her head that surpassed even the most gravity-defying av hairdos. She had the darkest skin Rosemary had ever seen outside hoodspace. "My name is Jeannie. I'll be your mama duck, and y'all will be my ducklings. Follow, ducklings."

They followed. Jeannie marched her gawking charges through

artist lounges, dressing rooms, practice rooms, and editing studios at a pace that left the group gasping for breath.

As they passed people in their work environments, Rosemary wondered how anyone had gotten the experience to wind up in these careers. She'd been led to computers the moment she had shown aptitude, and had never gotten any hint that any other path existed. High school funneled her classmates to one of eight concentrations: medicine/nursing, farming, military, construction, teaching, trade, computers, or some aspect of the Superwally empire, which technically bled over into the other seven. Did people teach themselves sound and makeup, or was there someplace they learned those things? She kept her mouth shut, afraid she'd sound silly or provincial, until Colton, the wardrobe guy, asked, "How do people become musicians, anyway?" and nobody laughed.

Jeannie stopped. The woman behind crashed into her, and Rosemary walked straight into both of them. She flinched at the contact, stepping backward onto someone else's foot. The unexpected touch left her so flustered she almost missed the response to Colton's question.

Jeannie answered without teasing, which suggested why she was the guide; it would be easy enough for someone working here to laugh, to forget what it had been like to be new. "Some were musicians already, Before, with live shows and everything. I know it's hard for some of you to imagine a time when people made a living playing live concerts for live audiences, but a lot of our musicians, even the younger ones, never stopped imagining it. They came to us, or we sought them out, because we're the ones who can make it happen for them."

She started walking again, and the group raced to keep up with her. "I know we promised to show you a live recording, and you're in luck. We have a very special performance today. If you've never seen Magritte play, you're in for a treat."

Colton gasped, and a couple of others perked up at the news. Rosemary pretended to be excited as well. She knew she had a lot of catching up to do in her musical education.

The narrow hallway ended in a locked door. Jeannie flashed a pass and ushered them into a space as big as a Superwally Fulfillment Center. The change from low-ceilinged hallway was drastic, but the soundstage itself wasn't so different from what Rosemary had expected. She'd pictured an auditorium, given the way Patent Medicine had played, or at least something the size of the Bloom Bar. All of their moves had been so much larger than life.

She'd expected the size, but not the silence. She'd imagined a set filled with people, bustle, music. Instead, the enormous space was filled with small modular rooms, like trailer homes. Rosemary looked for a stage. If not the exact one from the Bloom Bar, at least something similar. Speakers, amplifiers, lights. Something.

Jeannie spoke as if someone had asked a question. "You'll understand in a minute. Take it all in. There's a quiz later."

They all exchanged glances. Rosemary couldn't tell if the part about the quiz was true or not, so she tried to memorize the layout. The walls were lined with digital clocks stating the hour, minute, and second in three dozen cities around the world. Wires snaked everywhere from the trailer-boxes.

Jeannie glanced at her watch, smiled. "They'll arrive any second now."

As if on cue, a door opened on the hangar's far side, where the wardrobe and makeup wing branched off. A tall black woman entered, wearing a silk dress the color of rain. The man following her looked like he might be related—they had the same cheekbones, the same build—and a white woman trailed them waving a tablet. "Are you sure you want to change the order now?" she asked. "The techs aren't going to like it. You're on in ten minutes."

The tall woman had an accent Rosemary was unable to place, even after all her vendor services calls. Caribbean, maybe? "I am not interested in playing 'Warm Bed' tonight. I am not feeling that song. I want to play 'Misnomer' instead." She wasn't shouting, but her voice carried across the cavernous space.

"Mags," the man said, in a similar accent, matching her in volume, tone, and timbre. He wore a black suit with a stripe and tie the same color as the woman's dress. "Be reasonable. They don't have time to redo the cues for us."

"Asking to take one song off a set list is not unreasonable."

"Are you asking to remove the song, or replace it? Removing is easier than replacing."

"If we remove it, the set's too short." They neared Rosemary's group. Up close, the performers were even taller, and both faces were covered in thick makeup. The woman sighed dramatically, but didn't acknowledge the audience to her conversation. "We are artists, not trained dogs. I don't bark on command."

The man looked at the second woman, raised his eyebrows, then shrugged. "My sister says we aren't playing 'Warm Bed' tonight. Let us know if you prefer for us to cut it and run short, or substitute 'Misnomer.' It's the same length."

The second woman exited through a side door, leaving the performers—the artists—behind.

"I am not being unreasonable," the woman repeated as they walked over to two box-rooms, each entering one.

"You can move closer to take a look." Jeannie gestured for the group to follow the artists.

"Who are they?" Rosemary whispered to Colton. She chose him in part because he had reacted so dramatically to the performer's name, and in part because he'd been the one brave enough to ask anything. Not to mention he was the one she was least likely to ever interact with again if hers was a stupid question.

"Are you serious?" he whispered back. "She's the queen of Zoukhop. She and her brother practically invented it. She's like the national hero of Dominica."

As they got closer, Rosemary realized each trailer was an isolation booth, each with an array of cameras and lights and microphones orbiting a ministage. They had foam-padded walls, with windows into the booths on either side. She tried to reconcile the new information with her memory of Patent Medicine. The bassist's wink must have been to someone outside these windows.

"I don't understand," she said.

Jeannie heard her. "It's always a shock when you first see them. Like being handed a single puzzle piece and asked what the whole looks like."

Rosemary struggled to make sense of it. Inside the room on the left, the man stood just outside his spotlight, tuning his guitar. To the right, Magritte—Mags—sat on a stool, staring into a camera, arms crossed. Air conditioners whirred, creating more noise than any of the other equipment.

A voice boomed over an intercom, bouncing around the hangar. "We're cutting 'Warm Bed.' Please cut 'Warm Bed' from your cue sheets. The set will be two minutes and forty-seven seconds short. I want acknowledgment from every department in the next minute. Ping Control if there's a problem, but don't have any problems."

Rosemary didn't hear any acknowledgment, or any problems, so there must have been some other method of conveying those from each department to the mysterious intercom person. The guitarist moved into the spotlight in his tiny room. A light shifted a couple of inches along a track, then another did the same. The woman in the other booth still hadn't moved.

The air conditioners cut off and the hangar's overhead lights guttered, leaving machine silence, an absence of hum. Someone in the group giggled. Inside the booths, spotlights lit the performers, stark against the surrounding darkness. The man began playing his guitar. Mags must have stepped into her position in the moment the lights went off; now she swayed in time with her brother's syncopated strum.

"Why can't we hear them?" somebody asked. Rosemary was glad the question had come from someone else.

"Ssssssh," said a second person.

"Those are isolation booths," another voice whispered. "They're soundproof."

"In both directions?" the second one asked again.

"Ducklings," said Jeannie in a normal voice, cutting through the argument and answering in favor of soundproofing. "This way."

The group followed their guide away from the booths. Rosemary kept pace but glanced over her shoulder as she went. She still didn't understand how the pieces added up to the whole.

They went through yet another door. So many doors. Rosemary had no idea if they had already been down this hallway or seen this control room earlier. If they had, it had only been in passing. Now it was full of technicians and engineers, all in their own half-walled booths, all watching the two performers on monitor screens, from a hundred different angles.

She was grateful to have a wall at her back, and oriented herself to be the nearest of her group to the door, even if her view was now blocked. Way too many people. How did they all stand being in the same room? The heat of them, the air they displaced, somebody's cologne, somebody else's sweat, unless it was her own. Even in the packed Bloom Bar show, she hadn't felt so crowded, though of course that hadn't been real. Concentrate on the tech, she told herself. Find something to take your mind off it.

Jeannie whispered, "That bay over there is sound mixing." She pointed to a man in headphones behind a large screen filled with dancing meters, green cresting to yellow tips then falling back again.

An identical bay, with a young woman at the controls. "The one next to him is another mixing bay, for in-ear monitors, making sure the musicians hear what they need to hear. And that whole section is cameras." She pointed to the vast monitor bank covering two walls. "Some for the actual camera feed, some for what the audience sees, some for knitting it all together. The holo camera rig is automated, but we keep people at the controls in case anything needs a human touch. They're watching carefully during this particular set because there's a chance some camera may not follow the updated path for the new set list. Anytime you make last-minute changes you increase the likelihood things will go wrong. Remember that, kids."

Some monitors showed Magritte, some showed her brother, but the vast majority showed the two together. On a raised platform at the room's center, overhead projectors conjured a life-sized, living, breathing holo of the two performers without backdrop, knit seamlessly into one image.

Rosemary's jaw dropped. "How do they do that?"

"Do what?"

"Put them in one room together when they're not!"

Her eyes understood how. Each performer had their own camera array, with their own fake stage set behind them matching the others. The two were combined in studio. "How?" wasn't the question she wanted answered, though it was the first that had come out of her mouth. Not "Why?" either, since why was obvious: to make each performer look three-dimensional, they needed to be shot from all angles, with nobody else blocking them.

The question was a different "How?"—it was, How do those performers act as if they're interacting with each other when they're isolated? Patent Medicine must have been in booths like these as well. Those songs that had so moved her, the performance that had reached out and spoken to her; it had all been an elaborate ruse.

The musicians in the booths started a new song. The guitar had an effect on it that made it tremble. Magritte sang a line in some other language, something intense, with a dark turn at the end. The guitar echoed her, in her own voice, trembling, snarling. She looked at her brother, locked eyes with him. Cut him with another line, which his guitar tossed back at her. Their faces drew closer to each other. Inches apart.

Rosemary tore her eyes away from the holographic combined image to look at the individual monitors again. They were still in the same positions they had been in in the three-dimensional version, but now she internalized the isolation again.

"Can they see each other?" she asked, hoping it was a less naive question.

"Sometimes. They can't see much beyond the lights, but they have marks to show where they expect each other to be, and they do have visual monitors in their floors. We can correct if they're off by a few inches."

It was amazing. If either missed their mark, they'd look ridiculous. One singing to the other's nose, or playing guitar at nobody. Instead, this was a performance built in two halves, a relationship carried out by two people with complete faith that the other was where they were supposed to be.

The song ended, but the guitar continued into another song. The image flickered, jumped, then crumpled the two performers' images like paper. The holo in the room's center spun them into prismatic arcs, flattened Picasso figures given flesh: jaws elongated, limbs twisted, impossibly long shards of arm and body and guitar wound together.

"Fuck!" somebody shouted. "Nobody said they'd segue from 'Carajo' to 'Contagious.' Those were supposed to be hard stops."

"Cameras are three seconds behind cues."

"Jump forward."

"We'll miss a few seconds. There'll be a gap."

"Better than the paper dolls we have now." The paper dolls were creepy, distorted versions of the people in the booths. Rosemary slipped around her group to get a look at a console running code.

"On my mark, jump to the thirty-second cue for 'Contagious.' Five. Four. Three. Two. One."

The real-time monitors stayed on the performers. The holo took a stomach-churning leap to match up, then they were restored to three-dimensionality. It was a strange relief, an escape from an uncanny valley.

Magritte and her brother never lost a beat. If any control room stress had reached their earpieces, they showed no sign. The woman was a mesmerizing performer. It wasn't a matter of losing herself in the songs; she was part of the music, but she controlled it, used it. Something about the way she addressed the cameras said, "I am putting on this show for you." Not warmth, not connection. Power. Even in a setting this clinical, that much came through. Even in a playful song like the next one, or a quiet song like the one after that.

"And we're offline," announced someone in the room as the last song came to an end.

The holo faded out of existence, but the artists on monitor in the booths did not.

"What was that?" asked Magritte, looking straight into a camera as if she was about to reach through it. "That shouldn't have happened. Who missed the cue?"

Her brother lifted his guitar strap over his head, placed the guitar on a stand. Sweat shone on his face, dripping down his neck and into his collar. "Mags. It was our fault. My fault. We told them to cut a song, not to stitch the empty space."

She turned her glare on him. "If anybody complains, you can refund them yourself."

"Yes, yes." He waved a hand at her. "Now, can we please leave these sauna boxes and argue off camera?"

"Yes. Or the eavesdropping ghouls behind the cameras and mics could turn them off, since we're not talking to them anymore at this point."

Somebody shut the cameras off.

Jeannie turned to her tour group. "That's it, start to finish. Y'all will go off and learn the specifics of your jobs through online training modules. Then some of you'll recruit and you'll send people here, and then some will dress them and paint them and make them pretty, and the rest will mix them and film them and send them out to their fans. You've got the best gigs in the world. Have fun, learn your jobs well, and as you've seen tonight, don't ever let it be your fault something went wrong."

She said the last bit with a grin, but Rosemary couldn't tell if she was serious or not.

9

LUCE

Rip

Whatever April had hit three of my roommates over the next week, and whatever it was, it was bad. Started with chills and fever, same as April. I kept to myself, afraid to catch it, afraid I was the vector, afraid to infect the fourth, Jaspreet, the teacher-filmmaker.

She laughed when I told her as much. "I teach third grade, Luce. I have the immune system of a . . . what has a good immune system? Anyway, half my kids are out, too, and some had it before you went to New York. You're not Patient Zero. If anyone brought it into the house, it was me."

I allowed myself to be somewhat reassured, until the next day, when she fell down the stairs. I heard the crash from my room.

"I got dizzy," she said.

When I reached to help her up, she screamed like I'd hurt her. For a minute I thought she had injured herself falling, but then she tugged her sleeve back: her arm was covered with welts.

I drove her to the emergency room in her car, since I didn't have one. The ER was full. Every seat was occupied by someone in a state similar to Jaspreet's. Flushed, sweating, shivering, moaning.

Some tore at spots like hers, screaming like they were being stabbed or burned.

"I can call a friend," Jaspreet kept saying, but she didn't protest when I joined her on the floor of the waiting room.

"I'll stay until they show up." We weren't friends, but I regretted leaving April to her asshole roommates; I still hadn't heard from her. If I couldn't have been more helpful to April, the least I could do was stay here with Jaspreet until her friends came.

Nobody came. Hours passed. I read headlines on my phone. The president called for people to stay home, for health and safety. Schools closed again. Something something legislation something something. It all made me uneasy.

I glanced over to check on Jaspreet, who had her eyes closed and her head leaned back against the wall. "Um, you've got new spots. On your neck."

"I know. They feel like fucking cigarette burns." She tried to turn on her phone, but her hands shook. She thumbed it unlocked and then handed it to me. "Document this for me. I'll give you a producer credit if this turns out to be film-worthy."

I took the offered phone and panned over her spots as she displayed them. Recorded as they pulled her into a vestibule to get her blood pressure and temperature, both through the roof.

The nurse had obviously had a night of it already, but she mugged for the camera. "The good news is, your stats have won you a bump to the front of the triage line. Highest fever we've seen all night. The bad news is that we don't have enough beds. There's a chair in a hallway and a nice IV of fluids waiting for you."

"What is it?" Jaspreet asked. "I swear I had chicken pox, and I've had the measles vaccine. What else causes spots?"

The nurse shook her head. "We're not sure yet, but we're full of it tonight, whatever it is."

I waited with Jaspreet for another three hours. She slept. I watched a game show on an overhead TV with the sound off and tried my best not to touch surfaces. Whatever this was, I didn't want it.

The doctor who attended her—for all of two minutes—seemed more interested in cataloging and mitigating symptoms. Pill for the fever, fluids for dehydration, shot for the pain, cream to stop the itching if it started.

"And then I can go home?" Jaspreet asked. She considered the place we lived home, my distracted brain noticed.

The doctor shook her head. "And then we admit you. You're not going anywhere until your fever drops out of the danger zone."

"Can you say 'danger zone' again for my camera?" she asked, but the doctor had already left.

She turned to me. "You might as well go home. Thanks so much for hanging out all night and distracting me. It was nice getting to know you a little. I think this was the most we've ever chatted."

It was true. I gave her back her phone and told her to call if she needed anything, then returned to the house. Back to the moans of two other sick roommates and the place they considered a home but I didn't.

It had been midafternoon when I drove Jaspreet to the hospital, and it was nearly eleven now. Eight hours of hospital hum had exhausted me, but there was still one thing I wanted to do, since April's phone kept ringing through and I didn't know her roommates. We weren't even connected on any social media platforms, so I couldn't look to see who else knew her who I knew.

The plaque on the amp's back had read "Nico Lectrics," which was easy enough to search online. I'd hoped for a phone number, but settled for an email address. I dashed off a short message. "Hi, April Mennin loaned me one of your amps the other night—it was amazing, and I'd like to talk to you about buying one sometime—but mostly I wondered if you'd heard from April in the last few days or if you had any way of checking on her. She wasn't feeling well when I left." I closed with my name and phone number.

There. That was something, at least.

The phone woke me in the morning. I leaped from the bed, catching my feet in the sheet and tumbling to the floor, then scrambling to extricate it from my jeans pocket before the fourth ring. A New York number I didn't recognize.

"April?" I rubbed my bashed knee.

"Ah, shit, I'm so sorry."

"Sorry?" I repeated. "Who is this?"

"My name is Nico. You emailed me. I, uh, fuck. There's no good way to say this. April died five days ago."

I dropped the phone as if it had burned me. A spiderweb crack spread across the screen from one corner.

"Hello?" Came a muffled voice from the floor. "Luce? Hello?"

I stared at the crack until the screen lit to tell me the call had disconnected. Kept staring. It rang again, but I didn't answer. If I pretended I hadn't heard, if I didn't answer, it wouldn't be true. She'd died five days ago. Alive for me, dead for anyone who knew. Five days. I'd been home for a week. She'd died two days after I'd left New York.

I sat down on the floor. Retrieved the phone, traced the crack in its facade, hit redial. He answered on the third ring.

"Sorry," I said. "You took me by surprise . . . What happened?"

"It's this thing that's going around. She got a real bad case."

"Did she—did she go to the hospital?" I pictured her tossing and turning the night I'd spent on her floor. I should have tried harder to get her to a doctor.

"She wouldn't go. Said she couldn't afford it. One of her roommates called 911 on Tuesday when they found her in the bathroom. She'd passed out and hit her head. She was in the hospital for a day after that, but none of her friends knew. She was unconscious the whole time, anyway."

"I should have made her go to the hospital."

"You know she wasn't someone you could force. It's not your fault. Who dies of the flu? I thought that was old people and babies."

"Is that what it is? The flu?"

"No," he said. "Or, anyway, I have no idea. All they're saying is wash your hands and go to an emergency room if you get spots or a bad fever."

I nodded, then realized he couldn't see me. "Everyone here has that, too. Everyone but me."

"Yeah, I'm still okay, but it feels like a matter of time."

"Is there a funeral?" I didn't know if this was the right question to ask. I'd never known anyone near my own age who'd died before.

"In Nebraska or Arkansas or wherever it is she's from. Her parents claimed her body, I guess." From the sound of it, he was new at this, too. "Anyway, we wanted to have a memorial, but the newspapers say to avoid big gatherings right now, so I guess we'll do it . . . whenever this flu runs its course? Do you want me to let you know?"

I told him I'd appreciate it. I did want to buy one of his amps, too, but now wasn't the time. Guilt hit me that I was thinking about amps instead of April. I couldn't wrap my head around the idea, so my brain took me elsewhere. I sat on the floor and traced the crack in my phone, over and over again. It was readable, but fractured. Fitting. What wasn't broken at this point?

I called my aunt, who said she was fine, thanks for asking; she'd called an ambulance for a neighbor the day before. She hadn't heard from my family, but they didn't talk to her any more than they talked to me. My parents' number had never been in my phone, but I still knew it by heart. It rang eighteen times before I disconnected. I pictured the Hatzolah ambulances running themselves ragged shuttling people to hospitals, and feverish mothers tending to feverish children by the dozen. I didn't know what I would have said if they'd answered.

I fought the urge to chuck the phone across the room. What did it do for me anyway? It was a way for people to reach me with bad news at this point, nothing more. No more touring. No more April. Another way for me to lock myself in my room and avoid getting to know my roommates, and who knew if they were going to survive, either.

Ten a.m., and I'd left Jaspreet at eleven p.m. I searched for her number in my cracked phone and realized I didn't even have it. We weren't friends. I'd told her to call if she needed anything, but I didn't remember leaving my number. I called the hospital and asked them to connect me to her room. Waited to hear that she hadn't survived the night.

"Hello?"

I released a breath I hadn't realized I'd been holding. "Hey, Jaspreet, this is Luce. I'm just checking you're okay. You're okay?"

"Tired as fuck. They wake me every two hours for one thing or another. Blood, temperature. But yeah, otherwise okay. The fever is lower, and they have me on something for the nerve pain. The spots itch."

"I'm so glad." She couldn't have understood the relief in my voice, and I wasn't about to tell her. "Glad the fever is down, I mean, not the itchy spots. Listen, I realize I said last night for you to call me, but I didn't leave you my number, so I thought I'd give it to you. For anything."

"Sure. My brother is coming in a little bit, but thank you. I appreciate it. And thank you for bringing me in last night when nobody else could."

"No problem."

I hung on the line for a few more seconds, then said I had to go.

April and I had mostly spoken on the phone or in person. Our only text messages consisted of my last several attempts to reach her. I scrolled through the tour pictures on my phone; there weren't many. A couple from the backseat of the van to the front, a couple from the front seat to the back. One in a diner where she posed with an enormous banana split. She had her sticks in her hands in every picture, even with the ice cream.

She wasn't the best drummer I'd auditioned. Second best, but I'd liked her more, and I'd decided compatibility mattered more than perfection. We roomed together for eight months with no complaint, and I'd still held her at arm's length. Why?

I plugged my guitar in and sent silent apologies to the other sick roommates. Cranked the gain and the distortion, turned it up until the room hummed with potential noise. I stared at the neck, waiting for something that wanted to be played. Finally, I hit an E minor chord, all six strings, a wave, a wall. Hit it again and again, noise layered on noise, until it drowned out my head. Somewhere in the middle, the downbeats started sounding like words. Nobody is coming to save you, the chord told me, over and over again. Nobody is coming to save you. Chorus and verse.

I played until my B string snapped, slashing the meat of my right thumb, and kept playing with blood running over the pick guard. Didn't stop until my left hand was too sore to press the strings anymore, and my right hand's cuticles were seeping and raw. It felt good to bleed. Punishment for being the one left standing.

When I couldn't play anymore, I left a message for the entertainment lawyer who'd vetted the label contract for me, asking him to help me get out of the rest of the contract.

If the big clubs were closed, I'd play small ones again. I'd busk on the street. I'd open my own club if I had to. If having a label meant sitting on my hands I didn't want a label anymore. Whatever it took. I was a lousy friend, and I didn't know how to sit still. If all I was good at was being a vector for noise and hope, I'd be a vector. If nobody was coming to save me, I'd have to figure out a way to save myself. If I was lucky, I could do the same for some other people along the way.

And first, I was going to go downstairs and make a big pot of chicken soup for my sick roommates. This might have to be home for a little while.

10

ROSEMARY

Who Can You Trust

The online training modules could as easily have been done at home, but trainees were supposed to finish them on campus. Maybe so you'd still be there for them to call back in if you failed one, so they could offer you a different job or send you packing.

Rosemary didn't mind working in the private dorm room she'd been assigned. Instead of inspirational slogans like the ones Superwally issued, the posters depicted SHL musicians. The bed sagged, but not too badly, and the desk chair was comfortable. Nice view, too.

They'd even provided free Veneers! She'd never tried a Veneer before, since her old Hoodie didn't support the tech. Rosemary spent ten minutes cycling through the options for the room (monk's cell, tropical gazebo, Versailles bedroom, a dozen more) before settling on one called "Chelsea Hotel 1967." Now when she observed the room with her Hoodie on the next setting up from clear-view, the threadbare red carpet became a scuffed hardwood floor. The plywood headboard looked like wrought iron, velvet curtains filtered the sunlight, and every surface was draped with jewel-toned scarves. Given more time, she might have found one she liked more, but six years at Superwally told her not to waste company time on it, even if they offered the option.

Rosemary dedicated herself to doing well on her modules. She knew she'd made the right choice to take this job; now she had to prove it to them. It helped that the modules interested her, or some did, anyway, the ones that weren't about avoiding inappropriate relationships or how to log your expenses. She learned how to read a map, how to navigate interstate buses and city buses and trains, where to find information on schedules and safety. A training on what to wear would have been nice; she still didn't want to ask.

They had techniques for how to approach a band, how to recognize if a band had SHL potential. That part came down to, "We hired you to know it when you see it." There were a few suggestions about tip-offs for musicians who made bad SHL artists. They said not to waste time on alcoholics or drug addicts; now that Rosemary had seen the precision necessary to run an SHL concert, she understood the need for reliable talent. Nothing too political. Bring excitement, personality, charisma, the ability to connect with an audience, mainstream appeal, whatever that meant. Maybe it was code for some demographic? An age group, an economic class? If she had to guess, it was tied to the apolitical. They wanted excitement but not edge or danger or anything offensive.

The rules for contact were similar to the Superwally Ethics & Values Code, but less concerned with ethics than with line crossing. *You are not there to be anyone's friend. Observe. Don't be a stranger to them, but don't get too involved. There's always a temptation to sign acts because you like them. Sign them because we need them, because the world needs them, because they're wasting their talents in that dump they're playing.* No taking money or gifts from musicians you were pursuing. No promising attention in exchange for sex or favors. She wondered how many rules were based on experience.

Rosemary waited for them to tell her how to discover her exciting, personable, charismatic performers. When that information didn't come, she searched for a missing module, but the only clue she found was the line in the code of conduct that said "wasting their talents in that dump they're playing." Where was she supposed to find that dump?

"So . . . where do I go first?" Rosemary wrote to her new supervisors in Recruiter Management. She was too embarrassed to use the live interface. They had been sending her encouraging messages all day long, telling her no question was too basic, but this one might be.

"Anywhere you want!" came the unhelpful reply. Slightly more helpful: "There's a map"—a link lit on her screen—"showing where the current recruiters are. No sense duplicating their effort, but anyplace else is fair game. You let Logistics know, and they'll book your travel. Pick wherever your favorite band is from and start there. Or start with whatever's local to you."

It wasn't the best time to mention she didn't know any local bands. She pulled off her Hoodie, facing a momentary disorientation when she saw her room as it was instead of her scarf-draped Veneer. They had invited new employees to explore the campus if they needed a break; that sounded like as good an idea as any.

She had been surprised from the beginning at the campus's enormity.

"We need it, legally, to hit the legal ratio to the number of people here," Jeannie had explained. "But also, given how many people live and work here, the campus is considered a job perk."

The campus held not only the hangar and the studio wing, the offices and dorms and performer village, but also four hundred acres of pinewoods and paths. She chose the two-mile loop path marked with red circles. Two miles in brisk March air was a reasonable head-clearing distance.

The trails were wide and well-groomed, with footing that sprang back beneath her feet. A few yards past the first marker, she encountered an exercise station with metal bars fixed at two heights. A few minutes later, she came to a wooden beam anchored a few inches above the ground. She hopped onto it and walked its length, just for fun. The third structure, a little farther into the woods, was a byzantine jumble of lumber and metal.

"I've been walking past here for a year now and I can't figure this one out, either."

Rosemary turned to see a man standing in the path. He wore expensive-looking workout clothes, a lopsided smile, and hair that fell across his eyes in a way that looked both messy and deliberate. Latino, maybe, or Middle Eastern? She was much better at reading ethnicity in avatars. He looked familiar, but she couldn't quite place him. Not from her hiring group, but maybe she'd seen him in the control room or an office they'd toured through.

"Maybe this one isn't for exercising," she guessed. "Maybe it's art. I think I saw this on a museum site once."

He accepted the challenge. "Maybe a chin-up bar and a seesaw were spliced in a genetic experiment gone horribly awry."

"Maybe it's a torture device."

"Aren't all exercise machines?"

"I wouldn't know. This is my first—well, third if you count the others today. They seem friendly enough."

"Don't let them fool you."

She smiled. "I'll stay vigilant. Is it safe to continue toward the next one?"

"They're all safe compared to this one. Do you mind if I join you?"

She was supposed to be clearing her head, but it felt rude to say she didn't want company.

"Sorry," he said. "I'm Aran. I should introduce myself to people before I go inviting myself along on their walks. I never run into anyone out here, so I'm forgetting my manners. I mean, I come out here to get away from the folks in there, but it's nice to meet someone who had the same idea. That's what you're doing, too, yeah?"

Rosemary didn't know what to answer other than the last question, so she nodded. She also didn't have any clue about the etiquette of walking with a stranger in the woods. Did you talk? Walk in companionable silence? How close did you stand, and who got to set the pace? She started moving again, to let him fill in the blanks on distance, at least.

"You didn't say your name." He matched her stride, an arm's length away.

"Rosemary."

"Pretty name."

"Thanks. Um, my parents came up with it." She was flustered by the sudden suspicion he was flirting with her. She had no idea how to tell someone in person she was uninterested. In hoodspace you just threw a flag. "Um, I ought to tell you I'm not really into guys."

He cocked his head at her. "That's okay. I'm not often into girls, and anyway, if I was looking for somebody, this would be the worst place to look. I told you I never run into anyone out here."

She walked faster, embarrassed to have said anything at all.

"It's okay," he said. "I appreciate a person who's clear on her intentions. Let's go back to the part where we were just chatting. I don't recognize you, so I assume you're either new talent or new hire?"

"New hire."

"Let me guess: I don't think you're wardrobe or makeup. You don't have that look. You're a sound tech or something behind the scenes. Uploads, downloads, interfaces."

Rosemary tried to relax again, pretend she was chatting in hoodspace, instead of walking through an actual real-life forest with a total stranger who made surprisingly good guesses. "That's what I should be doing, only for some reason they gave me the artist recruiter job instead, and now I'm terrified they'll figure out I'm clueless."

She realized she hadn't asked him about his own job; that thought stopped her dead in her tracks. He was probably in office or logistics or people management, and now he'd know she was faking it. "So, um, how about you? What do you do here other than walk in the woods?"

He stopped to wait. "I make music."

"Like, you write? Or you play?"

He looked at her as if she'd missed a connection. It took her a minute. "Oh. You mean you play music for SHL? You're Talent?" She didn't know how she managed to put a capital *T* on a word as she spoke it, but that was how it sounded.

He looked more and more familiar, and she knew so few musicians by sight. "Wait. You're the singer for Patent Medicine!"

She knew it was true even before he answered. "I love 'The Crash.' I saw you play at the Bloom Bar. It sounded even better live. That thing where you drew out the ending was cool."

"Thanks!" He smiled. "That's the goal, I guess. If we make you think you're going to get something different on SHL than the recording, you're more likely to come to the show, yeah?"

"I'd go to another in a second." It was an honest answer, though she worried she sounded a little too earnest now.

"I look forward to seeing you there."

He was joking, obviously, but it led her to another question. "Is it weird playing in a box? Not being able to see your audience?"

"It took some getting used to. It closes down the conversation between performer and audience, which is a weird sensation. Like leaving a message for someone that they're going to read in real time. Not seeing each other while we play is the harder part. We have monitors, but learning how to cue each other in that situation is tricky, and we have to practice a lot more to get to a point where we can play something that sounds fresh or improvised."

"So it's not improvisation when you do something like that ending?"

"It can be, but we have to time it carefully. Like, if you say you want two minutes to talk to the audience you have to say where you want it, and you get exactly two minutes, with countdown. Or you say you're going to take *x* number of bars to solo at exactly this point. There's no room to let somebody keep going if they're on a roll, but I think that's more a problem for jazz than my kind of music. There, now that you're on the payroll, you get to hear all the trade secrets. I hope it doesn't ruin the experience."

She considered. "No. Not any more than learning you play in those tiny booths."

They came to another piece of exercise equipment, two sets of raised footsteps on hinges, with handholds beside them. "This one is more self-explanatory." Aran hopped onto one and began swinging his feet.

Rosemary climbed onto the other set. The machine's action was looser than she expected, moving her arms and legs out and away. "But why use a walking machine when you're already on a walk?"

"An excellent question. I don't have an answer."

"Hey, Aran, do you mind if I ask you something else?"

"Absolutely. Anything about music or exercise equipment is in my realm of expertise."

"My new job. I'm supposed to go someplace to look for musicians to sign, but I don't know where to start."

"I think most people start with the place they're from. A local singer you dig, maybe? Somebody flying under their radar?"

That was what she was afraid of. "I live on a wind farm in nowhereville. There are no local singers or bands. None I know of, anyway."

"There's no bar with bands playing in a secret room? No living room concerts?"

"If there are, nobody has ever invited me. There's only one bar. I've never been inside, but I can't imagine they have room for a stage."

She hopped off the machine and started walking again. When she heard his footsteps behind her, she asked, "So how did you get discovered? Living room concert?"

He laughed. "I came to them. That's not a recommended course of action, though. Most people who show up without an invitation get booted or arrested. There are procedures."

"How come you didn't get booted or arrested?"

"I was really, really good."

"And modest."

"If I was modest, I'd still be home in Baltimore playing basement shows."

Baltimore. She made a mental note.

"Well, Rosemary, it's been nice chatting with you, but we've reached the end of the road."

She realized the path had looped back. The SHL hangar loomed on the other side of the field.

"Thanks for keeping me company." Rosemary gave an awkward wave. It would have gone better in hoodspace. "I suppose I need to finish my trainings."

"And I suppose I'd better go back to the song I was working on. Hey, I don't know if you're allowed in the talent residences, or if they've got your evening booked, but I'm having a few people over at seven tonight. You're welcome to come. Sixth cottage on the right."

Once she'd made sure he wasn't hitting on her, she had enjoyed talking with him. He was easier to make conversation with than the others in her training group. Maybe because they were all as nervous as she was. "The trainings say we're not supposed to make friends with the talent we're trying to sign, but that's probably different once you're already here?"

"I'm sure," he said. "But you can check over your manual or whatever, make sure it's not against the rules. Consider it job training. You need to learn to talk with musicians, anyway. And how to 'be friendly without crossing the line,' right?"

"That's a good point." Her second wave went a little smoother.

11

ROSEMARY

Deep Water

She didn't know what you wore to a talent party, or to any real-life party, for that matter. He hadn't said "party," she didn't think. He'd said "having some friends over." Even though Aran had been wearing casual clothes in the woods, she pictured his friends lounging in their stage clothes. Magritte in her rain-colored dress and silver makeup, her brother in his impeccable suit. And would Aran's gorgeous bassist be there? She'd intimidate Rosemary whatever she wore.

She pulled out a pair of jeans and a new short-sleeved shirt from the Superwally SHL Social pack she'd bought before she left, "Guaranteed Cool for Any Occasion." The shirt had spangles. She tried it on, then stuffed it back into her bag and replaced it with a work-style polo and her farm jacket. She didn't want to stand out. Better to look less cool than like she was trying too hard. Spangles.

The Talent Village was on the opposite side of the hangar from the woods, behind its own security gate. She gave her badge to the guard, waiting to be refused entrance, but he waved her through. Inside the fence, a neighborhood of tiny cottages on the outside ring of a giant circle, and an interior ring of larger modular dwellings with narrow porches and three or four doors on the front. An older white woman in a suit and a fedora sat on the first porch strumming a guitar. The woman waved at Rosemary when she passed, and Rosemary waved back, starstruck. She'd heard the biggest performers lived in their own private compounds and only came to SHL for shows and rehearsals, but maybe some hung out here.

Sixth cottage on the right. The first few had painted trim, but Aran's was basic. She knocked on the door.

"Come in," he said.

She stepped inside, then took a step back as everyone turned to look at her. In hoodspace you didn't have to feel this exposed when you walked into a room. You spawned directly in to make a statement, or you walked in invisible and decloaked when you were ready. She wouldn't turn heel and leave. She could do this.

Aran sat on a queen-sized bed with his back against the headboard, his legs out in front of him. Rosemary had expected his bandmates to be the friends in attendance, but she didn't recognize the others. A black woman with short locs lay on her stomach crossways at the foot of the bed, head on elbows and Hoodie up, and a white guy with long blond hair sat on the floor, his mouth full of microwave pizza, using the box as a plate. She was glad she'd changed out of the spangled shirt. They all wore T-shirts and jeans, though Aran's T-shirt looked soft as a lamb and fit him as perfectly as an av's.

"Hey," said Aran. "I didn't think you'd come! Y'all, this is my friend Rosie. She's a new recruiter."

"Rosemary." She didn't want anyone getting ideas about nicknames.

He continued as if he'd never goofed. "Rosemary, this is Bailey. You might know her as MC Huntress. And that's Victor. He makes pop music."

The woman dropped her hood. Rosemary tried not to notice the once-over they gave her, or show that she'd recognized Victor Janssen. Half her classmates had crushes on him in high school.

"Hi." She wished they'd go back to whatever they'd been doing a moment before so she could figure out her place in the room. She wanted to flip up her Hoodie to see if the cottage had a Veneer, but didn't know if it would be rude, since nobody else was in theirs anymore. There was the bed, a little kitchen area with a sink, microwave, and minifridge, a bookshelf, a metal rod with clothes hung on it, a dresser. A door to the bed's left, which she assumed led to the bathroom. An acoustic guitar hung on one wall, and a keyboard rested on a stand beneath it with a paper notebook on its bench. Behind the front door, she spotted an empty chair with a jacket hung over the back and picked that as a reasonable place to situate herself.

"You don't have to sit in the coat closet," Aran said.

Rosemary jumped. She looked for another spot, but the keyboard bench was taken by the notebook, the bed was too awkward, and the rug too close to Victor. She sat down. "I'm fine here, thanks."

Aran shrugged. "Did you figure out where to go on your first trip? Rosemary is supposed to figure out for herself where to find musicians to sign, but she doesn't know where to start."

Bailey cocked her head. "But that's savage! You can go anywhere. Is there any city you've ever wanted to see? A scene you want to check out?"

"What's a scene?" Rosemary felt the color rising in her face again. The more she considered her situation, the more she felt in over her head. There was a whole vocabulary she didn't know.

"It's hard to know what a scene is unless you're in it, Bail. I know it's easy to forget when you've been here a hundred years. Rosemary's starting from scratch." Aran turned to Rosemary. "A scene is the bands and audience and venues of an area, all combined into a stew. Musicians inspiring each other, working with each other. Sometimes there's a similar sound or feel that gets associated with the place."

"I thought that was what I suggested," Bailey said. "I said, a city she wants to see."

"What's there to want to see?" asked Rosemary. "Anyway, I'm

not supposed to go see some city. I'm supposed to find local musicians, but I don't know how, so I guess I'm not going to have this job for long."

She crossed her arms over her chest and examined the book titles on the shelf on the opposite wall. Decided to take control of the conversation. "Aran said he just walked in here and told them to sign his band. How did you all get found?"

Victor snorted. "Aran's full of shit. Don't believe everything he says. I was one of the zillion people who are out there uploading music. Nobody hears it because if you don't have an SHL contract you have no access to Superwally distribution or audiences or anything but the tiniest streaming services, which you can't even access without hacking your own devices to ditch the proprietary stuff. SHL makes sure nobody hears you if you're not theirs. But I got to chatting with a recruiter when we both played on the same team in a shoot-'em-up, and she invited me to send her some of my stuff. Then I had to audition for an audience of one, which was weird, and then another audition as an opening act for Huntress here, and I got her fans dancing, so here I am."

That story calmed Rosemary's nerves a bit. If he had been discovered through a game, there was a chance she could start out online, from home. Baby steps.

Bailey rolled over onto her back and rested her head on her hands. "And I was playing in the Atlanta underground clubs when a recruiter told me he liked my stuff. I thought he was trying to scam me, but he kept coming round to shows 'til I started to believe him."

Rosemary filed that information away, too. What had the training packet said? Don't be a stranger to them, but don't get too involved. Bailey's story bore that out.

"How do you find underground clubs?" she asked. Better to sound ignorant in front of three people and learn something. If she asked anything too embarrassing, she'd have to make sure she never saw them again. "I'm sorry if it's a stupid question. I really don't know. Do you need a password? Aran mentioned earlier how some bars have secret music rooms, and I'd never have guessed that in a million years."

Bailey stood and stretched her legs. She was smaller than Rosemary expected, compact and muscular. "Sometimes you do need a password, or a person to vouch for you. Sometimes it's a matter of showing up in the right place on the right night. You wouldn't be there if you didn't know, so obviously you're meant to be there."

"I've never understood that logic," said Victor. "Anyone could be there if they did enough research. Cops, shooters."

Aran threw a pillow at him, which he ducked. "That's why nobody would've found you in a million years if you hadn't gotten lucky. Little bedroom geek making music in your room for nobody."

Victor threw the pillow back, with a little more force. It looked like Aran's comment had stung. "Better to be a bedroom geek than get arrested making music for slightly more than nobody. Why risk it?"

"And this is what you're up against, Rosemary. There are talented musicians hiding in their bedrooms, and talented musicians playing for ten or twenty people in hidden rooms all over the country. The company doesn't care where you find us, as long as you find us. Bring us in! Make us yours."

Aran tossed the pillow Rosemary's way, and she grabbed it and held on. She felt a little more comfortable now, a little less like a mouse for the cats to bat around. Still, if she asked another question, it would keep them from asking her any. They were performers. They didn't mind attention.

"So, what else can I tell the, ah, new talent about what they can expect if they come out here? They want me to sell something I've never seen. I think there's a talent FAQ, but maybe y'all can tell me more about what I'll be asked?"

"You can tell them all this can be theirs." Aran waved his hand at the room. "If they want. They can also live at home and travel in for shows, but if they're not a solo act, they'd be better off staying here for a while to practice in the isolation booths."

"Free food," said Victor. "Well, free-ish. It gets deducted from our pay, but the prices are reasonable, so it's not like owing the company store, unless you have fancy tastes or eat a ton."

"Or unless you're an alcoholic," said Aran. "If they drink a lot and buy at the commissary, they'll be poor very quickly. If they can wait the hour, they should drone it."

"It doesn't feed you in the same way a real live show does," said Bailey.

Victor squinted at her. "Superwally? The commissary? Are you still talking food?"

Bailey ignored him. "It's different from performing for an audience. More intimate, in a way, because it's more like playing for one person—the camera—than a whole crowd. If you're somebody who gets charged up by screaming fans or playing to the cutest person in the audience, you're not going to be fed."

"They do bring in audience for some people." Victor stood to toss his pizza box in the garbage, then returned to the floor.

"Yeah, but they don't like to, except on special occasions, and even then it's only, like, ten or twenty people. Cuts the profit margin. They have to screen everyone, and worry about security on campus . . ."

"But it can be worth it." Aran had a dreamy look in his eye.

Bailey swatted his leg. "You're only saying that 'cause you found a guy to hook up with at the festival last week."

"I used to meet someone at every show. Don't tell them that part or they won't come, Rosemary."

"That's the choice," Bailey said. "Fame and fortune, a chance to make an actual living playing music, but you have to give up the most fun parts of the job. I'm not even saying sex, but talking with fans after the show, signing stuff for them, watching their reactions . . ."

". . . Sex . . ." said Aran.

Bailey frowned at him. "Living here doesn't make you a monk. There are new hires all the time. It's a big campus."

"Not big enough when things don't turn out well."

"Not any smaller than the incestuous scene you came out of."

Aran nodded, conceding the point.

Rosemary listened in silence. She still had the sinking feeling she wasn't the person for this job. Who was she to tell some musician in some as-yet-undecided city that playing for millions on SHL made more sense than what they were doing? Not that she could speak from experience on any of the subjects they talked about, either; all of her dating had been within the safety of hoodspace.

She wasn't in a position to give anyone advice on music. She had expertise in other areas. Growing carrots. Solving database errors. Troubleshooting. That was what SHL had seen in her: good problem-solving skills, resourcefulness, enthusiasm. If they hired her, they must believe those skills carried over. She worked on memorizing what everyone had said, so she'd be able to repeat it back if she ever needed to have an opinion.

12

LUCE

Never Really Ever Had It

We had a large dry-erase board on the kitchen wall. On one side, roommates put notes about groceries needed and leftovers available and things like "Good luck on the interview, Jaspreet!" On the other side, we kept a running list titled "Don't Forget Normal."

The Don't Forget Normal list included: street festivals, Renaissance fairs, amusement parks, supermarket runs, movie theaters, malls in December, talking to strangers in a waiting room. We debated whether some of those were things we actually missed, but decided they all went on the list. Just because something had needed improvement didn't mean the solution was to cancel it entirely. Jaspreet, the public school teacher, had hated her school's principal and adored her students. She applied for the new virtual grade schools one after another, but there were far more teachers than spots, between the sick kids out of school and the ones who had died, and the constricting job market.

The whiteboard was impermanent, and some of the changes were clearly not going away. Plus, there were too many of them. They snowballed. We traded the dry-erase for permanent markers and expanded off the board and onto the kitchen wall, moving from generalities to specifics, good and bad. Pride parades, school assemblies, outdoor movies, outdoor concerts, baseball games, crowded trains, roller derby bouts, grocery store crowds before a snowstorm, and how the shelves emptied of bread and milk and bottled water and toilet paper. The "list" spread out of the kitchen and onto the dining room wall, black and blue and green and red against eggshell. We brought in a ladder.

With more room, it expanded into anecdotes, paragraphs, whole stories. Write it all down, we thought, so it would still exist somewhere. I found it safer to share there than to utter any of it out loud.

My first contributions were personal but distanced. *We used to play this room that had been a strip club in its previous life, the Wrecking Bar. Every surface was mirrored, and the bands played around the poles, and the stage extended out onto the bar, which worked better for a strip club than a music venue, but made for some interesting and unsanitary shows.*

I remember watching Patti Smith ride a bucking Stratocaster to a standstill, then rip the strings off one by one until she had nothing left to play.

The Patti Smith show had destroyed me in all the best ways, but I couldn't explain. I tried again, another day. *I remember Young Sport's set at Bumbershoot. I saw them a few other times as well, unmemorable shows, but for some reason that performance in Seattle was transcendent: the band was so present they moved a seated audience of thousands to dance in the aisles. Will we have festivals again? I miss joy sweeping through a crowd. The good contagion.*

I used to sneak into clubs without paying cover or showing ID by carrying my guitar in behind a band loading in. Some of them took pity on me and shared their fries and drinks. That was personal; so many kindnesses I'd never forget.

And finally, the most personal of all, though I wasn't ready to expand on it: *I wrote on another wall once, on the hardest night. I don't know if anyone ever noticed.*

Jaspreet photographed the whole thing and created an interactive online exhibit. She encouraged others to add to it, in comments or photos, which they did, by the thousands. We all felt our world slipping away, in cascades and cataracts, the promises of temporary change becoming less and less temporary. Didn't we feel so much safer? Weren't safe and healthy worth more to us than large weddings and overcrowded schools? Hadn't the pox been spread by people working and attending school when they should have stayed home? Never mind that they didn't stay home because they couldn't afford to. The talking heads were in agreement that necessity would fuel innovation. Good things were coming fast, they promised; I stopped watching the news.

My money was running out equally fast. The royalty checks still came, but they got smaller and smaller. My roommate Lexa, a nurse, suggested I look into getting certified as a nursing assistant, and it seemed as good an idea as any. I started taking online courses. It made sense on several levels, beyond just making sure I had cash coming in. As Lexa pointed out, no matter what happened, we'd still need medical professionals. I hadn't saved April, but maybe I could do some good for other people.

I threw myself into the nursing gig. If music wasn't going to be my thing anymore, I had to have a different thing. My world turned gray and quiet. Even when the roommates had parties (small parties, nothing to scare the neighbors into calling the police), I stayed upstairs or scheduled shifts to coincide. Better to leave it all behind completely. People, parties, fun. When I played music for myself, all I could manage was deep noise, mournful chords, janky tone. Every wanting sound.

I wasn't keeping track of time, so when Nora Bowles from Superwally's *Tuning Fork* ezine contacted me, I had no idea why she'd sought me out. She offered me six different platforms to talk, including one of those new Hoodie things some of my patients wore to distance themselves from their current reality, before I gave up and agreed to a phone call.

"You're hard to get hold of," she said without preamble. "Your old label didn't have any contact info for you."

I still had the same phone number and email; I'd told them not to pass my info along to anybody.

She continued. "I finally got your phone number from your old guitarist. He said to say hi."

Good old Hewitt. I'd never talked to him again, but he'd been a nice guy, when he wasn't drunk or stupid.

"Why are you calling?" I could tell she wanted me to ask.

"Well, as you know, we're coming up on the third anniversary of the Stadium Tragedy, and I pitched a story to my editors about finding the last musicians to play big live shows, and, well, as far as I can tell, you were the only one who actually played that night."

I didn't think that was true. She meant the only one who played a venue big enough to count by Superwally standards, and probably the smallest one of those. Surely there were others in living rooms and tiny clubs who'd had the same instinct as I'd had that night to push back against despair. Before I'd realized it was pointless. That I could make all the noise I wanted, and nobody would hear it anymore.

"Cool," I said.

"So are you still playing?"

"For myself. Sometimes."

"Writing new songs?"

"Yeah," I lied.

"I'd love to hear them sometime. I really liked 'Blood and Diamonds.' You should get with StageHolo to do a show sometime."

I remembered the name, but I hadn't kept up with any of the new platforms, so I made a sound of noncommittal agreement instead. We chatted a little longer, and hung up.

A week later, I heard a low whistle from one of my roommates, then a door creaked open.

"Luce!" yelled Lexa. "You're famous again!"

The article blew up. *Tuning Fork* had sold it to the other news outlets. The title was "The Last Power Chord," and we were indeed the only band of any renown that had played that night, according to Nora Bowles's research. The article linked readers to Superwally to buy the song, and the article went viral. I watched the song and the album climb their rankings. A couple of TV shows paid me to use it, then a movie. I even heard it playing in a car once as I biked to work. And still, I didn't realize the extent of its reach until I was bathing a patient and she reached over and touched my name tag. "Luce," she said. "Like the singer."

"Kinda," I said.

13

ROSEMARY

Adventures Close to Home

Leaving the highway for the county road, watching the county road roll into Jory's Main Street, Rosemary was struck by the emptiness. She'd never noticed before, or else she'd assumed the mix of dead businesses and thriving ones was normal. Now that she was supposed to seek out secret places, she had no idea where to find them. Were they hiding in the back rooms of the open stores or the boarded-up ones? Were there dance parties in the old high school gym? Rap battles on the playground after dark? She still couldn't figure out how to find what she'd been sent to look for.

Her mother was waiting for her in an isolation booth at Micky's. She unlocked the door and grabbed the handle of the rolling bag, squeezing Rosemary's hand for a moment before pulling the bag onto the seat beside her. Rosemary took the opposite bench. They both ordered the macaroni and cheese without even bothering to scroll through the menu screens, and she paid for both her own and her mother's meal, with a smile into the camera; it was nice to feel known.

"So tell me," her mother said. "Do you like the job? Are you glad you quit Superwally? Unless that's a bad question . . ."

"It's not a bad question at all, Mom. I'm glad I quit Superwally. It's an interesting job. I get to help people, kind of."

"Well, that's exciting. What's the downside?"

Their food arrived, looking and smelling like Micky's mac and cheese always looked and smelled, at exactly the right temperature. The SHL food had been fine, but different. Rosemary poked the edges with her fork. "It's a little overwhelming, but I'm willing to give it a try."

"Good. How long are you home for? Your father thought you were coming back for good, but I said I thought this was a visit."

"It'll depend, I guess. There's an assignment I have to do here, unless it goes badly."

Her mother cocked her head. "Well, eat and then I want to hear whatever you're willing to tell."

They got back to the farm in midafternoon. She took a moment as they stepped from the truck to appreciate what she had always taken for granted: home, the friendly ruckus of chickens conversing, people who loved her and didn't expect her to do miracles.

She dropped her bags in her room, where the Superwally customer support posters still decorated half her walls, and bands the other half. Funny how she'd always thought those bands lived in a different world from hers; she'd never considered them people before. They'd existed as verse and chorus, as notes and chords, as videos or recordings, as celebrities whose clothes and breakups were the subject of gossip, but never as people who had their own opinions and personalities outside the time they spent in public. The fact that she hadn't grown up watching them in glorious SHL quality probably contributed to her flat image of them. She lay back on her bed and imagined striking up a conversation with Iris Branches at a bar.

Her father was in the kitchen making dinner when she came out.

"What can I do?" she asked.

"Nothing." He didn't turn from grating potatoes.

It took her a moment to realize he was angry. Had he ever been angry with her before? Never in a way he'd let show. "I don't even get a hello?"

"Hello." He still didn't face her.

"Or an explanation of why you're not turning around? This is a weird welcome."

He slammed the grater onto the counter and turned to look at her. "Welcome home. I'm glad you're back. I'm pissed off."

"Pissed off?"

"You would be, too, if your daughter told you she was going to a training program at a protected compound, but secretly took a job requiring her to travel to places where she could be killed."

Ah. "Okay, first, I should have explained. I'm sorry I lied, but it's not like that. I'm here first, aren't I? This job could take me anywhere, but I'm starting at home, because I know it'll make you sleep easier if I can stick to towns near here. It's a good job, and I'm lucky to have gotten it."

If he hadn't started down this line, she might have talked to him about her fears about the job. Instead, she was stuck defending it. "Secondly, I could be killed anywhere. A blade could fall off a windmill and kill me tomorrow. Some chicken virus might mutate and kill more than the pox did. 'Safe' is not a reason to stay home."

"Statistically speaking . . ."

"Statistically speaking, you could have a heart attack tomorrow. Are you going to stay in bed waiting for it?"

He cocked his head. "I just don't understand why you'd put yourself in danger. We built this farm so you'd be safe. You can live here forever without any of these jobs between state basic income and the windmills."

"Because I'm twenty-four and my entire world for half my life has been these five rooms and this farm, and I like having a job. You got to live in the real world before you hid here. Why can't I have a chance to do the same?"

"It's more dangerous now, honey. You know that."

"Is it, though? How old are your statistics? I was terrified for the first few days, even on that compound, because you made me terrified to be there. Maybe I don't want to be terrified anymore."

"She's right, Dan." Rosemary hadn't heard her mother come into the kitchen.

"I don't care if she's right, Em. I'd rather she was safe."

He turned back to the potatoes. Her mother looked at her and shrugged. "I should have warned you he was upset. Go feed the animals. I'll talk to him."

Her father was still sullen over dinner, but her mother must have convinced him that being mad at her was pointless.

"So tell me about your job." It sounded like a forced line reading.

She explained the basics, putting the most positive spin on it, leaving out the cities. She wished she could tell him she understood his fears, that she'd felt them, too, but she thought she was better off taking a hard line. Talking about the job—even if it was still conceptual to her—made her feel braver and stronger. She concentrated on describing the bands she'd seen in the studio, the people she'd met, the compound itself.

"That's a lot of responsibility. I'm impressed, honey." At least that sounded genuine. Maybe he would come around. "So what are you back here for?"

"I'm supposed to try to find local musicians."

He cocked his head. "In Jory? There's nothing here."

"That's what I said, too, but everyone I talked to says there are hidden pockets of music everywhere. I wanted to give it a try. See what I can find."

"Like venues? Secret garage bands? Or people making professional-quality music on their computers?"

"Any of the above. Are garage bands a real thing?"

He nodded. "They used to be. I guess if it's 'any of the above' you'll find someone. Not necessarily anyone good, but someone."

She woke early to feed the chickens and clean their coop, the closest she was willing to come to apologizing for deceiving her parents—both the deceptions they knew about and the ones yet to come. She drove the farm truck toward town on an empty two-lane. High overhead, a hawk sketched circles in the cloudless blue, while a package drone took the more direct route at a lower altitude. She'd only witnessed a hawk attacking a drone once, years ago, but she always held her breath waiting to see it happen again.

A second bird darted low across the road, small and quick, brown with wings and tail tipped electric blue. Even though you weren't supposed to use a Hoodie for anything other than maps while driving, she asked for a quick ID: indigo bunting, male, winter plumage. A "First of the Season!" birding badge flashed in her peripheral vision, which wasn't an accomplishment anyone should be celebrating. Buntings never arrived before summer, and this one was here before it had even put on its breeding finery.

She drove through the license plate scanner at the north end of town, where the county road became Main, past the twelve stately houses lurking behind their security fences, houses that told of a past Jory she'd never known, ten of them now subdivided for multiple families. Then the municipal lot, where she parked the truck and continued on foot. What remained of Main Street was a long strip of vacant two-story buildings with signage nobody had bothered to remove, for types of stores she'd never seen. Ghosts: laundromat, Lucky Chinese, Carrie's Hair, Quigley Antique Mall. She didn't remember any of them ever having been open, though someone once graffitied KILL THE POXIES—SAVE A LIFE on the side of Quigley's, and her mother told her to look the other way, as if she hadn't already seen it, and it was gone the next time they returned to town.

There was still a feed store, a small grocery with a post office and health clinic inside, a gas station, a Micky's, and a bar. Of those, the only one she'd never been in was the bar. She wasn't going to find a secret venue in any of the others.

The bar was called Sweeney's, according to the marquee, and the Shamrock, according to the front door, propped open. It was a sunny day and dark inside, so her eyes took a minute to adjust. Inside, it looked like a replica of the one hoodspace Irish bar she'd been in, unless she had that backwards.

There were only two customers this early, both older white guys, on opposite ends of the wooden bar, with eight stools in between them. The rest of the room held six tables, separated and sealed by clear floor-to-ceiling booth isolators, like at Micky's. The bartender was middle-aged, another white guy, with more hair on his forearms than his head. She chose a stool midway between the two customers, realizing too late that it put her behind the tap handle contraption. She didn't want to move, so she stuck with her choice. Brave enough to not be isolated in a booth, but nowhere near the other customers.

"Can I help you?" the bartender asked.

She was on the clock, but she wanted to look like she belonged, and SHL had made it clear she should do what she needed to get the job done. She pointed to the tap handle shaped like an apple slice. The bartender poured a tall golden glass. She sipped cider, as she'd hoped. She rested one elbow on the narrow bar and tried to ignore the fact that her elbow was now sticky with who knew what. Exude nonchalance, that was the key.

"So, ah, anything interesting happening around here tonight?"

The bartender squinted at her. "Here, like this bar? Or in town?"

"Either?"

"Neither." He grinned like he'd been clever. "A new girl walking into my bar is enough to make the newspaper."

"We have a newspaper?" Even after over a decade here, her family was still not part of the town. Her parents would say it didn't matter because they had each other.

"Nah, figure of speech, sweetie."

Ugh. She couldn't tell now if the grin was a leer. Avs were so much easier to read than actual human faces.

It wasn't like she didn't know nothing happened here. She'd lived here forever, even if she was a stranger to the bartender. She remembered fragments of things before they'd moved to Jory: the water park, fireworks watched from a blanket on a crowded hillside. But here? No parades, no ball games, no dances. None of the stuff she'd read about or seen on-screen. This was a place where people followed the congregation laws. That was why her parents had moved here. Silly to think she'd find anything, even if everyone at SHL said all places had secrets.

Silly, too, to think even if the town did have secrets, anyone would tell them to her. Even here, in her own hometown, nobody knew her but the farm's most immediate neighbors and the staff at the feed store. Maybe that was the trick. Instead of marching into this bar and expecting people to tell all to a stranger, maybe she needed to start with people she knew. Let them connect her with others, who'd connect her with others. She put her drink on the bar and reached for the pay terminal.

Rosemary tried. She browsed the gas station's convenience store eavesdropping on other customers, but nobody talked about anything except the weather and the fishing. The grocery store was empty, except for a single bored-looking attendant and a security guard behind glass; if everyone else was like her family, they droned in most stuff they couldn't grow or raise. The attendant was in her eighties and didn't look like she'd be a source of hot leads.

She called her father. "Do you need anything at the feed store?"

"We're low on probiotics for the chickens, if you want to pick some up." She could tell he was surprised. She'd complained about going in there for years now.

Simmons's Feed smelled sweet as grain, but was always freezing in winter and sweltering in summer, thanks to the open door to the warehouse. This was the only store she'd ever spent much time in, before she'd started inventing excuses not to go.

She'd always resented being dragged along to load the truck. It didn't help that the Simmons kids never dropped their Hoodies, while Rosemary's parents still insisted she not use hers outside school. It took until she turned sixteen to convince them she had no social life because of that rule, and even then she was stuck with her lousy old Hoodie. "Why do we have to come here? Can't you just order it?" she would ask.

Her father would shake his head. "Feed, vitamins, salt. Too expensive to drone because of the weight."

At least his insistence she come along had bought her a passing familiarity in this one place, and at least it was spring, so the store's temperature was tolerable. She wasn't sure if luck or the opposite had put Tina Simmons behind the register. Tina was the closest person to her age she had ever known in person until the last few weeks. She was two years older than Rosemary, and had taken her to the one party Rosemary had ever been to, when Rosemary was eighteen. That party was the only proof she had that people did gather occasionally, even in a by-the-book town like Jory, and she had never even thought to ask Tina how she had met those guys.

She still remembered it with embarrassment. Eleven total strangers, the only other teenagers left in a fifty-mile radius who hadn't been killed by the pox or kept from leaving the house by their parents. It was nothing like hoodspace: a haze of too much beer; people sitting too close and talking too loud and calling one of their own friends Poxface, as if most of them didn't have scars under their clothes; boys who smelled of sweat and kept trying to put their hands on her; a five-mile walk home in the dark because she wanted to leave before Tina. Bodies. Her overwhelming impression had been bodies in proximity, and every motion having so much more impact than it had in hood.

"Hey!" Tina said. Apparently whatever memory Tina had of that party, it wasn't as awkward as Rosemary's. She was always friendly, even if she'd never invited Rosemary out again. "I heard you quit your job."

"Quit because I got a better one." Amazing how fast news traveled; her parents must have been in while she was gone.

"No kidding?"

"Yeah. Actually, I have a funny question, related. You know those people you used to hang out with?"

"My friends?"

Rosemary's cheeks burned. "Yeah. Your friends. Anyway, I was wondering, do any of them play music?"

Tina gave her a quizzical look.

"Like, a band," Rosemary said. "Or computer stuff. Anything. I've been told there are bands in Jory, playing in secret rooms or barns or garages."

"Sorry. I don't know of any. Mike Powell plays guitar, but he isn't exactly good. Oh! And Roberta Parker plays keyboard for her online church." Roberta Parker was the elderly attendant at the grocery.

"Thanks anyway. Can you charge five pounds of Fancy Feathers probiotics to our account?"

"No problem! Do you want me to invite you the next time we get together? I can tell Mike to bring his guitar."

"Sure." Rosemary hefted the tub of chicken vitamins into the truck bed and drove back to the farm. There was no way Mike Powell was what she was supposed to be looking for if even Tina admitted he wasn't any good. A church keyboard player wouldn't impress her bosses, either. She'd hit a dead end. She could call her high school friends, wherever they were, and ask if any played music, though that promised a long, awkward series of conversations with people she hadn't bothered to stay in touch with.

Back in her room, she pulled up her SHL Hoodie—they'd offered to issue her another new one, but she didn't see anything wrong with using the one that had been sent to her for the Bloom Bar. Aran had given her his number, and she found herself pinging him into an empty chat room.

He spawned into the empty space, glanced around, and with a quick swipe, conjured a woodsy background. "For old times' sake! I get nervous in empty rooms."

He had an expensive, photo-realistic av. His band did well

enough for him to afford it, or maybe SHL gave talent high-end looks to keep up appearances. Either way, she felt shoddy in comparison.

"What's up?" he asked.

"I have no idea what I'm doing. I've spent the whole day searching this stupid town trying to find musicians, and as far as I can tell there aren't any. I don't know what I'm supposed to do short of inspecting every barn and garage in the county for amps and drum kits."

He laughed. "That'd be some good detective work, but it does sound time-consuming. How big is the town you're in?"

"I don't know. Small." "I don't know" was a lie. Four hundred and ninety-three people within the town's outer limits. She didn't want to admit she'd gone home.

"Okay, if you're in a small town, you've got two options. If you think there's something to find, then hang around longer. Win trust. Watch people. Listen. It might take weeks."

Weeks. How long would they give her? "Or?"

"Or give up on that town and go somewhere else. You said you're from a farm, right? You know there are some places nothing grows, no matter how hard you try."

"Just give up? They won't be mad I wasted their money?"

"Not if you leave because you're following a lead."

"I don't have any leads."

"You do, because your buddy Aran is giving you one."

The background blanked out, then morphed into a cityscape she didn't recognize. She'd known sooner or later it would come to this. If she wanted to keep the job, if she wanted to get out of this town and this house, she had to leap. Somewhere out there, somebody waited for her to connect their dream of a life in music with the dream enablers at SHL. She had a mission to fulfill.

14

LUCE

Leather Jacket

The next royalty check was big enough that I called an accountant for advice. He told me to put a third of it away for taxes and pretend it didn't exist, to invest a third, and to use a third for living expenses or spending, however I saw fit.

That made as much sense as anything. I didn't feel bad taking money I'd earned, but I had mixed feelings about this particular windfall. People listening to my music again? Great. People only listening to that one song? That frustrated me. I wanted them to hear the other stuff, too, but most of all I still wanted to play. It wasn't fair that one old song kept rattling around like a dying echo of everything before, and I couldn't reach its listeners to introduce them to any of my other, better songs. Not in person, anyway.

My first thought was to buy a used van and hit the road again. But to where? There was still no place to tour. I missed music as sustenance, music as contact, music as currency; I had no idea how to make that happen again. I'd burned the bridge at my old label, so there'd be no help from them. My searches for open venues had come up blank. Anything that existed was flying under the radar, which meant there was no way to tour and capitalize on my new fame. Places would open again soon, I was sure, when people stopped accepting the government-fueled paranoia as normal.

Another thing had started bothering me, too. How many stories had I heard of musicians who achieved success and used their earnings to buy their parents a home or a car? I didn't even know if my family was still alive after the pox had swept the country. They were unsearchable, unconnected to the world outside their community. I sometimes rang the house to listen to my father's voice mail message, but nobody ever picked up the phone. Caller ID or nobody left to answer? There was only one way to know for sure.

I got to the bus early out of old habit, even though I had left my guitar home for once. I needn't have bothered; there were only four other people in line. They stood with oceans of space between them, so far from each other it could barely be called a line at all. I couldn't stand the suspicion in everyone's eyes, like the other travelers were there to kill them or infect them or both.

The day was supposed to get unseasonably warm for March, but it started out as a chilly morning. I'd dressed for my destination in a sweater and borrowed ankle-length skirt. The only part of my outfit that still felt like me was my combat boots, which I figured nobody would notice. Now I shivered and wished I'd worn my leather jacket, too.

"Coffee's on me," I said to the four others, pointing to the vending machine. "Then I can say I bought for the whole bus."

Nobody responded. I wondered if this was just the way things were these days, if I was violating some new travel protocol. I felt awkward, out of sorts; partly nerves from the trip I was embarking on, and partly the long skirt and cardigan, which made me feel like I was wearing a costume of the person I would have been if I'd never left Brooklyn. Were they all looking at me and thinking they knew something about me? They didn't. I bought a cup of bitter vending machine coffee for myself; it made a good hand warmer.

The bus arrived twenty minutes late. A sign on the side read THANK YOU FOR YOUR PATIENCE WHILE WE IMPROVE OUR FLEET.

There were a few people already on board, each in a separate row except for one couple and another pair that looked like a mother and child. Everyone else sat as far from each other as possible.

It was the quietest trip up I-95 I'd ever experienced. Nobody said a word, and if anyone was listening to headphones, they kept them at levels I couldn't perceive. All that silence made me want to scream, but I settled for looking out the window and willing a new song into existence. It didn't happen.

The corner where the bus dropped us normally bustled. There were still people out and about, and they still moved with proper New York speed and conviction, but I couldn't shake the feeling that this place, too, was diminished. I walked two blocks crosstown toward the train I wanted, noticing presences and absences: more police, no street vendors, shuttered stores, delivery bikes traveling in vast pelotons. No tourists as far as I could tell, though these weren't tourist-heavy blocks. It wasn't until I approached the subway entrance that I encountered a crowd.

"What's going on?" I asked a man standing at the group's edge.

He shrugged. "Same old."

"I haven't been in the city for a couple of years. What's 'same old'?"

"They meter the stations now, y'know? There's a bag scanner and a body scanner, and they only let a certain number of people down there at a time."

"That must take forever!"

Another shrug. "It's not so bad, as long as the weather's okay. It moves faster than you'd think. There'll be another wave in a second."

I didn't see how that could possibly work, but two minutes later, we moved forward. My backpack set off the scanner, and after I passed through the metal detector I had to argue that the wire cutter I used to clip new strings wasn't meant to cause trouble. I didn't even know why it was in my backpack instead of my gig bag where it belonged, but it had somehow hitched a ride. None of which swayed the officer, who confiscated it anyway.

The day up above had gotten sunny and warm, but the station was warmer still. I pushed my sleeves past my elbows. Once through security, the platform was surprisingly uncrowded, as was the train. There were seats for everyone. I held my backpack on my lap, but it wasn't in anyone's way. I remembered the last time I'd been here, leaving April's place, standing with guitar and coffee clutched close, and still feeling like I was taking up too much room.

Even after all that had happened, I'd somehow expected New York to be the same as always, unflappable. The subway had been overtaxed before, but the only way it could be this empty—the only way metering and inspecting could work without backing up the whole city—was if there were a whole lot fewer people using it. The pox, the people who'd shifted to working from home. I'd thought in a city this dense everyone would have just laughed at any proposed changes, but it felt like fear had made a dent even here.

As we crossed into Brooklyn, I realized I'd clenched my jaw tight enough to ache, and rubbed the joint to relax it. I didn't have to make this trip, but I wanted to. Needed to, to see for myself. I tugged my sweater sleeves back down to my wrists.

The subway hadn't been part of my childhood experience, so it wasn't until I was streetside again that the eeriness kicked in. One block from the station, then two, then I was on the tree-lined streets I remembered. A knot of teenage girls walked toward me; like me, they wore long skirts and sweaters even on this spring day. I examined their faces, looking for familiarity, before realizing that they would have been small children when I left.

As they passed, one of them said, "Her boots!" in Yiddish, and they all burst into laughter. They didn't even bother whispering; my boots marked me as an outsider.

The door to the girls' school I'd attended was chained shut; I'd assumed it would be open, that there would be exceptions for private religious schools. The streets were crowded with mothers pushing double strollers, toddlers walking alongside, and more clusters of girls and boys, everyone giving me a wide berth. It took me a minute to figure out that the kids were all coming out of houses. A neat solution in a community this small: classes around dining room tables. That was my guess, anyway. I'd been wrong to assume even this place would be unchanged.

Four more blocks, three more blocks, two more blocks, one. This street had been our street. These steps had been our steps. This door had been our door.

I knocked, waited, knocked again. I imagined one of my sisters ushering me in. Would we sit at the dining room table and drink tea? Or in the living room? I settled on the top step, wishing I had my guitar with me to play away my nervousness, though this wasn't the time or place. I traced arpeggiated patterns on my palm with my fingertips. Music only I could hear.

"Can I help you?"

I hadn't seen her approach, and now that my mother stood on the sidewalk, and I sat blocking her door, I couldn't move. She looked older, of course she did, and shorter, but maybe that was because I was on the top step. I didn't recognize the two children hiding behind her.

She tried again. "Are you looking for some—Chava Leah?"

I nodded, incapable of speech. And then she was hugging me, touching my face like she wasn't quite sure I was real. When she pulled away, it was to unlock the door. She looked up and down the block, then gestured me into the house behind the two boys. I wondered if they were my brothers or nephews, then was walloped by a wave of grief that I had created a situation where I didn't know the answer to that question. No, I reminded myself. This was never your path. You couldn't have stayed.

The door opened into a small vestibule filled with shoes. Just beyond it, to the left, the dining room, looking just as I remembered it. The dining room, the long table with the worn white tablecloth and a dozen mismatched chairs. The desk in the corner overflowing with books and papers. The side table displaying my great-great-grandmother's candlesticks. The boys had gone straight to the table, and one was standing on a chair to reach a jar of crayons.

I followed my mother into the living room. I moved automatically toward my spot on the couch, but she gestured for me to sit in the guest chair, which didn't creak or sag. She sat in my father's reading chair beside me and took my hand in hers.

"Are you coming home?" There was hope in her voice.

To stay, she meant. "I wanted to see how you're doing. I didn't know . . . So many people got sick, and you never answered the phone . . ."

Her face closed off. I hadn't given the answer she had hoped for; if I was returning, I would have led with that. "You shouldn't be here. The rabbi doesn't want outsiders coming here anymore. He says we're safer with no contact at all."

"I won't stay long." No wonder everyone had been eyeing me with suspicion. "I just want to know. Please."

Her face twisted. "Two little ones, Rachie's youngest daughter and Jacob, who was already so sick, may their memories be a blessing. Your sister Chana got a bad infection from it that spread to her brain; she has spells now, memory problems. Her boys are living with us so Eli doesn't have to take care of them all on top of his studies."

She kept going, listing friends and family. My oldest brother Avi's son Jacob had been born with spina bifida and a host of developmental disabilities; he was only a couple of years younger than me, and all of us who were old enough had taken turns babysitting him. At least I knew his name to mourn him; I felt terrible that I'd lost a niece whose name I didn't even know, and too ashamed to ask. "Is Chana in the house? Can I see her?"

She shook her head. "It's not a good idea. She's had a hard time."

I don't think I'd realized until that moment that this was it. She wouldn't introduce me to the boys, or let me upstairs to see my sister. We both looked at the door, looked at each other, looked away. She still held my hand.

"I'm doing well," I said. "I wanted to tell you. Do you need anything? Chana's care, doctor bills, anything at all? I want to help."

She lifted her chin. "We don't need. Give to others if you want to help."

Another mistake. I should have known I couldn't offer outright; she'd always been too proud to take anything. Clothes got handed down until they were scraps; toys and furniture, too. For other things, the community stepped in. Need to see a doctor? Too poor for a wedding? There were people who made that happen, out of love and support, without ever making it feel like charity. I'd offered charity. We'd never had money, but we'd never wanted for anything; the community provided. I'd loved all of that, even when I knew I couldn't stay.

"I'm sorry. I shouldn't have come," I said.

"No," she agreed. "But it's good to see you. You should probably go. It would hurt your father to see you."

He wouldn't be home for a couple of hours yet, if he still held the same job, so it was more than that. She didn't want any of the others to see me. Didn't want me confusing them; I was an aberration. Was I spoken of at all? Thought of, if not spoken of, judging from her expression. My being here was causing her pain.

I gently extricated my hand from hers. "I tried. I tried so hard to belong here, but it didn't work."

"I know."

She leaned over and threw her arms around me, pulling me tight to her. When she let go, I stood and walked toward the door. I paused before opening it, digging in my pocket for the wad of cash I'd hoped to give to her.

"I forgot," I said. "I wanted to return this money I borrowed from Chana. Will you make sure she gets it?"

Her chin lifted again, and I could tell she was about to refuse. We'd never had money as children; the idea that Chana would have had anything to lend me was ridiculous.

"I'll make sure," she said.

I wiped my eyes with my sleeve and headed back toward the subway. This trip was only slightly more familiar; this was the one

I'd taken the day I'd left, not before or since. It had felt permanent then, and more permanent now. I cataloged the streets, the stores, the faces, knowing this was the last time I would be here.

Once on the train, still not full even in late afternoon when it should have overflowed with students and day workers, I began to feel the burden of the costume I was wearing. I was not me in these clothes and I couldn't remember now why I'd worn them. Respect? A concession? I hitched the not-me skirt up a couple of inches and studied my thrift store boots, the scuffed toes, the too-long laces wrapped around my ankles. The other time I'd made this trip I hadn't had these boots yet, hadn't yet bought my leather jacket or my first guitar, hadn't known any of what lay ahead, for good and for bad. I pushed the sweater sleeves up over my elbows and wished again that I'd worn my jacket. My armor.

I'd promised my aunt I'd spend the night at her place at the northern end of Manhattan, but it hadn't struck me at the time we'd made the plan that I'd be re-creating my own exodus. By the time I got to her place, I was a mess. She fussed over me and fed me and made tea and listened as I recounted the visit.

"Oh, sweetie," she said when I finished. "We can't control what family we're born into, but we can choose what to take away from the experience. They love you. They just have no idea how to fit a gay daughter into their worldview. That's their problem, not yours."

We sat on her couch, the same couch I'd lived on after I'd left home. It had been donated to her by the nonprofit that had helped her start a new life when she'd made that same journey. In her case, she'd left behind a husband as well.

"Do you ever regret it?" I'd never asked her that question before.

"No." For a second I thought that was going to be her entire answer, but she sipped her tea and continued. "I miss some things about the celebrations, and some of the melodies, though my new shul community makes up for some of that. I miss family. But I can miss those things and those people and still know I didn't belong there. Right?"

"Right," I said. I'd known that when I still lived there, knew it when I left. It was only this extended unmoored moment that had me confused. "I almost apologized to her. I almost said it wasn't her fault."

"It is," she said. "If their worldview doesn't include their own daughter, they're the ones who need changing, not you. Anyway, it's probably good you went. Closure is good."

"What about you?" I asked. "You're the one I should be helping, after everything you've done for me."

She drained her cup and smiled. "I'm okay. I promise I won't be ashamed to ask if I ever need anything. Who knows, maybe someday you'll move back here, or I'll move to Maryland to be near you. In the meantime, you earned that money. You should use it to help with your own next chapter."

Whatever that was.

The next afternoon, I took the bus back to Baltimore. I arrived back at the house to find a half dozen bicycles on the front porch, and the owners of said bicycles inside. The table had been pushed to the side and the chairs arranged theater-style. Jaspreet had tacked a sheet over our graffitied dining room wall to show her friends the project she was working on: a documentary cataloging vacant houses, interspersed with interviews of wealthy residents packing up to leave the city.

"Why are you going?" Jaspreet would ask each interviewee.

"They say it's better to get some distance between people." Or "I just don't feel safe anymore." Or "People cross the street when they see my pox scars. It's not like I'm contagious anymore."

I pictured their grand pilgrimage, their stately moving trucks, an endless search for the place where fear wouldn't follow them. The homes she documented were a mix: large houses abandoned by the professors who no longer needed to live near their shuttered campuses; gentrified and ungentrified row homes; row homes that had been vacant long before any of the current troubles. Jaspreet gave statistics for the number of homeless people versus the number of available houses, the number of people who'd left in each of the previous four years.

The film was well made, but I was distracted. My mind kept juxtaposing my parents' neighborhood, where nobody was going anywhere. It kept playing with thoughts of family and community and what makes a place a home, all overlaid with this gathering of people whose lives had collided with mine, the potluck dishes on the table, the things we'd written on the wall, the cheering and the compliments for Jaspreet's work, their mutual understanding that this film was art and politics and a statement on what it took to stay, and what it took to leave, and what it meant to have no choice in the matter.

People chatted late into the evening, and for once I stayed downstairs, drinking and snacking and getting to know my roommates' friends. When everyone finally left, I asked Jaspreet a question I'd been waiting to ask. "That street in the scene with the community garden. Where's that?"

Jaspreet rewound to look at which one I was talking about. "Not all that far from here. A whole block of vacants in pretty decent shape."

I copied the address and looked it up after we were done cleaning. Then I started researching realty agents. I had a wonderful, terrible idea for how to use my "Blood and Diamonds" money.

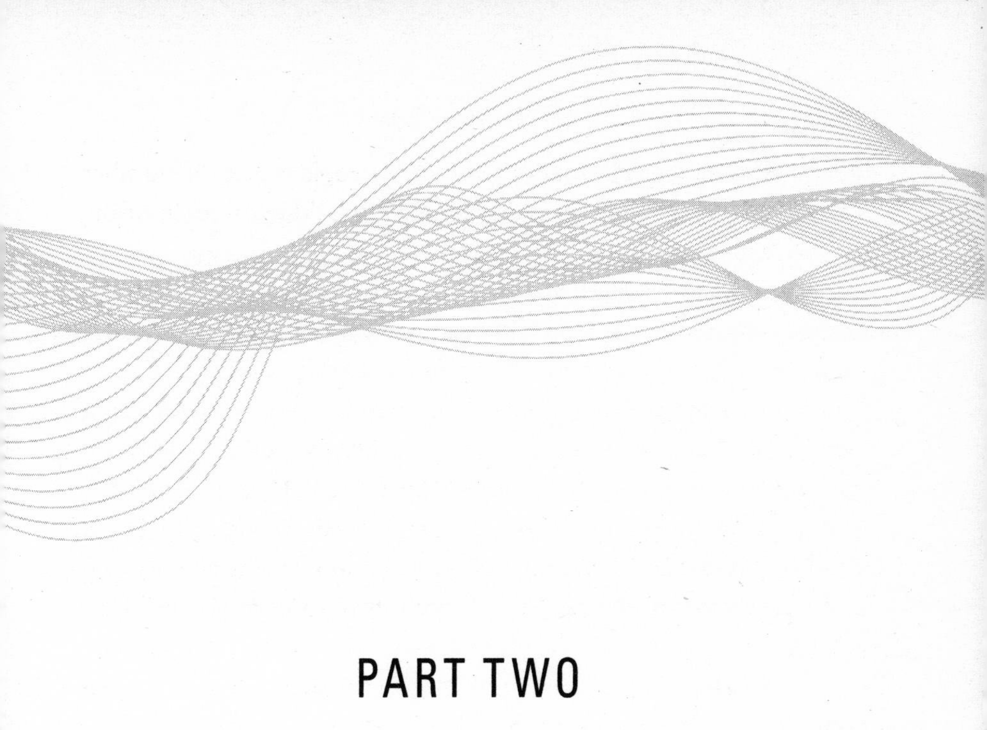

PART TWO

15

ROSEMARY

Baltimore

Rosemary's bus hit Baltimore as the sun began to set, lighting the skyscrapers in pink and gold and purple. She leaned against the window and wondered what it would be like to be in one of those rooms when the light struck this way. She didn't even know if those tall buildings were still in use. Were they residences or offices, and how were they counted in congregation laws?

"We'll be stopping in five minutes." The bus guard's voice, piped into each locked compartment, was loud enough to make her jump. It had been hours since he had spoken. "Please make sure to collect all of your belongings. Anything left behind will be destroyed."

They came off the highway exit, passed under a plate scanner, and were spit out beside a crumbling stadium. Two razor-wire fences formed a perimeter around it, even though it didn't look like there was much to scavenge. This wasn't one of the stadiums where SportHolo games happened, she was pretty sure. And how were they filmed, for that matter? The players couldn't all be in individual boxes like the musicians. Rosemary filed that question away for another time.

She remembered going to a baseball game once as a kid, in the

Before. The noise, the terrifying drop behind the bleachers, vendors hawking pretzels and ice cream and drinks, the players specks on the diamond far below. She wasn't sure why anyone used to pay to sit out in the weather and watch tiny people when SportHolo brought them right into your living room, large as life.

SportHolo hadn't yet taken off when the stadiums shut down, she guessed. Or there was some other aspect she had been too young to recognize, something sociological, ritual. Often when her parents talked fondly about the antecedent to something that was clearly better today, it was because of the nostalgia factor.

The bus lurched on into the city, catching seven red lights in a row. It had been a smooth ride for the most part, but now the seats rattled and knocked like the farm truck. Maybe they had switched to a human driver after exiting the freeway; maybe it was just bad roads. Rosemary tried to keep her stomach in its proper place, concentrated on the map overlaid by her Hoodie and finding the best route from the bus drop-off to her hotel.

By the time it stopped to discharge its passengers, on what looked to Rosemary like a random street corner, she was more than ready to get off the bus. She headed toward the exit holding her small bag in front of her to navigate the narrow aisle between compartments; it added a buffer between her and the person ahead if he stopped abruptly. She paused for a second on the last step, looking up at the buildings, down at the sidewalk. *I'm here,* she thought. *I can do this.*

After so many hours riding, her legs wobbled a bit with her first steps, like the ground beneath them was still moving. She walked three blocks to the hotel, enjoying the chance to stretch a bit.

The hoodmaps had left out pedestrians; they'd made her expect empty streets. Wide sidewalks let her keep her distance from the other walkers, but it was still a good reminder that even with all her preparation, real life was different. How did that Whileaway song go? *I walked in with open eyes / and still you caught me by surprise.* She didn't even know what to open her eyes to, so she guessed she'd be surprised a lot.

The hotel lobby was the most ostentatious nonvirtual space she'd ever been in; she checked to see if she'd forgotten to switch to clearview on her Hoodie. Chandeliers like constellations, casting a golden light over the slick white counters, all speaking cleanliness and warmth and comfort to an exhausted Rosemary. Too many firsts for one day.

She stepped into a service booth, tapped her phone on the pad. The low battery light flashed. She wiped it against her side and tucked it back in her pocket.

Reservation confirmed, the screen read. Welcome, Mx. StageHoloLive. Please confirm identity.

That didn't bode well. She tapped her ID to the reader, her heart sinking.

ID does not match name. Please place fingerprint against glass.

She put her finger on the smudged glass, trying not to dwell on all the other fingers that had touched it, then hit the button for assistance when it didn't accept her fingerprint, either. The screen switched over to a cheerful-looking av, a middle-aged Mexican guy. "How can I help you? *¿Cómo puedo ayudarle?* Please state another language if English or Spanish is not your preferred language."

Rosemary wondered how someone was supposed to parse that third sentence if English wasn't their preferred language. "I'm here on business. My company sent me, but I guess someone goofed and didn't put my name on the reservation."

"I'm sorry to hear about that mix-up on your company's part. Please be advised our hotel cannot be held responsible for mix-ups on your company's part."

The repetition clued her in that this was an assistance bot rather than an actual person's avatar. She wondered if there was a second button for human assistance if the bot didn't understand her situation. Surely this wasn't an uncommon occurrence.

"I'm sure if you call SHL they can verify I'm the person on the reservation," she said.

"I understand you want me to call essaychel to verify you are the person on the reservation."

"Yes!"

"That name is not a name we associate with this account. Please verify."

"StageHoloLive. SHL, not 'essaychel.'" She tried not to get too impatient with the machine. If bots improved their performance, companies would phase out their customer service specialists, and she'd have no Superwally job to fall back on. Maybe she ought to be celebrating its failure.

"Please wait while I call StageHoloLive."

Yes. "Thank you."

She waited a minute, two. Her phone buzzed. A single-word message from some nameless logistics assistant: "Sorry."

A moment later, the bot spoke again. "StageHoloLive has changed the name on the reservation to 'Rosemary Laws.' This identity matches your identity as confirmed by your identification, your fingerprint, and visual ID points."

"Yes. Thank you."

"Our records show you have not stayed at a hotel in our franchise before. Our hotel chain policy is to check the identity of all guests against all public lists of terrorists, sex offenders, and violent offenders. Please stand by. If your name is on the list of sex offenders or violent offenders, you will be placed in a special wing, provided you have no outstanding warrants. If you are on the list of terrorists, you will not be permitted to stay at our franchise."

Rosemary waited. She wondered whether the hotel pinged the police if somebody did have outstanding warrants—or if they were on an active terrorist list!—and what the special wing for violent offenders looked like, and if it counted people who had acted in self-defense. Pretty harsh to never be allowed on a regular hotel wing again if you'd served your time.

"Congratulations, your name is not on any lists of known terrorists or offenders. We apologize for the inconvenience of the wait. Your fingerprint will grant access to your floor and the lobby floor. Your room number is 2507. Welcome to the Marton family of residential experiences."

"Thank you. Um, what floor did you say?"

"Room 2507 is on the twenty-fifth floor. The elevators are past the service desk on the left. Have a good evening."

Rosemary slung her bag back over her shoulder and followed the bot's directions to a bank of doors she presumed were elevators. It was silly, but she hadn't wanted to admit to a machine that she didn't know how to operate an elevator.

"How many in your party?" a screen between two of the doors asked, in audio and visual.

"One."

A door to a small compartment opened and she stepped inside. The door closed behind her, faster than she expected. She pressed her finger to the ID pad, and the number 25 lit up. It was the top floor listed, but she had counted at least thirty from outside. Maybe this was like the SHL compound and they had extra floors to increase their square-footage-to-occupant ratio.

She steadied herself as she found herself pushed slightly toward the floor. It was a neat sensation. A screen at eye level proclaimed:

Every floor of our hotel is individually reinforced and blast-guarded.

Our elevators do not pick up more than one party at a time.

Marton hotels comply with all congregation and occupancy laws.

All surfaces in every room are sanitized between visits.

Please conserve water.

Your safety, health, and comfort are our primary concerns.

The door opened again on the twenty-fifth floor. She followed wall placards with numbers to her room and pressed her finger to the lockpad, saying a silent prayer that it recognize her so she didn't have to go back downstairs. It worked. The lights came on as she opened the door.

She locked both dead bolts and the chain behind her. There was a button marked Do Not Disturb beside the light switch. She didn't know why somebody would choose to be disturbed, but if there was a way to opt out, she approved. She dropped her bag on the bed and ducked into the bathroom to scrub the bus and strangers and fingerprint pads off her hands. The water shut off twice, and she had to wait a minute each time for the timer to reset; apparently even fancy hotels weren't immune to conservation laws. A little gold placard on the toilet tank informed her they used a gray-water system like the one at the farm.

The room itself was dominated by a vast ice-white bed. An all-in-one gym ate the remaining floor space. A quick glance in her Hoodie told her seven hundred Veneer options were available for this room, all for varying outrageous fees. She didn't think she'd be allowed to expense turning her room into an aquarium.

She crossed to the window instead. After a moment struggling to figure out how to operate the curtains, she gave up and slipped behind them.

Her window faced the city. The view from the twenty-fifth floor gave her a new angle on the world. She was in one of the high-rise windows she'd seen from the bus, the ones catching the sun and bending it. The buildings that filled in the grid spread before her, most shorter than her own. Some had decorative features: spires, gargoyles, things she didn't know how to name. Others were smooth, featureless, but no less beautiful in their attempts to reach the sky. One had a tower that spelled out BROMO SELTZER instead of numbers around an analog clockface; the clock was stopped, and she'd never learned to read one, anyway. Somehow the jumbled architecture combined for an aesthetically pleasing whole. She hadn't been more than a few blocks yet, but even way up here she felt a hum, an energy, from the collected presence of so many people in one place. Or maybe it was the whizzing flocks of package and surveillance drones, or maybe she imagined it.

She pulled up her hood and looked out the window with a map overlay. Two point three miles to her destination, straight north. The overlay highlighted the direct route and offered some transit options cross-referenced with a risk map, cross-referenced with time of day. It looked safe enough to walk, at least while it was still light out. Five p.m., so there'd be plenty of time to stretch her legs, get there in daylight, and get a sense of the city. That was her mother's phrase. After she had reassured her mother for the millionth time that she would be safe, her mother had said, "Well, if you have to go I'm so glad you'll be there long enough to get a sense of the city."

"What does that mean?" Rosemary had asked.

"Cities—at least how they used to be before, obviously I don't know how they are now—have, well, not personalities, but flavors, I guess you could say? Some felt like they had a lot of history. And some felt modern, and some felt quaint, and some felt touristy or trendy or busy or laid-back."

"Were you in that many?"

"It wasn't a big deal then. You know that. I grew up in Boston, went to school in Chicago, took a job in Atlanta, then another in Pittsburgh. You were a city kid until you were six. You'd have been one for real if I had convinced your father to stay there, but he wanted land . . ."

Rosemary had heard all that before. She couldn't imagine having grown up in a city. She'd gone to middle school and high school online, worked online, hung out with her friends online, dated online. She remembered classrooms from Before, had vague recollections of Fourth of July parades and the one baseball game. In her head, when she pictured those events now, she was the only one there.

"I thought you were glad we moved away, so you could raise me in a safe place."

"I've never been so glad of anything. Look, I'll deny this if you tell your father, but I like the idea of you having a little bit of adventure. Safe, controlled, message-your-mother-every-night-to-tell-her-you're-alive adventure."

Rosemary promised to be careful, promised to check in. Said she was tired, which was true, and probably going to bed early, which was not a lie because it had contained the word "probably." Her eagerness to make up for failure in Jory beat out her exhaustion. She was going out.

Now, climbing a steep hill, Rosemary wondered how much personality the cities still had left. The streets near the hotel were nearly empty, though blooming Bradford pear trees added a festive and pungent note. She wasn't sure whether people still worked in the office buildings towering overhead. The streets themselves looked well maintained—the asphalt glittered—and the shops looked closed for the evening, not forever.

She passed a museum, an honest-to-goodness museum, with thick security fencing. She wouldn't even have known what it was if her map hadn't told her. Inside, she pictured a few guards and an army of camera drones, showing the exhibits to the masses at home. She couldn't remember whether she had ever visited this particular museum in hoodspace. She'd never thought about what the museum buildings themselves looked like, either; all their class trips spawned inside, and the drones had their own paths, flying through long hallways, zooming in and out and around the art. This exterior was stately and serene, elegant even behind the razor wire. She examined it for a moment then kept walking, looking for the city to reveal itself.

Aran Randall's instructions guided her the last few blocks. *There's a row of empty storefronts on the block before,* he had said. *Notable for the fact that one was a clothing store, and before they locked the door they moved all the mannequins to the front.* He hadn't mentioned it had been a kids' clothing store, and the mannequins were all kid-sized zombies, posed in the window like they were trying to get out. A hand outstretched here, a forehead pressed to the glass there. Some of the other abandoned stores had broken glass, but maybe this one was too creepy for anyone to mess with.

Cross the street, and on the opposite side, there'll be a stretch of boarded-up row houses. They've all had their front steps stolen—they were marble, and don't ask me how somebody can steal giant marble slabs without anybody noticing or saying anything, it happened way before we were around. The doors looked bizarre, standing three feet above the sidewalk, opening onto empty space. Some had spray-painted messages on the plywood-covered doors and windows. "Want to buy this house?" asked one, with a smaller "Hell no—it has no floors inside" handwritten beneath. "If you hear an animal trapped in here call the city" read another.

The first-floor windows on 2020 are boarded up, too, and they've soundproofed it, so you won't see or hear much from the outside. You can tell which one it is because it still has its front steps, and the upstairs windows have glass. They turn on the outside light on nights when there are bands. Wednesdays and Saturdays. Rosemary had believed Aran's directions; she'd ridden hundreds of miles to follow them. Still, she was relieved they played out as he'd described. The mannequins, the empty houses with the floating front doors, the lamp like a beacon. She didn't know any reason why Aran would have taken the time to lie to her, but she hadn't allowed herself to dismiss that possibility until she had seen the place with her own eyes. What had Victor said about Aran? "Don't believe everything he says." She'd never pursued that particular comment.

Nobody was outside when she walked past, but the lamp reassured her, as did the two battered gas cars out front. Nobody would park on this block if there weren't something happening. Right? Of course, this was her first time here, and any absolutes crossing her mind were her own mind's devising. She had always invented rules for her own reassurance, though some had proven truer than others. Logic wasn't the point. Two cars might be a drug deal, or Aran could have sent her here to deliver her to a prostitution ring. That seemed too much trouble for him to go to.

Walking past, obviously too early, she realized there were details he hadn't provided, and she hadn't known to ask. What time they started, for example. She had never been to a live show, but StageHoloLive shows always took place at seven p.m. in their target time zone, so she had assumed music started at seven here as well.

It was almost seven now, but nobody went in or out. The city's midnight curfew had been posted on the highway signs, so she guessed that this show must end earlier. Somewhere between seven and midnight, then. She didn't want to miss it, but she didn't want to look overeager or do anything wrong.

She walked a little farther. She didn't see any dividers between neighborhoods, but she must have crossed some invisible line. Two blocks up, a few rowhouses had been replaced with garden plots, all awaiting their spring tilling. Another block along, the houses took on a more lived-in look. Some had window boxes with flowers, or screens painted with landscape scenes. Unlike the earlier places she'd passed, they had steps, though the steps were brick or wood rather than marble. Here and there somebody sat on a stoop or in a plastic chair, talking to neighbors. A vendor leading a pony cart full of apples and oranges rang a bell and shouted, "Fruit, fruit, get your fresh fruit." The chestnut pony and his harness gleamed with good care.

Kids on bicycles raced back and forth from the sidewalk to the street, enjoying the warm evening. Rosemary expected them to spook the fruit cart pony, but he didn't bat an eye. One house had its windows and door open and a SportHolo baseball game projected in the front room: a half dozen teenagers leaned in on the windowsills and doorframes, watching.

What was it like living this close to neighbors? More people were hanging around these five blocks than she usually encountered in an entire month. Living wall to wall with each other, breathing the same air. Technically they weren't congregating, they were all on different properties, but they were still interacting like they weren't strangers at all.

There was a small restaurant on the next corner. Rosemary didn't recognize the brand, but it looked safe and well lit, as good a place as any to kill some time and eat something. In a booth by the window sat people she guessed might be a band she'd be seeing later. They had a look she imagined bands had, like they were a misfit family rather than friends or colleagues, with all the accompanying family love-hate drama.

The door looked heavy, but when she pushed, it swung farther than she intended, crashing into the booth behind it with a jangling thud. Everyone in the place craned their necks to see who had made such a grand entrance, and Rosemary flushed with embarrassment, willing herself invisible. It didn't work. A tiny, elderly black woman with snow-white hair glanced up from behind the dining counter. Rosemary waited, letting the woman appraise her.

"Sit anywhere." The woman went back to filling salt shakers.

Rosemary walked past the band to the small booth beyond them, where she'd be able to eavesdrop. She slid onto the banquette, trying to be nonchalant about the fact that there were no isolation dividers. She tapped the table, but no menu appeared. Pulled up her Hoodie to get the overlay, but that didn't work, either. Her phone didn't suggest any link.

It took her another minute to notice a small laminated menu tucked behind the napkin dispenser. She pulled it free with two fingers, holding the smallest edge possible to avoid germs. It gave her three chilies to choose from (vegan, chicken, and burn-your-face-off) with options of rice, fries, hot dog (vegan, chicken) or pasta to put it over if she was so inclined. She flipped the menu over, but the other side was blank. Noticed the logo: the place was called the Heatwave Diner. A note at the bottom read "No Superwally? No problem. Cash only." Rosemary had brought cash, but she'd never been anyplace that didn't offer both options.

The woman from behind the counter walked over. "What can I get you, sweetie?"

Rosemary pointed to the coffee and the chicken chili over fries.

"Cheese? Vegan cheese? Sour cream?" the woman asked.

"Um, cheese, please. Thank you."

She pulled out her phone and sent a quick message home to say she'd arrived. No sense worrying anyone at SHL by mentioning she hadn't set foot in her target destination yet. Close enough.

The server deposited a mug and a miniature cream pitcher at the table. Rosemary took a test sip; the coffee tasted good enough to drink black, rich without bitterness. The group in the next booth were arguing over what to play that night, which meant Rosemary was right that they were a band.

". . . Luce, we haven't played that in months. I don't think this new kid has even heard it before."

"I've heard it, but I've never played it," someone who must have been the new kid agreed.

"See?" asked the first voice again.

". . . But I'm sure I can follow. It's straightforward, as I remember, except that weird bridge."

"See?" A new voice, a woman's, low and warm, echoing the first in a way that sounded closer to teasing than mocking, a laugh behind it. "It'll sound fresh. It'll be great."

"It's eight years old."

The woman again. "Eight years and still so relevant. I wish it would stop being relevant."

"We'll crash and burn."

"And nobody will care. I love a good crash and burn."

The waitress slid a chipped white bowl to Rosemary. "It's hot."

Rosemary stirred the cheese into the chili, poking underneath to see which fry cut they used. She usually knew what brand of potatoes a proper restaurant franchise ordered, could probably even still recite the Superwally product code from her first-year job checking orders, but these looked rough and house made.

The bowl wasn't as hot as she expected from the warning. She took a mouthful. Her first thought was that the chili wasn't all that hot, either. Her second thought was obliterated by peppers. Tears poured down her cheeks. She reached for the cream pitcher and chugged it.

"I told you it was hot," the waitress said.

Rosemary wiped her eyes with her sleeve. "But I didn't order the burn-your-face-off."

"That wasn't the burn-your-face-off. I make people sign a waiver the first time they try that one. Here, try it with sour cream."

Rosemary stirred in the sour cream and tentatively took another bite. The waitress was right. With the heat cut, the flavors spilled out: chili, paprika, cumin. She'd never had any food that packed that much punch. She took another spoonful and nodded at the waitress in appreciation. Another and she realized exactly how hungry she was. She had packed sandwiches for the bus, but she'd eaten the last one hours ago.

The band stood to leave, and Rosemary got her first good look at them. The guy with the blue hair wore a T-shirt with the arms torn off, the better to show off his tattoos. He had more tattoos than skin. Another looked younger than her, androgynous in a sundress and a denim jacket. They stacked their bowls on the counter as they left. Rosemary wondered if that was standard procedure; she'd never been in a restaurant where the customers cleaned up after themselves before.

The woman left last. She was maybe in her thirties, long ponytail, looking less dramatic than her companions, but exuding something Rosemary couldn't name. She shrugged on a leather jacket and winked at Rosemary as she straightened her collar. Reached into her pocket, grabbed a handful of cash, and tossed it on the table without counting. "See ya, Mary. Thanks!"

"Have a good show, Luce!" The waitress waved after them.

Rosemary didn't want to chance missing the band. She scarfed the rest of her chili, counted out cash to cover her check and tip, and then followed the others' lead and brought her dishes to the counter. The waitress smiled. If it wasn't standard procedure, it was at least appreciated.

"Um, do you know what band that was?" She was embarrassed to ask, in case they were super famous, but better to know.

"They go by 'Harriet' this week, but ask again soon and they'll have another name."

"Heretic?" Rosemary asked, searching for something that sounded like a band.

"Nope. Harriet. Like the girl's name. They've had better names, and worse. You should check them out. I think they're playing tonight."

"Yeah, I'm planning on it. Thanks!"

Rosemary retraced her route. She passed the members of Harriet, who had stopped on a corner to continue their argument.

A few more cars and vans dotted the street now. Rosemary glanced at her hood's display for the time: eight fifteen. A little more reasonable, maybe?

She dug an ancient piece of spearmint gum from the pack in her jacket pocket; the most important night of her life and she'd eaten dragon-breath chili.

16

ROSEMARY

2020

Aran had called it the 2020, and she hoped he wasn't messing with her; it wasn't a name that tripped off the tongue, like the Bloom Bar. Maybe it had a nickname, or maybe 2020 was the nickname, and she was inventing random worries to distract herself from her own nerves. The woman at the diner would probably have told her, but she hadn't thought to ask.

She approached from the side, as if she was trying to sneak up on the place. Willed someone else to walk in first, so she could study the method, aware she was acting overcautious again. She had taken the bus all the way here. She had walked in a strange city, eaten in a strange diner; surely it wasn't such a big deal to knock on the door. Or open the door? Too many options.

It was a venue, she told herself, even though it looked like a boarded-up vacant. She decided to push the door open, not knock, and found herself standing in somebody's sparsely furnished living room, a canned basic StageHolo show playing out on the tattered throw rug, some band she didn't recognize. The walls were bare and off-white, as was a painted-over fireplace. Nailheads poked out where pictures must have hung at some point, whiter white rectangles beneath them.

A tall, broad woman with the shoulders of a linebacker sat on the stained and sagging couch, her arms spreading over the back. "Can I help you, Officer?"

Rosemary took a step backward, almost off the doorstep. Looked behind her to see who the woman was addressing, only to realize the question was aimed at her. "I'm not an officer. Um, my friend told me bands play here."

The woman didn't move. "You know if you are police you are legally obligated to identify yourself now."

"I swear I'm not. Is this 2020? The 2020? I didn't mean to intrude if I'm wrong." Somewhere under their feet, feedback squalled. Rosemary looked down. "This is the right place, I'm pretty sure."

"Close the door a sec."

Rosemary closed it, happy to be on the inside, but the look on the woman's face didn't get any friendlier.

"You're not police, then, but I don't know what you're talking about. And I don't recognize you."

"Do you recognize everyone who comes to your club?" The front door creaked open again behind her, but Rosemary focused on the problem at hand.

"Club? This is my house. My spouse is down in the basement playing guitar."

This was getting exasperating. "Look. I know this is the address. Aran Randall from Patent Medicine told me to come. I drove eight hours to get here."

"Patent Medicine? You're going to mention a StageHolo band to get into my basement?"

"What's wrong with StageHolo? Some good bands play on there. You're watching one right now . . ." Rosemary pointed to the basic box on the woman's coffee table.

"Patent Medicine. Go back to wherever you came from."

A hand settled on Rosemary's shoulder, and she leaped sideways.

"Alice," a woman said behind her. "Are you harassing my new guitar tech?"

Rosemary turned. It was the woman from Harriet-the-band.

"You know her, Luce?"

"Yeah. She's tuning our guitars tonight. She's cool."

Alice frowned, then sighed and waved her hand. "I don't know why she didn't say so. She would have gotten a whole lot further mentioning you than mentioning Patent Medicine."

Luce lifted an eyebrow at the name. Rosemary made a mental note not to mention Aran's band again until she figured out why people here had that reaction.

Luce pushed past Rosemary. Her bandmates followed her in, and Rosemary trailed behind. They crossed the living room and entered a narrow kitchen, then turned 180 degrees to a basement stairwell beside the kitchen doorway.

The basement was at least as large as the house above, but still tiny compared to SHL venues. The ceiling was low, the floor packed clay. There was a faint odor of cat piss. A stage area filled one end, not any higher than the room, but differentiated by strands of LED lights and two bulky monitor speakers. SHL used those on the soundstage for effect, window dressing, even though the performers all had in-ear systems. The monitors looked good on the edge of a big stage, and served as a barrier. That was the one similarity between this and the Bloom Bar.

A banged-up drum kit lay in pieces at the stage's back, and a bass amp covered in stickers from a hundred bands sat tucked in beside the scattered drums. Guitar amps lined the wall beside the stage, and eight or ten guitar cases were piled in the corner. Microphone stands at various heights stood in stalagmite patterns on the stage perimeter, cords wound around them like vines. She fought disappointment that it was so cramped, an experience in miniature. Even though Aran had called it "a little underground space," she hadn't thought he meant it literally.

"What is this place?" she asked under her breath.

"It's either a shrine to rock as it was or an attempt to build something better. Some days one, some days the other. Are you gonna help or what?" Luce squatted a few feet away, rummaging in the pocket of a guitar bag.

"I—I thought you were kidding."

"Why kid? We don't have any comp tickets here. Either you're our guitar tech or you owe Alice eight bucks."

"She wasn't going to let me in."

"True. Maybe you don't owe Alice after all. You can go back to when she was telling you to get lost."

She said this matter-of-factly, though her eyes and the corners of her mouth hinted she was messing with Rosemary. The whole situation had gone wrong. Too fast, too aggressive, too jokey. She hadn't even had a chance to mention she worked for SHL. Or maybe she wasn't supposed to mention it yet; the training manuals left her a few different options.

"Okay," she said. "What do you want me to do?"

Luce held up a small box. "Do you know how to tune a guitar?"

"Nope."

"Change a string?"

"No." Rosemary's face flushed. She crossed her arms. "I'm not stupid. I'm just not a musician. Teach me whatever you need me to do. I'm a fast learner."

"That's better. Do you have a name, by the way?"

"Rosemary. Rosemary Laws."

"Cool name. Mind if I use it for a band sometime?"

"No, um, yes? Maybe?"

"You can get back to me on it. Okay, Rosemary Rosemary Laws. Lucky for you, tuning technology has advanced to a point where you don't need to know music, as long as you can read the alphabet and follow up and down arrows. You can read?"

"Yes." Maybe by the time the night ended she'd know whether to stop feeling offended.

A few more people straggled downstairs. One started assembling the drum kit, another taking microphones from pouches and attaching them to the cords on the stands. Luce pulled a black electric guitar from a case and plugged it into a pedal. She tuned two strings, then handed the guitar to Rosemary, who self-consciously turned the tuning keys, with the encouragement of Luce and the pedal. A red light with arrows told her which direction to twist, and a green light in the center blinked when she had it correct. She did the four remaining strings before handing the guitar back.

"Nice. If you can do that a few times when I hand you guitars during my set you're hired. I won't bother showing you how to string tonight—that guarantees I'll break one, you watch—but you can help us sell merch, too. Earn your keep."

Rosemary nodded. All she had to do was keep her mouth shut and observe, and if she liked the band she'd introduce herself again and explain why she was there. She had practiced that speech a hundred times in her head on the bus. Funny how now that she'd arrived she couldn't get enough words out of her mouth to say any of it.

The band finished setting up. Rosemary picked a wall to lean against where she could be unobtrusive.

"Excuse me, can I get in there?" A tall black man with a pierced septum and dreadlocks pointed behind her, and she realized she'd managed to block the soundboard.

"Sorry," she muttered, resituating herself in front of the board instead of behind, hoping she wasn't obstructing anything else.

"Come on, Rosemary Laws," said Luce from beside her. "Let me show you how our merch setup works."

Rosemary trailed her over to the stairs. There was an alcove underneath with a folding table in front of it. Luce hefted a suitcase onto the table and flipped it open. Inside, patches and stickers and download cards for Harriet, but also for Luce Cannon and Patient Zero and Last April and Typecast as Villains.

She pulled out some T-shirts, slipped them onto hangers, and hung them from the stair banister. They had DON'T EVEN THINK ABOUT IT screen-printed on them in block letters. The band names nagged at Rosemary.

"It's easy enough," Luce told her. "There's a price list in the suitcase. Cash only. Any questions, find me or one of the guys."

"Um, okay. When do I sit over here instead of over there helping you with your guitars?"

"For the whole night except when we're playing. Good question. Next?"

"Luce Cannon? Is that really you? Like, 'Blood and Diamonds' Luce Cannon?" As she said the name of the song, Rosemary remembered the way it had drifted into her hospital room, made itself part of her while her body fought the fever.

"In a previous incarnation. That song was a long time ago."

"Yeah! It came out when I was twelve, and then it got big again when I was in high school. It was my favorite song for ages."

The other woman winced. "I don't think of myself as old until somebody says something like that."

"Sorry. I didn't mean to say you're old. You were pretty young when it came out, right? So you're not old now. It's just I loved that song. I can't believe it's you. But—you're famous. What are you doing here?"

Luce cocked her head. Rosemary got the feeling she'd said something wrong. She changed the subject. "Um, are the other bands selling stuff, too?"

"Yeah, but that's not your problem. You keep my merch from walking off without cash in exchange."

Footsteps on the stairs behind them. Another band, more gear in the guitar pile by the stage. They all shared a drum kit, Rosemary had figured out by then, as well as the bass amp and mic stands. Luce turned to help them, and, Rosemary guessed, to step away from their conversation. She had probably blown it, saying she'd been twelve when "Blood and Diamonds" came out, and getting stuck on it. But Luce Cannon! What a coup if Rosemary brought her to SHL. Everyone knew that song.

Luce came back to the table a moment later, so Rosemary must not have insulted or embarrassed her as much as she'd worried.

"Do they all get soundchecks? All the bands?" she asked Luce, eager to show she wasn't hung up on the song. She had also decided to stop pretending like she knew anything.

"Naw. We do it to set the overall levels and the others get a line check. It's not worth the time to check everyone and move gear twice. The room sounds totally different with people in it, anyway, but it's ritual for me. Relaxes me a bit."

"You don't look nervous."

She laughed. "I don't get stage fright. Some anything-can-happen low-grade anxiety, maybe, but that burns off when we start playing."

Rosemary didn't know the difference, but she let it go.

The room began to fill. Rosemary was glad to be behind the merchandise table. She had dressed in what she thought people wore for shows, but it wasn't like what anybody else was wearing, and she felt more overdressed by the second. They all came downstairs and took positions in the room like they'd gotten a memo she had missed. Some stood alone, Hoodies up or checking their phones, leaning on walls, looking like they belonged.

The audience demographics varied more than she'd expected: black and brown and white, teenagers and seniors and all ages in between. At the Patent Medicine show, most of the avs had been young and white and had fit into the five basic av body types, since custom bodies cost so much more. She was struck again by how different real people could be.

She had expected people to be drinking, and some held bottles or flasks, but she hadn't spotted a bar. Whenever somebody stopped to look over the items on her table, she tried to exude a false front of confidence and belonging, smiling at them and waiting to see if they smiled back.

"What band are you here to see?" she asked one browser, trying to make conversation.

"All of them," the woman said, and Rosemary wasn't sure if that was a rebuke or an innocent answer. Maybe everyone came to hear everyone, not a particular favorite. Or maybe she'd made the woman uncomfortable, since she sat behind a particular band's table. Maybe she'd implied the woman wasn't fan enough. After that, she pressed her lips together, afraid she'd say something else stupid. What had Luce Cannon called it? Anything-can-happen low-grade anxiety.

The room now held more people than Rosemary had ever seen in one place. Each time she'd thought that recently, a new situation had come along to outdo it, but this was the most for sure. Fifty? Sixty? She had no idea how so many people fit in a space this size. She started to sweat. If she didn't have the table and the alcove to carve out some space for her, she wasn't sure what she'd do.

How did they stand it? Shoulder to shoulder, front to back with total strangers, with their heat and their odors. No clue if any of them had some new superbug, if a single sneeze might endanger the entire room. No clue if someone had a knife or a gun or a vendetta. If even one person panicked, the whole room would try to squeeze up that tiny staircase. People would be crushed. There were laws against this, laws to prevent gatherings like this one. She could pull out her phone and call in a violation. She held that consolation to her; the possibility obviated the need to do it. She had her space under the stairs, her table to keep her safe.

17

ROSEMARY

Shadow on the Wall

The first band started, and Rosemary turned her attention toward the stage area. She had to push the table forward a few inches in order to stand and see anything other than the hand-painted banner with the name "Kurtz" that now hung above the musicians. The shifting table earned her dirty looks from people who'd been standing in front of it, but she ignored them. Her first real live show!

The Patent Medicine show counted for something, of course; she wouldn't be here now if that experience hadn't blown her away. Even watching musicians record their set for SHL, with their individual camera arrays and sound booths, all knitted together to appear as if they were on a single stage; even that stirred something inside her. This had to be even better, with the band members close enough to interact with each other, and a real audience to feed off.

This band was a three-piece, drums and guitar and what sounded like a keyboard holding the low end where a bass usually rooted down, though she didn't see a keyboard onstage. The singer kept his eyes shut tight, gripping one arm with the other. He looked to be on the verge of tears, but when he opened his mouth, his voice came across controlled and intense, like a revival preacher's. The first song had a biblical fervor, but not from any Bible she had read. "These are my notes from the great upload," she caught on the second chorus. An interesting sound, but she wondered if a singer who didn't ever attempt to make eye contact with anyone would remind viewers that they weren't actually in the room with the band. His voice didn't match his face, either. It was a big voice, suited for someone with more personal charisma, and the lyrics worked better when she imagined some disembodied voice rather than a real person with a real body talking about an upload.

Really, this wasn't any better than StageHolo. With SHL she didn't need to worry about heat or crowds. She could adjust the volume, turn it off when she'd heard enough. She pulled up her Hoodie to check for messages, but she had no reception, maybe because of the alcove. Realizing she'd be unable to call for help if she needed it sent a new panic through her. She concentrated on making herself small and unnoticeable, concentrated on breathing the warm and sticky air, concentrated on the band again to distract herself.

Where was the keyboard? There were two amps. The guitar was plugged into one; the other had a box plugged into it. Nothing else onstage.

The singer twitched and she spotted it: a single-octave keyboard tattooed inside his right forearm. The fingers of his left hand roved over it, pressed down. She looked for somebody to ask, but everyone was paying attention to the band. She pulled up her Hoodie again to record a short clip. Amazing how this one difference changed the nature of the whole performance—she wished she could rewind and watch him from the beginning.

The crowd shifted, cycled, but didn't disperse, even when the band finished. She sat back down, and the singer with the playable tattoo walked over to her alcove with his own little case of vinyl records and CDs. Records and CDs! Rosemary's parents had a machine that played both, except when it skipped and stuttered. She wouldn't have thought anyone would bother, but a few people stopped to trade him cash for music, so more people must still own those devices than she thought. The singer caught her looking at him and flashed a grin. He had eyes after all. She wondered if his closed eyes while performing marked shyness or stage fright or a deliberate effect.

"What were you doing with your arm?" she asked, hoping it wasn't some fad everyone here had, yet another question to make her look ignorant.

He held out his arm for her to examine. Flat implants lay underneath the tattoo, one for each key. "Triggers and a transmitter. They send to a box synthesizer plugged into my amp. You can touch if you want."

Rosemary fought to keep her recoil internal, concentrated on the tech. "That's okay. Did you design it?"

"The trigger system idea was, uh, a friend's, but I designed the synthesizer. I'm working on a guitar fretboard next, but I can't decide where to put it. Here, maybe." He put his left hand to his chest and played an invisible riff. "Then a gyro in my right wrist to pick up the strum."

"Why not play a guitar instead of going to all that trouble?" Rosemary asked.

The singer gave her a funny look. "It's not trouble."

He moved away, leaving her wondering. She'd seen Tina Simmons's biometric tattoo and hadn't thought twice about that modification. What was wrong with trying to become your own instrument? She left the question alone to contemplate at a later time.

"Quick level check?" asked the sound guy over a PA talk-back audible to the room.

"Nah," said someone from the band moving onto the stage. "We'll start and you can adjust as we go. Hi, uh, we're the Coffee Cake Situation."

Rosemary barely had time to think that was a weird band name, when feedback filled the room. She put her fingers to her ears, some instinct telling her that the next sound would be unbearable. Instead, the band caught the feedback like a pro surfer catching a wave, riding it but not taming it. The feedback was the song. It was deliberate. She leaped to her feet, knocking her head on the slanted alcove.

"Damn," said the singer standing next to her. "Are you okay? That must've hurt."

Rosemary waved him away. "I'm okay. I'm okay."

She rubbed the spot where a solid egg was already forming. It didn't hurt; the noise pulled the pain away.

The band onstage had drums, bass, guitar, and cello. The cello ran through a distorted amplifier, long and low chords, bowed in such a way that they built to a crest and then crashed. The cello player had a mane of superhero-black hair with blue highlights, which fell over her face when she played.

Half an hour before, Rosemary would have thought closed eyes meant no connection with the audience. Now she realized it was a tool to draw the listener in, make the song more intimate. That cello player could wear a mask or a paper bag and people would still want to watch. There was something riveting about her confident hands, her posture, the sound she shaped and conducted.

After a minute or so, the guitar joined her, mimicking the cello but with its own distinct timbre. Drums and bass started rolling soon after, rising to meet the cello. The drummer, bassist, and guitarist were all women.

The cello player started singing. Rosemary hadn't even noticed the cellist had a mic until then, she'd been so drawn in to the hands, the bow, the heavy, mysterious drape of hair. Her voice was low and strange, a growl, a moan, every bit as pained as the sounds coming from her instrument. The cello and the voice came up through the trembling floor, up through Rosemary's bones. It was a physical sensation, a resonance taking place between her body and the instruments and the room. However long they played, it didn't feel long enough.

As the band left the stage, Rosemary tried to turn off her gut's instant reaction and picture them at the Bloom Bar. Would that bone-deep cello translate to SHL? Maybe they had some effect to approximate it. And was there some trend here for singers to hide their faces? All the SHL bands she'd researched were so perfect looking. Then again, maybe that was why she was here, to find some raw band and turn them over to the company. If she convinced SHL to take a look, they'd probably make the Coffee Cake Situation change their name. But that cello . . .

Luce appeared beside her. "Come on, Rosemary Laws. Our turn."

Rosemary had been so focused she'd forgotten she was supposed to help Luce's band. Blocked it out, maybe. She eyed the crowd. If possible, even more people had crammed into the space. "Are you sure you need me?"

"We can get by without you, but you'd make our set run smoother, and you did say you'd help."

Luce walked away then turned back, waiting. Rosemary assessed the distance between alcove and stage. Twenty steps would take her across the whole room.

So many people. Dozens, maybe hundreds. No, impossible. She'd seen the space empty. But it was so hot now, and everyone stood so close to each other. How did you get from one place to another in a crowd like that? If they didn't move, if they stood their ground, what happened to the person moving through? Worse yet, what if somebody else panicked while she was stranded in the middle of the sea of people? She'd be trapped, suffocated, crushed, trampled. Her breath caught in her throat.

"Are you okay?"

"Panic attack," said someone else. Voices floated to her, but she couldn't turn her head to see who'd spoken.

"Give her some room." Luce grabbed her elbow and guided her back to the chair in the alcove. "Sorry, I didn't realize. Look, if you can walk with me, there's even more room over at the side of the stage. You can have it all to yourself. You don't need to help us. We can handle our guitars."

Rosemary shook her head. Searched for her own voice. "I'm going to stay here, if that's okay. I wanted to help. I'm sorry."

"Don't worry about it. I'll check on you after the set. I've gotta go play."

Rosemary nodded. Settled back into her chair. Closed her eyes. She wasn't sure why crowds had never crossed her mind as a possibility. Of all the concerns she'd had when she applied for this job, she'd never considered that aspect. Underground club? Sure, I'd love to. She had pictured bands playing for her, but in her imagination there were never crowds. Never real people.

What had someone said a moment before, a panic attack? Maybe she was a person who got panic attacks in crowds. She'd never had one before, so she couldn't have known. Her career as a scout for SHL would be brief if she never actually saw the bands where they played. On the other hand, she'd made it through the first two bands without trouble. She would have been fine if Luce hadn't tried to make her walk across the room. No, that wasn't fair, either. She only had this alcove to herself because of Luce. She would have panicked way earlier if she hadn't had this space.

"Do you need some fresh air? You look like you need to get out of here." The cello player stood at the table. Her hair still fell in front of her face, her voice low and warm. "That's not a pickup line. Seriously, people have passed out from the heat in here before. Come upstairs."

"I shouldn't." Rosemary looked back at the alcove. "I told Luce I'd watch her stuff."

"Nobody needs to watch that old swag; anyone who'd want it has it already. It's an honor system around here anyhow."

Rosemary's cheeks burned. She might as well have NEW HERE tattooed on her forehead.

"Come upstairs," the cellist repeated. "It'll be okay. I promise."

"I really, um—" In the alcove, she had space all to herself. It would disappear the second she moved. If she stayed in place, all she had to do was wait until the entire crowd had left and then step out again and never come back.

The cellist tucked her hair behind her ears. Her face was all concern, all planes and angles. A constellation of pox scars marked her forehead and cheeks. She peered closer at Rosemary. "Oh. The crowd. You don't want to deal with the crowd. Come on, honey. Let me help."

"I want to hear them play," Rosemary said, but she let the cellist shift the table so she had room to get out. She let the woman take her elbow, fought the urge to pull it away. The cellist stood on the outside, forming a buffer, letting Rosemary have the space between her and the table, her and the stairs. Then they were at the stairs, up the stairs, and there was only one other person descending, and then they were in the narrow kitchen on the first floor, and closing the door on the crowd in the basement.

The cellist opened a cabinet, pulled out two glasses, spotty but clean, filled them both with tap water. She handed one to Rosemary, then opened the fridge and pulled two small yellow apples from a large bucket, offering one of those to Rosemary as well. Rosemary took the fruit and followed her to a back door, where they took one step down to a rickety porch. Two people talked in low voices at the far end, passing a joint between them in the near darkness. The cellist gestured Rosemary to the lone deck chair.

The other woman folded her legs to sit on the stoop, then pulled purple plugs out of her ears and stuffed them in her back pocket; Rosemary wondered why you would go to a rock show and then block out the sound, but decided to save that question for another time. The night air was cool in comparison with the basement. A siren wailed in the distance, and a dog matched its pitch. From the basement, a muffled "One-two-three-four" marked the beginning of Luce's set.

"I want to hear them play," Rosemary said again.

"Go ahead back down if you want." The cellist waved long fingers at the door.

Rosemary didn't budge. After another silent minute, she realized she'd been rude. "Sorry. I should've thanked you. And introduced myself. I'm Rosemary."

"Nice to meet you, Rosemary. I'm Joni." She offered a hand. Rosemary steeled herself for the contact. Joni's hand was big enough to envelop hers, strong and warm. "So where are you from?"

"What do you mean?"

"I've never seen you before. You obviously hate crowds, and your clothes are trying way too hard, like you read some article on what to wear to a rock show. No offense."

It was hard not to take offense, but it wasn't so far from the mark. "You're right. I'm not from here. I came for the music."

"And you didn't know an audience was part of the deal?"

"I didn't . . . I knew . . . I didn't know it would bother me."

"Which means you've never been to a live show before. Small town?" Joni took a bite of her apple.

"Very small town, and I'm pretty positive no bands are playing."

"Are you? There's nobody you can picture playing in their garage? Nobody they talked about with euphemisms like 'oh, he's a troublemaker'?"

"Nobody local to me. There were only a couple of kids from high school living anywhere near me. Anyway, even if there was some band making music in a garage, they'd be totally isolated. They wouldn't have what you have here. This is amazing."

Joni nodded. "It is amazing. I'd sure hate to find out you're here undercover to shut us down."

Rosemary frowned. "Wait, what? You think I'm a cop, too? Why do you all think that?"

"Nobody knows you, and you haven't mentioned how you found us."

"Look, if there's some secret password, nobody told me. I told that Alice lady I'm not a cop. Aran Randall from Patent Medicine gave me the address. He said if I came here I'd see real bands playing for real people, like Before."

A clatter from the dark alley at the back of the yard, like an animal knocking over a trash can. Rosemary wasn't sure what animals cities had. Raccoons? Possums? Coyotes? Cats? It distracted her for a moment.

"Aran Randall? Really?"

Rosemary sighed. "That's another thing. Why does everyone here roll their eyes when I mention his name?"

"Because he's a taker and a deserter. He borrowed money, went out to western Pennsylvania and knocked on the door at StageHolo until they answered, and left his band behind."

"No! He plays with his band. Patent Medicine."

"Sweetie, those are a bunch of hired hands that took the place of his real band. StageHolo told him they weren't photogenic enough, sent everyone home but the Great Aran Randall."

Rosemary started to protest. Then she thought about Patent Medicine, with their relentless good looks and studied moves. The bassist. That was what bands were supposed to be, as far as she knew, but they were nothing like the bands she'd seen tonight.

The other woman shrugged. "He had the right, but it was still a shitty move. He's good enough that he might have been able to fight for them."

"Maybe he did." A stubborn loyalty surged in Rosemary. Aran had taken the time to talk with her when nobody else had. "Maybe he tried but they didn't let him, and he thought he'd be better off getting popular and then helping his friends here."

She wasn't sure she believed that herself, and Joni definitely didn't. "'Helping his friends here'? What did he tell you about us?"

"I told you. That I'd see real bands playing."

"Like we're some living history holo? Are they teaching us in school now?"

"No! In my entire life until now, I had no idea anything like this existed."

"Where do you know Aran from, anyway? I thought he was holed up somewhere writing pop songs for other fake bands and playing on a fake stage."

This was not how Rosemary had hoped for this conversation to go. Her imagined version was far less hostile, with Aran's name serving as a blessing for her presence or a greeting from a far-off friend instead of another cause for suspicion. Did he know how his name went over here? As far as she could tell, he thought they remembered him fondly. She redirected the question. "What's wrong with StageHolo, anyway? They're paying musicians to be musicians. They're offering enough to live on. I'd think you'd all want that, but so far everyone I've mentioned it to tonight has been hostile."

"Not everyone. I'm sure those boys who played before me would answer if someone from StageHolo came knocking. But I'm happy here, playing for real people, calling the shots myself without regard to demographics or market share. They'd want me to pull my hair back. They'd smooth my face. Or they'd buy my songs but hire someone else to perform them."

"I don't think anyone else could play your songs," said Rosemary. "Unlike Aran's."

Which was true, but so was everything Joni had said. Rosemary realized she'd been rushing. Thinking about which bands to sign, when she had only just arrived. Thinking about the job first, when Joni was right—there was so much more to the question of who made a good addition to the StageHoloLive roster. She'd only seen three—no, two bands. She had time. Better to make sure she chose well. Musicians amenable to the idea of SHL, for starters; she hadn't realized some people thought of it less favorably.

"I get your point," Rosemary said. "Anyway, I swear to you, I'm not a cop. I had no idea crowds bothered me. I didn't even consider that might happen, since I've never been around so many people before."

"And knowing that you're not fond of crowds, will you be coming back?"

Rosemary grimaced, thinking of the room downstairs. "I will. Maybe I can get used to it."

"Let's hope so. Where are you staying?"

Mentioning the fancy hotel would only lead to follow-up questions she didn't want to answer. "I'm staying with friends." In the moment after she said it, she wished she hadn't lied, but it was too late.

"That's good. The motels near here give discounts to fleas and bedbugs. And I'm starting to believe you when you say you're not police, but I'm not ready to invite you to sleep on my couch."

"I wasn't asking you to, but, um, thanks. For believing me. Maybe."

"You're welcome." Joni stood and stretched. "Hey, if you're not going to eat that, I'll put it back in the fridge."

She held the remains of her apple in her left hand. She'd eaten every bite of it except the thinnest of cores. "I need to go pack up. Nice meeting you, Rosemary."

She grabbed both glasses and Rosemary's untouched apple and headed back into the building. The kitchen had filled with people, some grabbing sodas or water, some heading for the front door.

Rosemary debated going back downstairs to apologize to Luce, maybe help her carry her stuff to make amends, but the stream of departing audience members didn't abate, and she didn't know how to make it through the kitchen, let alone fight the current exiting the basement.

The deck overlooked a small kitchen garden with a paved path down the center. At the back, a parking pad and a chain-link fence with an unlocked gate. Wandering through alleys wasn't the smartest idea on her first night in a strange city, but she'd be better able to keep her wits about her out there than in the basement.

The alley was dark, but back home was darker. Here the shapes were cut and warped by shadows, more ominous than the all-encompassing blackness of the farm. Light seeped from the streetlights at the corners. A rat scuttled across her path, not in any particular hurry, but she'd seen bigger possums. She made her way to the cross street, then back out to the main drag, where people still straggled from the 2020.

According to her Hoodie, it was two miles' walk back to her hotel, but some neighborhoods in between had pretty lousy safety ratings at night—though none as bad as the alleys she'd just navigated, now that she looked. She walked a couple of blocks over to the main southbound route and waited for a bus.

She panicked when she raised her eyes from the payment pad and realized this was nothing like the interstate bus she had taken into town. No private compartments. People sitting elbow to elbow, a few slumped over like they were sleeping, threatening to collapse onto their neighbors. Some standing, clinging to poles or handholds, as if other strangers hadn't had their hands in the same places before them. Others checking phones or wearing Hoodies, eyes watchful. She followed their lead.

She made her way to an open seat, situating herself on the edge so her hip didn't touch the hip of the woman next to her. Left her hood down, kept her hand on her phone to feel it buzz when she reached the closest stop to her hotel. Repeated "Don't touch me, don't touch me" to herself, in the hope that the woman beside her wouldn't shift closer. She'd had enough proximity for one night.

After the club and the bus, her hotel room felt like an oasis. The air conditioner buzzed, but it was otherwise blissfully, blessedly silent. She was as tired as she had ever been, but she knew if she closed her eyes now she'd replay the night in her head over and over.

She slipped behind the heavy curtain to look out the window again. The view had changed from a few hours before—had it only been a few hours ago? Still the same buildings, but they had a different quality to them now. The dark backdrop let her see the whole city, no reflection, like there was no glass between her and the sky.

She followed the long, straight roads, the staggered traffic signals, the trails of brake lights and headlights, rivers of red and white and hazy yellow against deep black. Lights as far as she could see. In another hotel room across the street, backlit, someone stood in a bathrobe toweling her hair, looking out her own window. Did their eyes meet? The other turned away, closed her blinds. All the way down, at street level, tiny people made their way along the sidewalk, the last few postcurfew pedestrians. From up here, the city took on a romantic aspect, a language worth learning to speak.

She was exhausted, but she'd promised daily check-ins, and now it wasn't even the same day anymore. She pulled her Hoodie up and summarized the evening for Management, leaving out her terror, her failure to even make it to the third band. *Three interesting bands played tonight,* she settled on. *At least one was a definite possibility. I'd like to hear a little more from them before broaching the subject or wasting SHL time if they don't work out. Settled into hotel room. No prob re hotel mix-up. Have a good night!*

She didn't think anyone would bother reading it until morning, but at least she'd sent it. Maybe she'd even impress somebody that she'd gone scouting on her first night here. She collapsed into the bed without even bothering to brush her teeth. For one moment, as her head hit the pillow and she sank into the bed the size of her bedroom at home, she registered the fact that it was the most comfortable mattress she'd ever slept on, and that maybe, maybe, she could get used to this; and then she was asleep.

18

ROSEMARY

Germfree Adolescence

According to Aran, the 2020 held shows on Saturday and Wednesday nights. That gave Rosemary two days and two nights to figure out if there were any other less crowded places to hear live music and/or to come up with strategies for how to brave the crowds again. She tried not to be a total drain on company resources. Even walking the hotel's neighborhood was an exercise in desensitization and discovery, worth her time and energy. There weren't many people on the streets, but enough to unsettle her stomach.

Finding music proved impossible. She tried the hotel's e-concierge, which reminded her gatherings larger than thirty people were illegal and unsanitary. The human concierge gave her the same line, but she thought his answer might change once she'd been there a little while. The 2020 couldn't be the only place with live music. There had to be other places where jazz or classical music fans risked arrest to hear their favorites live, or underground dance or rap clubs like the ones Bailey had described.

Or maybe this was all that remained. Except there were still jazz musicians on StageHolo, which must mean people played jazz somewhere, or they wouldn't be able to hone their craft. Unless they did it all online? But how could they do that and still be sure they weren't broadcasting their existence to the very people who'd shut them down? She had these conversations with herself, alone in her room. As if it even mattered. She worked for the rock division, and she knew even less about jazz than rock.

She found a proper branded restaurant a few blocks from the hotel. She hadn't realized how much she had missed the familiarity until she slid into a red vinyl Micky's booth and shut the isolation door. In-booth ordering made so much more sense than sending an employee around like at the Heatwave. The server had said she'd have warned her if Rosemary had ordered the burn-your-face-off chili, but Micky's could place a warning on a dish, too, not subject to the waitress's whims or sense of humor. Not that she'd need warnings at Micky's, where she knew every dish on this menu by heart. Comfort slathered with comfort, served in a bowl.

On the way back to her hotel, a man walking in the opposite direction sneezed as he passed her. She didn't think his sneeze hit her, but her skin crawled for the duration of the walk, and she had to use her day's water allotment to wash herself and her clothes.

Afterward, she called her mother. She had left her ancient school Hoodie at home for her mom to use, so they'd be able to sit together and chat even when she was far away. Her mother had held it like a dead thing—no, like less than a dead thing, their chickens were handled respectfully—but agreed to try it.

"How did you deal with it?" she asked, when they were both seated in the space they had agreed on before she left, a static kitchen with padded wooden chairs and a picture window facing out on a field of winter wheat. It was the closest hoodspace template they had found to their own comfortable kitchen. Maybe if she made enough money at her job she could get their home done up as a custom environment.

"Deal with what? What happened?" The old Hoodie couldn't handle photo-realistic avatars, either, so the other av didn't look much like her mother at all. Same hairstyle, but different body type, wrong height, wrong face. Two legs. Cheap and generic, with only her real voice to reassure Rosemary. Her worried voice. "Is everything okay?"

Rosemary held up placating hands. "Mom. If I needed help, I would have called you direct, not invited you for a sit-down. I promise. Somebody sneezed near me, and my brain went all flu and pox and disease vectors. How did you stand being so close to people all the time? They're so . . . warm."

Her mother shrugged a cartoon shrug. "We didn't think about it. We went to movie theaters where hundreds of people sat in the same room and stadiums where thousands sat next to each other. We rode in airplanes and buses and trains, in open compartments, where strangers sat next to strangers."

"The city buses are like that! People sitting and standing right next to each other."

"I thought you were taking single-cells once you got there."

"I was—I was going to—but there weren't any around that night so I thought I'd try it."

The avatar's frown looked nothing like her mother's. The mouth bent in a strange way. "What are you there for again? You didn't say you'd be taking public buses."

"Mom. We've gone over this. It's a business trip. SHL sent me here to take some meetings."

"I still don't understand why they have to have meetings in person. Nobody else does."

"It's part of what makes them the best, Mom. The personal touch." She had decided not to mention the club or the bands even before coming here. The part she most wanted to ask about, the crowds, she couldn't except obliquely without heightening her mother's concern. "How did you keep from panicking around so many people, though? On the bus, in the old days?"

"It's so hard to explain. People were everywhere. Some were sick, sure. Maybe we washed our hands a lot, I don't know. I had a friend who didn't like touching people, even back then. She used to imagine a bubble surrounding her, a bubble that grew and shrank, but was always there. Even if somebody tried to hug her, or bumped into her on the street, a thin layer of the bubble was still there between them."

"Huh. But there wasn't one?"

"No, of course not. It was a psychological technique. It wouldn't have protected her from anything, but it kept her functional."

"Huh." She filed that tip away.

"Rosemary?" her mother said after a minute. "I still don't understand why we're talking through cartoon characters instead of face-to-face by phone."

"A phone can't do this." Rosemary switched to clearview and shared her feed from her own perspective for the grand tour: the gym in the corner, the fingerprint lock, the magnificent view out the window.

Her mother sighed. "I do miss it."

"Miss what?"

"I don't know. All of it. Everything."

Saturday night loomed closer. It hung over Rosemary, exciting and terrifying in equal parts. She wanted to go back. She wanted to hear the music, but each time she thought about the people in the room, even sitting alone in her hotel, she had to fight panic. It didn't seem possible that the two feelings existed so close to each other, the excitement and the fear.

Still, she had to go. If she framed it as a chore, an inevitability, it became a thing she'd have to cope with, rather than a thing to avoid. If she didn't go, she didn't talk to the bands. If she didn't talk to the bands, she didn't sign the bands. If she didn't sign the bands, she didn't have a job. The company would decide she'd taken the job fraudulently and bill her for her magnificent hotel room, and she didn't have the money for that, so she had to go. No other option.

She didn't go. Seven p.m. passed. She was a fraud. A cheater. A shirker. A chicken. A liar. A thief. Eight p.m. It was raining. She'd be forgiven for not wanting to go out in the rain. Wait until Wednesday, unless it rained Wednesday, too.

Her mother had told her to put herself in a mental bubble,

though she'd be horrified to know her advice was being used to go to the 2020. Her father would tell her to go with her gut, stay safe in the hotel, come home. Nobody else in her life would bother to make the case. Aran, maybe, if he didn't laugh, but she had asked him enough already. She had to be the one to convince herself.

At nine o'clock she dumped all her clothes onto her bed. Closed her eyes, tried to picture what the audience at the 2020 had worn. This could be her do-over, her chance to blend in. She'd be the last person down the stairs instead of the first, coming in this late. If she stayed in the back, she'd keep out of the crush.

She put on her Hoodie, realized she'd forgotten to charge it, and took it off again. She'd have to do without. Stuffed her wallet and phone into a small bag, then realized an umbrella made sense, too, and repacked into her backpack. Another advantage SHL and hoodspace had over real-life excursions: everything you'd ever need fit into a bag of holding.

City rain bounced off surfaces instead of settling into them like farm rain; it stained the buildings and sidewalks gray and grayer. She splurged on a single-cell to keep from getting soaked, and to delay dealing with other people for as long as possible. This way she wouldn't be lying to her mother when she said how she'd traveled. The backseat was more worn than the one she'd taken to her orientation, and smelled like artificial flowers on top of fried chicken.

She spent the short ride psyching herself up. She was a woman alone in the city. How cool was that? Had she ever in her life imagined herself someplace like this, doing something like this? I belong here, she repeated. I'm here to help people. To bring music to the masses, musicians that deserve to be heard. I will walk into that building as if I have the same right to be there as everyone else.

Alice was lying on the couch watching another prerecorded band on the living room rig when Rosemary opened the door. "You again?"

"Do you know everyone here?" Rosemary asked in return.

"Yes, and you don't belong."

"I'm not police. I told you."

"Fine. You're not police, but you're something. I'm sure of it."

"I can't imagine you give this hard a time to every new person who shows up. I just want to hear some music tonight. Please?"

"You're not going to be tuning for Luce tonight?" Alice smirked, and Rosemary's cheeks warmed. Before she could defend herself, the woman pointed toward the front door. "You can come in when someone else vouches for you. Not Aran Randall, not Luce. She's way too trusting."

"Is Joni here? Joni would . . ."

"Joni's not here."

"I don't know how you have anybody here at all if this is how you treat people."

"This is how I keep us from getting shut down."

"Look, I already know where you are. If I were a cop, I'd have busted you already, wouldn't I?"

"I don't know, but you're not welcome without an escort."

Rosemary knew she'd been beaten; she left the way she had come in. What were her options now? Head back to the hotel, admit total defeat. Troll the web for uploads, hope to find the next Victor Janssen somewhere in hoodspace.

She caught movement in the corner of her eye. A man on the opposite side of the street, lit by a streetlight, lifting a rifle. She shrank back into the doorway in panic, trying to make herself invisible. A second look showed it wasn't a rifle; he was closing an umbrella. He had a little girl with him, five or six years old. The rain had stopped for the moment.

Something rattled, and she looked down to see her hand shaking, knocking against her bag, the buckle of which knocked against her own umbrella. An umbrella looked like a gun at the right angle, in the right moment, but it wasn't a weapon. Nobody was trying to hurt anybody here. It was some guy trying to get his kid home. She had no reason to overwrite him with her own groundless fears.

She would have given up and gone back to the hotel if she hadn't mistaken that umbrella for a gun. Somewhere inside her the shame of her own paranoia hot-wired a new determination. She was here for a purpose. She wanted to be good at her job, and being good at her job meant finding music that couldn't be found by someone sitting in their bedroom with a Hoodie. She'd been given a chance to do something new and different with her life. She wouldn't allow herself—or Alice—to squander it.

Where did Alice get off keeping her out, anyhow? Assuming Rosemary was other than what she claimed to be? Never mind that her suspicions were correct; that didn't give her permission to make snap judgments about people she didn't know.

She reversed her steps from a few nights before, rounding the corner into the darkened alley. The precise backyard count from the corner to 2020 escaped her, but she recognized the chain-link fence, the garden, the steps to the back door. The gate's padlock was in place this time.

A broken link at the top snagged her pants cuff and raked her leg when she clambered over. Her plan to land lightly on her feet was upended, and she dropped headfirst into the paved yard, pants still caught like a trophy fish. She stayed that way for ten seconds, or ten minutes, eyes closed, head spinning, before getting one leg under her and hopping to free the other. When it pulled clear, she lost her balance and fell backward again, this time into the soft garden soil.

The whole sequence had gone much better in her mind when she'd looked at the padlocked gate. She examined the muddy, torn mess she had made of herself and did her best to wipe the dirt off with a sodden sleeve. Her head rang with a mild urgency.

The back door was unlocked. Two people stood in the kitchen, drinking water and arguing in low tones. They gave her an odd look, but didn't question her presence. Alice the door dragon still sat in the front room, guarding the entrance and maintaining her charade of a person lounging at home watching canned StageHolo shows at high volume. Nobody stood between Rosemary and the basement stairs; all she had to do was convince herself to go down there. Given the trouble she'd gone to, she wasn't turning back.

She opened the door to the basement and was greeted by noise cut short, then clapping and cheering. A good time to slip in; time for a new song to begin.

Rosemary had hoped the rain might keep people away, but if anything, the basement was more packed than it had been for the previous show. A new musty scent mixed with the sweat and cat pee odors for which she had already prepared herself. Wet dog? Wet clothes. Wet clay. Wet everything.

She lingered at the bottom landing. Nobody was going in or out, and she was more than happy to stay in that spot, with easy escape at the ready. She didn't know how long the band had been playing already. Luce stood onstage, tuning, her hair flattened to her forehead with sweat. Rosemary swung around to inspect the alcove where she'd spent the previous show: nobody sat behind the merchandise table. She hadn't been needed after all, as Joni had said.

"One-two-three-four!" shouted Luce, and the room changed again. Rosemary turned her attention to the stage. She expected "Blood and Diamonds," but this song sounded nothing like that; a different genre altogether, even with the familiar voice cutting through. She hadn't believed it was the same person, couldn't reconcile her mental image with the ordinary-looking woman she'd met. Luce's ponytail flipped and bucked as she sang, punctuating her lines. A fierce ponytail. A hype man of a ponytail.

Craning her neck, Rosemary identified the whole group from the diner. They all looked different now. The laid-back teasing had been replaced by something knife-edged. She wasn't sure what could be dangerous about music, but that thought lodged in her mind, and once there, it didn't shake.

She had loved music her entire life, even if the live type had never been an option. She thought she knew what music sounded like in a fair number of forms: the stuff her parents had introduced her to, the songs she had found on her own, the life-changing Patent Medicine show, where she'd felt for the first time like she was inside a song, that a song was a living thing. Magritte's performance in the SHL tanks, compelling even in isolation. The bands from the other night, each special in their own way.

This was another thing altogether. Loud, for one. The guitars swallowed every inch of space in the room, filling the air, replacing the oxygen in her lungs. She put her fingers to her ears, but the guitars kept coming. The kick drum rose up through her bones; the bass mimicked her pulse, or her pulse mimicked the bass.

People danced all around her. They held the inches they had carved from the crowd, but moved within that space, some bouncing on their toes, some shifting their torsos, their hips. She moved, too; the song demanded it. It blocked everything else out.

The song ended, but the drums kept going, rolling forward then shifting to a new beat, with a new urgency. The audience adapted. Rosemary found herself moving forward with the crowd, pressing toward the stage, dancing, dancing with real people, in real life. The bubble her mother had told her to imagine had formed around her; she was in the crowd, but untouchable. She had space.

Except thinking about the bubble made her think about the reason she had needed the bubble, which made the fear real again. She hadn't noticed that her baseline panic had subsided as she listened, but now she noticed its return, a tidal wave that had sucked the ocean miles out to sea and now returned it as a solid wall.

She stood in the middle of the basement, surrounded. If she fell, she'd be trampled. If someone shouted "Fire!" they'd crush each other in the rush for the stairs. The music held her upright, but she was no longer dancing. The exit was too far. Her knees buckled and the music stopped, or the music stopped and her knees buckled.

"What the hell?" someone said, above the crowd noise.

Hands grasped her arms and forearms, reached under her armpits, pulled her to her feet. She didn't know whose, tried to slap away whatever stranger was touching her, but they dragged her toward the stage area. The song stopped short and the musicians cleared to the sides. She found herself sitting on a buzzing amplifier.

The bassist stood over her. "Hey, this is the woman from the other night."

"There's a first aid kit in the kitchen, under the sink," Luce said. "Somebody grab it for me?"

"I'm okay," Rosemary said. "I'm okay."

"You are not okay. You're bleeding from at least two places, one of which is your head. Did you get beat up?" To someone else: "Did anyone see what happened to her?"

"No, I'm not bleeding, I—" She put her muddy palm to her head; it came away bloody.

Luce glanced at her, then spoke into her mic. "We're going to call it for tonight, friends. Sorry. See you next time. Thanks for coming out on a rainy night."

She turned to Rosemary. "Can you walk?"

Rosemary nodded, though she wasn't sure.

An aisle formed through the crowd, and Luce and someone else helped her up the basement stairs. At the top, someone pressed a plastic box into Luce's hands, then they rounded a corner and climbed another flight. Alice in the background saying, "Shit. I told that kid not to come in tonight, maybe thirty or forty minutes ago, but she wasn't bleeding when I talked to her, I swear. I don't know how she got downstairs."

Luce fumbled with a lock on the top landing, touched a small box mounted on the doorframe and put her finger to her lips, and then they were on the second floor.

If the first floor was sparse, this room was the opposite. The same basic furniture categories, an entirely different effect. Hardwood floor with a plush throw rug under a low table. Bookshelves full of actual print books. A deep purple couch. Scarves draped over the lampshades. She went to check her Hoodie to see if this was the Chelsea Hotel 1967 Veneer from SHL headquarters, then remembered she'd left it at the hotel. Momentary panic: did she still have her bag? Amazingly, yes.

The walls were a warm red-purple, with white trim. They were lined with pictures, dozens of pictures, snapshots of bands caught in midsong, sweaty close-ups, blood-covered guitars. The guitar picture made Rosemary touch her head again.

"First things first, let's get you cleaned up before you bleed all over my furniture. Unless you think you need a hospital? You don't have one of those biometric tattoos, do you? The ones that call your doctor if you get a boo-boo?"

Rosemary looked at her hand, the blood, the mud. She realized she was supposed to answer. She hadn't been in a hospital since the pox. Her case had been relatively mild, the fever worse than the nerve pain, but she remembered the other kids clawing at their faces and arms, screaming, babbling from fever. And before that, the emergency room full of adults whose moans had unsettled her far more than the crying children. She shuddered. "No hospital. I'll be okay. No tattoo."

Luce gave her a close look, then nodded. Led her down a short hall and into a small bathroom, and put enough pressure on Rosemary's shoulder to encourage her to take a seat on the closed toilet.

"How about I'll clean this out, see how deep it is. If it needs stitches, or if you're still loopy when I'm done, we'll reconsider the hospital idea. I'm pretty sure you have a concussion, and whatever got your leg had teeth. Should I be worried about rabies? Werewolves? Zombies?"

As she talked, Luce opened her first aid kit and laid it on the sink rim. She put on gloves and opened a packet of antiseptic wipes. "This is where you tell me what happened."

"I, uh, I climbed a fence, but I caught my leg on the top, and I must have landed on my head, but I didn't—ow!—I didn't realize it? So I guess I landed harder than I thought, and then—ow!—I guess I wasn't thinking straight, and I came inside, and it sounded really good and—ow! Would you stop poking at my head?"

"Almost done." Luce tossed the wipes in the garbage. "It's not that deep, but I made it bleed again. Head wounds always bleed worse than they are. I can stitch it if you want."

"Does it—does it need stitches? Are you a doctor?"

Luce laughed. "I used to be certified as a nurse assistant, and I did a year of actual nursing school when I was trying to sort myself out, but more importantly, I've cleaned up my share of musicians. Head meets headstock, hand meets ceiling, drumstick projectile. Anyway, I've seen worse. I think you'll get by without stitches. It may scar either way, but it's at your hairline, so it won't be too noticeable. You've also got an impressive lump, which is what bothered you when I poked it, not the cut."

"No stitches."

"Fair enough. In that case, can you hold this gauze for me while I tape it shut?"

Rosemary let Luce guide her hand to her head.

"Let's take a look at your leg now. Your pants may be a lost cause." She inverted the pants leg and tugged it up Rosemary's calf, then grabbed some more wipes. "Also, let's go back to the part where you said you climbed a fence. I'm assuming you mean my back fence, and I'm helping you after you broke into my club, after you ditched me the other night, after I vouched for you with Alice?"

That summed it up pretty well, so Rosemary didn't say anything.

"Have you had a tetanus shot recently?"

Rosemary nodded, peered down at her bloody leg, then looked away. "My parents have a farm. We keep current on tetanus."

"Okay, good. You've got a puncture I'm going to flush out, but I won't stitch this, either. Then there's the question of the concussion. I don't suppose you have anybody who can come get you, keep you awake?"

"No—I don't know anybody here."

"Right-o. I guess we're going to be best buddies tonight."

Rosemary opened her mouth to protest, to say she needed to get back to her hotel, but Luce shut her up with, "Unless you'd rather hang out with Alice?"

"No, I'll stay here," Rosemary said. "What does Alice have against me, though?"

"Now, or before? Because now she'll add sneaking past her to the list. Before, I think she didn't trust you. Now I'm guessing she really doesn't trust you. Hang on—let me find you some clothes."

Luce washed her hands, then left Rosemary in the bathroom. Rosemary listened to footsteps down the hall, then to a hollow knock in the pipes under the sink.

Luce returned with a small pile of clothes. "Shorts or sweatpants? Anything else I own won't fit you."

"Sweatpants, thanks."

Luce handed her Option B and left Rosemary alone in the bathroom to peel off her ruined pants and ease the sweats over the bandage on her leg. She washed her face and dried it with toilet paper to keep from bloodying a towel, then made her way out to the living room, where the musician had collapsed across the couch. There were two water glasses on the table. Rosemary assumed the fuller one was for her, and drained it in a single gulp. She chose a worn velour recliner and sank into it.

"Don't get too comfortable. We're staying up." Luce's voice came from deep within the couch.

19

LUCE

Where Is My Mind

It took the kid so long to change and make her way out of the bathroom that I almost went in again after her. It gave me enough time to wonder what I was doing. I should have insisted on taking her to the hospital; it was the responsible thing to do. When I thought back on mistakes I'd made, more than one had started from not taking somebody to a hospital when they needed it. Still, she was so insistent. Terrified. So I settled into the couch to wait, and eventually she wandered out of the bathroom, downed a glass of water, and sat. I told her we were staying up.

"Is that medically advised? Is that a thing people do?"

"What some people do is go to the hospital and get a CT scan, but I get the not-wanting-to-go-to-the-hospital part. Hence my solution."

"Isn't there a concussion app I can use?" She reached for a Hoodie she wasn't wearing, a panicked expression crossing her face. She definitely wasn't operating at full capacity.

"Anything like that depends on knowing your baseline function, sweetie. I'm guessing you don't have that recorded anywhere."

Rosemary shook her head, then stilled it, looking like she regretted the motion.

"If you think you might puke, I'll grab a bucket. Anyway, the staying-up thing's probably been disproven for twenty years, but I think the main point is to make sure your brain isn't swelling or bleeding, by interacting with you. If you start slurring or dropping thoughts, I take you to somebody who actually knows what they're doing."

"You sure there's no such thing as an online CT or something else from this century?"

"There's no such thing as an online CT. Anyway, if you disappear into one of those ridiculous hoods, I won't be able to tell how you're doing. So, Rosemary, tell me about yourself. What are you doing here in our fair city?"

Rosemary picked gravel from her palm. It left tiny indents. "I'm here for the music."

"Why here? Why not New York? You could see a dozen bands a night."

Rosemary shuddered.

"Ah. Too many people? That's why you left the other night, too?"

"I thought I'd be able to handle it. I need to hear the bands. I had no idea . . ."

"That's what Joni said."

"Joni mentioned me?"

The kid looked delighted; she didn't have much of a poker face.

I wasn't about to tell her Joni had said she was cute. "She said she didn't know how you were going to reconcile your issue with crowds, but you seemed cool unless you're a cop."

"You people take a lot of convincing. I'm a little sick of the questioning. Tell me . . ." Rosemary scanned the walls, clearly looking for a change of subject. ". . . How did you end up here?"

I rolled back to a sitting position, debating what to say, as I usually did when anyone asked anything remotely personal. Even now, after all this time, it felt too raw. "After the . . . After we couldn't tour anymore, I was at a low point for a while and I wanted to find a way to be useful. Then there was a bump in my royalties, enough to buy this place, and I found a way to be useful that was a little more my style."

"You own it? The whole building?"

"I do," I said, with no small pride. "It's nicer than it looks. Good bones. I keep it a little decrepit for deception's sake, and I bought the vacants on either side so there'd be nobody to complain about noise. Anyway, music doesn't make any money anymore if you don't do StageHolo, so I thought I'd give nursing a shot. Except I wasn't much good at it. I could handle the people part, but not the chemistry and math." At Rosemary's obvious alarm, I added, "And the practical. I was good at the practical part."

"So what did you do instead? If you don't mind my asking."

"A bit of this, a bit of that. I work a few days a week taking care of two adult brothers with developmental disabilities. Nothing as secure as nursing would have been, but I'm still here, and I still have this place, so I guess I'm doing okay."

"You're doing *okay*? What you've got here is amazing."

I smiled. "Thanks. It makes me think I'm making a difference."

"Making a difference?"

"For the music. For the city. For the people who come twice a week looking for connection."

"Is that why they come? Connection?"

"You tell me. You came here from wherever you're from, looking for music you'd never heard before. Maybe that's about songs, but you can get songs online if that's all that matters to you. You're here for something more, the same as we all are. A chance to create something."

As I said it, I thought it was true. I found myself deeply curious; as curious as I'd been about anything for a while. She'd clearly stepped out of her comfort zone, and it meant enough to her that she hadn't let Alice dissuade her. Something about her made me feel a kinship. I was pretty sure she was a lot older than I'd been when I left home, but she came across every bit as cloistered. *Did you feel it, too? Did a song call you and claim you for its own?* I'd met a lot of musicians since then, but none of them ever used those words.

"What's in it for you?" Rosemary asked.

Her eyes were closed, or she would have seen the disappointment in my face; she'd asked the wrong question. "I thought I said. The people. The connection. The music."

"Sorry, that came across strangely. I guess I'm asking this because I'm not a musician myself—do you play to make them happy, or do you play because it makes you happy?"

"I guess . . . it's . . . it's a little of both. I love to play. I love connecting with other musicians onstage. I love that the audience pushes me to write new material because it's the same people week after week, and they trust I'll never bore them, but I do miss the new audiences. I miss winning over people who've never heard me before. So I guess I play to make these few people happy, and sometimes if I'm lucky it wears off on me."

"When you were onstage tonight you looked like you were exactly where you were supposed to be. Like you were a character in a video game who absorbed every single bit of energy you were offered, and you were all powered up, and it was just sitting there under your skin ready to be released. I looked at you tonight and I thought, 'I've never been that complete in my entire life.' I don't know where I'm supposed to be." It was an intimate admission. I could tell if I mocked her now, she'd leave and never come back.

"Complete. I like that word." Rosemary exhaled as I continued. "I suppose that's true . . . This isn't for public consumption, okay? I don't think I've ever told this to anybody here. I grew up in a huge family, with a bunch of siblings. I shared a room with three of my sisters, two older and one a year younger. I loved them more than anybody, but there was part of me that I knew I couldn't share with them. I don't know why I knew that. It was something I knew wasn't allowed, and it got all tangled up in my mind.

"My first crush was on a melody—you wouldn't know the song. It was klezmer, Phrygian, this Jewish song that still lights me up. I thought at first it was the clarinet player, and people would understand that. Then I realized it was the sounds that came out of his clarinet, mixed with the sounds from the rest of the band, and I wanted to be part of the music itself, and that was never going to be allowed, and there was so much that must be wrong with me. Then I saw a woman playing electric guitar, and I got even more confused, and it wasn't until I figured out who I was, who I couldn't be if I stayed, until I finally got to play guitar with a band, with all that power and noise, with people shaping the same sounds at the same time, making something together . . . like I'd spent my entire life in a country where everyone spoke a different language than I did, and suddenly I was home. I never put a word on it like you did, but . . . I hope you find it somewhere, whatever your thing is."

I paused and looked down at my hands, which were forming chords on their own. "There used to be a musician named Neil Young—have you heard of him?"

Rosemary shook her head.

"He was this crochety old man by the time I started paying attention to music, but he used to go out on tour with this raggedy garage band called Crazy Horse. He'd play these ridiculous solos. He said to play a guitar solo all you had to do was grab the neck of the guitar and start wailing on the first note you found. If it sounded good with what the others were playing, you hung on it for a while longer. If it didn't, slide one fret up or down. When you got bored of that note, move to another one and start the same process. I guess I'm looking at this period of my life as one extended Neil Young solo. A note that's still working for me, for now, because it fits so well with the chord around it." This was officially more than I'd talked to anybody about anything in a long time.

"I'm not entirely sure I understand."

"You're a captive audience, sorry. And really, I'm supposed to keep you talking, not the other way around, but you don't sound impaired. I'll chalk 'I don't understand' up to a faulty metaphor, not brain injury."

Rosemary stifled a yawn. "I still have doubts about this concussion theory."

"No yawning! The night is still young." I stood, stretched, and left the room to get a snack and some tea.

When I came back, she was standing, too, examining the photos on the walls. They were mostly pictures of bands playing downstairs. She stood in front of the only picture of me; my body facing the camera and my face in profile, sweaty, hair plastered to my face and arms, looking at someone just out of the shot, smiling. I wasn't sure who I'd been smiling at, or anything about the night it was taken as different from any other night, but I liked it. It looked like the inside of my head when a song lifted off.

"Why do you hide that?" she asked when she noticed I'd returned. She pointed at the framed platinum record peeking out from behind the bookshelf.

I put down the tray I'd brought, piled with crackers and cheese and apple slices, and two mugs of tea, and climbed into my cozy couch again. "Because it's irrelevant. I mean, I wouldn't have this place if it weren't for 'Blood and Diamonds,' but the award, the context it was given in, was a little weird. The gold record—you can't see that one from where you're standing—came during the tour, and I got nominated for a bunch of awards that all got canceled later that year when people started dying. The song was years old by the time it went platinum, and only because of a nostalgia piece. A journalist figured out we played the last show Before, did a big article, and the next thing you know, the song is charting again, higher than the first time. If I got half that attention for one of the new songs, like 'Choose,' I think I could make a real difference."

"How?"

"It's the best song I've ever written. I think it speaks to something that's going on. The feeling that you want to create something but you don't have the tools, you've lost the language."

"Did you play it tonight before I interrupted your set?"

I nodded.

"If it was the one I'm thinking of, that song was amazing. I couldn't stand still."

"That's the point! We're all standing still, and we shouldn't be."

"So how do you get it out there? How do you get people to hear it?" Rosemary picked up a mug, peered into it.

"Mint tea. From my garden you fell into. And I don't know anymore. Anyway, the best way to hear it is live. Person-to-person transmission."

Rosemary warmed her hands on the mug, took a sip. "Like a virus."

"Fear is a virus. Music is a virus and a vaccine and a cure."

"Live music only?"

"No, but that shared experience is special. Being in a room with other people when something happens that will never happen the same way ever again."

"What about StageHolo? Is that the same?" Rosemary hid her face behind the mug, breathing the steam.

I shrugged. "I don't know. I've only seen Alice's living room rig. I hear Hoodies are immersive, but I don't know how that can replace what we do here. I guess it already has, pretty much everywhere. Doesn't it give the opposite message, though? That people should stay isolated?"

"My first live musical experience was SHL, and it was fantastic. I felt like I was there."

"How does it compare now that you've been to a real show?

When a song blew your mind, did you and the person beside you turn to each other and grin because you knew what you had just shared?"

"No," Rosemary admitted. "And the drums didn't play in my bones the way they do here. But it beat the hell out of anything else I'd heard 'til now, and it brings music to lots of people who live in places where there isn't any."

"Right! But they'd have music if people hadn't been conditioned to stay inside! If it wasn't illegal. It's a cycle. It's ridiculous to still have congregation laws ten years after the guys who caused most of the trouble got put away. People are social."

"People like being safe."

"The two are not mutually exclusive."

Rosemary sipped her tea. Again, I couldn't decide if I'd been wrong about her.

By the time I let Rosemary leave, the sun was testing the edges of the drawn curtains. We stood at the front door, suddenly awkward despite the night's conversation.

"Promise me you'll get checked out if your head goes wonky. Blurred vision, dizziness, altered thinking, bad headache, anything like that."

"Will do. Thank you for keeping an eye on me, I guess."

"My pleasure. It could have been way worse. You could've been a total ass and I'd still have been stuck talking to you all night."

Rosemary squinted and smiled. "Thanks, I think? Um, this might sound stupid, but am I allowed back here? After breaking in, I mean? I'll pay the eight dollars for tonight."

"I'll tell Alice to take you off the blacklist. Then you only have to work on the crowd phobia."

"Thank you!"

I reached out an arm. Rosemary stared for a minute before she understood. "Um," she said. "I've never hugged anyone who wasn't family before, not in real-space, and even my parents aren't much for hugging."

My arms dropped to my sides. "I'm sorry. Hug not required. Not everyone likes them."

"No, it's okay. I just didn't know what to do." She mimicked my gesture, and we wound up in a weird, brief half-embrace, shoulder bouncing off shoulder, before she ducked out the door.

20

ROSEMARY

Come See Me for Real

Back at her hotel room, Rosemary lowered herself gingerly onto the bed. She didn't remember the last time she'd stayed awake all night. Her body existed as one giant ache, and her eyes begged to close. She wanted a bath, even if it ate a few days' water credits, but she didn't recall if Luce had told her not to get the cuts wet. Or was that stitches? Casts? How were you supposed to know if your thinking was altered when you were this tired?

She lay back for a minute, then groaned and reached for her Hoodie.

You didn't check in, the first message accused. *Please report.*

She missed knowing the person on the other side of her work correspondence. SHL handled her by group. If she needed something tangible, she called Logistics. If she wanted a supervisor's opinion, she called Recruiter Management. If she ran into someone who didn't want to sign the standard contract, she'd call Legal to negotiate. Nowhere a single name, a single person to trust or not trust with a question or a problem. Maybe that was the point. At least she didn't have to put energy into talking face-to-face with a management avatar at this time of morning.

Sorry. Spent all night talking with a singer after a show. They didn't need to know about the fence incident or the reason she'd spent all night talking.

Good lead? came an immediate reply.

Rosemary groaned again. She should have waited to respond after she'd gotten some sleep. *Maybe.*

Keep us posted. Sooner than later. We're eager to see what you're capable of.

What was the proper response? *Will do.*

She was eager to see what she was capable of, too, for her own sake. Luce had said she left home because she knew she couldn't be herself if she stayed. Maybe, even if Rosemary was still looking for her thing, she could start with the knowledge she'd done right in taking a chance on this job.

On her next attempt to get in the 2020, Rosemary didn't trust that she wouldn't have trouble until she was through the door. Alice gave her a scowl and a salute from her couch that suggested grudging approval. She supposed that was enough; she didn't need to be friends with everyone. The company didn't even encourage it. *You are not there to be anyone's friend. Observe. Don't be a stranger to them, but don't get too involved.*

But surely it didn't matter so much. People had been so kind to her already, except for Alice. What was the harm in being friendly back? Everyone here knew each other. Maybe they didn't all like each other, but they trusted on some level or they wouldn't be here. Trusted that they were all here to listen, and that nobody would tell the wrong person. Even Alice was doing her job, playing her part night after night in case the wrong person stumbled in.

So much trust and care. If that many people put their safety—their freedom, their lives—in each other's hands, who was she to doubt them? Nobody planned to start a stampede or a fire. They were mechanics, teachers, techies, nurses, musicians. They came because they loved music, loved these bands, felt some piece of the music belonged to them.

As she descended the basement stairs for the third time, she decided it was okay to be scared, but not to let fear keep her from the music she'd come to hear. Fear of bees was reasonable, but running from bees got you stung. Fear of crowds was reasonable, too, or so she'd been taught. Crowds spread disease. Crowds concealed attackers. Crowds attracted the attention of people who might do you harm. She could worry about all that or walk downstairs and do her job.

She still aimed for her protected spot below the stairs, armed with her mother's invisible bubble, for whatever good that did. She had no illusion she'd stay calm in a crush, but maybe she could extend the limits of what was panic-worthy and make it through one full show.

She stood in her safe zone. She had been so focused on the room in the past—the stage, the musicians, the nearest exits—that she'd never taken a close look at the crowd before. It struck her that part of the job involved gauging the audience, too. It wasn't only about her assessment of the band, her reaction to the music. Who did the audience respond to? Who made them dance, or press closer to the stage? A puzzle piece clicked into place. She thought back to the bands from the first night, tried to remember what the crowd reactions had been.

The audience had an even wider age variety tonight, or a wider variety than she remembered. In her mind, the menace of the second night's crowd clouded everything. They were big, young, broad-shouldered, heavy-footed, in her recollection. Tonight a few people leaned against the walls, chatting with each other. More gray hair than she remembered. Nobody who wanted to hurt her. Not deliberately, anyway.

Joni came around the corner and stopped beside her. "Rosemary! Back for more punishment?"

"Desensitization. Are you playing tonight?"

"Nah. I don't want people to get sick of us."

"How could they? You were wonderful. I was hoping to see you again."

"Thanks. I'm flattered."

Someone touched Rosemary's arm. She flinched, turned.

"You came through the front door this time, I hope?" asked Luce. "How's the head?"

Rosemary put her hand to the adhesive bandage at her hairline. "Much better, thanks."

"So you think you'll make it through a whole set?"

"I'm going to try."

"Good. It's nice playing for new people. Just stand your ground, so I don't have to clean you off the floor again. Stand firm and people will bounce off you."

Luce melted into the crowd.

"So how come she can play practically every time this place is open, but not you? Because she owns the place?"

"No, she can play because her band is amazing and she spends all her time writing new stuff and experimenting musically and no two shows are ever alike. We don't have enough material to play more than one show a month. We've only been together for a year."

"I'd never have guessed."

"That's because you heard us once. Come back in a month, and it'll be the exact same songs. Maybe one new one if you're lucky. We don't have time to work up more. Most of the bands here are on a one-month rotation, except Luce's. She calls it her 'extended residency.'"

Rosemary didn't know what that meant, but she nodded. If that was the case, if she wouldn't see some of these bands again for weeks, she'd have to practice making faster decisions on which she thought were StageHoloLive material.

She had another question. "Is the crowd mostly the same night after night, or do people turn up for specific bands? I asked somebody the first night I was here who she'd come to see, and she said 'everyone.'"

Joni shrugged. "A mix. I think Luce is smart to only open the place twice a week. There are regulars who are here every night it opens, and musicians like me whose bands play monthly, but we come out other nights, too. I sit in with some of the others if they need cello. Then there are friends and family members and big-*F* Fans who only come for the bands they love. Luce tries to juggle the combinations so Fans hear different bands when they turn out for the ones they know, so maybe they'll fall for somebody else as well. Cross-pollination, she says."

The first act started, and they both turned their attention to the stage. An elderly black woman stood there on her own, wielding a sleek burgundy electric bass twice as long as she was tall. She wore cowboy boots, jeans, and a fringed red and black shirt. How old was she? Seventies, maybe even eighties, her hair a silver cloud around a lined face. She looked familiar.

From the clothing, Rosemary expected country, but from the first notes she realized her impression was wrong. The woman had some sort of effects station. She started a bass loop, sinuous and funky. Put down the bass, the loop continuing, and picked up an electric guitar. She attacked it in the same way she had the bass, echoing the line and embellishing it in a higher range.

When she sang, her voice had the same rich timbre as the bass. She shaped notes in her mouth, pushed them out from somewhere deeper, drawing out vowels and then clipping them off. She layered and looped the vocals as well, harmonizing with herself, making sounds that were words and not words. Each time Rosemary thought the song was as full as it could get, another part came in. Her ear followed the layers, seeking specific sounds, delighting when they appeared, reaching a strange and thrilling completeness when certain phrases resolved.

When a solid wall of harmony and guitar had built, the musician hit her foot pedal. Everything stopped.

"This is the sentence we brought on ourselves," she whisper-sang. Her guitar echoed the melody, then punctuated the line like a challenge. "We did nothing to stop it / We shaped it / We bought it / We gave it a home and a name." She hit the foot pedal again and the loop wall rushed back in to fill the silence. She took off the guitar, laid it strings-down against her amp, where a growl of feedback began to form beneath the music. She looped that noise, too. Noise on top of noise. She hit one more foot trigger and walked away, leaving the layers to loop and loop and then stop. The room stayed silent for a moment, then erupted in cheers.

"Who. Was. That?" Rosemary asked Joni, eyes still on the empty stage.

"Mary Hastings. She's been playing in Baltimore for decades. She's not in any rotation, though. She plays when she feels like it. Sometimes it's six months, sometimes it's two weeks. We always make room for her. Amazing, isn't she?"

"Completely amazing." Rosemary tried to figure out why the woman looked familiar. "Wait—does she work at the diner up the street?"

"Yeah, she and her sister and brother own it. She gives us all discounts on the nights we play."

"Does she always play one long song?"

"She plays whatever she wants. One song or three, ten minutes or an hour. I've never heard her do a song the same way twice. I've never seen her do one song with no verse or chorus before, either, but that was badass."

Somebody—not Mary Hastings—started putting her guitars into cases. The performer stood chatting in a corner. Rosemary wandered over to the merchandise table, but there wasn't anything labeled "Mary Hastings."

She tried to picture the woman on an SHL stage. She could command a room, that was for sure; Rosemary still had goose bumps. She had the charisma, the presence, the musical chops, but Rosemary wasn't sure about that mainstream appeal factor she was supposed to consider. Nothing too political, they'd said, and this had felt political even if the only lyrics were five whispered lines.

Her biggest concern was Joni's comment that Mary Hastings never played the same song the same way twice. She remembered what had happened when Magritte had gone off script. SHL wanted musicians to bring something special, but maybe there was a different kind of control to their brand of special. In any case, now she had four very different bands to tell them about.

And perhaps she would have a fifth? The next band looked more conventional than any she had seen here. Drums, bass, two guitars. The lead singer was a good-looking guy, blond and tall enough to touch the ceiling without straightening his arm. The bassist had heavy pox scars on every visible patch of skin. The drummer looked older than the others, around fifty, maybe, bald. The second guitarist leaned over and whispered to him, and he barked a laugh.

They tested their instruments, then started playing. It was the closest sound to Patent Medicine she'd heard since arriving, enough so that she realized she'd been wondering for a while now how a band that conventional had come from this scene. Their first song was a love song, three minutes of catchy, straightforward pop. Rosemary waited for some trick, some hint they were making a comment on politics or taxes or art, but the next song didn't have any deeper meaning, either. Pure candy.

Joni leaned toward Rosemary. "The bassist and drummer are the rhythm section your buddy Aran left behind."

Rosemary appraised them again with the knowledge that this was the original Patent Medicine. The SHL version was much better looking, and their moves were more polished, but underneath they had similar blueprints.

She actually preferred this singer's voice to Aran's. It held a bluesy richness, a worn quality. She would have recommended this band based on their sound, but she wasn't sure if that was wise if they had already refused to go audition for StageHolo when Aran stormed the gates.

"They're better than Patent Medicine," Rosemary whispered into Joni's ear. "This guy is better than Aran."

Joni stayed silent for a moment, then turned to her again with a sly look. "I probably shouldn't say this and spoil your impression, but there's this game I play watching some of these bands. It's a friend's theory she told me a long time ago, that musicians make love the way they play their instruments. When I see certain people play, I can't help but—" She pointed at the drummer, partially obscured by the singer. Rosemary hadn't taken a good look at him before, but his movement was oddly loose and frenetic, like he was playing with more limbs than could be seen.

"He's an octopus. I don't think I want to picture . . ."

"Exactly." They both laughed. Rosemary looked at the others in the band using that same lens, then considered the other bands she had seen so far. The frantic players, the intense ones. Joni and her cello, her warm, sure hands. She looked away in case Joni could read her thoughts on her face.

The people in front of her started dancing. Rosemary felt the urge to join them, but she remembered the other night and knew she'd be better off taking baby steps. Get through one full night on the room's edge before venturing into the middle. She tapped her toe and stayed put. The band—the Handsome Mosquitoes, by their own introduction—played a ten-song set, crisp and punchy. Ten perfect pop songs, all exuding mainstream appeal.

Rosemary pictured the Bloom Bar crowd leaping to buy all their merchandise as they finished a show. Their T-shirts looked like they had been hand silk-screened, and the art on the download card was amateur at best, a juvenile pun on a juvenile album name. Nothing like their polished songs. Hopefully the album's production quality was as good as their show, but if not, SHL producers could help, and their professional graphics people would design a better logo for the merchandise. If. If she recommended them, and if SHL was willing to look past the rougher aspects.

Luce's band took the stage. They started with a song they hadn't played at the previous show. It launched from nothing: no audible count, no instrumental intro. Drums, bass, guitar, and straight into a chorus, zero to sixty with no warning, the sonic opposite of Mary Hastings's slow build, hooky without being poppy, loud and loose and ragged.

It was strange to reconcile the woman she had chatted so easily with a few nights before with the person onstage now, staring down her audience like she didn't care what anybody thought of her, like she dared them to disagree with what she was singing, dared them to look away. Nobody did.

"Was that new?" someone asked from somewhere near Rosemary as the song slid to a stop.

"I haven't heard it before," said someone else. "Damn."

She recognized the second piece from the previous show, before she had gone stupid. It was hard to believe they could ramp up from the first song, but this was the one that had run away with her a few days before. It threatened to do the same again. The beat was close to a heartbeat but not quite, inviting her body to adapt itself to the song rather than the other way around.

Rosemary remembered her panic from the other night, but it felt distant now, like she'd decided to be a different person. Rosemary had been replaced with someone who was okay in crowds, someone who didn't grow up under a failing Hoodie in the middle of nowhere. City Rosemary, with drums for a heartbeat and bass for a pulse. The volume that had felt crushing wasn't crushing at all. It pushed from underneath her skin, making her stronger, pushing the bad stuff out. She needed to put it on repeat until it became her own personal armor. What had Luce called it? "Choose." She pulled up her Hoodie to record.

The song ended, and its absence nagged at Rosemary like a missing tooth. The third one was quieter, a respite. The fourth song had a spoken-word interlude, preplanned but stream-of-consciousness, with a rhythm to it. Luce came across both tough and vulnerable, inviting the audience in. Nobody in the crowd talked, even though they'd all heard this band dozens of times.

Rosemary found herself wishing that she played an instrument. Bass, maybe. That rooting of the song, the tight communication between bassist and drummer. How long would she have to stay here before some band accepted her, let her play with them? Or maybe she'd buy a bass and go home and practice and return in a few months or a year. She had a job to do, but the two weren't mutually exclusive.

The last song ended with an extended coda. The drummer and second guitarist had a wordless *la la* part, echoing the melody Luce had been carrying. Luce stalked the stage. She climbed onto her amp, then stretched one foot out to rest on the bass drum. She stood there, balanced between amp and drum, head inches below the ceiling, strumming harder and harder. One of her strings broke and she pulled it loose to dangle from her guitar. Another string, then another, all three trailing from her headstock, whipping with her movement, flashing when they caught light.

The guitar became more and more discordant, but it didn't matter. None of it felt like performance, though she posed unanswered questions of how she didn't fall over, how the bass drum didn't crack or spill her, how she played that hard in that precarious a position without losing her footing or looking like she cared about anything other than the sounds she dragged out of her guitar. It was as if Luce had become a conduit for something bigger than her, and it didn't matter what she wanted or where she was or how she had gotten there.

At the last possible moment, as the song built to its inevitable conclusion, she pushed off the drum, knocking it into the drummer, who leaped backward off his throne but managed still to bring his sticks down on the cymbals for one last crash. The whole band cracked up in laughter; they all looked surprised-pleased-relieved it had ended as well as it had.

Rosemary dragged herself back to the analytical. She was supposed to pay attention to the whole package, not just her own response, the better to explain what she was selling—what she was buying—when she talked to her employers. She thought she knew how to pitch it. Sure, they were political, but maybe that was acceptable, as long as she'd play "Blood and Diamonds," too? Their songs were catchy, and they were compelling to watch. Everything she could ask for.

"That was amazing," she told Luce after the show. "What you said the other night—about wanting to make people realize they want to make something themselves? I think I get it."

Luce looked exhausted, though she'd been full of energy a minute before. "Thanks. Glad you made it through one. You going to hang out a while?"

"Uh, this is the first time I've gotten to the end, so I didn't know that was a thing. People hang out now?"

"Some do. At the Heatwave. You're welcome to join us." She paused, cocked her head. "I'd like that."

Rosemary nodded and retreated to the back of the basement while the musicians packed their gear. She started to offer help, but their movements were so precise she knew she'd be in the way; she preferred keeping to the edge while the audience exited, in any case. Luce packed up her merchandise last, folding the case and sliding it into the alcove behind the table.

"The benefits of playing in my own house." Luce grinned. "Let's get out of here."

The end-of-night stragglers headed up the street. Luce's band walked together, speaking in low voices; the other band chatted with the two strangers, leaving Rosemary alone. If she dropped out of the group and headed back to her hotel nobody would notice.

"Rosemary, catch up. I want you to meet people."

Or not. She walked faster, and allowed Luce to introduce her around. The guy with the tattoos, the drummer, was Dor. The teenage bassist, in a yellow sundress over jeans, with supermodel cheekbones and a cascade of chestnut hair, Andy.

"You're all so intense onstage," Rosemary said.

"That's because we have to concentrate on not being killed by our singer." Dor drew his face into a caricature of sheer concentration.

"You look constipated," said Luce. "I hope that isn't what you look like onstage behind my back."

"Nah, he's more like this." Andy made a worse face.

It was hard to be intimidated by people who mocked each

other so lovingly. Rosemary smiled and kept quiet, happy to be included.

The shades were drawn at the Heatwave. Rosemary waited for someone to say it was closed, but when the door swung open, she realized the place was full, even though the city curfew was fast approaching. There were at least fifteen or twenty people inside, some she recognized by sight, if not by name.

Mary Hastings sat in the first booth on the left with three other women. Two people stood behind the counter handling orders, both of whom looked to be the musician's siblings. The crowd dispersed among the tables and barstools, but everyone chatted cross-group. She looked for a familiar face—Joni, maybe, or the singer with the keyboard tattoo, but she didn't see anyone she recognized except Alice, who sat on a stool at the bar. She wasn't about to go chat with Alice, so she stayed by Luce's side.

Luce stopped at Mary Hastings's booth first. The other woman was tinier than Rosemary remembered. When she stood for a hug, she reached Luce's chin, and Luce herself wasn't tall.

"You were awesome." Luce sounded like a giddy fan. "Every time you step up there, I have to pinch myself. Thank you."

"Luce, you know I'm just happy you haven't yet kicked this old woman off your stage yet. I should be thanking you."

"You have a place to play as long as I have a stage to put you on."

They hugged again, then Hastings sat down and Luce moved along. Here and there people waved or gave her a thumbs-up, but it didn't take her long to slide into the last booth. Rosemary lingered, not sure if it was reserved for the band, though they had all stopped to chat.

"Slide in, Rosemary. There are no reserved seats."

Rosemary moved toward the opposite bench, but the bassist from the second band got there before she did. She didn't want to risk being squeezed between two guys she didn't know if a third person tried to sit on that side, so she slid in next to Luce instead, trying to gauge the appropriate distance to leave between herself and the other woman.

"Do I smell? Eh, scratch that. I probably do."

"Sorry," said Rosemary. "I was trying to give you enough space."

The Harriet drummer—she had already forgotten names—no, Dor: *D* was for drummer—slid in after her, trapping her. She scooted a little closer to Luce and tried not to panic. They'd let her out anytime she wanted, or else she could always slide under the table, or onto the table and out the door. She'd never be able to return if she did that, but the option reassured her.

The bassist across the booth pulled a flask from his jacket pocket. "To another great show." He took a swig and passed it around. It got to Rosemary fifth. Four sets of lips—that she had seen—and four mouths' germs. Had the pox never reached this place? No, she'd seen evidence that it had. Or maybe they had all forgotten already, or been even younger than her. Luce wasn't younger, though, and she didn't think any of these guys were, either. Whatever they were drinking was powerful enough to disinfect . . . or it was worth the risk.

Tonight, for once, she wasn't going to be her usual anxious self. She held the flask up, trying to keep it away from her lips. She spilled a little but not too much as she gulped a solid mouthful. It tasted like gasoline, but left a warm sensation in its wake. She wiped her face with her sleeve and passed it on.

Mary Hastings's brother came to take their order, starting with Luce. When he got to Rosemary, she said, "Chicken chili with sour cream," remembering the last bowl. "And a glass of milk."

She glanced around to see if anyone mocked her for the milk, but nobody did. They all ordered sodas or water themselves; this wasn't a bar. When the flask came back a second time, she let her lips touch it as she took a longer swig. The burn spread pleasantly.

She turned to Luce. "Your band was wonderful. I'm so glad I got to be there. I wish everyone could see you play."

"Ha. You and me both, friend."

"The room would get awfully crowded, though," joked the guitarist across the booth. "Poor Alice would have her hands full."

"First, we clone Alice, then we invite the world."

"Agreed."

They passed the flask around again. Rosemary didn't feel altered, but something inside her unclenched. The proximity of those seated on either side grew more tolerable.

She excused herself to go to the bathroom. Pushed through the people in the aisle with a confidence she didn't wear every day. Maybe she could. If this person was inside her, why did she only get released with a drink and a good show? She was obviously there beneath the surface.

Joni stood in line inside the bathroom door. Rosemary hadn't seen a multistall bathroom since she was a kid.

"Hey," said Rosemary. "I didn't see you after the show."

Joni shrugged. "I don't like standing around doing nothing." She tucked her hair behind her ear. She had dimples Rosemary hadn't noticed before.

They both stood in silence for a moment. A song played over a tinny speaker in the corner above the sink, and Rosemary recognized it. "Come See Me for Real" by the Iris Branches Band. She'd listened to it all the time in high school.

Another wave of confidence washed over her. The crowded restaurant didn't feel oppressive anymore; in this corner, it was protection. She leaned back against the hand dryer to steady herself. "So, uh, what you said earlier, about people playing the way they . . . I, uh, I like the way you play."

"Yeah?"

"Yeah. You're . . . deliberate. Careful, but sure."

Joni cocked her head, stepped closer. "Yeah?"

Even bolder now. "Deliberate is nice. Quiet confidence. People who are loud confident make me nervous."

"Loud confident?"

"Nervous that they aren't nervous. As opposed to nervous like something good is about to happen."

"Like now?"

"Like now."

They both leaned in. Rosemary's heart quickened, and she closed her eyes. Lips brushed hers, parted hers, electric. Real lips, a real person, a touch she didn't want to move away from.

"You drank Mikey Lee's hooch," Joni said.

"Sorry."

"I didn't say it was a bad thing." Joni kissed her again. "But are you drunk? I don't want to think you're drunk and doing something you'll regret later."

"I only had a little to drink. I'm kissing you because of how you play your cello."

"What about that touching thing? I've noticed the flinch."

"I just don't like it when I'm not expecting it."

A stall door swung open, and the person ahead of Joni traded places with the person leaving. Joni and Rosemary broke apart for her to wash her hands. Joni had a contemplative spark in her eye, like she was sizing Rosemary up. The far stall opened, and Joni grabbed her hand and pulled her in. Kissed her again.

"Is this okay?" she whispered. "It's gauche, but I have roommates and you said you're staying with friends, and I kind of want you right now."

Rosemary nodded. She could say she had a bed in a room overlooking the entire city, but it might spoil if she tried to trade this moment for a different one in another place. A wrong word, an awkwardness interjected on the ride to the hotel. A chance for her head to catch up with her body and remind her she wasn't supposed to get involved with the artists, a chance for her usual walls to reappear. *Now now now* sang inside her, alongside Iris Branches Band's "Come See Me for Real." She pulled Joni closer.

The bathroom door opened again, and more people walked in, talking.

"Shit," said one of them. "Get a room, yo."

The toilet in the next stall flushed, and Rosemary giggled and then they both did, and Joni pressed her mouth to Rosemary's shoulder, and Rosemary bit her own lip, trying to keep herself quiet.

Running water, the hand dryer, the door, and they were both giggling, the moment gone.

"I'm glad you came here, Rosemary Laws," Joni whispered.

"Me, too," Rosemary whispered back.

Joni kissed her again, then slipped out of the stall, leaving Rosemary reeling against the wall.

"Your chili's cold," Luce said when she returned. The others at the table were done with their food.

"There was a line in the bathroom."

"Ah."

Rosemary mixed sour cream into cold chili. She hadn't even realized how hungry she was until she took her first bite. She worked to catch up. "So what happens next?"

The Mosquitoes bassist dragged a hand across his throat. "It's Wednesday night. Most of us have to work tomorrow. Sleep happens next."

"Oh."

"I can introduce you to someone from one of the collectives if you want to hang out later. I'm sure some of them will party. Or, I think you know Joni? Ask her."

Rosemary glanced over to see if Luce said that in a teasing way, but she didn't seem to be suggesting anything.

"It's not that I need to party. It's just been a really nice night. I don't want it to be over."

"Even nice nights have to end. That's what makes them nice. Otherwise they'd roll right into the next shitty day without anything to differentiate."

The bassist across the booth grimaced. "Or you can do the endless-awesome-night thing, but that takes a lot of drugs to maintain."

"Does anybody do that anymore?" asked his drummer, the octopus.

They exchanged a look. Rosemary wondered if they were thinking about Aran. It's not like that for him, either, she wanted to say, but she thought better of it.

The bassist lifted the flask again. "To great nights with good friends, to great nights ending, to the next great night." He passed the drink, and they all toasted.

They all started sliding out of the booth. Joni stepped behind Rosemary as she shrugged her jacket on. "So, uh, do you want to hang out sometime?"

Rosemary understood the question behind the question. "I'd love to see you again. Can I find you online, or do you want to make a date now? Not a date, but, you know what I mean."

"Let's decide now. I'm noncomm. Well, semi-noncomm."

" 'Semi-noncomm'?"

"A lot of people are completely noncomm. No Hoodie, no phone. I keep a phone for emergencies, so I can't say I'm the real deal, but I don't have an av or anything."

"Gotcha," said Rosemary. She'd never heard of such a thing. She knew people who weren't connected—her parents, for starters—but she'd never thought their stubbornness was part of a movement.

"Have you walked around Baltimore at all? I have to work tomorrow and Friday, but I could play tour guide Saturday if you wanted."

"I'd like that."

"Meet me here at ten a.m.?"

A vision of the two of them in her hotel room flitted through Rosemary's head, and she shuddered. Not yet. She nodded.

Joni grinned, then leaned over and gave her a quick kiss, long enough to be more than friendly. "Sweet."

21

ROSEMARY

A Selection

Curfew had long since passed. Rosemary was surprised to find the bus still running, but she supposed there were people who needed to get home even at that hour. She rode back to her hotel still feeling she'd been inoculated against her own fear. Sure, there were people out to do harm to others, but a city bus at two a.m. wasn't where they would choose to do it. She didn't need a bubble. She had common sense. She still chose a seat where she'd be able to watch the other passengers, where she didn't have to come into contact with anyone, but she chose not to be concerned about the lack of barriers and compartments. Everyone was trying to get home.

Back at the hotel, she looked out her window at the city laid out beneath her. The headlights, the hotel windows, the streetlamps capturing tiny figures then releasing them into the dark: even this late, there was still so much movement. Maybe she'd never go back. She was a different person here, and she liked this person. No other night in her life came close to this one. She was a note that hadn't ever known it fit into a chord. The music, the invitation, Joni. A tiny involuntary shudder at that last thought, an echo, shadow lips on her own.

She woke to her phone chiming.

Good time for a report?

The clock read ten a.m. She reached for her Hoodie and dragged it over her head. Happy her avatar looked work appropriate without any effort on her part, glad this wasn't Superwally Vendor Services with its daily photos and techwear and insistence on propriety.

The StageHolo virtual meeting spaces were meant to evoke their beautiful campuses. A green and grassy meadow, a single bench. She sat next to an avatar of a slim middle-aged white man. He had perfect chestnut hair streaked with gray, and a neatly trimmed beard and mustache. The hair showed he was high-end, reacting to the same code-wind that rustled the grass. Untucked dress shirt over a T-shirt and jeans. He didn't introduce himself. She pulled up his information, but it only said "Recruiter Management—Generic Male (1 of 5)." More group management.

"So, what have you got for us? Your reports have been exciting."

"I don't even know where to start."

"Tell us about the acts you've seen."

"All of them, or just the ones I think are worth considering?"

"Whichever you want."

She considered. Easiest to go in chronological order so she didn't miss anyone. Better not to mention that these were all of them, too; she didn't know how many they expected her to have seen in eight days. "So there's a band with this intense preacher vibe, kinda, but not religious, and the singer has this tattoo implant controller in his arm that he plays. He's building other ones on his body."

"So it's performance art? His body is his instrument?"

"No! Well, yes, but the songs were good, too. Intense." She flashed on Joni's line about people playing instruments the way they made love, and then an image of this singer playing his own arm with ecclesiastic fervor. She laughed to herself.

"Okay. What are they called?"

"Kurtz."

A white block appeared in the fake sky, with "Kurtz" written on it, a question mark after it.

"Next?"

"The Coffee Cake Situation. It's an awful name, I know"—she interrupted herself as Management opened his mouth—"but their sound is fantastic. The singer plays cello, and she's absolutely riveting to watch."

"The Coffee Cake Situation" appeared in the air above "Kurtz." "Do I have the order of preference correct?" Management asked.

Rosemary considered. Both bands had interesting sounds, singers who were compelling for different reasons. She wasn't sure if her judgment was clouded or if this was the proper order. Which band's music had she enjoyed more before Joni had kissed her? Joni's, she thought. The main selling point for Kurtz was the singer's unique implants, not their songs. She couldn't picture either band without their lead performer, and neither was about the songs so much as the sounds they created, and the ways they made people react. She had no idea which had a better chance with StageHoloLive.

"They both have potential," she said carefully. "Do you mind if I list the rest and then sort the order?"

"Fair enough. Next?"

The next night was the one where she had fallen over the fence. She skipped that one for the time being.

"Mary Hastings. Tiny little old woman with a giant sound. She's a one-woman band, uses lots of effects. Absolutely phenomenal."

"But?"

"But I saw how much trouble it was when Magritte went off script, and she didn't act like somebody willing to stick to a plan. They said Mary Hastings plays as long as she wants, when she wants. She's worth it, if you want something different."

"I'll pass that along to Specialty Acts. Maybe there's a niche for her somewhere."

The name "Mary Hastings" wrote itself on the white square with a line through it and an arrow beside it.

"Next?"

"The Handsome Mosquitoes."

"These bands are better than their names?"

"I promise. These guys are really talented. Poppy, um, anthemic. The singer's a good-looking guy with an amazing voice and a ton of charisma, and the band is really tight." She didn't mention they had been Aran's band, the former Patent Medicine. They were excellent. They deserved another chance.

"Nice. Did any of the acts you've mentioned look like they have habits that might keep them from fulfilling obligations?"

"I didn't see anything that rang any alarm bells for me. The bands were on time. This scene is about the music, not any side benefits, I think." She was echoing something someone had said, but it sounded good.

He flashed a smile. "Ah, those are great when you can find them. Was that the last one?"

"One more." She paused. "Do you remember 'Blood and Diamonds'?"

"Of course. Hell of a song."

"Yeah, so, I found Luce Cannon. She's playing here, under a different band name. She's amazing."

"Saving the best for last, huh? Wow. Nice job, Rosemary." The management avatar shimmered a bit, like it was vibrating with excitement. "That was a killer song. We can build a whole mystique around her, like 'whatever happened to . . . ?' Then a rediscovery special, emphasize how she hasn't played or released a song in years."

"She has, though. Twice a week, every week, practically. She's put out a ton of music on some weird platform."

He wasn't listening to her. "Not with us or anyplace else that matters. How do we reach her? And the rest of the bands you found?"

She hesitated. It felt wrong to make this connection without giving the musicians a heads-up, and she hadn't collected contact info for any of them yet. A little lie wouldn't hurt.

"Uh, most of them are noncomm. Do you know what that is?"

He sighed. "A pain in the ass. Why do they always have to be noncomm? Alright. You're authorized to offer an audition to any of the rest, as long as you connect us with Luce Cannon. She's a done deal. Tell the rest they have to un-noncomm long enough to talk to us, if they're interested. Once you've signed them they have to borrow a phone, borrow a Hoodie, whatever it takes to get them in contact with Logistics. Do you have any videos?"

"A couple." She sent them his way.

"Thanks. We'll review those, but we assume they'll back up what you've already said. Make sure they know we may have to discuss other band names for, oh, probably all of them. The Coffee Cake Situation. Saints preserve."

She didn't know what to say, so she stayed silent.

"Good job, Rosemary. We look forward to getting those contacts in the next few days."

"How soon?" A new panic gripped her. She'd expected weeks to figure out how to make the approach.

"By the end of this weekend." He paused, went still. Probably consulting with someone else. "Yeah. Tell them they have to give us a decision by the end of the weekend. No point in giving them longer."

"Shouldn't I have seen them each a few more times, though?"

"Do you think you need more time? Your descriptions make it sound like you've got a good handle on it already."

The edge in his voice made her think more time was not advisable. "No, this weekend's fine. Thank you for your trust."

"We were surprised when you picked Baltimore. Most people pick something close to their home region for their first time out. This is better than expected."

When the connection terminated and the grass faded from view, she was left with all the questions she hadn't been willing to pose. How was she supposed to approach everyone by the weekend? What music had she missed in her own "home region"? Not to mention she no longer understood why anyone stayed in said home region when they had the option of going almost anywhere.

The bassist for the band that had been Aran Randall's original Patent Medicine, the Handsome Mosquitoes, had said at the diner that they all worked on Thursdays, and the singer had worn a T-shirt for Blackner's Lumber & Salvage, an odd thing to advertise if you weren't an employee. An odd thing to wear for a rock show, really, unless maybe there was a point where you were cool enough that whatever you wore was cool by default. Or maybe it wasn't strange at all, and she still didn't know the rules, which was a distinct possibility. Rosemary looked up the location, which turned out to be a mile west of her hotel. The day looked inviting from her vantage point in the sky, and she decided to walk.

Walking made her wish she knew more about Baltimore. She'd chosen it based on Aran's suggestion without researching further. She knew it had been a significant city at several points in history, but she couldn't dredge up the whys from high school. Strolling the wide sidewalk, waving back to strangers who sat on their stoops, she wished she remembered the details. The picture in her head was so different from this friendly place. It had been put there by her parents and teachers, and it was nothing like reality.

She hadn't caught the singer's name, so she wound up asking if a tall, good-looking blond guy worked there, which won her a knowing look from the cashier. "If you want my advice, forget him. He's a player. You're not the first one to come here, though you're not his usual type."

Color rose to Rosemary's cheeks. "No! I'm not . . . I just need to talk with him."

Another look told her the cashier didn't buy it, but she pressed an intercom button below her register and paged Josh diSouza. Rosemary stood awkwardly to the side, willing the other woman not to tell her any more. How awkward would it be if the person paged didn't turn out to be him? Sorry, didn't mean to bother you, but I hear you're a hit with the ladies.

She was relieved when the tall blond guy walking from the back was the right tall blond guy. He wore the same T-shirt, or an identical one, and there were wood shavings in his tangled hair.

He glared at the cashier, then appraised Rosemary. "Do I know you?"

She spoke low, in case his band was a secret. "My name is Rosemary Laws. I was at your show last night, and then at the Heatwave. I hung out with the other guys from your band, but you'd left already, I think."

He took her elbow, his grasp firm but not rough; it didn't lend a favorable impression, since she hadn't given him permission to touch her. He led her to an area that was outdoors but fenced in. She'd never been in a lumberyard, but she liked the sweet piney scent, the sawdust underfoot. It reminded her of her family's barn.

"Sorry," he said. "I don't usually talk music here. How can I help you?"

"I've got a proposition for you. For your band, I mean. I didn't know how to find the other guys."

He sat on a stack of pallets and gestured for her to do the same. "A proposition."

"Yeah. I . . . Are you familiar with StageHoloLive?"

"Of course."

"I'm a . . . They call us artist recruiters. I travel the country looking for bands to bring into the SHL family." After all the times she had practiced this in her head, it proved remarkably easy to say, at least to this guy. Maybe because she hadn't talked to him before, so she hadn't yet presented herself as anything else to him. Easier, too, to pretend he wasn't the first one she had ever attempted to recruit. "I think you guys are the complete package, and I'm authorized to offer you a chance to audition for my bosses."

"You're kidding." He stared at her. "Really?"

"Really."

"Can I, uh, two of the other guys work here as well. That's how I met them. Can I bring them in on this conversation? You're making this offer to all of us, not only me?" He had gone from confident to all nerves.

"All of you. I know what happened with Patent Medicine."

He looked relieved. "Be right back."

She waited. Rosemary imagined herself vacuuming up all his confidence to use for her own. The power position.

He returned a moment later with the bassist, the one who had offered his flask the night before, and the octopus-drummer. Kenny and Marcus, if she remembered. Kenny looked entirely changed from the diner, his body language closed off, scarred arms folded across his chest. The drummer looked a little less tightly wound, but no less wary.

"You?" asked Kenny. "I shared my flask with you. Luce said you were cool."

"Easy, Kenny," said Marcus. "She never lied. We didn't ask her what had brought her here, or what she did for a living."

"She should volunteer it. Otherwise we met under false pretenses. She was a fan, far as I knew."

"Look." Rosemary tried to get the conversation back under control. "I apologize if I misled you in any way. That wasn't my intent, but I truly do want to talk to all of you about SHL."

Kenny didn't relax. "All of us? Or are you going to make us drive out to your headquarters and audition and then tell us you want our singer?"

"All of you. And is that what actually happened with Patent Medicine? That isn't the story I heard."

Marcus shook his head. "Come on, Kenny. You know that isn't what happened. Aran screwed us, not SHL. Do you really think he fought for us? He drove out there on his own."

"He told me he was going," Kenny said. "He said he was bringing video of the whole band."

"Maybe he did, maybe he didn't. Maybe if we had gone with him, they'd have been impressed by all of us instead of only Aran, but we didn't go. This chick is here in front of us right now. Let's maybe talk to her instead of convincing her we're dysfunctional."

Josh raised his hands, a placating gesture. "I promise, I'm not looking to ditch you guys. She's offering all of us."

Rosemary shot him a grateful look. "All of you, as I said. Your songs are super catchy."

"So what's the deal?" Kenny didn't unfold his arms.

"A second audition at SHL, expenses paid. You already passed the first one, since I like your stuff. You have to show that your sound plays well to the cameras as well as it does to a live crowd. That's it. If they like you as much as I do, you get a contract."

"Enough to live on?"

"As I understand it. The terms are between you and Legal, but they want their musicians happy and focused on making music."

"Do we have to move out there? Live in some little artist village with Aran as a next-door neighbor?" Kenny's hostility hadn't faded.

"Not if you don't want to, I don't think. You can commute."

"How long do we have to decide?" asked Marcus.

"Sunday at the latest."

"Fuck! How do you expect us to make a decision that fast?"

She shrugged. "I know it's short, but how much deciding do you have to do? It's an audition, not a commitment. Contract comes later. You can walk away if you get there and change your minds."

She turned away and studied the sky while they talked in low voices.

"An audition," Marcus said at last. "What do we have to do?"

Rosemary smiled. "First of all, do any of you have a phone or a Hoodie?"

Josh returned her smile. "You think we're all in that noncomm cult? This is a connected band, friend. We're on board, ready to promote."

She gave them the contact information for Logistics, and her employee ID as reference. It had gone well, or as well as expected, considering the Aran complication. If she had thought about it more, she'd have waited to talk to them after Kurtz. Maybe she'd gotten the most difficult out of the way first. She hadn't mentioned the possibility of a name change, either, but she'd leave that to somebody more experienced.

She had assumed none of the bands were online, but the Handsome Mosquitoes made her realize she'd generalized. To find Kurtz, she tried the old-fashioned way: head in hoodspace. She scrolled through body-mod sites until she located one that intersected with music. He was right there, contact information and everything. How many guys could there be with a piano in their arm and a desire to turn their whole body into a trigger system? "KurtZ OMB," he called himself online. One-Man Band.

It was easy enough to ask him into a private room to discuss his music. His avatar had even more mods than he had, though they came across a little more cartoonish. Anyone could have piano keyboards for arms if they paid enough for the customizations, or a guitar for a body. When he walked, his footsteps triggered drum hits. A map of what he yet wanted to do to his real body, perhaps. Beside him, she felt generic.

The room was his choice, paneled with colored squares that lit when he moved. The different colors corresponded to different notes. The discord gave Rosemary a headache, but it made sense to make him comfortable by letting him choose the space.

"Hi," she said. "I met you at the 2020 last week. I liked your band, and the body-mod thing is awesome."

"Thanks. Do you look like your avatar?" He tapped on his arm as he talked, little trills.

"Close."

"No music mods?"

"Sorry, no. I hope I didn't misrepresent myself when I contacted you."

"Nah. I was hoping. I love to see what other people come up with."

"Sorry," she repeated. "But I'm here to offer you a chance to audition for StageHoloLive."

His tapping trills ceased. "You're joking."

"Dead serious. I'm an artist recruiter." She pushed her professional credential to him.

"Whoa. For real."

"For real. You and your band are invited to audition. Logistics can get in touch with you about travel arrangements if you're interested."

His hand went to his arm. "Will they have any trouble with my trigger system?"

"It was part of the appeal, so I assume they'll find a way to make it work."

"Is there room to improvise? To do new mods and stuff?"

"It's harder. I think you'd have to talk to somebody who knows the tech side, but I think as long as you keep them in the loop, it can happen." She repeated some of what Aran had told her. "Structured creativity, if that makes sense. That's how it was explained to me, anyway. I'm not a musician."

"And it's only an audition? If I don't like the situation, I can still walk?"

"Absolutely."

He took a deep breath. "Okay. Tell me who to talk to."

"Will do," said Rosemary. "But, um, what's your name? I got the name of the band and your avatar, but I think I should give my bosses your actual name."

"Kurt Zell."

Kurt Zell. KurtZ. She thanked him, and let him show her what he'd been working on, a guitar fretboard mapped over his avatar's torso, as he'd mentioned at the club. In hoodspace, it represented layers of modification she couldn't even imagine. He played his own body to play his brain to play his avatar's body, translating it all into an eerie and off-putting sound. All without even opening his mouth. She realized she hadn't even mentioned his voice to Management. Let that surprise them.

22

ROSEMARY

You're Only Here to Know

She hadn't been given the go-ahead for Mary Hastings, so the last two bands on her list were Joni's and Luce's. For some reason she felt apprehensive about both those conversations. Not because she didn't think she had fair offers for them, but because of the Handsome Mosquitoes' reaction. False pretenses, they had said, or one had, and left it to the others to argue him down. Her pretenses weren't false, though. She genuinely appreciated their sound, and she had tangible benefits to offer. If she was in the room on business, she was also in the room as a music fan. She hadn't faked anything, she told herself.

Joni. She wondered if she had made an awful mistake with Joni on Wednesday. It had felt right at the time. She liked her, really liked her, thought she was impossibly talented and sexy and kind. Not enough credit was ever given to simple kindness. And yet, the words "false pretenses" colored her Friday and made her dread meeting Joni the next day. False pretenses would have been if she wasn't a recruiter but told them she was. She pictured the note-perfect Management avatar walking through the 2020, offering people auditions in exchange for cash, auditions for sex, auditions for drugs. She hadn't misrepresented herself. She had never been anything but herself.

She toyed with the idea of inviting Joni back to her room instead of touring the city. If there was any active lie she had told, it was that one, about staying with a friend. She should have said she had a hotel through work. Then she could have shown off the room, the view, the bed.

But then Joni might have asked about her job, and would she have told the truth? All anyone had ever asked her was whether she was a cop. She'd have been truthful if they had asked the right question, she was certain. That made it Joni's and Luce's fault they hadn't questioned her more specifically. They'd asked her about music where she came from, but not about her. She would have told them. Maybe.

Anyway, this was the day to come clean. She took the bus to the Heatwave to meet Joni. Pulled up her Hoodie and rewatched the videos she'd taken of the 2020 bands. Her recordings captured the bands well enough. They all sounded good. Management would have told her by now if they thought any of her offers were mistakes. The company must be happy with her performance.

Her Hoodie buzzed her to leave the bus, and she tucked it back and rang for her stop. Joni leaned against the diner's facade, reading a paperback. She looked up and smiled when she saw Rosemary, sliding the book into her bag.

"I hope you weren't waiting long," said Rosemary.

Joni shook her head. "Nope. Walked faster than I expected, but it's a nice day, and I never mind a few minutes to read. Look, um, I'm going to be direct: I like you, but I think I made a mistake the other night."

Lightning shot through Rosemary's chest. Joni continued. "I thought maybe we'd walk, get some lunch, go to the show tonight, but maybe take it a little slower? You haven't even mentioned how long you're staying around, and I have a tendency to throw my heart into things."

Rosemary bit her lip. She didn't want to say she didn't know how much longer she'd be in town. Didn't know if her nerve had been fortified by alcohol or the wonderful show or something else that might not be present again. She nodded, and Joni exhaled.

"Okay, good. I'm glad that's settled. Anyway, I've been trying to think of what I wanted to show you. Do you want to see where all the jazz musicians played? The area was bad for a while, but it's being restored. Not with jazz clubs, of course, or none that aren't hidden, anyway." She gestured in one direction, then another. "Or I can show you the Peabody Library. It's gorgeous. Closed to the public now, but I have a friend who works security there who would let you have a peek . . ."

"Whatever you want to show me, honest." *I have something to ask you, too,* she didn't say.

"Okay. We can figure it out as we go."

Joni started walking. Rosemary was caught a step behind, but jogged a few steps to meet her stride. These blocks between the diner and the 2020 had become familiar, at least. She wondered what it was like to know a city well, or a neighborhood.

"There's a lot still wrong, obviously, but in some ways it's gotten better here since we were kids. My neighborhood growing up was over there." She pointed southwest. "It was pretty rough Before, but by the time I was in high school, with better schools online and less gentrification some of the disparities had evened out. My mom worked, so I went to school from a friend's house. I know it's bad form in some circles to say anything is better in the After, and there are new things that are fucked up, and some of the same old problems, but there are a few things that've improved. I don't think they should have closed everything down, just that there've been some interesting side effects that I don't entirely hate. I'm sure if they relaxed the laws and let us open clubs and museums and stuff again, we could fix some of the other stuff, too."

"My parents always told me people were safer with the congregation laws in effect. You think people have changed?" She'd learned in school that the time Before was terrifying and anxious, full of shootings and bombings and crowd-borne disease.

"I do. Look around. Kids have access to good schools, regardless of where they live. People have better access to jobs and housing. We're working on federal basic income. There's way less desperation."

"My Hoodie still tells me to avoid certain streets."

"I'm not saying everything is perfect. You'd have to have seen the Before to know how much better this After is, here at least. The prison cycle's got a flat tire. The rents went back to manageable when all the rich people left. City resources were reallocated more fairly."

Joni walked her through a community garden on the next block, talking about cleaning the city soil. Rosemary could hold her own on gardening, but she kept wondering when she'd have a chance to raise the StageHoloLive proposition. She tried to steer the conversation back to music.

"Your band is the only one I've seen here that's all women. Is that on purpose?"

"Yeah. There's something about playing with all women that's . . . a different dynamic. An all-queer band like Luce's changes the dynamic, too. And Luce curates her space in a way that puts us in the majority, which is nice. She says it's one of the perks of being in charge. Some people think it's a political statement, too, but that didn't really come into it."

"Huh. I don't even know what you mean by a 'political statement,' let alone the rest of that."

Joni laughed, then stopped when she realized Rosemary wasn't joking. "I can't ever decide if you're adorably naive or if I should feel sadder about it. Or maybe happy that you don't know why this matters."

"Educate me?"

"Maybe later. You do get why the 2020 is so special, though? Luce created a place where it doesn't matter at all who's performing on a given night. It's not driven by who can sell the most tickets, or what you play, only that you care enough to throw yourself into it. That doesn't exist everywhere."

Rosemary still didn't understand. She thought it might be a dig at StageHolo, or at something from the distant past, but she didn't want to clarify and risk getting an earful about her employers. She changed the subject back to urban farming.

They had lunch in a little Ethiopian restaurant. Rosemary had never had Ethiopian food, but she let Joni order, and followed her lead in eating it. The flavors were unusual but comforting, sour and savory. She even managed not to stress over the fact that they were both tearing and dipping their bread into the same mounds of split peas and beef. Neither mentioned Wednesday night.

Joni chatted on about the city instead. Her day job involved preventing homelessness, and she tied the tour together in a context of racial history, queer history, social history, politics, and even music history that left Rosemary exhausted and amazed.

"I had no idea," Rosemary admitted. "I thought a city was just a place with more people crowded in together."

"Stick around, kid," said Joni. "There's hope for you yet."

An Ethiopian teenager stood in the corner rapping to prerecorded tracks while they ate. Rosemary must have been staring, because after a while, Joni leaned over. "It's not *music* that's illegal, you know. Just gathering to listen to it. He's totally legit."

It was easy to forget that. When Joni went to find the bathroom, Rosemary took the opportunity to Hoodie up and see if he was online. She blinked past an ad for Superwally's Foods of the World drone subscription, but got an error when she tried to get the artist's name based on the song he was playing: not in the StageHolo or Superwally databases.

She mentioned it as Joni slid back into her seat. Having established that she knew nothing was liberating; she could ask so many questions, freed of the burden of pretending worldliness.

"You do know there's still music changing hands on other platforms?"

"I thought everything existed between those two databases

unless it hadn't been uploaded yet. I mean, I understand Live is selective, but I don't get why recordings wouldn't be available through Superwally or basic StageHolo."

Joni still didn't laugh at her, but she gave a curious look. "Not everyone buys into that system."

"Huh. I mean, my parents don't, but I thought that was only on the consumer end. Like you noncomm people."

"Noncomm is a philosophy. It's not anticonsumerism. We still buy stuff, but we don't want our purchases tracked, and we don't think we always need to be in contact and trackable ourselves. You said you tried to find his song while I was away from the table?"

Rosemary nodded.

"So now Superwally and StageHolo both know you're on the lookout for Ethiopian hip-hop, and they know you're at this restaurant. Even if you're paying for ad-free, they're adding to their profile of you, waiting for a moment to sell it back to you in some way, or sell you to somebody else."

"What's so bad about that? I'd rather get ads for stuff I'm interested in than for stuff I'm not."

"Sure, but what if you want to research something without your information being commodified? What if you don't want to put money in the pockets of a company that donates to sketchy political candidates?"

Rosemary lost the thread. "They do what?"

"They give money to candidates on both sides of the aisle who want to keep the status quo. Candidates who want to keep the congregation laws in place, the curfews, anything that keeps people inside and using their products."

"How do you know?"

"It's still on the free web, public knowledge, if you know where to look. Look, you obviously enjoy their products. I'm not trying to tear down your idols, but you should know they have a vested interest in keeping you scared. The fact that you're here with me, eating new food in a new place, gives me hope. You don't have to give up your Hoodie: just open your eyes to the fact that you're being bought and sold along with whatever you buy when you're in there. Me, I'd rather work on making the world out here a better place for when people come back to it."

"So where do you buy music?"

"You mean other than from the artists directly at shows? That's it for me, but there are sites. If you hack a Hoodie or phone to disable the proprietary stuff, you can shop at a bunch of cool places." Joni tore the last sodden piece of injera in two and handed one piece to Rosemary, balling the other and stuffing it in her mouth.

They spent the rest of the afternoon walking off the heavy meal. Rosemary tried to absorb what Joni had said. Were congregation laws so bad? There hadn't been any bombs or major outbreaks since they'd been enacted. She'd grown up feeling safe. Still, here she was, so maybe safety wasn't everything. Anyway, why care that ads tracked your interests if you had nothing to hide? There were issues she still didn't understand, clearly. Meanwhile, Joni showed her an art gallery where you looked at art in person, instead of through bot cameras, and a bookstore with shelving units on wheels.

"They have speakers and discussion panels here a couple of times a month." Joni pantomimed rolling the shelves away.

"On what?"

"The economy, the future, books, politics, art . . . you name it."

"And I'm guessing the reason you'd go hear somebody talk instead of watching them online is that these talks aren't available in hoodspace? Either the speakers are noncomm or there's a reason they're not online?"

Joni grinned. "You're starting to get it! Come on, I have one more thing to show you."

They walked north and east. Rosemary still turned her head constantly to try to catch the sights: tiny ethnic grocery stores, coffee shops, restaurants, hair salons, all small enough to skirt the congregation laws.

They turned onto a residential street. A few houses down, Joni slid the latch of a wire gate and let Rosemary into a yard, more crocuses than grass. Someone stood in a corner—no, that was a gold-painted mannequin waving to her from beneath a small dead tree mosaicked roots to crown in blue glass. Another mannequin sat in a claw-footed bathtub, up to her neck in dirt, which Rosemary guessed would be full of flowers in another month or two. Where would she be by then?

"One of my roommates is an artist," Joni said.

They entered through a small vestibule ringed with mannequin-hand coat hooks. Rosemary pulled up her Hoodie to see the place as the residents wanted it seen.

"No Veneer here, Rosemary. All the art is here for real."

She'd spent her whole adult life wishing she had a proper Hoodie to keep up with the world, and now that she had one, she hung out with people who had another idea entirely.

They walked through a dining room with walls covered in text, tiny faded notes in multiple colors of marker—more art, Rosemary supposed—and entered a tiny kitchen.

"Hey, Javi, is there enough for an extra person?" Joni asked.

The man in the kitchen, Javi, presumably, was stirring a large pot. "No problem! There's plenty, as long as she likes lentil stew."

"Excellent. Rosemary, this is Javi. It's his night to cook, lucky for you. He's the best in the house."

"Nice to meet you." Rosemary contemplated whether she'd ever eaten a stranger's cooking before. Not counting restaurants, of course, but that was different. Everything looked clean enough.

She stood out of the way while Javi stirred in spices and Joni took bowls from the cabinet. A bulletin board on the refrigerator held chore and meal charts.

Two other people materialized the moment Javi declared his stew done, and Rosemary was introduced to Lexa and Clothilde. Clothilde was the artist, and Lexa owned the house. Rosemary followed their lead and filled a bowl straight from the stewpot. She still felt full from lunch, but it smelled delicious. She wouldn't even dwell on being the fourth person to touch the ladle.

They all sat at the dining room table together to eat, talking about how they'd spent the day. Clothilde teased Javi for making stew off-season, and Javi retorted that there was no wrong season for stew. Lexa, an older trans woman who worked as an administrator at a health clinic, was celebrating a new grant for her workplace. Joni listed all the places she'd taken Rosemary, and they critiqued her choices and added more sights for her to see.

"I love when my dishes night coincides with Javi's cooking night," Joni said, stacking the bowls at meal's end. "He's a one-pot cook, and he cleans as he goes. Not like some people around here."

Clothilde laughed. "You're talking about yourself? The kitchen always looks like a hurricane hit it when you're done cooking."

"Can I help?" Rosemary held on to her own bowl.

Joni snatched it from her. "Nah. There's a machine."

Rosemary trailed her into the kitchen anyway, still awkward despite the warm welcome. "Is that why you brought me here? To show me you live with a bunch of people who treat each other like family?"

"No, but that's sweet, and I hate that it's a surprise to you. If you want to help, you can dole out one more serving in a fresh bowl."

Rosemary did as she was told, as Joni loaded the dishwasher, then emptied the leftovers into a large glass jar.

"Come on," Joni said. "I can wash the pot later."

She followed through the dining room, which now smelled like stew, up a stew-scented staircase. The upstairs hallway was narrow and low ceilinged. Joni knocked on the second door on the right.

They stepped in and closed the door behind them. This time, Rosemary resisted the urge to look for a Veneer and accepted it at face value. The room was small but cozy, lit by a desk lamp. It was hotter than outside, probably from the electronics: the flat surfaces were all covered with what looked like science experiments. Boxes with dials and wires connected to other boxes, amplifiers, a small keyboard. Fans whirred amid the other machine noise.

A woman sat in a desk chair in a tank top and shorts, legs

crossed, head bent over a circuit board. She swiveled her chair to greet them.

"Rosemary, Katja. Katja, Rosemary." Joni put the bowl of stew on the desk beside the electronics.

Katja waved a greeting, then raised an eyebrow at Joni.

"Rosemary, I wanted to introduce you to Katja to show you there's amazing music being made here that doesn't translate well to your formats of choice. K, do you mind being used as an example?"

Katja shrugged. "I never mind a chance to play. Bass is in the closet."

Joni rummaged in a large wardrobe and pulled out an electric bass, which she plugged into one of the amps before sitting on the bed. "Key?"

"I'm feeling D minor." Katja pulled up her Hoodie—Joni had said not all her friends were noncomm—and fiddled with wires and boxes for a minute. A computerized beat emerged from another amp. Rosemary sat on the far edge of the bed from Joni, the only other clear space.

Joni started to play a simple bass riff, nothing like the sound she had ripped from her cello, though she still carried the same intensity of purpose that Rosemary had found so entrancing. Then the other instrument started, one she didn't recognize, something bowed mated with something brassy. Rosemary turned, remembering she was supposed to be listening to Katja this time, not Joni. She expected to see Katja playing an instrument, but her hands were empty. The sound itself came from a small amplifier on the desk.

The pitch changed, and Rosemary looked closer, determined to figure out what she'd missed. Katja massaged her own wrist and . . . was that it? Yes. She ran her hand up and down her other arm, drawing notes, changing the pitch and velocity. Somehow it all worked with Joni's bass. She slapped her own shoulders, her forearms, her thighs. Her entire body made music. Everywhere she touched produced sound. Rosemary looked for something like Kurt Zell's keyboard tattoo.

Katja held out her right arm, and Rosemary realized it was an invitation. She was repulsed for a moment at the idea of touching a stranger so intimately, but Joni whispered, "Go on, it's okay," without missing a note, and Rosemary pushed her fear aside and reached out.

She used one finger to stroke Katja's forearm. Katja shuddered, and the amp emitted a ripple of notes, barely audible, all in key. "Harder, please. That tickled."

Three fingers, pressed down. A chord, insistent, dying the second she lifted her hand away. Katja smiled and pushed her chair backward again, to indicate she no longer needed Rosemary's touch. She played for a couple more minutes, then nodded to Joni, who ran through her riff two more times, then stopped. The beat kept going, but both women looked at Rosemary expectantly.

"Wow," she said. "How do you do that?"

"Trigger implants under my skin. Processor translates them all into key and then out to the amp." Katja leaned over and hit a button to cut off the beat.

"Like that Kurtz guy?"

"Not 'like that Kurtz guy.' That ass stole my idea."

Joni slapped the bass strings, making a rude noise. "But if he hadn't stolen your idea, you'd never have gotten a better one."

"This is way cooler than his little keyboard," Rosemary said, hoping to repair whatever insult she'd made mentioning him.

"True." Katja ran her hand across her forearm again, though it no longer made a sound. "And he wouldn't have gotten kicked out of the house, and you wouldn't have moved in, so I guess it's a win for everyone."

"Now show her the vid," Joni said.

Katja pulled up her Hoodie, and Rosemary took the hint to do the same. Katja pushed a video her way.

"Are you watching it?" Joni asked.

"Give her a sec."

The clip lasted a minute. It had been filmed at the 2020, on a third party's Hoodie, since she was seeing Katja from a few feet away. Rosemary watched hood-Katja throw herself into the crowd, allowing them to play her the way Rosemary had. They were respectful, but not as shy as she had been. It felt intimate, as it had in real life, but also voyeuristic to watch other people do the touching on a recording. She shut it off.

"That's amazing, and I get why you're showing it to me. The video doesn't capture it. But SHL . . ."

"SHL would program it so avatars could touch an avatar of me, and it would lose all meaning."

Rosemary closed her eyes and pictured the code, then tried to picture Katja in the Bloom Bar. She imagined reaching out, avatar to avatar, and how the illusion would crumble. They were right: not everything was meant to be an SHL experience. She already knew that, had already been through the motions of choosing bands specifically for hoodspace, but none of those decisions had been based on a performance like this. You had to be in the room to experience this tactile connection. She understood: sometimes the performance was the music, and vice versa, and the two couldn't be separated.

23

ROSEMARY

Hold On, Hold On

They walked back to the 2020 in silence. Rosemary had too much to say, so she didn't speak.

When they reached the door, she mustered, "I had a wonderful day. Thanks for showing me around."

Joni smiled. "There's more I can show you if you want to do it again sometime."

"That would be lovely."

The evening's first band was a teenaged-looking sextet of assorted gender presentations playing hip-hop on toy instruments: a plastic drum kit, a plastic ukulele, a tiny xylophone, etc. They turned their joke instruments into a catchy sound, and the ukulele player was a talented rapper. They all wore Superwally warehouse uniforms—ironically, Rosemary thought, since if the techwear in the uniforms was still activated they'd be fired—and the first song gave a hilarious takedown of Superwally customer service. What if one of them was Jeremy from Quality Control? Rosemary laughed out loud at the thought. She didn't think SHL would condone mockery of Superwally, but she made a mental note to find out their name and mention it as one to watch. Now that she had an idea how SHL worked, she thought it would be easy enough to add other bands as she found them.

After a couple of songs, she spotted Joni chatting with someone she didn't recognize, a stocky black guy with a shaved head, and made her way over.

"Rosemary, this is Mark Grail. He's been coming here since Luce started bringing in music. He took most of the pictures on Luce's walls. Mark, this is Rosemary. She's visiting from out of town. I was just saying I hadn't seen Mark in a while," Joni said.

"And I said I got a little burned out on the scene. There's only so many times I can watch the same bands in the same room."

"What did you do instead?" asked Rosemary.

"Hung out in a jazz joint for a while. Found a good monthly house concert."

"And why did you come back?"

"Because he missed me," Joni teased.

Mark waved her off. "My buddy Dex is in the next band. It's their first time here."

"I've been meaning to ask," said Rosemary. "How do you know who's playing on any given night? I've been trying and trying to figure it out."

"There's a calendar on the fridge upstairs."

"A calendar?"

"Paper. Old like Main Street, but it works."

"Okay, but how did Mark know his friend's band was playing without coming here to look on the fridge?"

Mark smiled. "I think it went something like, 'Hey, Mark, my band's first show is Saturday night. Please come.' "

"I wonder if I'll ever get to a point where I'm not asking stupid questions."

"That wasn't stupid," said Joni. "Silly, not stupid. Just because we don't have Hoodies doesn't mean we don't communicate."

"And not all of us are noncomm." Mark gestured at his Hoodie. "I just choose to leave it down when I venture out into the real world. Like you, I see."

A siren whooped, and Rosemary glanced at the stage to see what the teenage band was playing now. A few other people looked in that direction as well. They were still on their toy instruments.

"Must have been passing by outside," said Joni.

Another whoop. Then another. At the stage's back, a tear in the paper covering the window let through a small arc of blue and red light.

"I'm going to go take a look outside. Mark, why don't you open the back door, to be safe?" Joni headed up the stairs.

"There's a back door?" Rosemary asked.

"Under the porch. For band load-ins and wheelchairs and people who can't climb stairs." Mark pointed in the direction he was already walking. "And safety's sake. Luce has been around long enough to think of that stuff. No firetraps."

Rosemary followed him a few steps and then stopped, unsure what to do next.

Joni returned. Rosemary took a step toward her, but Joni walked past her as if she were invisible. She walked onto the stage, interrupting the band in midsong. "Hey, everyone, Code Blue. There's no danger, but I need you all to quietly leave out the kitchen door or the back. Code Blue."

She made a slashing motion across her neck and the sound guy cut off the mics. For a second, nobody moved. Then a middle-aged white guy pushed past the stage and dashed up the stairs. The crowd followed, moving as a wave toward the two doors, flowing around Rosemary, jostling her. Her stomach dropped, and she found herself rooted to the spot. It couldn't be a fire. There were fire alarms, but they hadn't gone off. If somebody was hurt they wouldn't evacuate; they'd leave everyone where they were. If fire and ambulance were ruled out, that left police. In any of those scenarios, if Joni said to leave, she should go. If her feet worked.

A loud but muffled voice came through the ceiling.

"Turn around!" said somebody on the stairs. "They're coming in the front door." The tide swirled. Rosemary was shoved against the merchandise table.

"Stop pushing," someone said, but nobody did. She squeezed into the alcove she had sat in the first night, trying to put some space between herself and the others. The crowd pushed toward the door. She pressed herself back, deeper. Whatever it was that everyone was trying to escape, it couldn't be as bad as getting trampled or crushed. She waited, listening to the shouts upstairs.

The last audience members trickled out. More footsteps on the stairs above her head. A small chunk of plaster dislodged.

"Anybody down here?" somebody asked.

"Status?" she heard over a walkie-talkie.

"They all went out the back. Basement's empty. You catch any?"

"A few."

"Enough to make the count?"

"Probably. Find anything?"

"Some sound equipment. Definitely being operated as a club. I'll be up as soon as I take a few pictures."

Rosemary stayed put. She hoped Joni had gotten out, and Luce, who must have been in the building somewhere. She even worried for Alice. She pictured the scene: Alice sitting in her living room, telling the cops she was home alone. Alice taking on the entire police force single-handedly. Rosemary wondered if one had dressed as an attendee, and if Alice had sniffed them out before they made it through the door.

She had no idea how much time passed. Ten minutes, an hour. An eternity. The blue and red slivers of light reflected on the stage wall until they didn't anymore. Distant voices drifted downstairs through the disturbing quiet until they were silent, too. She'd never have imagined she might get to a point where she missed a crowd.

At some point, in the millionth minute of eternity, a hinge squeal, then the tumble of a lock. A moment later, Luce appeared in the room, pulling the plug on the lights that marked the stage.

"Are they gone?" Rosemary asked.

Luce dropped the cord and whirled. "Jesus, Rosemary. You nearly gave me a heart attack. Everybody's gone."

"I was afraid you got arrested." Rosemary stepped from the alcove, rolling her head side to side to unkink her neck.

"Not arrested. Cited. Closed down."

"Closed down like permanently?"

"Probably. I was stupid to run this from my house. Better to rent or squat somewhere, so when they cite you, you can move on to another place. Me, this is all I've got. Now the city can seize it if they decide I was involved, which I was, of course, and if they think that's the best way to keep me from doing it again, which it is."

Rosemary couldn't find a word to convey how awful the prospect was, and she'd only been here a short time. This wasn't another shuttered storefront; this was a community. Anything she said would be inadequate. "Shit."

"Shit," Luce agreed. "Do you want a drink? I need a drink."

"Sure, but shouldn't we be doing something? Calling lawyers? Making sure everyone's okay?"

"You're sweet. As far as I know, they only arrested two guys stupid enough to break away and run because they were carrying hard drugs. A few more got cited for congregating, but that's a misdemeanor, and I should have enough to cover their fines. Did you see who got people out in time?"

"Joni. She told that Mark guy to open the back door. She isn't in trouble, is she?"

"I don't think so. I didn't see any sign of her. Come on."

Rosemary followed Luce to the second-floor apartment.

"What can I get you? I'm going for whiskey myself."

She'd never tried it before. "Whiskey is fine."

Luce opened a cabinet in her living room, poured two amber tumblers. Shot one, poured another. She gave the other glass to Rosemary, put hers on the coffee table, and flopped face-first onto the couch. Rosemary chose the same chair she'd sat in the last time.

She sipped her drink and winced. It had an eye-watering burn to it, but the aftereffect left her strangely calm.

"What I don't get," said Luce after a minute, eyes still closed. "What I don't get is why they busted us on this night of all nights. That was about the quietest band in the rotation. There's no way anyone complained."

It wasn't a question, so Rosemary sipped her drink and stayed silent.

"It's not the end of the month, and they didn't go out of their way to bust anyone, so I don't think it was a quota thing. If there's somebody wanting to be paid off, they didn't make it known."

"Have you had to pay someone off before?"

"Nah. I went to so much trouble to make sure we didn't bother anyone. Soundproofing. Shows don't go super late. I own the vacants on both sides and the only people who sleep in them are in bands that play here. Nobody knows about us who shouldn't. There's nobody fighting that I know of, and even if they were, they'd take it out on each other, not the show space. This is just shitting where you eat. Sorry—did I say something?"

"No—I, uh, it's been an upsetting night." Rosemary's stomach flipped. She didn't want to put her horrible thought into words. "Do you mind if I use your bathroom?"

Luce waved her glass toward the hall.

In the bathroom, Rosemary raised her Hoodie and pinged Recruiter Management.

"Hi, Rosemary, what's up?" The same generic avatar spawned, though she had no way to know if the same person controlled it. "We've been contacted by those Mosquito guys, and Kurt Zell. Nice work."

"The performance space where I've been recruiting was raided tonight. While I was in it. We didn't have anything to do with that, did we?"

A frown crossed his perfect face. "Let me check."

For a moment, his avatar stood vacant, not blinking or moving other than the fake wind through his fake hair. "I think there's been a misunderstanding," he said when he returned. "That wasn't supposed to happen until next Saturday."

"What do you mean 'supposed to happen'? What wasn't supposed to happen?"

"You were supposed to be given until tomorrow to sign any of the four acts we discussed. They weren't supposed to be raided until after relationships were established. Somebody entered the wrong date."

"I don't understand."

"We owe you an apology. You weren't arrested, were you? Do you need me to transfer you to Legal?"

Her frustration bested her. "No. I wasn't arrested, but some people I know probably were, and this whole place is probably shutting permanently. Can you explain to me what's going on? Really slowly?"

Luce called down the hallway, "Are you okay?"

"I'm fine!" Rosemary called back without putting her hood down, making Management wince at the volume. Then, to the avatar, "Explain. Please."

"Standard protocol. Recruiter goes in, finds new talent, recruits talent. Once everyone is on board . . ."

". . . You shut the place down so they can't compete with you, and the audiences are forced to see their favorite bands on SHL instead of in person, because you've taken that option away."

"We, Rosemary. You work here."

"We." Oh, God. "So what do people in my position do now? Quit in disgust? Is this why there was an opening for me, you burn through recruiters?"

"Some quit. Some realize their outrage is temporary but quitting is permanent, and buckle down and get on with their job. You didn't do anything wrong. You found some great acts—"

"Bands," said Rosemary. "Not acts."

Management continued as if she hadn't interrupted. "—and you hooked them up with us. They'll be so much better off here. Think about it. All the fans they can reach. They're spinning their wheels playing for the same people in the same city. Please tell us you got to talk to Luce Cannon before the police came?"

"As a matter of fact, I didn't. I was going to talk with her tonight."

"Shit. Did she get arrested? Will you be able to find her again? I can get Legal on assistance for her, too, if you think that would help."

Find her yourself, she wanted to say. "I know where she is."

He looked relieved. The first genuine emotion she thought she had ever gotten from him. "Thanks. We know it can be upsetting the first time you hear this, but it's a good system, we promise."

"Really? Does this 'good system' take into account the fact that Luce owns the venue you closed? Is that supposed to help me convince her to do business with us?"

"Ah. Um." He seemed flustered. Left his avatar empty again momentarily, returned contrite. "Was that in the information you gave us?"

"It wasn't, because I didn't know it was relevant. You sent me here without full information."

"It works best that way for the first trip. Otherwise the recruiter gets nervous and telegraphs."

"This is messed up. What if people stampeded to get out and somebody got hurt? What if I got hurt?"

He shrugged. "It works. Nobody's ever been injured as far as we know. Anyway, maybe now she won't be tied to her venue. Tell her we'd love to have her on board. Give her some bright sides."

Rosemary put her hands to her head. "I don't think she's going to be as enthusiastic as you imagine, but I'll give it a try."

"Thanks for being a team player."

She dropped her hood again without saying another word.

The bathroom swayed. She wished she could have told him where to shove it, to say she wanted no more part in this. At least not in putting people in danger and closing performance spaces. She considered her beautiful hotel room, the weeks of meals. She would be in debt forever trying to pay it off if she left without completing a single assignment. She couldn't walk away. Anyway, connecting musicians with SHL was still a good thing. Maybe? Getting them the huge audiences they deserved. Putting them in the position to live off their music. Those were all positives.

She composed herself. Walked back into the living room, where Luce still lay on the couch, a pillow over her head. She sat again and drained her glass. There was no other way to do this.

"Luce, I need to tell you something."

The pillow shifted to one side, and Luce raised her head. She looked exhausted, and not in the sated postshow way. Her tone was light, but her voice was weary. "You're a cop after all. You've been here undercover this whole time and now you're going to arrest me."

"No."

"Good. I don't think I could take that."

This wasn't going to be easy. "The night is still young. Can I ask you a serious question?"

Luce levered herself back into a sitting position. "Hit me."

"I had something to ask you, before any of this happened."

"Okay . . ."

"You said the other night if you could get half the attention you got for 'Blood and Diamonds' for 'Choose,' you thought you'd be able to make a difference. Were you serious?"

"Yeah, of course. It's the best song I've ever written."

"Do you still want to get your music in front of new audiences? Big ones?"

"Sure. Why?"

Rosemary took a deep breath. "What if I offered that to you?"

"What are you, a genie? A hidden-camera-show host?"

"Not a genie, and I don't know what that second one is. What if I, uh, could put you in touch with StageHoloLive? If I told you they were interested in you and your new stuff."

Luce stood and poured herself another drink without offering Rosemary one. "Did they say both of those things? Me and my new stuff?"

"They were happy to think whatever you'd put out recently wasn't widely distributed yet, so they could rerelease it in a package with live stuff, and, ah, 'a rediscovery special.' "

"A rediscovery special. Do you know what that means?"

"They want to introduce you to a new generation of listeners?"

"They want to package me as a nostalgia act. They want me to play the same music I played back then. You've heard me. Do I sound the same?"

"No," Rosemary admitted. "It's not even the same genre."

"I wrote one good folk-pop song, and the next thing I knew I was playing sit-down theaters all over the country for a company that only knew how to market me if I stayed in their little box forever. Now StageHoloLive wants me but only if I get back in the little box again?"

"They didn't say that. They were excited to know you're still playing. I'm sure you could set terms."

"Set terms for what?"

"Whatever you want. Money, artistic freedom. You can quit your day job and make music full-time again. There are so many people who'd love to hear you."

"In their little hood-worlds and their living rooms."

Rosemary bit her lip. "You play for the same people night after night. You've been holding a wake for music you think is dead."

"Do you really think that's what we're doing?" The weariness was gone from Luce's voice, replaced by something hard-edged. Disbelief, disappointment. Conviction. "I don't think you do, and I don't think we are. Playing for the same people every week is a different challenge from touring. I have to make every night interesting. It pushes me to keep writing."

"Your songs deserve a bigger audience. If I hadn't come here I'd think you were still 'Blood and Diamonds,' not all your amazing new stuff. I'd never have heard you again if I hadn't come here."

"And why did you come? You said you were here to check out music. You meant for StageHolo, not for yourself." It wasn't a question.

"For both. I'd never have been able to leave home if it hadn't been for this job. I wanted to go places. I wanted to hear music I hadn't heard before, and see stuff I hadn't seen."

"Ha. They sent you on tour." There was no humor in her laugh. "Did they know I was here all along? How did you find my place?"

"Aran Randall told me to come here."

"That figures."

"He said there was great music happening. He was right."

"And you thought you'd come in and convince me to leave everything I had going here? Or did you arrange the raid tonight, too, to give me impetus?"

"I had no idea about the raid," Rosemary said with what she hoped was believable sincerity. "I swear. And Aran didn't mention you, only the 2020. I was the one who decided which bands to pass along."

"Wait—so if I agreed to sign, but only as 'Harriet' without the nostalgia factor, would the offer still stand?"

"*Mine* stands," said Rosemary. "I told them about you because you make amazing music, not because of your name."

"But you recognized me your first night. Did it color your opinion at all?"

"It made me excited to hear you, but I wouldn't have bothered telling them about you if you'd sucked."

"That's comforting. Did you make this offer to any other bands here, or just me?"

"You, the Handsome Mosquitoes, and Kurtz. Both of them have live auditions arranged. I was supposed to offer Joni's band as well, but I never got the chance."

"So even if we hadn't been raided tonight, you were taking my bands."

"Some of your bands, and only if they wanted to go. I have a feeling Joni wouldn't have been interested."

"I'd guess you're right. Okay. What's the next step?"

"The next step?"

"Do you tell them I'm interested, or do I put on your hood thingy, or do they send lawyers to darken my doorstep?"

"You're interested? For real? I can reach them now if you'd like."

"Not tonight. Jesus. Come back tomorrow after I get some sleep and we can figure it out. Right now you should go home."

Rosemary let Luce walk her from the apartment, out the front door. "See you tomorrow," she said. "I'm sorry this place is over."

"Me, too, Rosemary Laws. Me, too."

24

ROSEMARY

Walk Away

Walking back to the hotel drunk wasn't the smartest idea, but when she checked the time, it was later than the last buses, and she didn't feel like waiting for a single-cell. She was waiting for the elevator, debating whether to send a message about Luce now or let Management stew on what they had done, when a hand touched her back. She jumped.

"Nice place," said Joni. She put her hands on her hips and made an exaggerated show of examining the vestibule. "Is this where your friends live?"

"You scared me."

"Good."

"Why are you angry?"

"Because after the police left, I called a cop I know, and she said the raid tonight was a tip called in from outside the city. You're the only one who's shown up lately from outside the city. And I went back to check on Luce, and I saw you walking out, and I thought I'd follow you a couple blocks, but you kept walking, so I kept walking to keep an eye on you, and sure enough, here we are at a hotel that I'm doubting is where your friends live."

"Can I explain?"

"Please."

"Do you want to come upstairs so the lobby doesn't call security because your voice is raised?"

Joni shrugged and didn't speak. Rosemary took the opportunity to cancel her elevator call for a single-person party, and call again for two, with an extra thumb-swipe to confirm.

She'd finally figured out how to open the shades the day before, and had left them open. When they got into the room, Joni walked straight to the window. "I haven't seen the city from this angle since I was a kid. It's beautiful."

"Yeah. I stare out there every night."

Neither spoke for a minute, then Joni broke the silence. "So. Explain?"

"I wasn't the one who called for the raid. I swear I had no idea they would do that. I didn't ever tell them where the 2020 was—not even the name!" She wracked her brain for anything she might have said to betray Luce and her club. "I work for SHL, but my job is to recruit new talent."

"Are you good at it?"

"I don't know. This was my first assignment."

"Were you successful? Did you bring back heads for your trophy wall?"

No point lying. "Kurtz. The Handsome Mosquitoes. Luce. And I was going to ask you, only I never found a way to ask."

"Yeah?"

"Your band is awesome. There isn't anybody on SHL doing what you're doing."

"Well, thanks. Did Luce really say yes?"

"She said she'd talk to them."

"She said that before or after the raid?"

"After. Joni, I really, truly didn't know they were going to shut the place down."

"Huh. So you told them about all of us, but you never mentioned the club?"

"I didn't. They knew I had found a place here, but I only sent them names of bands and vid—" Oh. "The videos. I sent them footage of Kurtz, but I didn't scrub the location. I forgot about the metadata." She sat on the bed, covered her face with her hands. "I can't believe I did this. But they would have found a way no matter what, I think. Whether or not I had done something stupid. They'd have tracked my Hoodie or asked the bands or something. I didn't know 'til tonight, but I think they do that everywhere." Rosemary didn't open her eyes. She didn't want to look at Joni. "So, do you have any interest? In being a trophy on my wall?"

"Being a StageHolo musician? No, thanks. I can't believe you're still asking."

"You won't even consider it? Making music full-time? Getting paid? Getting your songs in front of millions of people?"

"I told you the night we met. They won't want me. They'll want to fix me in ways I'm not interested in being fixed."

"You won't know until you try."

"No. I do. I'd rather play in my living room for six people than be a moneymaker for a company that deliberately ends scenes like ours or tells us we need to work on our sex appeal. They don't understand that music isn't just the notes we play. It's the room and the band and the crowd. I'm not interested in faking any of that."

"But the room is gone." Rosemary's fault, even if she hadn't called it in. "Maybe I can convince them to tell the cops it was a mistake. They raided the wrong place. I can still get Luce out of trouble."

"You do not get to fix this, Rosemary. You broke it, but it's not yours to fix. You've done enough damage. That room is gone, but there are others. Or there will be. Maybe I'll start one, but if I do, you're not invited." There were tears in Joni's eyes, but she blinked them away. "What are you going to do? You've got your bands. What happens now?"

"I hadn't considered what's next. I guess they grade my performance and then send me somewhere else."

"To poach more bands and ruin more live venues? Force them

further underground until nobody can find them at all and everyone has to pony up to StageHoloLive?"

"I don't want to go back to Superwally. What else am I supposed to do? I think I'm good at choosing bands—and yes, I understand not all of you want to be chosen—but I don't want to shut places down. This isn't what I thought I'd be doing at all." She paused. "I'm so sorry, Joni. For everything."

"You should be. Whatever you do right now isn't going to make up for it. Remember that."

Both of them were silent for a while, until Joni shook her head and walked out without saying another word. If Rosemary had known a single thing to say to make things better, she would have said it. She walked over to the window. It faced the wrong way for the sunrise, but the building across the street reflected it back at an angle, orange-gold on glass. Joni was ant-sized at ground level. An angry ant-sized woman. Rosemary followed her progress up the street until she disappeared from view.

PART THREE

25

LUCE

Are You Ready

Any note can be played over any chord and any chord can be played over any note. I read that in a book about jazz. It doesn't quite jibe with the Neil Young solo theory; that one implies there is such thing as a wrong note, one you move through if you hit it: dissonant, discordant. A pebble, a splinter, something stuck between the song's teeth. Yes, live songs have teeth, and teeth are messy things, tearing and rending and helping spit ideas into the world. A live song has notes that don't want to be there, that call attention to themselves in their wrongness. A botched chord, a chorus taken too soon, a forgotten lyric. I love those moments.

Sometimes everything goes well, too. It doesn't matter where you are, or how many people are in the room. The stars align, the band locks in, the audience gets what you're trying to do, and you transcend bodies and bad days. The song is you, and you are more than yourself.

If I can only express myself in song (or in words that describe song) please take these notes as a eulogy for people and places I've lost or left behind: my family, and that entire community that I grew up in, which took care of everyone but had no space for me;

April, whose friends never held a memorial; the basement in Baltimore where I rebuilt myself, where I redefined community for myself in a way that I actually felt included. They're all gone now. They simmer under my surface, boil over as chords wrung with bleeding fingers from a battered old guitar.

When Rosemary came back for me the day after the raid, I didn't answer the door.

I watched her from behind my curtains on the second floor, waited for her to pound harder, call attention, try going around the back again. She did none of those things. She knocked, then paused, then knocked again, three times, harder. She looked up once, and I recognized the look on her face, even if I hadn't seen it on her before. She looked hopeful.

For a moment, just that moment, I hated her. What gave her the right to be hopeful, when she had so casually, so effortlessly, destroyed everything I'd created? She hadn't meant to, I know; she thought she was helping. It was my fault for thinking I'd seen myself in her: the desire to exert some control over circumstances, to not be bound by a life planned by well-meaning others, to find community of her own choosing. I wasn't sure how much of that was her, and how much I had overlaid.

I hadn't hated many people in my life; even when I ran from my family, it hadn't been hate that drove me; it had been the fear that I would never get to be myself if I stayed. Their refusal to talk to me afterward had been on them. Pain, not hate.

Hate was reserved for front-page villains. Abstractions: the pox, the bombers, the bombs, the gunmen, the guns, the chaos they sowed, the politicians who wielded restriction in the name of freedom and safety, or the ones who didn't stop them, or the ones who were sure it would only be temporary. I could hate StageHolo and the other companies that sold the restriction back to people as convenience. I'd already been suspicious of their effect on our community, but now that I knew how they operated, I could spare some disgust, too.

The last time Rosemary knocked, her face changed. She didn't look hopeful any longer; she looked lost. And I thought: maybe she had been right to hope. We'd had a connection. The offer she'd made me had been sincere and generous. She could recognize what she had done but still hope to make amends for some of it. By hiding, I was denying her that chance. Even seeing all that, I couldn't call down. I recognized her desire to make amends without being ready to forgive.

She raised her arm to knock one more time, then looked down at her fist, unclenched it, and walked away. I thought of that often over the years that followed: the conscious letting-go. I wrote it into the song "Leaving Town" a few weeks later. I didn't realize it would link me to her forever, but every time I sang that song there she was again, opening her hand, letting go. Letting me go. It was in that moment I knew I couldn't stay.

What else do I love about live music? I love when a band segues from one song to another, blending the two, highlighting their similarities before breaking them apart. I love when a band throws a snippet of a cover into one of their own tunes, gives away a piece of their musical identity, shows they know that those chords—the I, the IV, the V—share an unbroken lineage with almost every rock song ever written. It says I dare you to call me derivative, when I know better than anyone that they are all one song. Pick a note, any note. Wear it out. Play it again.

I could have made a different choice. Opened the door for Rosemary. Offered myself to StageHolo in exchange for keeping my space. Started a new venue, improved security, developed new layers of Alice. Those options would have made more sense than leaving, but I couldn't bear to see that basement sitting empty on a Saturday night or my own failures laid bare, and I couldn't imagine ever saying yes to a company that had turned an enthusiastic kid into a weapon without her consent.

If I had it to do over, would I save the 2020? The space shuttering pushed me back out into the world, out of my comfort zone. I had become complacent. I'd hidden behind my conviction that keeping the 2020 going was a public service. I loved that room and everybody who played there. I was glad I'd had the opportunity to give that gift to my community—and to myself—for as long as it lasted.

I thought, too, of how Rosemary had come looking for music because she didn't find it at home. I'd thought of myself as a vector for noise, and then I'd settled for being a vector for noise in one city, for the people who sought me out, for the people we trusted enough to let into the room. That was a slow way to pass a message, when there were kids like Rosemary out there waiting to receive it.

Once I had that idea, I realized the road made more sense. Time to unclench my fist and let go of the comforts I'd accumulated. If the only constant is change, why fight it? Embrace the change, outpace the change, be the change, change the lineup, change the locks, change the key, change everything but the melody and the message.

Daisy the Diesel Van was Alice's discovery, at a city impound auction. Ten years old, with only three thousand miles on her, and not a dent or speck of rust; I guess nobody wanted to bid with the diesel price being what it was. What did anyone need with a fifteen-passenger van these days, anyway? I bought her on the spot. One of the kids who came to our shows worked at a garage that did biodiesel conversions. Some others helped pull out the middle seats and put in a bed, and then a cage at the back for my gear.

Alice moved into 2022, one of the vacants I owned on either side of the performance space. I left a lawyer friend—his band was called Octopus Sex Arm—fighting to keep the 2020 from being seized, but he said I didn't have to be there for that, and I didn't think I could bear to be.

I left Baltimore with: two guitars, acoustic and electric; my old

Marshall amp; a week's worth of clothing, plus leather jacket and two sweaters; stage boots, snow boots, sneakers; four paperback books; my swag suitcases; a case of fresh strings for each guitar; a drive containing every song I could imagine wanting to listen to; my writing notebook; my bike; the ancient annotated Rand McNally USA atlas I had bought on the last tour Before. I sold or gave away the rest of the instruments and music gear, and boxed all my personal stuff to put in a friend's garage. Not the first time I'd pared my life down to what I could carry.

How do you find a place to play in a new city when everything is underground? Rosemary never did have to figure that out. We were handed to her on a silver platter. If she had known where to look, she'd have found the others. Step one: You scope out all the coffeehouses. All the dive bars. The bike co-ops. You know the look when you see it, the kids who share a collective secret. Getting them to trust you is harder. It takes time, but once you're in, you're in.

The first destination I chose was Pittsburgh, Baltimore's sister in rough-hewn beauty. Philadelphia or D.C. would've been closer, but I needed to feel like I'd gone somewhere I couldn't turn around and head back from the same night. It had been so long since I'd been anywhere. I drove through Baltimore toward I-70 saying mental farewells: goodbye, 2020; goodbye, Heatwave; goodbye, adopted home. How many times had I left before? I could do it again. Reframe it to be about the place I was going, instead of the place I was leaving. Pittsburgh bands and clubs had always been unpretentiously fun. And all those rivers! I remembered driving through Pittsburgh on the last tour, seeing the venue from a bridge heading in the opposite direction, with no clue how to get turned around again. April drumming on the back of my seat, Hewitt repeating directions given by his phone as it rerouted us again and again. This time I couldn't really get lost, since I didn't have a set destination beyond the city itself.

I had been on I-70 for five miles when I saw flashing lights behind me in the side mirror. I pulled over with a sigh, unsure what I'd done wrong. Both hands on the wheel, mentally reviewing the locations of wallet, phone, registration.

After determining that my van was mine and I was me, the trooper returned to my window.

"Do you know why I pulled you over?" he asked.

I resisted the urge to catalog all the possible reasons. "No, sir."

"Did you notice anything about the other cars around you?"

"No, sir. There've barely been any."

"This highway is restricted to self-driving vehicles."

"I had no idea," I said, in all honesty.

"It's been restricted for eight years."

Oh. "Officer, I haven't been anywhere in ten. You can see how new my registration is."

He sighed. "I think I actually believe you, but I have to write this ticket."

He took a few minutes writing it up, long enough that I worried that he might have seen something to do with the venue and decided to cause me more trouble, but eventually he returned to my window. I stuffed the ticket into the glove compartment; I wasn't planning on returning to Maryland anytime soon.

The trooper thoughtfully provided me with a personal escort to the next exit. I waved him a cheery goodbye and pulled into the first parking lot to look at my ancient atlas. I drew several X marks on I-70. An updated online map would have been helpful in investigating alternate routes, but I was stubborn. Roads might change, but the basics of A to B were still the same.

The old pike that ran parallel still existed; maybe it was good for me to be on a smaller road. It would let me see how people like Rosemary lived, instead of bypassing the small towns. Prove that farms were still farms, fields were still fields. Until, near Frederick, an enormous building rose out of the flatness. The biggest building I'd ever seen. An airplane hangar? A server center? No: Superwally distribution. As I got closer, I saw that what I'd assumed were starlings or sparrows were in fact drones, rising in a stream, a flock, a cloud, to head to points unknown. Self-driving trucks, drone delivery. No jobs for the humans, other than consumption, which was itself a full-time occupation.

What a weird world we'd created. As I drove through Frederick's empty downtown to pick up my next small road, I was struck by the reasonableness of it all. The transaction we'd made. Of course it made sense to trade company for safety. To trade jobs as makers for jobs as consumers, consuming from the comfort of our homes. We'd set ourselves up.

Maybe I was stupid for pushing back against this system, still looking for a place for myself. Stubborn in this, just as I was stubborn about my atlas or buying a van that needed a human behind the wheel. Left behind. Nothing to do for it now but keep going and get left behind somewhere new.

Pittsburgh welcomed me with signs saying to smile for the cameras. I slept in the van behind an abandoned-looking church, and spent the next few days haunting the streets. Took tiny notes in the tiny inset map in my atlas: this bar is smaller on the inside than the outside, maybe has a secret room; this place where I changed my bike chain has a raised platform in the back, for no discernible reason.

My third week of morning coffee at a coffeehouse playing the Shondes over speakers, I complimented the music. Was rewarded with, "Come back tonight after we close." I returned that evening to blackout curtains and an unlocked side door and a succession of solo musicians. It was a weekly series.

On my second week in the audience, somebody asked me if I played. By the end of the night I had an invitation to do a set the following week. Nerves gnawed at me; I hadn't played a solo show in years, not since that night with April in New York. I had always preferred the safety of numbers. Not just the actual physical security of having people on the road with me. With a band, if nobody came we'd still have a good time. We could treat it as a glorified practice; we still had each other. If someone messed up, they could hide behind the others. What I had forgotten: on your own, nobody needed to know you messed up. There's no chord to make your note dissonant. Nobody to look askance when you forget a verse and go straight to chorus.

I told myself the Pittsburgh crowds were hungry for new music, the same as I'd been when I started the 2020, the same as I was playing in the same space with the same bands cycling through, week after week. I loved all my bands, don't get me wrong. I loved the way they pushed themselves—the way we pushed ourselves—the way we pushed each other—to bring something fresh to each show. To make sure the audience had a reason to come and listen. Still, hearing a band you know and love play something new is not the same thrill as falling in love with a band you've never heard before. It's a tamer joy.

I framed that from the audience's perspective. The truth for me was that every time I stood in front of our 2020 crowd, I was challenged to dig deeper into myself, to find words I hadn't already said in all the weeks and months and years before. That, too, provided a different challenge from the one of facing a new audience and knowing I had one song, at most two, to convince them I was worth their time. They didn't know me; when I stood on the stage in Pittsburgh for the first time, I gave a chord-by-chord introduction.

Nerves punched my chest from the inside and made my legs shake. I played bare-bones versions of the songs we had played full band in Baltimore, which calmed me somewhat, and "Don't Even Think About It," the only song from Before that I still tolerated. No one booed.

I sold fifteen album codes and five T-shirts that night. Three kids asked for records, which I hadn't brought. Made enough to cover the coffees I had bought over the previous weeks.

"Will you play again next week?" the barista asked.

I shook my head. "I want to see what's going on in other cities."

"Come back anytime. I've got a friend with a basement house concert in Cleveland, if you want me to tell them you're coming."

I hadn't decided which way to go yet.

"Perfect," I said.

26

ROSEMARY

Bridge

The sign read OUT OF ORDER, like the bridge was an elevator or an automatic teller. Do Not Trespass would have made more sense, or Authorized Access Only, or even a simple Danger, or Keep Out. "Out of Order" wasn't intimidating at all. Beneath it, someone had scrawled *Ce n'est pas un pont*.

Rosemary scaled the chain-link fence, careful where she placed her feet, remembering the last fence she had climbed. She made it over this one with her feet below her head where they belonged. On the other side, stone steps crumbled, the mortar between shifting slabs gritty underfoot. Easy to see why they didn't want people trespassing in this area of the SHL compound. Out of order, out of time. It didn't even span water anymore. This bridge had been here long before SHL, long before congregation laws, long before an After had been made by a Before.

She knew this wasn't the smartest idea, hiking into parts unknown without telling anyone where she'd gone, but she didn't know her destination, other than someplace to pretend she was unreachable. She knew people now who lived their entire lives noncomm or semi-noncomm, people who might never speak to her again. Luce, Joni. They had only been in her life a few weeks, but their absence still stung, as did her part in it.

She'd omitted that from her debriefing. Omitted the fact that she'd caught movement in the upstairs window when she knocked on the door at 2020, that for one moment she'd glimpsed Luce behind the curtain and thought maybe she hadn't broken everything. She had. She knew now that it was all on her.

They had brought her back to the campus, back to a room identical to the room she'd stayed in the previous time, but on the compound's far side, a small building called the Retreat Center. She was the sole inhabitant, with food droned in from the other side. It wasn't a prison, but it matched her mood: she was a part of nothing, and better left where she couldn't taint everything she touched.

Management met with her in hood, in a virtual replica of an office in the building across campus, complete with meadow and woods out the window. Their avatar sat in a leather office chair, a massive oak desk between them and Rosemary. The furniture and the avatar were overlarge, so slightly as to be almost imperceptible, obviously meant to leave her feeling small.

"Why do you do that?" she asked Generic Management—Male (1 of 5). "Why are we meeting in hood when the real me is here, and the real you is here? It's a nice day outside."

"I'm at a different compound. Washington State."

Oh. "Then why bring me back here at all? We could be having this conversation anywhere."

The fake breeze through the fake window rustled in his fake hair. "Best practices dictate bringing recruiters back to decompress after their first successful acquisition. We can send you home if you'd like, too, but that tends to be trickier emotionally."

"A little vacation while we struggle with our consciences? What percentage of us come back?"

"Sixty percent."

Enough to justify their ridiculous policies. Enough turnover to teach them they shouldn't waste too much time on training. A perfect system. "At this moment I'm wondering why anyone keeps this job."

"Most don't actually see a venue shut down on their first assignment—it's not supposed to happen until after you're gone. The reaction is less visceral if you hear about it from afar. Anyway, it's a good job, and you know it. Money, travel, expense account, excitement, music. We'd like you to stay. You didn't disappoint."

"How could I disappoint?" Rosemary dug her fingers into her palms; her av echoed the motion, though it was too cheap to bleed. "You only hired me because I liked music and I looked naive enough to lead you straight to a venue for you to close."

"We hired you because you were competent in your old job, in a way that usually translates to competence in this one. Which it did. We got two promising new acts from you, and would have gotten more if it hadn't been for our own screwup."

At least they acknowledged their screwup, even if their apology had to do with timing, rather than the act itself. And she'd connected SHL with the Handsome Mosquitoes and Kurtz, both of whom wanted the connection. "They both passed the audition?"

"Yes. We're signing Kurtz and Josh diSouza. They both show tremendous star potential."

One of her nails broke skin. "Josh diSouza—not the Handsome Mosquitoes?"

"He's the whole package. Looks, voice, presence. He's a little tall for the cameras, but we can make adjustments."

"But the band wrote the songs. The band is amazing."

"If he can't write, we'll get someone to write for him. The band was sharp, but they had bad optics." Management held up his thumbs and forefingers to form a box, squinted at it. "He's the real find."

"Did he fight for them?"

"A little, but we told him he'd go further without them, and he saw reason. He was beyond excited, really."

"I need to finish this debrief later." She tried to control her voice.

He gave an oblivious wave. "I'll be here all day. Buzz me when you're ready to finish."

Rosemary studied the map and then headed off through the woods in the opposite direction of the manicured walking trails, into the unmapped areas, which was how she found the old, unmarked path, and then the cordoned-off bridge.

She stood on the bridge and peered over. The width and height suggested it had spanned a decent-sized body of water in the past, but the river was at this point nothing more than dried mud. Maybe it came back after rainfall. Or maybe it was like so much else she'd encountered, forever diminished.

At least this wasn't her fault. She pictured the looks on the faces of the Handsome Mosquitoes when they were told their singer had signed on without them again. Did they blame her? Would they go back to Baltimore and keep playing? Not that they had a place to play anymore. She kicked the bridge, then again, harder, until her toes protested.

Her phone buzzed, surprising her since she'd had no reception last she checked. She expected it to be Management, telling her she had strayed too far, telling her to make a decision, to stay and accept what she'd need to become, or go home and try to forget all the destruction she'd caused. It was her mother.

She wasn't ready to talk to her mother yet, either, to put her complicity into words, so she ignored it. Kept the phone in her hand as she leaned on her elbows. She contemplated tossing it off the bridge, watching it smash on the rocks, running away into the forest to live on tubers and berries. The Ghost of the SHL Woods.

It was as reasonable an alternative as any, and at least she wouldn't be able to cause any more trouble. SHL would hire somebody to take her place. She'd haunt their windows at night, whispering warnings, so they knew what they were committing to, so they'd go to their first assignment with their eyes open, or quit before going at all.

Or, more realistically, she could go home. Her parents would listen sympathetically and tell her she'd made the right choice to quit, and maybe she'd get her old job back if she groveled enough. Her father would try to hide his relief that she'd returned to "live happy in hoodspace!" like the old ads said. She'd pretend she hadn't found anything better in her travels. She'd live happy in hoodspace as long as she didn't think about how monumentally she'd screwed things up for people who'd opened themselves up to her.

That return to status quo offered so much comfort. No crowds, no umbrellas that looked like guns, no police sirens, no strangers sneezing on her. If she still had a musical itch to scratch, she could save up for some SHL shows, if she could stomach supporting the company, knowing what she knew.

Except when she thought about stepping back into her old life, she felt like she was watching an avatar of herself go through the motions of putting on her work Hoodie, waiting for the Quality Control call, meals with her parents. Everything felt small and dulled. Now she understood how much she'd missed; how much had been taken from her in the name of safety and control. That knowledge meant she'd even ruined home.

If she left the company they'd hire someone else to take her place. Someone new and naive, as she had been a few weeks ago. Someone who'd destroy something, somewhere, and then face this same decision. The job would still need to get done, and the cycle would continue whether she stayed in the position or someone else took it. Maybe it was better for her to stay, to save somebody else the heartache and guilt. Maybe the whole sixty percent stayed by saying, "If I don't do it, somebody will." Maybe this was who she was meant to be: a person who blighted everything she touched, for the benefit of her corporate overlord.

She studied the maps of where artist recruiters had been recently. Some embedded themselves in a single large city, which presumably meant that they managed to make themselves invisible, so nobody connected them with venue closings. Some crisscrossed the country, taking full advantage of the opportunity to travel. The maps color-coded them, but she couldn't find any further information on who they were. She wasn't supposed to know.

At the time she'd gone through training, she'd noticed that the others in her group had been hired as makeup techs and audio and such, and she'd been the only recruiter. She'd assumed they were trained in batches based on hire date, but now she wondered if the company had deliberately isolated her from other recruiters, the way they'd isolated her now. No chance to talk to other employees, compare notes. If she'd quit, she guessed she'd have been shuttled out with no chance to talk to anyone, and maybe a nondisclosure agreement held over her head in exchange for debt forgiveness. Even now, when she'd agreed to stay on, they weren't giving her any chance to tell anyone what she had done. Maybe they assumed by the time she'd completed her second or third assignment, her complicity would keep her from sharing. No wonder their system worked.

So, where to go next on her tour of destruction? First option, close her eyes and pick a target at random. Second option, call Aran, though then she'd want to ask him why he hadn't told her his name would close doors rather than open them, or if he'd known what they'd make her do. Third option, search interviews of SHL bands to see where they came from, under the assumption that where there was one there might be others, if their scene hadn't already been picked over. Maybe the trick was finding a place that had produced good music before, but hadn't been visited in a while.

What was she doing even thinking about trying again in a new city, or approaching it like something with a good solution? She put the puzzle aside. It felt wrong to hack a Hoodie that still technically belonged to the company, so she hacked her own phone, a small illicit thrill. She looked up the underground music site Joni had mentioned, now unblocked. The Coffee Cake Situation had a page, just like any band on Superwally, except this wasn't Superwally. They had three songs for sale and one awkward band photo.

The recordings had nothing on the live show. She wrote an apology to Joni, then deleted it. Joni didn't want to hear from her.

The Handsome Mosquitoes had a page, though Josh diSouza's name was missing from the band lineup. She wanted to apologize to them, too, but she didn't think they'd want to hear from her any more than Joni would. Luce's band Harriet was on there, and Rosemary bought an album download, meager penance. She could throw every penny she made at Luce's bands and it still wouldn't make up for what she'd done. "Not knowing is not an excuse," she started writing to Luce, though she didn't know who monitored this page. And if Luce wrote back, could she really justify that she was still with SHL after what they'd done? She deleted that message without sending it, same as the others; all her apologies were worthless, sent or unsent. She might as well embrace that she was everything they said she was.

Maybe she'd find a way to make it up to them, she told herself as she walked through the maps again, as she chose a new city, as she resigned herself to being disappointed in herself no matter what she chose.

27

LUCE

Sixteen-Bar Solo

The basement series in Cleveland charged admission. Ten dollars cash a head, fifty-three people, three acts to divide the $530 between. The homeowner didn't keep a dime, and the two local bands were sweet enough to offer me their shares, which I turned down. I'd never have found the place if it wasn't for the barista in Pittsburgh, and the homeowner gave me a note that would open doors if I headed to Columbus. Notes and passwords and names to buy entrance: after what happened with the 2020, I understood.

The road had changed since I'd been on it last. Most freeways had lanes reserved for self-driving cars; in some places, as I'd already seen, entire highways were closed to Daisy the Diesel, part of the reason I'd gotten her so cheap. I got an unwanted police escort through some towns that weren't big on strangers. Ate dinner in chain restaurant isolation booths when I couldn't find anyplace local and slept in the van in parking lots when there were no motels. Only the smallest motels had avoided shuttering over anti-congregation laws, those and the big chains that made the necessary renovations. I kept my old road atlas next to me, the one we had bought on tour Before, and started taking notes in it again: which towns were safe to pass through, where I found a decent meal. Circle marked the venue, hopefully not to be crossed out by SHL before I passed through again.

There was an odd déjà vu in entering cities I'd toured through long before and seeing them so changed. Sometimes the bones of the places I remembered were still there, signage fading and drooping, parking lots gone grassy. I never minded seeing a Superwally or one of the other big-box stores reclaimed by nature, but the little places made me sad. I told myself that if I knew these cities like I knew Baltimore, I might see the secret life hidden under the decaying surfaces.

I did odd jobs in the long gaps between shows, washing dishes and tending bar for spending money so as not to dip too far into my remaining savings. The veggie oil reduced the one big expense; the other, food, couldn't be helped. I slept in the van when I had to, or crashed on couches like I had starting out. Slow and steady, making friends as I went, doing my best to win invitations back.

I spent two weeks in St. Louis after playing there, sleeping in the van and tending bar, then headed to Memphis for a show set up by a friend of a friend, a tiny dance studio that hosted acoustic shows at night. I waited around for the instructor to take a break and turn off the camera, but when she finally did, she had only bad news for me. "Sorry. The police came by a couple of nights ago. We have to lie low for a while."

She didn't say StageHolo had instigated the raid, possibly didn't know, but I knew.

It was only midday, and I had nothing to do, so I drove out to Graceland, parking on the empty shoulder of the empty road. There was razor wire on the fence, and through the shuttered gate I saw drones darting around the grounds, letting Elvis into hearts and Hoodies through the magic of some StageHolo subsidiary or another. They were getting a better show than those who had made the pilgrimage in person Before; their tours ended with a real live Elvis holo show, decade of choice. Interesting to see how they integrated the new into the old.

Elvis died before I was born; I had no beef with Elvis. I'd left Baltimore angry, driven angry, played angry, but I wasn't even sure where to place it. Angry with StageHolo for being the actual force of destruction, for shutting something vital down while they shuttled people around this ancient shrine, and with Rosemary, the conduit. With myself, for not finding a way to protect what I had. With myself, for driving from city to city holding this in, when I could be using it, channeling it into song.

I grabbed my guitar out of the van and stood in front of the gate again. Played the first two lines of "Suspicious Minds," the only Elvis song I knew, because the songwriter got that one right, about the trap we can't escape. Just substitute fear for love.

A couple of drones turned toward the sound. I gave them the finger, even though that wasn't fair, it wasn't the Elvis fans I was mad at. A few more gathered.

"We're still here," I said to them. "We're still playing music in real life. Come find us. Music is a living thing. Fuck StageHolo."

That felt better. "Fuck StageHolo. Don't give them your money. Learn an instrument. Go see a real band play. Get this place reopened and walk around it in real life. Everybody is afraid; it's what you do when you're afraid that counts. The world isn't over yet." That "everybody is afraid" bit sounded like it wanted to be a song. No, it was one; a fragment of something I'd written a long time ago and hidden away behind a hotel dresser. That's how songs always happened: it might take years to come right, but if I sat on a line or a rhythm long enough, it revealed what it wanted to be. I was writing my way back into it in real time, for a bunch of Elvis drones.

"The world isn't over yet. We don't need to keep all the old things, but we need something new. Borrow a guitar and learn how to use it. If that isn't your thing, figure out what is. Invent your own genre. Carve your initials into something. Brand them, paint them, shoot them, transpose them, change them entirely and sculpt yourself out of a new medium. Instrument and tool are synonyms: we can still construct ways to belong. Our song is a work in progress."

Elvis fans were not the ones I needed to reach, but it helped me focus to say it out loud. I grabbed my guitar's neck and started playing, looking for the chords and melody that would make me feel complete in the moment.

A siren wailed in the distance. When I looked up, the drones had multiplied. An army of drones, all waiting for my next move. One of them, or maybe the static security camera, must have called the police. I hadn't trespassed, but they could probably get me on disturbing the peace or illegal parking or something.

"Good night, Memphis!" I waved to the airborne crowd, then cased my guitar and took off before they could find some reason to arrest me. I wasn't really sure which direction I was heading until I hit a park on the banks of the Mississippi.

I saw a small cluster of people leaning against the railing. From a distance, I couldn't tell what they were doing, but as I got closer I heard a familiar murmur, and I saw someone toss something into the water. I didn't know the exact dates of the holidays this year, but it was the right season for this to be Rosh Hashanah, the Jewish new year. They were here for tashlich, casting their sins into the river. I dug in my backpack for a granola bar, ate most of it, then followed their lead, emptying the crumbs over the edge. Opening my hand, releasing.

I didn't remember if there was a prayer I was supposed to say. My memories of doing the same at the East River as a kid were hazy at best. Still, it was a ritual I understood. It's hard to hold a grudge standing beside a river. A river says move on, move on, move on. Flood your banks, alter your borders. I tossed away my anger at Rosemary and my anger at myself, though I kept the resentment of StageHolo. To my mind, that was a righteous fight.

I sat there for the whole afternoon, watching the sun set in blue and gold, then pink and purple. I wrote "Leaving Town" sitting beside the Mississippi, thinking of Rosemary's unclenched fist, opening my hands, letting go. Then the start of "Manifest Independence," incorporating the stuff I'd shouted at the Graceland gates.

In the morning, I headed to Nashville.

28

ROSEMARY

More Rock, More Talk

If a hood backdrop existed for "Mountains as Far as the Eye Can See," Rosemary had never known to look for it. Roads that rolled and turned on a hairpin, trees thick with summer, vistas stretching from one state into another. She alternated between clearview, capturing the scenery as it was, and a map overlay displaying the names of mountains and valleys: Fancy Gap, Meadows of Dan, Rocky Knob, Fairy Stone, Woolwine. She loved the names, loved the ways the peaks layered green to blue to purple in the distance. Some turns made her stomach flip, made her brace against her compartment's sides, but she tried to turn it into a game. A long, long, roller coaster sim with an impressive view, leading into the small city of Asheville, North Carolina, which hadn't been visited by a recruiter in two years. For a few minutes, riding a bus around mountains, she regained some of the excited anticipation she'd had on her first trip. If they had taken away her illusion that she was doing some good in her job, at least she could still appreciate the places it allowed her to see.

She'd figured out that Logistics gave new recruiters the fanciest hotels to make them feel they owed the company from the start. This time, she'd asked for lodgings that let her fit in better, and Logistics had said, "If that's what you really want . . ." They'd found her a tiny apartment above a convenience store, the type of place somebody moving to town might realistically afford. It could benefit from a Veneer: it had stained carpet, burned-bottom pots, a hot plate, a microwave crusty with other people's culinary disasters, sour-smelling minifridge, box fan in the window. Maybe this was their attempt to show her she'd overcorrected, but it felt right. She didn't deserve better after what she'd done.

In the store downstairs, she bought a Micky's-2-Go microwave mac 'n' cheese, almost as good as the real thing, and then settled onto the sagging bed. The bus still rattled through her. When she finally fell asleep, she dreamed that Luce had ridden into Asheville on top of her bus, playing guitar to the mountains, shouting down to Rosemary that nobody had to hide anymore.

She woke to sun and music streaming through the unshaded window. The old overeager Rosemary would have rushed out to find the source, but she took her time dressing. Two doorways down, a tall black man with long dreadlocks played a fiddle, his instrument case open before him, as if it was legal to play on the street. People walking past tossed change in the case or nodded at the VCash code taped to the lid, doing the same in hoodspace.

She leaned against a wall to listen, but the fiddler glared at her and gestured her along with his bow in between phrases. Nobody else stopped for more than a second. Local ordinances must allow music as long as nobody congregated. She wandered the compact downtown area in circles that led back to her block, hoping to catch the fiddler on a break. Most stores hadn't opened yet, but she cataloged them for possible return. One sold paper books, another musical instruments, another sex toys. Small restaurants she didn't recognize offered every cuisine from Thai to Tex-Mex. The fiddler was gone when she turned the corner the fourth time, but at least now she knew there were definitely musicians around. It was only after she went to bed that night that she realized she might have scared him away by circling the block so many times. Stalking street musicians wasn't the way to engage them. What was? She had no clue.

She developed a routine. She drank coffee at the bookstore each morning, pulling up her Hoodie and pretending to work while watching the half dozen other customers, trying to figure out what kinds of jobs people might bring people to work at a coffee shop instead of their homes. Not Superwally customer service, even if some had the jawbone implants that let you chat subvocally; Superwally mandated their uniforms and dedicated space. Writers, students, tech. She wondered why you'd choose to work in the company of one to nineteen strangers instead of the comfort of your home.

Except, as the days went on, she started to get it. She liked how the woman behind the counter, Sadie, greeted her by name after the first week. Her latte art changed from a question mark to a fuzzy branch which Rosemary thought might be her namesake herb. She was still getting used to sitting at tables without isolation booths, inches away from other customers, but she liked recognizing the others in the room, and the feeling that they were slogging through the same kind of day, even if she was pretending.

She started using the time to peek into her Hoodie's code. She listened to music on her hacked phone while she explored, sending notes to herself about local bands, careful to change their names in her notes in case somebody at SHL spied on what she wrote. She found a way to freeze the tracking app without turning it off, so it looked like she was still sitting at French Broads Coffee & Books after she'd gone home. That might come in handy. She still felt terrible that the info her Hoodie collected automatically had been used to target the 2020.

She people-watched, and explored, and stewed over what she'd learned. She had been sold a bill of goods, since she was a little kid, that said nobody anywhere did anything together. That you could do it all from the comfort and safety of home: work, date, play games, hang out, listen to bands, watch sports or television or movies, have sex ("Superwally Stim Accessories for all budgets—whatever you're into!"), maybe eventually visit your partners to figure out if you were as compatible in the flesh as in hoodspace. Who needed the real world when all that was at your wired fingertips?

And she'd bought into it all. If her parents told her cities were dangerous hotbeds of violence and disease, why would she have any reason to believe otherwise? If they said there was nothing more to life than farming and family and whatever job she could get from Superwally, and be grateful for that, who was she to argue?

When she called home, she found herself short-tempered. She was angry at the fiction they'd created; her father was angry the fiction hadn't been enough for her. She knew that was unfair, that the entirety of hoodspace had been built to feed this narrative, to keep them all scared and complacent and docile consumers. Maybe she was mad they'd fallen for it and taken her with them.

In the afternoons and evenings, she walked the downtown blocks listening for music. The street musicians made her check-ins easy. It took her two weeks to figure out she could bring them coffee instead of stalking them. She learned their names, mentioned them to Management in categories of "no" and "maybe" so SHL would see she was working. The fiddle player from her first day in town was Nolan James, who taught music in hood and to local kids. Then there was Annika, who figured out any song anybody requested on her keyboard, but insisted the requester join her to sing; an old woman named Laurian, who played Appalachian murder ballads on banjo, an enormous dog asleep at her feet; Mercury Retrograde, who candidly discussed his mental health diagnoses over double espressos, and played ukulele in the costume of a superhero he'd invented. At least the street musicians were legal; if she found one she enjoyed enough, she wouldn't be wrecking a venue when she sealed the deal.

As it got later, she tried to tune the street players out, hoping for a glimpse of movement behind a shutter, or music wafting from a closed shop. She wandered out of downtown and across the river, past warehouses and parks, in ever widening circles and ever longer spokes, looking unsuccessfully for the elusive crowds, listening for the low thump of bass rising from a basement.

29

LUCE

Cool Out

Pittsburgh, Cleveland, Columbus, Toledo, Detroit, Ann Arbor, Chicago, Milwaukee, Madison, Minneapolis, Des Moines, Kansas City, Lawrence, Columbia, St. Louis, Nashville. Sixteen solo shows, five months. A slow passage. I needed those sixteen solo shows in those months after the 2020 died, and they were a necessary intimacy. All those couches, all those new friends, all those people who felt good for having helped me make a connection down the road; it wouldn't have been the same if I'd had a band along. By the sixteenth show I'd be lying if I said I wasn't itching for a beat beneath me.

That was when I found Silva again, the sound guy from that fateful show at the Peach; or he found me, I guess. It was pouring rain the night I played Nashville, and I was glad for decent road cases as I shuttled my gear out of the antique store where I'd played between racks of vintage clothing to wet people in Eames chairs. I'd seen him there, a familiar face I couldn't quite place.

"Can I help?"

"Sure." I nodded toward my amp. "Remind me where I know you from?"

In the second I asked, I remembered. "Scratch that. Just remind me your name. I'd never forget that show."

"Silva," he said, hoisting my Marshall into its wheeled case. "How's it been going? I was so excited when the Bowmans said you were coming to their place. If anybody had the nerve to tour again, I should've known it would be you."

I invited him into the van to get out of the rain. We sat cross-legged on the bed, sharing a joint he pulled from his shirt pocket.

"How's Nashville dealing with the new world order?" I asked. "It was harder than I expected to find a place to play. I figured here of all places . . ."

"StageHolo songwriter pipeline. This city is crawling. I've done some sessions for them."

He must have seen my distaste flash across my face, because he added, "They're keeping music going."

"Fuck StageHolo."

"No, seriously, they have problems, but they're making sure there's still a path for pros, so I can't call them all bad . . . but I miss playing live. Actually, I came to see you because I was hoping you might be, ah, looking for a bassist."

"Huh. Bass without drums?"

He grinned. "I figured you'd say that. I know a drummer who's looking to get out for a while, too."

"I like playing as a trio . . ." In the back of my brain, songs started stripping down and rearranging themselves.

Two days after the antique store show, I drove out to the tiny cottage where Silva's friend Marcia Januarie lived. She answered the door in shorts and tank top. "Sorry in advance for the heat inside. AC broke and I was hoping to get away with not turning it on again. Fall isn't supposed to be this humid."

When we shook hands, I glimpsed a small sliver of a possible future: the bright urgent heat of a new musical collaboration blurred with the bright urgent heat of a new love; a collision that would work for a while, until it didn't; a map to a new and uncharted place. It was a terrible idea to mix the two, when drummers willing to tour were so thin on the ground, when anything that tanked us might tank the band, but really, nothing about this idea wasn't a terrible idea, so we might as well go all in, especially when one handshake said so much. She'd sized me up in the same way, I could tell, leaving us in one of those rare instant mutual attractions. I hadn't felt that in a while.

Silva showed up a minute later and we set up our gear in a loose circle with the drum kit that already took up a large portion of the room. Marcia was right about the heat; the room was stifling.

"Can we open a window?" Silva asked.

She shook her head. "Only until we start playing. I found the farthest place from neighbors I could, but they still complain. I've got it pretty soundproofed as long as we keep 'em closed. That okay? I've got fans."

"It's not any worse than my club was in summer. I'll survive." It was a little hot for me, but I was feeling her enough to agree to anything.

We played a few covers and one of my songs. Silva'd been a good bassist all those years ago, and now he played even better, filling in spots in the song where I might have missed a second guitar. Marcia's drumming was compact and spare, perfectly in the pocket. Three songs in, I thought it would work; four songs in I knew.

After, we opened all the windows and ordered pizza and poured bourbon over ice, tossing around possible band names, laying out a loose practice schedule and our expectations for each other and the band. When Silva headed out again, I caught him winking at Marcia on his way out the door.

She returned to the couch with a second drink for each of us. The glass was sweating.

"So," she said. "I'm not reading this wrong, am I?"

I'd always appreciated direct women.

My van stayed parked at Marcia's for five days: five days of sex and music and getting to know each other, in no particular order. When we finally dragged ourselves from the cottage, it was for her to show me how Nashville had changed. Silva had said as much, but I had to see it for myself: the walled-off estates, the enormous StageHolo compound, the Ryman and Opry turned drone-infested shrines, all the clubs gone the way of all the other clubs. I shouldn't have thought it would be any different here. The songwriting community hadn't had to change too much; they were just working for a different kind of publishing company from the one Before.

It made sense if I thought about it that way, but it still made me angry. That night, the power died halfway through practice, and I said it was time to discuss where we were going and when.

"We're going to need a name," Silva said.

I pictured another hour lost to tossing random phrases at each other. "I don't care what we're called."

"Luce Cannon? It worked before."

"Not Luce Cannon. Not any of my old band names. This is something new and it deserves to stand on its own."

Marcia stood and stretched behind her drums. "Ice cream, anyone? If this is like last time, I'm losing everything in the fridge again, so we might as well eat it now."

Silva and I put down our guitars, turning off the amps so they wouldn't surge if the power came back. We leaned over the kitchen bar, where some light came in from the moon. I took the offered spoon, but Silva passed on the ice cream and poured himself a bourbon.

"Dessert Spoon," I said. "The Countertops."

"Is that how you came up with all your band names? Random items in front of you?" I didn't need light to catch Marcia's disapproval.

"None of them mean anything until people notice you. Sure, there are some awesome names, but some of them are only awesome because you like the music."

"But the other side is true, too." Silva dipped into the nearest pint. "There are good bands with names you can't forgive."

I took the pistachio ice cream and roamed the room, naming things. "The Festival Owls. The Thesauri. Carpet Cleaners—hmm."

Marcia laughed. "Those are awful. We might as well start throwing random words together. Lunchpocket. Powersuck. Cassisfire."

I walked into her crash cymbal and had to grab for it to keep from starting a chain reaction. When I'd extricated myself, I asked, "What was that last one?"

"Cassisfire. Cassis and Fire. The two flavors you're not eating since you stole the pistachio."

"What's cassis?" Silva asked.

"A berry. The 'fire' is cinnamon chocolate chile. Y'all are both missing out."

I said it a few times under my breath. "Two words, not one. Cassis Fire. Like 'cease fire.' It's not awful."

"Better than any of those others," Silva agreed.

"Sweet," said Marcia. "Can I have some of the pistachio now?"

The power didn't come back on, but by the end of the evening we'd finished all three pints and come up with a plan for a minitour to test the waters. They were both interested, ready in the abstract, but I was the one pushing. The thought of that StageHolo compound in the same city had me itching to get out again, like they could infect us if we were too close for too long. Sixteen solo shows had been enough to tell me I'd missed both road and band, not one or the other. The two combined, plus the new connections, the reconnections, the audiences, the kind strangers, the people who became less than strangers in days spread out over years: those were the things that could fill the hole inside me called home. Nothing else gave me that fix.

30

ROSEMARY

Badge

She was working up to asking one of the street musicians outright when the barista, Sadie, invited Rosemary to her band's show. After all her searching, it was as easy as an invitation; it had taken exactly what she'd been told all along. Get involved, get to know people, and you'll find out what's happening. Sadie might have been flirting with her, too; Rosemary still found it maddening that people in the real world didn't use the same markers they did in hoodspace. Anyway, she wasn't getting involved this time.

She thought of everything that had gone wrong in Baltimore, and debated not even going. It was one thing to stumble across a venue and later give it up to her bosses; it was another to come in as an invited guest, knowing she was a Trojan horse. She settled on attending with her new precautions in place. When she put her Hoodie on that night, she altered the settings to make the GPS tracker mirror her phone's location on her bedside table. She'd left her wallet there as well, taking only cash and her driver's license, so her spending couldn't be tracked. As far as the company was concerned, she'd taken the evening off.

The address was a warehouse by the river. The thought occurred to her as she walked through the dark that Sadie could be a serial killer luring her to a deserted location. Then she remembered she'd had the same thought about Aran as she approached the 2020 for the first time, and remembered the way Luce had welcomed her, and her heart ached. She wondered if she'd ever think about it without shame.

"You'll know it because it's a giant building painted the ugliest shade of yellow-brown in existence." Sadie had leaned over the counter and pressed a plastic coin into Rosemary's hand. "Repeat the directions back to me so I'm sure you've got it? We're trying to keep too many people from searching the address."

It was hard to discern the color with the sun down and the security lamps in the parking lot throwing a sodium-yellow glow, but she was confident she'd found the right place. Other people arrived on bicycles and on foot from other directions, most in twos and threes. The parking lot was weedy and overgrown, every inch of the chain-link fence hosting a locked bicycle. As she passed under a security camera, she noticed it was aimed at the sky instead of the entrance, if it was on at all.

She followed the others to a door on the building's far side and into a low-ceilinged office. Passed her invitation chip to the Door Alice, played in this instance by a fit and pox-scarred boy in his late teens. He gave her a curious look.

"Sadie invited me." She waited for him to say, "Go back to wherever you came from," or "I don't know who that is, Officer."

"Welcome to my shitty warehouse," he said.

"Yours?"

"Yep. Hey, don't look so surprised. Brown people can own warehouses."

"Sorry! It's because you look so young, not because you're brown . . ." She started to explain, but he'd already moved on to the next person waiting to enter. Her record for insulting gatekeepers she should befriend was now two for two.

She walked through the next door, and the office gave way to a warehouse. The space had been divided at some point; it was nowhere near as large as the building's footprint, though still bigger than anyplace she'd ever been other than the SHL hangar. She made out two orange Exit signs along the opposite wall from where she'd entered; nice to know there were other ways out. There were probably fewer people inside than had crowded into the 2020, dispersed over a larger area. She still felt more comfortable on the fringe and didn't see a strong reason to press forward toward the low stage on the interior wall.

It reminded her of the hoodspace club where she'd seen Patent Medicine, the Bloom Bar. There was even a bar along the side, or at least an old conveyor belt studded with a dozen picnic coolers. People shoved their hands into the ice for drinks, then tossed cash into fishbowls interspersed between the coolers. An honor system. She glanced at the bills in the fishbowls and tossed a five into the nearest one, choosing an icy cider from among the beers and soft drinks.

She spotted Sadie at the same time Sadie spotted her. "You came! Do you hug?"

Rosemary nodded, still pushing her own limits. Sadie was a big woman, even bigger without the coffee counter in between them. The hug was strong and solid, and not long enough for her to get uncomfortable with the contact. She managed to return a one-armed squeeze with the hand that wasn't holding a drink.

"Did you have trouble finding it?"

"You were right about the color."

"Ha!" Sadie had great dimples, but Rosemary was Not Getting Involved. "True, but that doesn't make it any easier to find."

"Your directions were fine, thanks. Um, what's the order?"

"We play first, then a duo from Charlotte, then the Simrats. You'll like them."

"Oh! I've listened to one of their songs! I can't wait to hear you all," Rosemary said in all sincerity. She was curious what to expect. She'd found the Simrats on the same underground site where Joni's band had a page; they had a trippy sound, with better production than a lot of the other stuff she'd heard. They'd been on her maybe list, depending on how they came across live, if she could find them playing somewhere, which she finally had.

She had another thought. "Do bands from other cities play here often?"

"Not very. Lucien used to live here before he moved to Charlotte for love"—she elongated the last word, bringing her hands up under her chin in a mock swoon—"so when he wants to visit we build a show for him."

Sadie excused herself to get ready, and Rosemary was alone again. All around her, people chatted with each other. She still envied the ease with which they navigated the space. Did anybody else here feel as awkward as she did? She scanned the room's edges, looking for someone else hugging the wall, and was surprised to find several. One corner held an entire herd of office chairs gone feral. Three people raced chairs down the far side of the room, leaning over the seatbacks like jockeys, with their friends cheering them on.

Sadie's band started playing. The chair racers kept racing, and a few others continued chatting near the drinks. Rosemary triangulated between the stage and the emergency exits.

She hadn't asked Sadie her band's name or their genre, and now that she heard it she had no category for it. Sadie played bass, and Nolan James played fiddle, with a guy she'd never seen before on guitar, and a woman she recognized as one of the coffee shop Hoodie-workers on drums. Despite the acoustic instruments, they had a looping, funky groove, and harmonies that reminded her more of R & B than rock or pop or folk. An intriguing sound, and they had a good interplay onstage, and most of the audience was up and dancing. Even though she had told herself to stay analytical, to hold herself back from feeling anything for these bands, she couldn't help moving with the music. Forget analytics; they were fun.

The second group turned out to be a married couple, two handsome trans cowboys from Charlotte. Both guys played acoustic guitar, and their songs were catchy and clever. She filed them into her mental maybe box. She sometimes thought she was too easy to please, but she recognized the difference between liking a band and thinking they were SHL material. Two different things, especially when a definite yes came along to recalibrate her.

The last band took a little longer to set up than the others had. The guy who owned the place stood watching from the doorway, so Rosemary walked over to talk. If she was going to practice chatting with strangers, it made sense to start with the ones she had questions for. "So, uh, I didn't mean to doubt this was your place. I just didn't figure the owner was involved. I thought maybe an employee was letting people in, or it was an abandoned building."

He smiled back. "It's not abandoned. My mom has a bunch of empties, though this is the only one with power. She's been trying to get Superwally to buy it for a distribution center, but they say it isn't quite large enough, and it costs too much to bring up to code. It's been years now. She said I could skate in here in the meantime, so here I am, 'skating.' You're friends with Sadie?"

"Yeah." Better not to say new friends. "Rosemary. Nice to meet you. Do you do this a lot?"

"Tomás. Twice a month."

"Are there other places doing this, too?"

"Acoustic rooms, yeah, people's living rooms, but as far as I know, this is the only one big enough for bands. I've got the space, why not use it?"

"You're not worried about getting raided?"

"Dude, I'm terrified of getting raided, but if we all live the way they want us to, all scared and alone, nobody would ever hear a band like the Simrats." He nodded toward the stage and grinned at his timing.

"Friends, Romans, Countrymice," whispered the lead singer. "Lend me your ears."

The lights went out at the moment they hit their first chord. The band's clothing glowed under black light. Their instruments, too, painted to shine, and streaks on their faces. It reminded Rosemary of phosphorescent underwater habitats in aquarium vids. The band had at least ten members; it was hard to tell exactly how many in the mass of glowing limbs and instruments. Drums, two guitars, samples, a horn section. Their sound filled every corner of the room. The singer had a voice as good as any Rosemary had ever heard, slippery and strong, twining around and over the instruments without ever getting lost behind them.

On a hunch, she pulled up her Hoodie. Sure enough, a free local Veneer was available. She accepted it, and the space went even wilder. Now strange glowing cloud-animals drifted through the air above her head, dipping and diving, chasing each other. She dropped out of hoodspace again; she didn't need the distraction from their sound.

This couldn't be the same band she'd listened to on the drive. The fantastic live sound was nothing like the recording, which had been interesting at best. They deserved a larger audience than the group dancing in this room. She debated filming a clip, but didn't want to risk it if she hadn't managed to turn off the metadata the way she thought she had. Her description would have to do, packed with as many superlatives as she could provide.

Their third song sounded familiar. It took her a minute to recognize Luce Cannon's "Blood and Diamonds" filled out and swung, the horn section adding something she wouldn't even have guessed could be added. She forgot her professional reserve and screamed the words along with the others in the room: part of the song, part of the band, part of the moment. Part of other moments, too: the first time she heard "Blood and Diamonds," in her mother's car on the way to get ice cream a month before everything went bad; "Blood and Diamonds" playing hourly on the nurses' station radio in the hospital, telling her she was stronger than she knew, strong enough to walk out someday soon. It didn't matter that this wasn't Luce's original; this was a new version for the new Rosemary. She had room in her life for both.

Maybe this was why people risked arrest to come out to these shows. You could do the same thing at an SHL show, and if you'd never been in this room you might not even know the difference, but there was a difference.

Walking back toward her rented room after the show, she tried to analyze her exhilaration. She'd arrived here down on her job, but she could still take some selfish joy in the perks, when the perks involved spending her nights listening to amazing bands. Beyond how much she'd loved the music, she genuinely liked the idea of creating opportunities for musicians who had worked hard despite there being no end goal; they couldn't be playing music in hopes of someone like her walking in the door. It wasn't a money thing, either. They had to be playing because they loved to play, or believed in their songs, or something like that, which meant she got to ride in and change their world—not that they had any obligation to say yes when she offered it. This time, she'd find a way to do it right. She couldn't fix what she'd done to Luce, but surely there was a way to get these bands attention without ruining what they had; there had to be a solution somewhere, if she could just think of it.

Someone called, "Hey!" from the darkness ahead, where a streetlight had shattered, the glass strewn on the asphalt below it. She looked up, assuming the voice was Sadie's. In the moment she registered it was a stranger, someone else hit her from behind.

It wasn't a hard shove, but she wasn't expecting it, and it knocked her off her feet. She put her hands out to catch herself, jamming her left pinkie hard against the cement, a white flash of pain. She scrambled to stand, clutching her hand, but someone pushed on her head, so she sat.

"Stay down." She couldn't see the second guy's face. He had his right hand in the pocket of an ancient jacket, denim with white leather sleeves, unless they were yellow. Hard to tell in the dark beneath the shattered streetlight. He had a logo over his heart, a jumble of letters she didn't recognize. Her brain started untangling them because it didn't want to think about the gun that he did or did not have.

"Cash, Hoodie, phone," he said, as if placing an order.

"I don't want any trouble," she said, like someone out of her parents' movies.

She dug in her pocket for the bills she'd wadded there in case she needed to pay to get into the show, and handed the money to him. He accepted with his left hand, the right still in his pocket. His hand was white, with short, dirty nails. She disentangled her Hoodie and passed that over as well. "I left my phone at home. I'm sorry."

I'm sorry. Who said "I'm sorry" to a mugger? She sounded ridiculous to her own ears, and fought down the urge to apologize for the apology.

For a moment she worried he didn't believe her, but then he shoved her to the pavement again and took off running in the direction she'd been heading. She sat watching until he was out of sight, then a little while longer. She had no idea how long. She didn't see any sign of the first guy, either, the one who'd said "Hey."

What were you supposed to do after a robbery? Nobody else was around, which meant nobody else had chosen this route. She hadn't bothered to check the crime maps for this particular jaunt, after all her wanderings. She'd gotten cocky, or careless, or overconfident. Lucky, too, she supposed. He hadn't shot her, or even taken her keys or wallet. No, he couldn't have taken the wallet; she'd left it in the apartment. He'd only asked for the stuff he could wipe clean and use, or wipe clean and sell. Her Hoodie would reset if someone else put it on, so she didn't have to worry he'd track her. Best possible mugging.

She didn't want to walk down the same street they'd taken anymore, even if it led back to her room, so she took the next right, then a left to parallel the road she'd been walking. She wished she'd brought a jacket; her teeth were chattering for some reason.

Temporary noncomm. For this minute, putting one foot after the other, heading more or less in the correct direction to get herself back to her room, she was alone in the world. No way to call anybody. No way to check the safety maps if she wanted to, now, or summon a ride, or call the police. Joni's way made more sense, carrying an emergency phone, but if she'd had an emergency phone they would have taken that, too.

A brightly lit diner sat at the next intersection, ten or twelve people inside despite the late hour. She swung the door open, searched faces for her mugger, or at least his jacket, and when she didn't spot him, slid into the nearest open isolation booth and locked the door.

The menu was embedded into the tabletop. She expected offerings like Heatwave's, but it was basically the same as a Micky's. She ordered a grilled cheese sandwich, tomato soup, and hot chocolate, then pressed the panic button.

The response came quickly. "Do you have an emergency, Table Four?"

Was it an emergency? "I think I was robbed. I mean, I was robbed."

"In your booth?"

"No. Sorry." Apologies again. "On the next block over, before I came in. They took my Hoodie."

"And your first thought was to order soup and a sandwich?"

It had seemed like a good idea. She didn't speak.

The voice disappeared, then returned a moment later. "I've called the police for you. They'll be here in five minutes. Is there anything you need, um, other than soup, sandwich, hot chocolate?"

"Nothing I can think of, thank you."

She hugged herself for warmth and studied the menu. It felt strange not to have a phone or Hoodie to pass the time. How did noncomm people do it? Joni had carried a book. Maybe she should start carrying a book.

The hot chocolate arrived with so much whipped cream that the top sheared off in the pass-through. The server lingered longer than necessary. Gawking, probably, at the woman stupid enough to get mugged because she'd stopped paying attention to her surroundings.

The police officer arrived at the same time as the food—"Officer Selsor" and "They" read their badge and a pronoun pin—prompting an awkward moment as they squeezed into the booth opposite her, then turned and took the food from the staring server, putting it on the table in front of her. The officer was middle height, middle weight, acorn brown, with a shaved head and kind eyes of the exact same shade as their skin.

"You reported a robbery?" The officer wore a Hoodie but didn't raise it, instead placing an old-fashioned tablet on the table to take notes. Less intimidating, she guessed. They had a smooth Southern accent.

"Yes."

"Did they do that to you?" The officer pointed at her left hand.

Her pinkie looked like a swollen sausage, the skin tight and angry. Now that they mentioned it, pain came rushing in. She nodded.

The officer rapped on the wall of the booth. "Can you grab a bag of ice and a towel?"

The server, who'd lingered by the table, disappeared in the direction of the kitchen, and returned a moment later. Rosemary accepted the ice and towel through the pass, and held it against her finger.

Officer Selsor started with the basics. Rosemary gave her local address, hoping to avoid questions about why she'd come to town.

"Okay, now, can you tell me what happened?"

She recounted the moment. The details felt useless now—a young white guy she'd barely seen, an attacker she could only describe by his clothing and his left hand.

"What about when he ran away? Did you get a sense of his height? His hair?"

She shook her head. "Baseball cap, red maybe. Short hair, I guess, since I didn't see it? The jacket was bulky so I don't know his build. Hard to tell how tall he was because he was standing over me. Five-eight, maybe?"

"And the other guy? Any other details?"

"I barely glimpsed him. I don't even know if he was trying to help me or working with the second guy."

"Working with," said Officer Selsor. "We've heard similar from a few people over the last couple weeks. What were you doing out this late? It's close to curfew."

"Close to curfew isn't past curfew. I had the right to be out."

"Of course. I was just curious what you were doing on that street."

Rosemary had no reason to withhold any information from the officer, but the question reminded her of her last encounter with the police, when they'd chased everyone out of the 2020. "I was walking. I like to walk at night."

Officer Selsor opened their mouth, closed it, paused like they were trying to decide what to ask next. "Can I take you to the hospital for your finger?"

"No, thank you. I'll ice it." Change of subject worked for her.

"Look, maybe it's only jammed, or maybe it's broken. That's way easier to fix earlier than later." They lifted their left hand. The middle finger bent back at a bizarre angle before joining the other fingers again, taking the long way when the rest had gone direct.

"No hospital. It's not that bad. I can go to a clinic tomorrow if it's still swollen."

They shrugged. "Your choice. Can I give you a ride back to your apartment?"

Rosemary considered the blocks between the diner and her room. "Thanks, yeah. And, um, I forgot my cash had been stolen when I ordered this food. What should I do?"

"I'll talk to the manager. I'm sure they'd be fine if you sent them money when you got home."

The officer left the booth, and returned a minute later with a takeaway box. "It's on the house. Manager said come back sometime and buy a sandwich under better circumstances."

The handful of people still in the diner all watched Rosemary go. She followed Officer Selsor out to their patrol car, where they opened the back door. "Sorry, protocol. I can't have you in the front seat."

She didn't really care. She watched out her window, examining the shadows for people.

Her street was dark and quiet. She groped for the door handle and realized there were none; she was in the seat where suspects rode. She waited for Officer Selsor to let her out.

"You're okay? Do you need to call anyone to stay with you?"

"No, Officer. Thank you for your help."

The muggers hadn't taken her keys. Really, they'd caused her as few problems as a mugger could. She didn't have to apply for a new ID or deal with reaching her landlord to say the keys were gone. She didn't have to worry that they'd followed her home or knew where she lived.

She poured herself a glass of water, drank it, filled another, then flopped onto the bed. Her energy drained away, leaving only her throbbing finger. She reached for her phone to report her stolen Hoodie to SHL, then realized that if Management looked at its location, it would say she'd been in her room all night. Crap.

All she wanted was to sleep. Instead, she rummaged in her bag for a pen and paper and wrote out the phone numbers for SHL Emergency, Logistics, and Management from her phone. Checked the time: 12:40 a.m. Twenty minutes until Asheville's curfew, an hour later than Baltimore's. She filled a pot with water, grabbed a tissue, and headed back downstairs one more time. Looked both ways, but the street was deserted. She probably made a strange picture, wandering the street with a pot of water and a finger like a sausage. Somebody could do her a favor and steal the phone now, too, but nobody came along. She was oddly calm. Impervious.

She walked three blocks, to a restaurant where she'd had tacos two days before, and ducked around the back to the dumpster. She removed the data chip first and put it in the pot, then took it out and snapped it in two. She used the tissue to wipe her own fingerprints off her own phone.

The screen spiderwebbed as it hit the ground. Her heel did more significant damage, grinding it into the pavement, which was strangely satisfying. When she picked it up with the tissue and tossed the pieces in the dumpster, she knew she had finished it off.

Now she was noncomm for real, at least for the night. She made it back to her room a minute before curfew. Iced her finger, took two anti-inflammatories, and passed out.

31

ROSEMARY

Career Suicide

The usual combination of violin and sunlight woke Rosemary. She pulled the pillow over her head, a movement that brought the events of the previous night back to her with finger-screaming clarity. She raised her hand to her face: still swollen, but maybe a little less? Maybe.

She iced it while she rummaged through the kitchen drawers, eventually finding a roll of masking tape, which had enough adhesive left for her to bind the pinkie to its neighbor. Good enough.

She was waiting at the coffee shop door when it opened.

"Thanks for coming last night! You look like hell," Sadie said. "And you're not usually here this early. What's up?"

Rosemary told her about the mugging. "Can I use your phone to call my work and my parents so they don't worry?"

"Of course. God, I feel awful that happened on your way back from my show. I shouldn't have let you leave alone."

"Did you leave alone?"

"Yeah."

"See, it could've happened to you, too. Freak thing." She'd walked down the wrong street at the wrong moment. For all her worry about strangers with guns and strangers with germs, she'd never even noticed how other people also added safety to a situation. Sure, it wouldn't have happened if she hadn't left Jory, but she couldn't imagine not having left anymore.

She called home and told her mother she'd smashed her phone (true!), and could she drone one to French Broads Coffee, Rosemary would send her the money when she got back to her room, and yes, she was fine and she'd talk for longer as soon as she had a phone again, sorry for the long silence. Management got a different story: She'd been heading out to a late show when she'd been mugged. She'd given a police report. She'd hurt a finger, but it was okay, and yes, she'd go to a clinic if she needed. They wanted to send an incident report immediately, but she pointed out she had no device with her. They promised to send a new Hoodie right away.

It was the first time she'd ever been anywhere without both her devices, and now she had neither, at least for an hour or so. She ordered a latte and watched the others trickle into the café. She felt alert, present, disconnected, tired; an odd jumble. Not bored, though. Her mind was unknotting the problem she'd been thinking about since Baltimore, adding to it the muggers, the quick "Hey," the distraction before she'd been hit, the GPS tracking.

Her packages arrived in one delivery from Superwally an hour later. *Our goals are speed and efficiency.* She busied herself recovering info from hoodspace and setting up both devices with her preferred settings, then sent a quick thank-you to her mother and a quick "back in business" to Management.

Most people working at French Broads kept their Hoodies in some percentage of clearview, to still be aware of their surroundings. She felt safe enough to go full for a few minutes. She paged through the StageHoloLive archives looking for the Patent Medicine concert she'd attended all those months ago.

The recorded version started her off front and center, a perfect viewing location, but not the one she remembered. This time, she spawned after the band; she was the illusion here, not them. The same start to "The Crash": three voices and two huge guitars, holding a note for ten seconds before the drums rolled in. It still hit her like a wave, but when she looked to the side to see if the others in the room had felt it, she found herself in a sea of bots. They bobbed their heads in time to the music, but none of them turned to exchange glances with her.

The song ended, and Aran Randall's ghost said, "Good to see you all. Good to be here."

They had edited out "at the Bloom Bar." She knew now that he must have recorded the names of a whole list of SHL venues. His hair fell in his eyes again, and he brushed it aside again. "We're going to go ahead and play some songs for you, yeah?"

The gorgeous bassist opened her eyes again, but this time Rosemary wasn't in the wink's path. It had never been meant for her. The second song's bass groove began, and Rosemary exited the concert.

She pulled up her own recording of Luce's band, that special night at the 2020. Flat video, not the immersion of the Patent Medicine show, but even seeing it brought her the physical memory of being there. The electricity, the immediacy, the thrill, the heat of the room. It was all there for her recollection.

She searched another band, another song. The Iris Branches Band, "Come See Me for Real." Audio only, the way she'd heard it in the diner bathroom. She didn't care what Iris Branches looked like. She flipped back to clearview and closed her eyes. The song used to remind her of high school, but now it sounded like the bathroom at Heatwave, like her heart beating faster, like Joni's lips pressed to her own.

She almost had a plan. When she closed her eyes, she could see the result she wanted, the way she used to envision perfect code before looking at the flawed version. She'd repaid Luce's kindness by killing her venue, and Joni had said she couldn't undo what she'd done in Baltimore, but maybe she knew a way to make a difference. This time, she'd tell Sadie, because it wasn't a plan she could implement on her own, and it wasn't a thing she wanted to do without permission. Plus, she needed bait.

Rosemary met with Management a week later. A busy week, giving her a new respect for logistics. Event planning turned out to be hard work.

This Management rep had chosen a different background. No breezy meadow here, and no replica of an office to intimidate her and make her small. They were both seated at a small table in a bare but cozy room, in identical chairs, a pleasant blue sky visible out a large window. She guessed she'd passed the point where they thought they needed to scare her into submission; this was meant to convey a meeting of colleagues.

Generic Management—Female (2 of 5) was built on the same lines as Generic Management—Male (1 of 5). Slim, generic white person features, chestnut hair with a deliberate touch of gray, expensive-looking haircut and clothes. Rosemary wondered if the other three avatars were white as well. Most of her coworkers she'd met on campus were nonwhite, but every avatar she'd met in Management was white and thin and able-bodied. Superwally had played with age but otherwise left people as they were, as far as she knew. She tucked that information away for further pondering.

"Hi, Rosemary. How's it been going in"—she paused—"Asheville? Good weather?"

She'd graduated to collegial chitchat as well. "Yeah, the weather's been lovely. It's a nice little city. Full of music."

"Good, good."

"Have you ever been to this area?"

"Um, no."

Rosemary wanted to follow up, to ask if this Management person had ever been a recruiter, what scenes she'd destroyed to get promoted, but that would mar the illusion of model employee she was trying to project. "You should check it out sometime. It's beautiful. There are real waterfalls and stuff in the area, too, but I've been too busy with work to see them."

"Sounds nice. Whatcha got for us?"

She imagined the faceless manager sitting somewhere in a childhood bedroom turned workplace, points flashing across her vision for a perfect pivot from pleasure to business.

"Two acts." She used their word back at them. "I've seen a ton of musicians here, but I think these two groups are SHL material. The first is called Way Way Down. R & B grooves on folk instruments. Catchy stuff." She wasn't sure they'd be pretty enough, but she was willing to stand behind their sound.

"Sounds interesting. Got video?"

"Sure. This is from a practice, since I got nervous taking my new Hoodie to a show after . . ." She let her voice trail off.

Generic Management gave a good simulation of a sympathetic smile. "Yeah, we heard what happened. Glad you're okay."

"Thanks. The other is called the Simrats. You're going to love them. I'll send along a vid someone else recorded at their last show. Twelve-piece band, sound as big as any room you want to fill. The singer's voice is amazing, and they do this glo-paint thing that will translate well. People will line up to see them." She was proud of having figured out how to alter the metadata on the video the band had given her, but that was another in a long list of tech victories nobody but her would ever celebrate. Maybe she should design a hoodbot to follow her around complimenting her code-tweaking.

"Wow—a twelve-piece. I don't think anyone's brought in a rock band that big in ages."

"But it's okay?"

"Sure, in the right circumstances. Expensive, but worth it if they're as good as you say they are."

"They are."

"Nice job, Rosemary. You have contact info? No noncomm bullshit?"

Rosemary didn't let her avatar wince. She passed their contact info along. "They're all reachable. They're doing a big show together a week from Saturday, too, if you want to send someone to watch."

"No need. I'm sure your report and the videos will be enough,"

Management repeated. "Hey, you haven't heard from Luce Cannon, have you?"

"Sorry, no."

"Too bad. The one that got away. Anyway, you can contact Logistics to get out of there anytime you want, now."

"Is it okay if I stay a few days? To see those waterfalls I mentioned? My room is paid through the end of the month."

Management shrugged her too-perfect shoulders. "I don't see why not."

Management thanked her again, said she looked forward to checking out the videos, signed off. The space resolved to blank. Rosemary switched to clearview and looked over at the coffee counter.

Sadie leaned on her forearms, watching her. "How did it go?"

"Good, I think. If they like you, they'll contact you within the next few days."

"And I don't have to say yes?"

"Nah. They'll offer you an audition or a contract, and either way, you don't have to say yes. Thank you for helping, either way."

"My pleasure. Gumming the works while negotiating with the Man. I'm into it."

Rosemary grinned. She'd been terrified to explain her plan, nervous Sadie would share Joni's or Luce's reaction, though their reactions might have been different if Rosemary had been this honest with them. Maybe.

She'd tried to keep some distance, but it was hard not to consider Sadie a friend. The planning had made them closer, though she no longer had the impression Sadie was hitting on her, either because she now knew who Rosemary was or because she'd be leaving town soon. They'd settled into the roles of friendly coconspirators. "How are the invitations coming?"

"Rad," said Sadie. "The warehouse concert of the year *and* group action. Spread the word."

32

LUCE

Fix My Life

Silva booked our first shows as a band, calling around to old friends until we had gigs lined up in Atlanta, Athens, and Dahlonega. He called it the Georgia, I Must Be Out of My Mind tour.

"Don't expect much," he said, hoisting his amp into the back of the van beside mine as we packed to leave.

Marcia joined us, staggering slightly under the weight of her drum hardware bag. They looked nothing alike, but I felt a strange déjà vu thinking of April and the massive duffel she always insisted on carrying for herself.

She gave me an expectant look. "A little help here?"

"Sorry!" I grabbed one handle and helped her lift it.

"Just saying," said Silva, lending a third set of hands. "Keep your expectations low. These places aren't what you're used to."

"I'm not used to what I'm used to anymore, either. You were there when I rocked out at an antique store. They said to keep the volume down so I didn't rattle anything off the shelves."

"I played backline for live karaoke behind chicken wire at a country-western bar." Marcia put a hand around my waist.

Silva grinned, getting into the game. "I played an airport baggage claim. I don't know why they thought people might want to listen to live music while they waited for their bags."

They'd shifted into Before, so I did, too. "Busking in Manhattan. August. Garbage day."

"Oooh, you win." Marcia pinched her nose. "C'mon. There's more gear and I'm not carrying it all."

I watched the two of them head back toward the cottage, memorizing the moment because I didn't know how long it would last. It felt good to inhabit that space again. My favorite space, with its shorthand of shared experience. I picked up my pace so nobody would accuse me of not pulling my weight.

In the old days, on a highway, the trip to Atlanta would've taken a little more than four hours, but it took us nearly seven on the back roads, between the speed limits, the meandering roads, and the overzealous cops.

"Don't you need to have a reason to stop us?" I asked in frustration the third time we were pulled over. The first one had claimed he thought we weren't wearing seat belts; the second said I'd been weaving, but declined to test me; the third said she'd had a call about a suspicious van.

The fourth one didn't even pretend. "A van with Maryland plates this far from home is reason enough," he said before asking for my license and registration. When everything checked out, he followed us through town, stopping only when we passed under their second license plate reader. I'd wanted to grab lunch, but he made it clear we weren't stopping in his town. We ate premade sandwiches from a gas station automat a few miles down the road instead.

"Can we skip the towns entirely?" Marcia asked, as yet another trooper deigned to follow.

I concentrated on maintaining the speed limit and the straightest line possible.

"Not if we want to get there in time for the show," Silva said.

"But this is definitely getting old. Was it like this up north, too, Luce?"

"Not this bad. Dammit." Lights behind me again. I sighed and pulled over. Again.

The Atlanta show took place in the windowless back room of a luthier's workshop in Little Five Points. Walking past the workbench, the neat tubs of hardware, the cubbies full of guitars with labels saying where they'd been sent from and where they went back to, I couldn't help salivating. It had been over a decade since I'd seen a guitar store; the guitars I'd bought and sold since coming off the road I'd bought from and sold to friends. This wasn't a guitar store, but it was akin, and the owner clearly had her own custom projects going as well as the repairs. My own guitars could probably use some of the luthier's TLC, but that involved being in one place long enough to come back for them, or having an address to send them back to. Someday, maybe.

We were slotted with two local bands, one of which had a drummer Silva had played with once upon a time. They were kind enough to offer us the middle spot, so that their fans didn't get the idea to show up late or leave early and skip the band they didn't know. We soundchecked, then ordered pizza together from three different pizza places, so that anyone monitoring deliveries wouldn't think we were ordering for a crowd. It was good to get a chance to chat with other bands, even if neither was considering touring. They were happy playing this place and one or two others on a semiregular basis, the way I'd been happy at the 2020. Controlled danger; nothing like the vagaries I'd experienced since leaving home.

I watched the audience enter with the curiosity of someone who had developed her own security without consultation or any knowledge of best practices. Mine had been named Alice. If it hadn't been for her amazing facial recognition and deep suspicion of humanity, I knew my place would have been raided long before

Rosemary's arrival. This place seemed far more regulated, and as I watched people enter, I tried to figure out the system. It seemed to involve key fobs, a scanner, and a question. I finally gave up and asked about the last part.

The luthier's wife grinned. "On any days without a show, the landing page on our website is one of Mary's custom guitars. On show days, she throws a picture of an old Bacon mandolin up in the morning, then at noon, some vintage piece or another. It's a splash page with alternate text saying the make and year—doesn't say that we have one. They have to come in and ask about that particular vintage instrument. Once we get to recognize somebody, they can buy a key chain that gets them in without having to jump through hoops."

"What's today's vintage?"

"A 1959 Gibson Explorer."

My jaw dropped. "You have one of those? Aren't they worth like half a million dollars?"

"Of course we don't! She repaired one once and snapped a picture. But anyone actually looking for one would call to ask, not show up in person, since we're mostly a repair shop, not a store. It's not listed on our sale page, and we mostly sell Mary's work, not vintage."

The system seemed complicated to me, but they still had a venue and I didn't, so I wasn't in a place to critique. I had one other question. "How do new people find out you're here?"

"They don't." She shrugged, then reconsidered. "I mean, if a band is playing here and has somebody new to invite, they can vouch and we'll start the vetting process, but we try to keep it pretty limited. No sense risking everything."

Alice had wanted me to be that careful; she hated when I brought in strays. I'd argued that communities needed new blood or they stagnated, and that there was no point having the place if we couldn't serve as an escape for people who needed it, no matter whether they knew us or not. Better safe than sorry, she'd said, and of course, she'd been right. I'd been too trusting.

The back room would've fit about thirty people in addition to the three bands and owners, and twelve showed up. Twenty minutes after the show was supposed to start, despite the low turnout, they locked the front door and turned out the shop lights. The venue space had a nicer smell than the 2020: wood and oil with a faint undertone of solder. The audience settled themselves into three small risers' worth of thrift store couches and lounge chairs. A ceiling fan creaked overhead, stirring the air.

I leaned against the back wall and watched the first band. They were young, not much more than teenaged, and it would've cheered me somewhat to think that they'd found a way in here if one of them hadn't called Silva's drummer friend "Dad" over pizza. Still, they were decent performers, even if their songwriting was trite. They were here, and trying, and that was all I ever asked of anybody, and the idea of parents who encouraged their kids to break the law for music gave me hope for the future. I listened to their first two songs before slipping into the tiny green room.

The last band had vacated—to watch their kids play, I guessed—and I'd seen Silva sitting in the front row with his buddy. Marcia was alone in the band room, Hoodie up, drumming air. I couldn't recognize the song from her pattern. I kissed her and she leaped a foot off the couch.

"Anybody could sneak up on you in that thing," I said as she took it off. "I don't get how people use them in public."

"That's because you're old." She looked miffed, but not overly so.

"You're two years older than me."

"Wouldn't know it. You're a dinosaur."

"I'm not! I just don't see the point of those things."

"It's awesome tech, Luce. I still think you should try it sometime. Here, put mine on for a sec. The women's national team is a goal up on Canada."

She held the Hoodie out, but I clasped her hand to my chest and then gently pushed it back in her direction. "I don't want to watch people fake soccer for cameras. You have fun, though, if that's what gets you ready to play."

"They're not faking just because they're playing for cameras, any more than you're faking if you play to an empty room. Anyway, I don't like to hear the band that plays before me, so I don't have to know if they've laid down something too amazing to follow."

I grabbed my guitar from its case and sat down opposite her on the couch to tune. "Huh. I'd rather know, so I can up my game if I need to. Not that it's a competition."

"Girl, everything's a competition."

She settled back into her game, and I noodled on my guitar while I listened to the band. They finished to familial-level enthusiasm. I nudged Marcia that it was time.

"We have a treat tonight," Mary the luthier said as we stepped into the stage area, such as it was. "They're called Cassis Fire, and they're from out of town."

Not a superlative introduction. I guessed from it that Silva hadn't sent music; his friend's introduction had probably been enough to get us in the door. It didn't bother me. I'd always loved winning over the audience.

I hadn't given a ton of weight to the fact that this was our first show together, but as I jacked my guitar and hit a test chord, it struck me. We'd spent the last few weeks practicing in a circle for each other, and now we got to turn outward again. To see if the cues that worked at home carried to this context, too. The songs were still fresh to Silva and Marcia, and the arrangements made them feel fresh to me as well, even the ones I'd played before. A small thrill hit me, stage fright of the sort that could be tamed and harnessed and turned into energy. Even if we were still rough around the edges, we'd conjure something. A new band, a new tour, a dozen new people to win over. My favorite challenge; the one I would break any law to experience again.

"Hey," I said, stepping to the mic.

The next chord was for real.

33

ROSEMARY

Pressure Drop

Rosemary waited for the concert with a combination of excitement and trepidation. Only her career on the line, no big deal. She checked in with Sadie and the Simrats constantly, and was relieved when they both got their calls. The Simrats were signed on the spot—she even got a bonus added to her paycheck. Sadie's band was asked to audition, which they were still debating. The clock had started ticking.

"My nerves have nerves today," Sadie said in the cab they shared to the warehouse. "I'm usually anxious before a show, but my butterflies are wearing butterfly hats."

Rosemary felt the same way. "Mine, too, and I'm not even playing. I guess this is what it's like to put on a show? Worried everyone won't be in the right place at the right time, or that nobody will come at all."

"Sounds about right." When Sadie grabbed her hand, Rosemary squeezed back. A solidarity squeeze.

The cab arrived at the warehouse, low and gray, like a thunderstorm. Sadie grabbed her bass and let Rosemary carry the box she called her bass head. Someday, Rosemary needed to learn all the terms.

"It's weird to ride a cab to the front door of a show without worrying about leading cops here," Sadie said. "One time only, right?"

"One time only," Rosemary repeated, hoping she hadn't screwed everything up for everybody again.

They walked in through the front door, with Sadie muttering under her breath, "That's a weird feeling, too."

The scent of decaying rubber hit them as they entered. The foyer was two stories tall, with light streaming in through a skylight, and dominated by a pink and blue pile taking up most of the floor with its deflated footprint. She spotted turrets: a giant inflatable castle. They tracked around it instead of through; behind it, the ceilings dropped back to a normal height.

"What the hell did they make here?" Sadie asked.

"Tomás said they sold something called 'party rentals.'" Rosemary had spent a fair bit of time with the kid who put the shows on over the last week.

"That explains it, I guess." Sadie pointed to a glassed-in showroom with three enormous tables, each employing a different decorating scheme. One was red and gold, one silver and glass, and the third one a beachscape, littered with seashells and sand. Up close, thick dust covered everything. "Can we help you choose a theme for your party?"

Rosemary scratched her head. "What've you got in 'rock concert'?"

"Allow me to show you! Walk this way."

They passed a few more showrooms before they got to a door marked Employees. When Rosemary pushed it open, they found themselves in blackness with a bright spot at the far end—an open door.

"Welcome! Step into the light!" Tomás shouted from that direction. They traipsed across the empty space, using their phones as flashlights.

"You found it okay?" he asked when they got closer.

"No problem," Sadie said. "How's setup going?"

He gestured toward two people moving among piled cables and speakers and lights and stands. A thick line ran out the open door. "Fine. We scrounged some crap PA equipment for the occasion, in case we lose it. We've got everything else we need. Extra generators, water to flush the toilets."

"Yay." Rosemary tried to hide her own nerves in front of people other than Sadie. If she were in his shoes, she'd want to know that she was confident this would work. Besides, he was smart; no sense risking more than needed to be risked.

She'd wanted to be early, but watching everything come together so slowly made her even more nervous. She pulled out her phone and checked her bus ticket.

"I can't believe you're leaving tomorrow." Sadie peered over her shoulder, bass in hand.

"My work here is done."

"Almost done. You haven't done the part where you leave destruction in your wake yet."

Rosemary's stomach turned, but she forced a smile. "Oh, yeah, I forgot."

By seven, they'd completed setup. Both bands had soundchecked. They sounded weak and flat; hopefully that was the emptiness of the space, not the sound equipment. If the plan doesn't work, they'll still get a show, Rosemary told herself, even if a crappy one. Bands will play and then go home.

And live with the undetonated threat she'd brought hanging over their heads every night, waiting for it to go off. It had to be tonight. She'd altered the metadata on the Simrats video she'd handed over so that it showed these GPS coordinates. She'd made sure to mention this show. That would be enough. She waited.

One of Tomás's friends arrived with coolers. Soda and water only, so if they got busted it wouldn't be for serving alcohol.

"What if nobody comes?" she asked at seven thirty.

"Relax," Tomás said. "We told people eight so they'd be here by nine. They'll come. If not for the music, then for the bouncy castle."

"You inflated that thing?" Rosemary pictured people trying to escape a crush and running straight into a giant blue and pink roadblock.

He laughed. "That castle probably has more holes than the *Titanic*. Or did the *Titanic* only have one big hole? In either case, I didn't. Yet."

She was beginning to think nobody took this as seriously as she did. It was an abstraction to them, even if it would affect them and leave her unscathed. She hoped the joking was his way of hiding nervousness. Nervous was better.

At eight fifteen, people started trickling in, and she mentally crossed "no audience" off her worry list. She moved on to the next item, walking the perimeter to make sure all the doors had been unlocked. They'd told the audience members—friends of the bands, all—to come in through the staff door on the south side, and told them where to find all twelve emergency doors. When she came back from her tour, the space had filled. Fifty or so people milled in front of the stage, and a few more hung in the corners in the dark, if the glowing screens were any judge. A good number: enough to suggest this was a legit show, but few enough to make it safely out the doors as necessary. The whole audience knew what might happen and had chosen to take the risk.

By nine, about sixty people had arrived. Rosemary settled against a back wall, out of the light. As she'd hoped, Sadie's band, Way Way Down, sounded way, way better than they had in soundcheck. The audience soaked up the sound and kept it from bouncing around the walls. They danced and swayed. She was too anxious to do anything but wait for uninvited guests. They didn't come.

The band finished their set. Sadie packed her stuff and walked over to where Rosemary stood, lugging her gig bag and the heavy bass head by her side. "No sign?"

"No sign."

"They might still come."

Rosemary nodded. "This is the weirdest thing I've ever wanted."

"Look," Sadie said. "My oldest sister is a forest ranger. The preserve she works on sets their own brushfires sometimes. If you do a controlled burn, you get way less damage than if you let brush accumulate and wait for a wildfire to break out. I'm looking at this as a controlled burn."

"A controlled burn." The comparison did actually give Rosemary some relief.

The lights on the stage switched over to black light.

"Friends, Romans, Countrymice," said the lead singer, face aswirl with color. "Lend me your ears."

The drummer counted four on sticks, and the entire band kicked in at once. A cover Rosemary recognized from her parents' records. "I Fought the Law."

"Very funny," she whispered. She wished she could enjoy this.

They played a second song, and a third song, and a fourth. Rosemary didn't recognize them, but she caught a law enforcement theme. She didn't remember the band being this political, but it was a special occasion. She still harbored a perverse pride in finding a good band for SHL, and a perverse concern that all this had been for nothing if they weren't willing to toe the populist line needed for an SHL band. No, her instincts were good. This was a command performance for her special event.

And then a whoop outside the building—Rosemary flashed for one moment to the 2020 raid. And then the far door opened and flashlights poured through. A megaphone or speaker squawked: "Stop playing. This is an illegal gathering." And then everyone was running, to all the doors, all unlocked. They'd positioned the stage so the audience got a head start on the police. Somebody swung a spotlight around to temporarily blind the cops as they entered.

The Simrats, under their black lights, a knot of painted bodies and instruments, played like the band on the *Titanic*, going down with the ship. A horn section soundtrack for a police raid. They had nothing to worry about; SHL would bail them out. If it went as she hoped, nobody would get hurt, nobody would get caught, and no scene would get ruined. Just a bunch of kids trespassing at one of Tomás's mother's warehouses; she wouldn't lose it since she'd had nothing to do with the show. It wouldn't be this easy in other cities, but if this worked tonight, she'd find ways. Like her muggers, this show was one big shouted "hey" to distract from the real shows. A controlled burn, as Sadie had said.

Someone cut the PA. The band played on through their amps, without vocals, until the generator shut off as well, killing all the lights and sound at once except the drums. People scattered. A thrilled panic surged through Rosemary, and she worked on harnessing it rather than letting it run away with her. She looked over at Sadie, who flashed a nervous smile.

Rosemary reached for Sadie's bass head, but Sadie stopped her hand and grabbed it herself. "I'd rather have all my stuff with me if we get separated."

A bobbing light came toward them, making Rosemary's heart leap again. The closest exit was the one they'd walked in through, the one leading out past the showrooms and the two-story entrance.

"It's been nice knowing you, Rosemary," Sadie said as they moved closer to the exit. "Keep in touch."

She swung open the door. The space ahead was dark; the sun through the skylight had been the only illumination earlier, and there was no electricity now that the generator was off. She hadn't taken into account how dark it would be in a power-dead warehouse on a moonless night. Ahead, red and blue lights bounced at the edges of a monumental blackness, and a loud hum filled the air.

"Ah, shit, they're out front." Sadie stopped.

"Exit eleven is down that hall." Rosemary put a hand on Sadie's elbow to guide her. "There's no parking lot on that side, so maybe they don't have cars out there."

"Thanks! Are you coming?"

"In a minute. You should go." Rosemary hugged Sadie. "Thank you for your help. Good luck!"

Sadie disappeared down the dark hallway; she had no way of knowing that act was the first time Rosemary had ever instigated a hug outside of her family. Big nights seemed to have a weird effect on her, making her try all kinds of things outside her comfort zone. As long as she was scared, excited, worried, adrenaline fueled, she might as well double down. She wouldn't declare this operation a success until it was behind her, but so far it looked like everything was going as smoothly as induced chaos could go. She didn't deserve for it to go this well.

Rosemary turned back to the main entrance, where an enormous inflated castle dwarfed the vestibule. It looked intact other than two drooping turrets. She had seen these in old movies, in school carnival scenes and birthday parties, but never in person. That was a different kind of childhood, a different kind of growing up, a Before to her After, full of real human bodies navigating the space between each other. One bounce, just to try it, and then she'd run.

34

ROSEMARY

Free Will Astrology

This time Rosemary couldn't avoid the hospital. The cop waiting for her below the castle insisted, so she couldn't say she got hurt during arrest or intake. He recorded the whole interaction, for his own protection, he said, though she imagined his buddies might get a laugh out of her misstep.

He also insisted on waiting for an ambulance rather than driving her himself. Everyone else had scattered, leaving Rosemary and a couple of others who must have been too close to the door the cops came in. The only one she recognized was the Simrats' singer, who gave her a salute as he was loaded into a van. The van was mostly empty; they must have been expecting to pick up more people, which they probably would have if this had been a normal show and not a controlled burn. Hopefully the police weren't suspicious.

When the ambulance finally arrived, the cop watched them load her, then followed in his own car.

The EMT who rode in the back with her was friendly and curious. "How did you do this?"

"I turned my ankle."

"Well, yeah, I can see that. But how?"

"Have you ever seen a bouncy castle?"

The EMT laughed. "Not in a million years."

"Me neither. I couldn't resist."

"And that's why you're being arrested?"

She tried to play it cool, like she did this every night. "Nah. That's for trespassing and congregation. And, uh, resisting arrest. He said I shouldn't have kept bouncing."

"Huh. Must've been a fun night."

"It was! We could make it more fun if you want to slip me out the door somehow."

That was the end of the friendliness. "Can't do that."

"Sorry. I was kidding. I just didn't plan on getting arrested tonight." Then why had she stopped to bounce? She'd wanted to. And maybe part of her wanted to be caught, to be punished, for what she had done in Baltimore.

"You're not going to get far on that foot, in any case."

When they'd taken off her shoe to apply ice, she'd caught a glimpse, purple and swollen, majestically damaged. One look was enough; two would remind her where they were going, and she was trying very hard not to think about that. She loathed doctors. And hospitals. Probably nobody liked them, but the cocktail of hate and fear that her mind concocted on the drive made her queasier than the injury. It's only your foot, she told herself. They won't keep you.

The hospital wasn't far. Certainly not far enough to hatch some grand escape plan. She let them wheel her off the ambulance and into the emergency bay. Her escorted entrance must have gotten her some kind of preferential treatment, because she was whisked right into the examination area. A nurse took her medical history, gave her another ice pack and a painkiller, then showed her to a sealed exam room to wait for them to call her to X-ray. She waited. And waited.

A quiet night, or just the way hospitals were these days? She had a closed door instead of a curtain; maybe the rooms isolated noise as well as germs. Her last reference point was a dozen years in the past. It involved halls lined with screaming people, the pox burning nerve-imagined holes in their skin; her own screaming, too, the sounds you made because your body had to make them, the knowledge that the doctors were doing everything they could, but it didn't touch the pain, and they didn't believe you when you said you were on fire. The thought of it made her want to run, but the cop was sitting in the bedside chair.

A diversion wasn't a bad idea. What she wanted to hear right now was "Blood and Diamonds." She raised her Hoodie and put it in clearview, keeping an eye on the cop to see if he objected. The song reminded her of hospitals—she'd been humming it since she walked in the door, she realized—but not in a bad way. It reminded her of nurses, of people who had tried to cheer the kids in their care without condescension. Safety, recovery, strength.

She played it twice. The song still retained its magic, but now it made her want to hear Luce's newer songs again. She had an album on her hacked phone, old-school, which she didn't want to listen to right now in front of the cop; she didn't want her behavior to stand out in any way. She searched to see if anyone had ever uploaded any footage of Luce's shows to the usual channels, but all she could find was stuff from Before. A different Luce.

Luce performed in spaces where people didn't upload to hoodspace. Why would there be anything? Try again. And, wait—she played in bands. Rosemary was looking for Luce Cannon. She tried "Harriet" and "music" instead.

Her search returned dozens of versions of a single immersive video labeled some variant on "Harriet—live—do something!" "Harriet speaks truth!"

The cop was off in his own Hoodie—maybe doing paperwork, from the way his hand moved on his thigh—and surely somebody would get her attention when it was X-ray time. She entered the video.

Drone-shot. That much was obvious from the swift and steady pace. They moved through a wooded estate, toward a gate covered in musical notes. Other drones flew into view, aiming for the same location.

Someone asked, "What is it?" Someone else answered, "I dunno. Somebody's losing it outside the gate. GlitterFan said to come see."

Then they arrived at the gate, hovering, the noise of dozens of drones drowning out the person on the other side. This drone surged forward, until it was almost touching the gate, and its microphone must have been unidirectional, because the other noise fell away.

Luce stood on the other side, her hair greasy and disheveled, her middle finger raised in the gate's direction. "Fuck StageHolo. Don't give them your money. Learn an instrument. Go see a real band play. Get this place reopened and walk around it in real life. Everybody is afraid; it's what you do when you're afraid that counts. The world isn't over yet."

"This chick is crazy," the operator said.

"Nah—wouldn't it be awesome to be here for real?"

"Ssh," said someone else.

Luce continued. "The world isn't over yet. We don't need to keep all the old things, but we need something new. Borrow a guitar and learn how to use it. If that isn't your thing, figure out what is. Invent your own genre. Carve your initials into something. Brand them, paint them, shoot them, transpose them, change them entirely and sculpt yourself out of a new medium. Instrument and tool are synonyms: we can still construct ways to belong. Our song is a work in progress."

She started playing, something Rosemary hadn't heard before: angry, dark chords. A minute later, she looked up like she heard something, and then Rosemary heard the sirens, too.

"Good night, Memphis!" Luce said, waving in Rosemary's direction, then running for a nondescript van parked up the road.

Memphis. She was in Memphis, which was in—Rosemary had to look it up—Tennessee. That wasn't far from Asheville at all, but if she was traveling, she might be gone by the time Rosemary got there. If she was traveling, maybe that meant Rosemary hadn't ruined her life. Or maybe she had, and this was a filmed breakdown. It didn't look like a breakdown. She came across sincere and driven, if not entirely in control.

Her location wasn't the thing that mattered, anyway. Message transcended location, even if it was a message saying to be somewhere and do something. And this message was reaching people. Four hundred thousand views and climbing.

She played it again, listening carefully, then dropped her Hoodie to think. We need something new. Create something better. Construct ways to belong. That was a message directly to Rosemary. Not only to her; she knew that. It would take more than just her, anyway. The concert tonight had been one step in the right direction, but only one step. What was the next one? She groaned in frustration.

The cop looked over. "Ankle hurting?"

"Yeah." It wasn't a lie, even if it wasn't the whole truth.

She kept thinking it over. Thought about it as they came to get her for X-rays, as they mashed her foot into the right position for the X-ray, as a doctor eventually showed up and confirmed she had a bad sprain, not a break. They wrapped it tightly, told her to ice it and elevate it and try to stay off of it. When the doctor wrote a prescription for a painkiller, the cop interjected that she would probably be better off waiting to get it filled, if she could stand the pain.

"Are you really supposed to have a say in my care?" she asked, as if it had been her plan to go to the hospital.

"No. I'm not telling you what to do. I'm just saying less paperwork, less chance of your pills getting lost, less delay in getting you out the door after you're arraigned. Speaking of which, are you ready to go?"

She wasn't, but she supposed that didn't really matter.

Lockup hadn't been on the list of things Rosemary had been dying to experience in her travels, and afterward it made her list of things she'd prefer not to experience again. Jails had their own exceptions to congregation laws, with the result that she spent the night with thirty other women in a cell that wasn't nearly large enough for thirty women standing, let alone sitting or trying to close their eyes. Only three others looked like they might've been at the warehouse concert, and she was glad North Carolina had recently done away with cash bail, according to the officer who'd done her intake, so she wouldn't have to worry if they had the money to get themselves out; it was her fault they were there. When Management had shown all that concern about getting Legal involved after the raid in Baltimore, it had been only for her and Luce, not for anyone else who got caught up in their net. She hadn't even considered that before.

She carved a few inches out for herself on the questionable cement floor and waited, which was an interesting exercise in itself. She had no idea how to keep her mind occupied with no Hoodie, no phone, no job, no music, no chores. Her foot throbbed, and she tried to get someone to bring her ice, but the request was ignored. Nothing to do but wait and hold on to her space and second-guess her life decisions.

Waking disoriented her; she hadn't planned on falling asleep. She started to stand up before her foot reminded her to stay on the floor a little longer. Breakfast was a square eggish patty on square white bread, which she gave to another woman who looked hungrier than she was.

They'd done away with cash bond, but left a complicated recognizance system. The district court commissioner didn't like that she had no personal ties in the state. He asked her not to leave the city until her court date; she successfully argued that her job demanded travel, and the restriction was amended to staying in state. It helped that she had nothing on her record, and that the charges were only congregation and trespassing, both level-three misdemeanors; apparently the cop had only said resisting arrest to scare her. Legal would have gotten her out faster, but she hadn't wanted them to know she had stayed. It was possible they knew already, if they tracked her company Hoodie even when she was on vacation. She still wanted to pretend they wouldn't do that.

So she was stuck in North Carolina for the time being. On vacation as far as the company was concerned, which was good, because she was still weighing out the ramifications of what she'd done. She had no way of knowing if anyone had gotten hurt, if anyone had picked up weightier charges, if Tomás would get in trouble—at least he was only seventeen—or his mother had lost her building. Tomás had promised she had others; he'd liked the subterfuge. Rosemary still couldn't tell if she had the stomach for this, though it still felt better than the alternative. The waste she'd laid to Luce's life and the scene she'd built so carefully.

She hobbled back to her room. Arranged to have her pills droned in. Realized she had no ice in her tiny fridge's tinier freezer, and added a chemical ice pack to her Superwally order. What she wanted to do was go see if Sadie was at work, but that would involve walking. She collapsed on her bed and set her mind to work on a question that had been nagging her: Why was the video labeled "Harriet"?

The video she watched didn't provide the answer, but one of the others did. From that drone's angle, a large "Harriet" sticker was visible on Luce's guitar case, and after much discussion, the uploaders had decided that was her name. None of them connected her with Luce Cannon, one-hit wonder, and if anyone from Baltimore was watching, they weren't spilling. It added to the mystery. Between all of the versions, Rosemary counted over three million views. Three million people watching in amusement, or three million people taking it to heart, or some lower number of viewers watching it on repeat as she had done? She had no way of knowing. All she knew was she needed to do something to help; to answer the call to action.

She had one tiny grain of power: recommending bands to SHL. Two if you counted the trick she'd pulled on the company here. Was there any medium in which she could follow Luce's instructions? A thing she burned to do? More than anything, she wanted to be a conduit for Luce's message, to shout it from the rooftops in a way that it might be heard. Maybe, maybe she had a way.

It started with a twofold apology.

"Baltimore Homelessness Prevention Services, this is Joni speaking."

"Don't hang up. I'm sorry to call you at work."

"Sorry? Who is this?"

"Joni, this is Rosemary. Please don't hang up."

There was a sigh on the other end, but the call didn't disconnect. Rosemary took that as a positive sign.

"If you think the statute of limitations on my anger has expired, you're wrong."

Or not. "Look, you don't have to accept my apology. I don't think I would, either, under the circumstances. I'm calling because there's a thing I want to do for Luce, but I need to find her to do it."

"I don't know where she is. She left town right after you killed her space."

"I know. I was hoping you'd have a way of reaching her. Somebody has to, right? Somebody knows where to reach her if something happens with the 2020?"

"There's a lawyer," Joni admitted.

"So you could get the lawyer to pass a message for me?"

"I could, but I still don't know why I would. What could you possibly offer her that she hasn't already turned down?"

"A way to do it without selling out. A platform. Have you seen her vid at Graceland?"

"Her what?"

"I'll send you a link. Borrow a Hoodie and check it out, and then call me back if you're willing to help me reach her. And again, I can't even tell you how sorry I am for what I did. You said I couldn't fix it, and I can't, but maybe I can make something else happen. Watch and call me back if you're willing to let me try."

Rosemary hung up. She still wanted Joni to like her again, to forgive her, but she'd settle for a return call, for now.

35

LUCE

Crying in the Wilderness

Nobody answered the door at the Athens venue and Silva couldn't get ahold of his friend who'd gotten us the gig. We'd planned on splurging on motel rooms, but the motels we found said we had to have booked in advance to clear their background checks. We ended up spending the night in the van, which we figured we'd be doing more of in the future, so we might as well get used to it. In Dahlonega we played to a cold and empty campground, where at least the owners were enthusiastic; they fed us and let us stay for free.

After those shows, we headed back to Nashville for a couple of weeks while Silva lined up some Tennessee shows. The Knoxville mansion show went well, except that the PA picked up police radio and broadcast it through every silence between songs. They said it was a bug and a feature, an annoyance that kept them apprised if the cops were headed their way. I didn't think they had that much to worry about in any case; they were obviously rich enough to buy their way out of any trouble.

A pounding rain caught us as we left Knoxville, and continued into the mountains. It thankfully put a stop to our random police encounters; they didn't want to stand around getting wet while they asked us questions about nothing, I guessed. I'd bought new tires for the van, and they seemed grippy enough, but it made me wonder where we should be when winter hit. Not these mountains. Not up north.

After all the back rooms and basements, I would've thought I'd seen the worst venues the country had to offer. I'd never played this particular barn, though, and this particular barn smelled like the cows had only recently vacated, and left a present on their way out the door. It was a modern milk cow shed, with rows of pumps and gutters running full with rain and manure. How could they not even have bothered to flush them out when guests were coming? I couldn't imagine an audience would want to sit there to listen any more than I wanted to smell that while I played. Its only selling point was a roof.

"Really?" I asked Silva.

"A gig is a gig, right?"

I sighed and followed him, choosing my steps with care. We walked out the other end of the barn and down a set of limestone steps set onto a hill, slippery even with the single galvanized pipe railing. I picked my way carefully behind Silva, with Marcia behind me. The gig bag on my shoulder was waterproof, and so was my amp's case, but it was going to be a long way down wheeling that heavy thing, not to mention Silva's amp, which did not have a case. Also not to mention that it would be an even longer trip back up if it was still raining. Still thinking, my head down, hood up to keep the water off my face, I ran straight into Silva when he stopped.

"Ta-da," he said.

I'd been concentrating so hard on the footing, I hadn't noticed we'd arrived at another building. Looking down, the ground still looked the same, grass clinging for purchase as its substrate became mud. We stepped into an older barn, though, or a new barn designed to look like an old barn, since this one didn't smell like cows. The tin roof amplified the rain to a near deafening volume, but there were no leaks. Fall dampness pervaded everything—rain was the overwhelming scent now—but the metal folding chairs laid out in neat rows were dry. So was the stage, an honest-to-goodness raised stage at the far end of the building. Lights hung from each support beam, and a couple of high-end speakers pointed out toward the audience seating.

"It's a real venue." I took it all in. "You were messing with me?"

Silva grinned.

"A real venue in a cow pasture," Marcia said. "How are we supposed to get my drums down here? Or your amps?"

Silva was still smiling. "There's a driveway that leads down to the side door. I thought it would be more fun to bring you down this way."

Marcia leaned against a post and examined the muck on her boots. "You mean we didn't have to walk down the Staircase of Doom? Or get soaked?"

"I'm still stuck on you making us think we were going to play in that cow palace. I'm not sure we're at the point in our relationship where you can drag me like that. You can bring the van down. I'm not going out in that monsoon again." I tossed the key at him and he snatched it out of the air.

"Fine, fine. It was worth it." He disappeared into the rain.

I shook my head again. I wasn't really annoyed; more relieved, really. Relieved I hadn't sunken to playing for a mooing audience. Relieved we didn't have to breathe cow for two hours. Underneath that, a little pleased to have people back in my life who felt comfortable enough to prank me. Nobody would go to that trouble if they didn't care.

"You must be Eric Silva's new band," somebody called across the room. An older man, in his sixties maybe, wearing jeans and a Hawaiian shirt.

"Yep," I said.

"Welcome to Music City. Have you played here before?"

"Years ago, with a different band."

"Glad to have you back, then. I'm Dave."

"Is this your place?"

"Yeah. The dairy is my cousin's, but he let me build this place. It looks like a barn to any drone passing overhead, and it's too far out in the country for anyone to complain about noise."

In the last few months' travels, I'd discovered that people had endless creativity when it came to carving out space for music. I told him about the 2020; he frowned sympathetically.

Silva backed the van up to the side door, and we went to drag the gear inside. The soundcheck went quickly and proved Dave a good engineer. After that, there was nothing to do but wait to see if anyone showed up in the rain.

I was curious to see who our audience would be. In this age of flying under the radar, it was hard to tell who to expect. The venues had their own methods of spreading the word, their own local networks. In several places, I'd played to only a handful of listeners, but I didn't mind. I'd play to whoever wanted to listen.

People began trickling in. This audience fell on the older age of the spectrum, like the antique store had. There were probably twenty of them visible from the brightly lit stage as we picked up our instruments to play. Silva had said to expect a musician's crowd, and we'd rehearsed based on that knowledge.

I was so caught up in the joy of playing again that it took me a few songs to notice that the audience wasn't really responding. A smattering of applause, but it felt polite. Obligatory. I tried not to let it bring me down. The rain added a cool ambience, and the barn was cozy and dry. We sounded good. Don't take it personally.

Dave had said to play for an hour, but by thirty minutes I felt like we'd overstayed our welcome. Metal folding chairs become instruments themselves when people start shifting in them. I couldn't figure out why they were bored.

"Should we cut it short?" I whispered to Silva between songs. "I don't think they're into us."

"Finish the set. They paid, so we should play. And Dave's enjoying himself, and it's his place. Play to him."

It was an odd feeling. I tried to put myself fully in the music, as I usually did, but there was a part of me observing us critically. We weren't doing anything wrong; it just wasn't our night. Only toward the end did I start to feel like there was somebody out there for us. The stage lights were bright enough that we couldn't see into the crowd, but for the last three songs one person made up for the others with their enthusiasm. It cheered me, and gave me the energy to finish on a high note.

There was no other band following us, so we didn't need to hurry to strike our gear. I hopped down from the stage to hang out by the merchandise table, which looked lonely in the corner. Nobody headed that way. Instead, they were rearranging the chairs into a circle. Chatting, then sitting down again, pulling cases out from under their seats. It suddenly became clear.

I walked back to where Silva and Dave chatted. "What kind of music do you usually have here?"

"Old-time and blues."

So that was the problem. They'd been polite, but we were just the opening act for a jam session. They wanted to play, not to listen. They probably weren't even into the kind of music we were playing. Oh, well. A practice in front of people wasn't a bad thing. A fiddle tune picked up, and I turned to listen.

They were excellent musicians, and their instruments filled the room in a way that felt organic.

I reminded myself that I needed to try to win every crowd, but I wasn't always going to succeed.

We packed our gear into the van, careful to be quiet so we didn't disturb the musicians, though they didn't look like anything would distract them. When our instruments were stashed, we went back in to graze at the potluck table. I filled my plate and leaned against a beam to listen while I ate.

Someone approached from the direction of the music.

"Hey," said Rosemary. "I missed most of your set trying to find this place, but you sounded great. I don't know why they weren't into you."

"It happens."

She shrugged and smiled. "I wasn't too obnoxious, was I?"

"No—I guess I appreciated someone cheering for us. Um, what are you doing here?"

"I've been trying to get in touch with you for months. Nobody would give me your phone number, which I suppose is fair, but I finally convinced Joni to give me your lawyer friend's contact info, and he said he wouldn't give me a way to reach you, either, but he'd tell me where you were playing, on the condition that if I went to see you I couldn't bring any device with me—I'm noncomm for the night."

My lip twitched at her use of the phrase; it sounded too casual from the person whose Hoodie recording had killed my venue. She must've mistaken it for a different objection, because she rushed to add, "Sorry. I know noncomm is a philosophy, and I know I'm basically the antithesis. I shouldn't have said that. I meant my Hoodie and my phone are both back at my place. No chance I'll lead anyone here other than the people I came with. I'm still horrified that I did that, even accidentally."

It still hurt too much to talk about the 2020. "How did you get here? Don't you need a device to operate most cars these days?" I'd only recently learned that, riding around Nashville in Marcia's little self-driving Chauffeur.

She waved in the direction of the musicians. "My friends Nolan and Sadie brought me. Nolan has a car, and he wasn't hard to convince after I found out there'd be a jam."

We both watched the fiddlers through their next song.

"So, Rosemary, are you still working for them?" I didn't even want to invoke the name, lest I bring them down upon this lovely space.

"Yeah, but that's what I wanted to talk—"

"You didn't drive all the way out here to convince me to play for those bastards. Tell me you didn't."

"It's not like that."

I turned my attention to the casserole on my plate. "I'm going to eat my dinner now. Thanks for coming. Have a good drive back."

"I didn't come out here to convince you to play for them."

"'For them' or 'for us'? You can't distance yourself if you're still working for them after what you did."

She sighed. "For us, then. But it's not like that. I've figured out a trick. I find a place that's got shows going on, and then I make offers if I see anyone good, and then I fake StageHolo out with a fake venue to raid. I've done it in Asheville and Charlotte now. Everybody wins. The bands that want a deal get a chance, the venue stays safe, StageHolo is off everybody's backs for a while."

I was a little impressed, but I didn't let her see it. "Has anybody been hurt? Or arrested?"

She looked down at her left ankle. "Me. Both. Getting hurt was my fault, and the charges are minor."

"Minor to you, but not to somebody who can't pay the fines, or got in trouble in the past. Or the wrong officer gets called in on the raid, and somebody gets hurt for real. That sounds like a fun bait and switch, but you can't possibly see yourself doing that forever. They'll catch on if you get even a little sloppy."

"I know, I know. I know it's not a real solution. I'm still trying. That's why I'm here."

She'd clenched her fists into balls, the knuckles whitening. I softened my tone. "What's why you're here?"

"I came to tell you I have another idea. Something bigger. First I need to ask: have you seen 'Harriet speaks truth'?"

"What's that?"

"It's a vid you need to see." She reached toward her neck, then dropped her hands. "Oh, crap."

I recognized the gesture for what it was: she was so rarely without her Hoodie that she hadn't connected her promise not to bring it with her need to show me something.

"Give me a minute." She waited for their song to end, then headed into the musicians' scrum to talk with her friend Nolan. I took the time to finally finish my dinner.

She put his Hoodie on herself as she returned to my leaning post, then took it off to present it to me like a trophy. I'd never actually handled one before. I put my plate on the corner of the potluck table and accepted the thing from her like it was something unclean; in point of fact, it was vaguely damp, from either the rain or Nolan's sweat. My choices were to hand it back or to put it on and find out what had her going, and I was curious. Once wouldn't hurt, as long as Marcia and Silva didn't see me; they'd never stop teasing me for my hypocrisy.

The only impediment was my complete cluelessness. After I wrestled with it for what must have seemed to Rosemary an eon, she reached over and put it right. "You don't have to do anything. I already queued it up."

The barn fell away. For one long second, I stood in blackout darkness. A moment later, I whizzed through the air just above the ground, following a drone that was following a noise. Oh. I was a drone, following a drone, hurtling across a lawn toward a wall. The sensation was disorienting and exhilarating at once. How had I never realized that all those hooded kids knew what it felt like to fly?

Then I recognized the gate, and I knew where I was, and when. The disturbance was me. Graceland. However many months ago. This video was shot by one of the drones hovering on the other side of the gate, watching me lose my cool. "We're still playing music in real life. Come find us."

I'd been eloquent that day. Poetic in my anger. I hadn't thought about it since, but now, watching myself, it was memory and artifact at once, filling in things I'd forgotten. Some of it had been pulled from my song notes, from things I'd thought but never said aloud. It mostly left me thinking I'd neglected finishing that song for far too long.

I struggled out of the Hoodie, momentarily disoriented. The other place had almost felt more real; no wonder these things were so popular.

"So what? The video's gone viral?" I couldn't think of the modern term, but I figured she'd follow.

"It's everywhere. Millions of views. Not only that, though. Here, I'll queue up—"

I hung on to the Hoodie when she reached for it. "You can tell me without showing. It's okay."

"You've got followers. People posting responses, saying what they're going to do, like your instructions said. 'Carve your initials into something. Brand them, paint them, shoot them, transpose them, change them entirely and sculpt yourself out of a new medium.' "

Fuck. Up until that moment, I hadn't entirely understood, but she had it memorized.

"Do they, uh, know who I am? Or am I just some woman yelling at a locked gate?"

"Nobody knew at first, but then somebody said you were a musician from Baltimore, and then there was a bunch of arguments about your band name, and they've decided your name is Harriet. All the videos say 'Harriet speaks truth' or 'Harriet is right' or 'Be like Harriet.' Well, except the ones that say 'Lady loses it outside Graceland.' "

Which meant in either case they hadn't connected my name, or "Blood and Diamonds." It wasn't a nostalgia thing. They were watching because they believed in what I was saying. Or because they got amusement out of watching what they thought was a breakdown; I couldn't help those people. But the others . . . the others were my people.

She recognized the look on my face. "You're thinking, 'How do I reach them?' "

"Yeah," I admitted.

"That's why I wanted to talk to you. I have an idea. We need you to say all that again for SHL."

I couldn't believe we'd come round to the same thing again. "You said that wasn't the idea."

"Not you signing for them—not you signing for us, I mean. You agreeing to do a one-time show."

"A, no, and B, didn't you say those things are choreographed and timed? Am I supposed to ask them to block five minutes for me to trash them?" I handed her the Hoodie and retrieved my plate to make a leisurely circuit of the potluck offerings. I wasn't hungry, but I put a sugar cookie on my plate to justify the movement.

"You call it 'five-minute vamp on D' or 'sixteen-bar intro' so that everyone knows when to come back in," she said when I circled round to her. "They won't pay attention to the content as long as the time is built in."

"This is ridiculous. Why would you think I'd want to do that?"

"Because it's the largest platform you could possibly get. You could subvert it."

I put the plate with the uneaten cookie on the table corner again. "It's not subversion. You keep working inside the system thinking you can change it from the inside. This works for them. They have zero incentive to change the way they do business."

"Better than not trying at all!" She waved Nolan's Hoodie at the musicians. "These people are nice, but is playing for this group getting you anywhere?"

We had reached an impasse. "Rosemary, you're not listening to me. If you think I said something so important, why are you ignoring the actual message? I said fuck StageHolo and I meant it. I'd rather play barns and back rooms for a hundred years."

"And you're not listening to me. You're being stubborn. You want to burn it down, but you're not interested in saving the people inside before you light the match? Take us with you! Tell us where to go." A tear ran down her face and she wiped it away with the back of her hand. "Tell me what it would take to get you to do one show. One show where I promise I'd make a way for you to tell them what you thought of them, for everyone to hear."

"I'd still be taking their money. I'd be endorsing them."

"You don't have to take their money. Or you could take the money and donate it somewhere. Argh. I didn't come here to argue with you. Why are you so stubborn?"

"And why are you so naive?" A couple of musicians tossed glares in our direction. I hadn't meant to raise my voice.

"You've given up on ninety-nine percent of the people out there, Luce. You're playing to the people who know to come find you. You would've missed me entirely. Or I would have missed you. I don't even know which it is. Forget it. If you can't understand this doesn't have to make you compromise yourself, I don't know how to explain."

She unclenched her fists and walked away. I thought of her making that same gesture as I watched her from my window at the 2020. She was letting me go again.

I didn't see her again that evening. She must've been somewhere around, since her friends hadn't left the jam, but she didn't come near me again.

Our plan had been to sleep in the van, then drive back in daylight. At one a.m., having driven all day and played a show, I slipped out. The ground between the barn and the van's side door was getting muddy, and I kicked my boots off under the bed before crawling into the backseat bed, hoping the others would do the same. Marcia appeared not long after, and we made out until Silva climbed into the front passenger seat a little while later, reclining it as far as it would go. The fiddlers were still playing, but it was a distant sound, a lovely soundtrack for sleep. One thing was for sure, they had more stamina than I'd ever had; my fingers would've fallen off hours before. I made a silent toast to musicians of all stripes before passing out.

I woke before the others. It wasn't physically possible to get out without climbing over Marcia. I tried to wait out my bladder, but that wasn't physically possible, either.

"Sorry . . ." I threw a leg over, searching on the floor for my boots, then reaching for the door handle. I slid out backward, feet first, into at least five inches of mud. It filled my low boots even as they sank. When I tried to step out of it, my left boot stayed behind.

"Ack." There was no place for my foot to go, and it was already covered in muck. I tried to find my boot with my toes, with no luck. At least it seemed to be mud run down the unpaved driveway, not manure. I gave up and settled my foot down into it.

The passenger door opened. "Don't step out," I said, too late.

"Well, that's fun." Silva lifted one muddy foot then the other, squelching. His sneakers had stayed on better than my boots.

"Getting out of here is going to be even more fun." The van was hubcap-deep. Had it been that muddy the night before? I didn't think so. I looked up the hill. "It looks like the entire road washed out down here."

When I slid the barn's side door open, the mud followed at a slow ooze. It had already made its way under the door and a few feet in. I used the bathroom, then investigated what remained of the evening's potluck: chips, a bowl of apples and oranges, chocolate chip cookies; all of those looked safer than the potato salad. I chose an apple and a hamburger roll.

"That's a good look," Marcia said, pointing at my feet. Hers were covered in mud, too, but her shoes had stayed on.

"Everybody's a critic," I muttered.

She joined me in snacking, then we busied ourselves looking for the tools to get the van out of the mud. She found some lumber behind the stage. I found a spade. I wasn't sure where Silva had disappeared to, so I got to work digging, starting with the spot where I'd lost my boot. I found it after a few minutes, though the digging itself felt Sisyphean. Every spadeful replaced itself. It didn't help that the rain hadn't stopped.

"I chose this life," I repeated to myself. A mantra. "This is my journey."

Marcia had joined me with a rake. Neither of us seemed to be getting anywhere. The lumber would help under the wheels, maybe, but I didn't want to try moving before Silva returned.

About twenty minutes later, he came around the side of the

barn, followed by a young man on a tractor, a long-haired blond farm boy out of central casting. The kid's eyes went wide. "I've seen you!" he said. In this setting, after the biblical rains, I half expected him to say my ghost was roaming the hilltops.

"You're famous," he said next, still staring. He turned off his tractor.

"That song was a long time ago."

I started to say more, but he shook his head, dismissing my protest.

"You're, like, everywhere famous." He motioned at his Hoodie. The video. "My dad said I'd like the music for once, but I didn't bother to come down the hill. He usually has fiddle jams. Did you play last night?"

"We did . . ." I almost apologized, then wondered what I was apologizing for. His fault he missed us, not mine.

"Can you say all that stuff from the vid again for me to record? So I can say you were here?"

That felt odd. Performative. "Let me think about how best to do that. I wouldn't want to get this place in any trouble."

"What if you bought eggs from me up at the farm stand and I recognized you?"

That seemed reasonable. "Okay, but after we get the van out of the mud."

His tractor made short work of the problem of our stuck van. We followed him up the hill at tractor's pace.

"What exactly are we doing right now?" Marcia asked.

I scraped at the mud on my boot. "I'm not entirely clear on that myself."

The eggs he was selling at the top of the hill were multicolored, heirloom. He handed me a carton and I stared at them while he filmed me, wondering what I was supposed to say. It felt weird trying to repeat whatever I'd said on the video; profundities on demand were not my wheelhouse. I put down the eggs and grabbed my guitar.

"This is a work in progress," I said, launching into "Manifest

Independence," the half-finished song I'd started writing by the Mississippi. I still didn't know how it ended.

The kid thanked me and promised to wait until the next day to post the video, so we'd have time to make our getaway.

"So you're in the prophet business now?" Silva asked from behind the wheel as I got back in the van. "What's the deal?"

"Not prophecy. I'm taking advantage of a platform. Time-honored tradition."

"If you say so. That boy was ready to follow you anywhere."

I'd gotten the same feeling. I turned an imaginary mic on myself, trying to turn it into a joke. " 'Ms. Cannon, you've just found out that ones, if not tens, of modern youths found a video of you making a fool of yourself. How does that make you feel?' 'I'm glad you asked, Bob.' "

"You can joke, but why? This might be a good thing."

"Hey, if I finish this song, do you want to record it sometime soon?" I asked to change the subject.

Silva and Marcia both responded enthusiastically, and we spent the drive home discussing album concepts—in between the flashing lights, pull over, rinse, repeat.

36

ROSEMARY

Remember Who You Are

The second she stepped out of the barn, Rosemary realized her error. She hadn't needed to leave. She could've sat with the musicians. She could've asked Nolan for his keys, or asked him to leave, though she'd have felt bad doing that when he looked so happy. She could've coolly approached the buffet and loaded a plate. Instead, she'd flounced out into the downpour.

Her pride kept her from turning around, and her pride was not waterproof; she was drenched in seconds. The roof overhang didn't help when rain came down sideways. Not just that; the floodlights outside the barn showed the entire road washing out down toward them in muddy cataracts. Not just that; this rain was cold.

Her healing ankle complained as she followed a pipe railing uphill to an empty dairy barn. The smell was a familiar one if not one she particularly liked: she'd grown up with three milk cows. One produced more than enough milk for their family—they bartered the excess milk with neighbors or turned it into cheese and butter—but her parents believed that cows were herd animals and deserved a herd; funny how they didn't apply the same logic to children.

From the dry doorway, she watched the lower barn's lights

flicker as people moved around. The sound didn't carry. Here she was again, watching community happen from afar, unable to take part. She didn't play an instrument. Everybody said that didn't matter. They said things like, "Not everyone needs to play—we need an audience, too!" But how did that jibe with Luce's carve something/play something speech? Was that screed only about music, or did it apply to other things, too? Maybe she was still getting it wrong, and that was why Luce wouldn't listen to her.

A big orange cat approached from the barn's interior, and let her stroke his back before stalking away with his tail held high. She missed the farm more than she had in a while. Missing it somehow made her resolve stronger. She had to figure out what her life was supposed to be. Some combination of these things that she loved.

Headlights appeared down below, then another pair, and she realized the jam must be breaking up. What time was it? She had no device to tell her. Late, anyhow.

Three a.m., according to Nolan's car. He had to manually drive it the first fifteen minutes, thanks to an error message with the navigation system, which kept telling them to find the road to proceed. It left her time to rant at him and Sadie about her conversation.

"What's so bad about working within the system, anyhow? The system pays us, and keeps our cars from crashing, and delivers groceries to people who can't leave their houses. Sure, it needs a little subverting here and there, but that improves the system. What does she want me to do? I can't do anything to help if I quit. The only power I have is in this job."

"Why do you want to please her so much anyway? Do you have a thing for her?"

Sadie looked unusually interested in Rosemary's answer to Nolan's question. "No! I . . . I want to help her, and I want her to help me. I think if we work together, we can make bigger things happen. And anyway, she makes me want to be better. I'm not even sure if she's as good a person as the image she projects, but when she sings she makes me want to fix the things she says are broken."

"Well, that's a powerful gift, to make somebody want all that."

"You heard her, too. Did you feel it?"

"Sure, a little. The band was a little raggedy, which makes sense since it was one of their first shows together, but I can see what you mean about her charisma. Hey! The car figured out where we are!"

He turned to her as the car took over driving. "So what's your plan?"

"I don't know. My plan hinged on getting her to agree to play. Without her, I've got nothing but what I've already been doing."

Sadie said, "That's not so bad, though. You get to listen to music and plan some fun shows and keep people out of trouble. That's not nothing."

"It's nothing if it goes on that way forever."

"You don't have to be the change all by yourself. You need to find people to help you."

"Like you guys did."

"That, and more. You need people who will call legislators, and people who will run for office, and people who will write articles and—"

"What you're talking about will take forever!"

"Maybe, maybe not. But I'll bet you somebody out there is already working on it, and could use whatever boost you give."

Rosemary wasn't convinced.

They rolled in late, and Rosemary slept most of the day away on Sadie's couch while Sadie dragged herself off to the coffee shop. When she woke in the evening, there was a text message on her phone from an unknown number.

Look I've been thinking. U said a 1 time show maybe I can do 1 time, my way

It could only be Luce. The time stamp said it had arrived two hours before. She immediately texted a response. I'm interested—tell me more!

"I'll tell Luce." It must have been a bandmate's phone.

"You look excited about something," Sadie said, coming through the door.

"I don't know yet."

"You don't know if you're excited?"

"I don't want to get my hopes up."

Rosemary spent the next day waiting for the call and trying to decide where to go. She didn't have to stay in North Carolina any longer—the cop hadn't shown up and her charges had been dismissed—but she wasn't sure where to go with the whole country in front of her. She couldn't stay on Sadie's couch much longer.

The bus took the better part of a day, giving Rosemary time to listen to Wilmington bands. Logistics took her new plans in stride. She asked for a room on the ocean and, after looking at maps, picked an area called Carolina Beach because it had "beach" in the name.

"It's, like, fifteen miles away from Wilmington," they warned. "There's not much out there."

"You let me go to my hometown without telling me it was too far from anything. Maybe I have a lead." She didn't, but that was beside the point.

"Do you know it's hurricane season?"

"Of course," she lied. She pulled up a weather map. "I don't plan on being there long, and there's nothing brewing."

From the bus drop-off, she called a single-cell to take her to the motel Logistics had booked. When she stepped out of the vehicle, the sun felt hotter on her skin than it had in weeks, brighter, and the air tasted like salt.

The Silver Bell Motel was two stories tall, with the first floor on stilts ten feet above ground level and rooms that opened directly to the outdoor walkway, unlike her fortress-like hotel in Baltimore. It was possible she was the only guest; the parking lot was empty and the whole area looked deserted.

She found the beach across the street and over a small dune

from the motel. Found. It hadn't been lost. You couldn't lose an ocean. She climbed the dune and caught her breath. How had she not expected it to be this big?

She pulled up her Hoodie and looked for an ocean backdrop she'd played before, just for reference, then dropped it again. There was no comparison. They'd gotten the horizon right, the colors, the sky. She remembered walking along the simulated beach, getting points for finding fancy shells and treasures washed in by the tide, listening to the waves lapping the shore.

What they'd missed: the wind, strong enough to freeze-frame the gulls as they took off and landed; the volume; the sand she kicked into her shoes within the first three steps, so that she had to take them off, then her socks, which she stuffed into the shoes to carry; the frigid water; the irregularity of the shells and other debris, when she'd always imagined each one perfect; the way the sea came closer, then receded, leaving her feet to sink in the muck. The multiple textures of sand: the dry dunes, the gritty debris that marked higher tides, the velvet damp closer in, if she braved getting wave-hit, which she did. The weight of the ocean. In the distance, the remains of houses on stilts, collapsed into themselves. Here was a thing that people had sullied, but you couldn't tell it if you didn't look that way. From where she stood, looking outward, the ocean won.

What was she doing here? That was the question of the hour. She'd arrived to find bands and to destroy their scene, or to fake the same. Was it such a bad future? Not if she could travel to places like this.

Her phone buzzed in her pocket, and when she looked, there was a message from the same mystery number giving a download code for one of the sites she could only access outside the Superwally/StageHolo networks. She entered the code, shielding her screen in the bright sun.

"Cassis Fire—Manifest Independence" appeared. The beach was empty, so she turned the volume up and played the song to the ocean.

When the last chord rang, she played it again. And again. And again, and again, until a low battery warning appeared. It didn't matter; the song was part of her now. She would never hear it without thinking of the beach, the gulls, and the absolute, boundless joy that started at her chest and expanded outward to fill her entirely when a song connected perfectly with a moment.

The lyrics were taken from the things Luce had said at Graceland, or else the things she said had been taken from the lyrics. It was instructive without being pedantic: an invitation, a challenge, a call.

Her phone died. She hadn't even responded yet. Hopefully Luce wouldn't think that was rude. She knew she should head back and charge her phone so she could write back, but the ocean was too much for her. She zipped her jacket up to her neck and lowered herself to the sand.

Rosemary requested a meeting with Management the next morning. Something big, she'd said, trying to see if she could rustle up a nongeneric manager in the process, if such a person actually existed. They didn't; not today, at least. Generic Management—Male (1 of 5) met her in the nonintimidating, regular-office setting.

"That was fast! You've only been in"—he paused before continuing—"Wilmington one night."

"It's not about here," she said.

"Oh? The message said you had something. We figured—"

"Luce Cannon."

"You found her again? In Wilmington?"

"I said it wasn't about here. I know where she is."

"And she's willing to sign?"

"She's willing to do one big show, then gone again."

His gears were clearly turning. "Luce Cannon: One Night Only. We do a special on that big song, maybe make up something forensic about tracking her down, lead it all up to a show . . . What was the name of that famous article? 'The Last Power Chord'? We call the concert the Last Last Power Chord, or the Next Power Chord, something like that, that she's coming out of retirement for one show only . . ."

"She'll be fine with all of that." They'd had this talk and figured it would go this way. Luce was not a fan of the coming-out-of-retirement angle, but it fed into the fiction of the thing. "She does have some specific guidelines for how it has to go down, though."

"The money, you mean? We'll have Contracts make her a good offer."

"No. She'll only do it under certain conditions."

"We'll see what Legal says."

Rosemary continued. "There has to be a live audience—"

Generic Management Man sighed. "Of course there does. Why should it matter if that's illegal?"

"—and she wants to choose the location."

"You mean which campus will host? That's not a problem."

"She doesn't want to do it on a campus. She wants to do it at a real venue." Those were Luce's words, real venue. "Nonnegotiable."

"We can't do that."

"Sure we can. We can do all of that. Patent Medicine did a 'music festival' on campus with an audience. It shouldn't be impossible to transport a camera rig somewhere."

"We have to apply for waivers from the state and federal government every time we do something like that. It's not simple."

"Who said anything about simple? This is going to be a logistical bear, and we're going to do it because this concert is going to make us a ton of money." She was careful to say us, not you. Rosemary Laws, Model Employee.

"Anything else?"

"We'll own the concert recording, but we point song links to her own site."

"Legal will *never* agree to that."

"They can hash it out, then, and see if she walks, but she'll probably give up merchandising if we give her that much."

He sighed again. "You're still on our side, right? It almost sounds like you're working for her."

"I'm not working for her. Let me know what you decide."

She disconnected and dropped her Hoodie. The ocean greeted her with a roar.

37

LUCE

Manifest Independence

The marquee from that last night Before still had my name on it. Of all the changes and incongruities and instances of past overlying present, I'd never once considered that one. It made perfect sense. The last show before we collectively gave up on trusting each other in proximity, captured in time. A memorial plaque for who we used to be.

"Oh, man," said Silva, and I realized whatever I was feeling as we approached must be even stranger for him, since he had worked there. He would have been the one waiting every day for the go-ahead to change the sign during that hellish upheaval.

The C and H from the name had fallen or been stolen, leaving THE PEA. Grackles nested in the remaining letters and most of the bulbs surrounding the sign looked like they'd been shot out. Somehow, nobody had stolen the movable letters that read TONIGHT: LUCE CANNON.

Looking closer, we saw the marquee was propped up by a couple of new-looking jacks. The posters were gone, the glass ticket booth boarded up, the sidewalk cracked. Time was a bastard on the best of days.

"This poor old girl." Silva shook his head as we turned down the alley.

Marcia watched us both with curiosity. "Why is it always 'she'? I don't think I've heard someone call a building she before, but ships and guitars . . ."

Silva shrugged. "I have no idea, but if the outside looks this bad, I'm a little nervous about the inside."

"They would have taken any opportunity to move us to their campus if it wasn't possible to play here," I said, though I was wondering the same thing. I had pictured the place frozen in time, perfectly preserved. Stupid. Preservation is an action, not a state.

We turned another corner, and I was surprised to see that the back was as busy as the front was deserted. A dozen trucks and vans crowded the loading dock. We had to block one of them in, but it was reasonable to think they wouldn't be leaving before us.

I shouldered my guitar and looked at the others. "Last chance to turn around."

"This was your idea, not ours," Marcia said. "That's completely your call."

"Silva?"

"I want to see what she looks like inside."

Backstage bustled with activity. Nobody gave us a second glance; if we were there, we belonged. Some of them were assembling camera rigs, others trying to raise a new curtain, others loading more equipment in through a side door halfway down the room. We walked past and onto the proscenium.

"Oh, man," Silva repeated.

The seats were gone. Paint hung from the walls in long strips, and the place carried a vague smell of—water? Trash? There was a stain in the shape of Australia on the ceiling above the balcony. A couple of workers snaked wires off the stage and around the wall to a corner in the back, where they'd set up a makeshift control booth.

Still, it was beautiful. The wall sconces, the stage, the elegant balcony molding, the chandeliers. A thought crossed my mind that if someone had been using it as a secret venue, I might have ruined everything for them by choosing to play here when I could have picked anyplace. I could have made them film me at the 2020. Why had I chosen this? Because, I told myself, you wanted to show them a past that didn't have to be past. Or something like that.

"You made it! And you were right: this place is beautiful! I've never seen anything like it."

I turned to see Rosemary approaching from the wing. Funny how I always heard her before I saw her. You had to give the kid this: she was enthusiastic. I felt a pang of sympathy for her "never seen anything like it." It had been a beautiful room, but not unique in its day.

"Is everything going okay?" I asked.

"Yeah. It's all working out pretty well. The city owns the building, and they had no problem turning on the electricity as long as we were willing to pay to get everything inspected. It mostly needed a good cleaning. The company liked that the chairs were gone. Said it'll be easier to film. All the sound equipment was sold off a long time ago, but we would've brought ours in either way. And you should've seen how excited they were about that marquee with your name on it. It was like they'd discovered an intact dinosaur fossil. Um, you're not the fossil in that scenario. The marquee is."

I sighed. More nostalgia. Maybe I brought it on myself by picking this place, this format.

"So, um, thank you for telling them to make me your artist liaison for this gig. I don't really know what that entails, since it isn't part of my normal job, but tell me what you need from me and I'll do it."

It wasn't like we'd ever had an artist liaison for anything before. A host supplied by the enemy. I didn't really know what to ask for, but scrambled for something to make her feel useful. "Could you rustle up some people to get our gear inside? It's faster with help."

She saluted and disappeared, returning with two burly guys and a burlier woman.

"Minions! Excellent!" Marcia led them out the door. I followed, but they picked up two more people along the way, and I didn't end up needing to carry anything. One trip, and everything was in for us to assemble.

"Closer to the front," I said to Marcia as she unrolled the rug that kept her drums from moving. "I want us all tight and intimate if we're playing for cameras."

She saluted and dragged her rug closer to me. Techs began to circle us, taping marks onto the wooden floor.

"Hi, I'm Luce," I said to the guy miking my amp.

"Hey," he said without introducing himself.

It took a while for them to get the sound under control, the speakers emitting earsplitting crackles and squeals like creatures that didn't want to be tamed. The challenge would be creating a mix that worked both for their recording and for the live space. I was more worried about the latter.

"Rosemary, how many tickets did you sell?" I asked the question into the mic and she appeared in front of me instantly.

She gestured out into the empty room. "They gave away ten pairs of tickets in a contest, along with transportation to get here."

Ten pairs. "What was the contest?"

"They had to say where they first heard 'Blood and Diamonds.' I know that's not what you would have wanted, but Promotions insisted that was the best way. There were a lot of entries, for what it's worth."

This was the first I was hearing about it, but the contest was a distraction. "What I'm trying to say is it's going to sound awfully boomy in here with no seats and no bodies to absorb the sound. Twenty is nothing in a room this size."

"Maybe it'll work itself out?" She looked away again.

"Twenty isn't what I had in mind when I told you I needed a live audience."

"I know, but it's all I could get them to agree to. Better than none, right?"

"I guess it is what it is. We'll make it work." Not much choice.

We eventually came to a point where I was satisfied with the live sound and the nameless soundperson adjusting levels didn't seem to be fiddling anymore. Then we went through it again for the recording rigs and the lights. Beneath it all, I heard the grumbling of the techs as they repositioned their equipment. "What the fuck are we doing here?" one of them muttered to another, and I wondered the same. What was the point of my insisting we do this here if there wasn't any audience? No, twenty wasn't nothing. I'd play for ten or five or two if they were into it. I'd just have to convince these contest winners that the recent stuff was as good as the song they knew.

When the techs were finally done, I asked into the mic if I could have a minute to play.

"Sorry," came the voice I'd started thinking of as the Director, since he hadn't bothered to introduce himself. "No time."

I remembered standing on this stage, playing for myself and nobody, in the last minutes before the world changed. This was the problem with trying to re-create a memory: the overwrite took the memory down with it.

The Director himself approached from the booth, carrying a printed set list with times for our songs, and a stack of lyric sheets. I'd submitted it all two weeks before. "This is all still good, right? No changes?"

"No changes, unless you'll let me drop 'Blood and Diamonds,'" I said. It sat there at the end of the set, taunting me. The one thing SHL wouldn't budge on: no show unless I closed with it.

He opened his mouth.

"I'm kidding," I said, before he could tell me what I already knew. "I wouldn't dream of dropping the big finale."

Maybe because of my joke, he insisted we go over details for every song in the set; by the time that was over, it was almost time for the doors to open. For all twenty people.

A nice spread awaited us in the green room, every single item from the ancient rider I'd sent them. Rosemary's doing, I was pretty sure. The room looked the same except the pictures were gone. I looked around the space remembering other people, another time, the last minutes Before. When I sat on the couch, a cloud of dust rose up around me. "Tell me one more time why we're here?"

"Dude," Silva said. "You keep asking that like this wasn't your doing. I have no problem with it, and I hope it goes down like you're planning, but maybe it's time to own it either way."

"I know. I know. It'll be worth it. It's not selling out."

"It's kind of selling out," Marcia said, "but that term needs redefining anyhow. This is temporary selling out for a good cause. It's not a permanent state."

"That helps a lot," I told her, sticking out my tongue. "Hey, Silva, what happened to the eight-by-tens?"

He surveyed the bare nails on the walls, then turned and winked at me. "I have no idea what you're talking about. I'm sure nobody who worked here would have taken them home for safekeeping."

Somebody knocked on the door, and my stomach flipped. This is not a conjuring, I told myself. It goes down differently.

Marcia said, "Come in," and Rosemary entered. She looked nervous, but not upset. I waited for her to tell us to turn on the news. "Do you need anything?"

Relief washed over me. "An audience."

"There are twenty very excited contest winners on their way."

"You know that wasn't what I meant."

"I'm doing what I can, Luce. And I did the other thing! Everyone who shared the Harriet video knows that's you now. I've been gearing them up for this for weeks. I said if they waited for the end of the show they wouldn't be disappointed."

I kept forgetting the audience I couldn't see.

"SHL is kind of confused about the numbers, to be honest," she said, as if she'd heard my thought. "Way more first-time viewers than they expected, and the demographics are wild in every category."

Huh.

She ducked out of the room again, and I squeezed into the bathroom to change. Nobody had cleaned the toilet in years.

"Isn't that a little on the nose?" Marcia asked, pointing at my shirt when I emerged. I'd painted "Is this real?" on the front and "This is not real" on the back.

"You should've seen the runners-up." I'd made and discarded "Fuck StageHolo," "Burn yr Hoodie," "Ask me about my corporate overlords," and "You are a wholly owned subsidiary" before deciding they might blur those out.

Another knock on the door. Another moment where I steeled myself for bad news, but it was only a tech giving a five-minute warning. Silva left the room to tune his bass and my guitar one more time, so they'd be ready when we stepped out. Marcia and I followed.

The last time I'd been here, the last time I'd looked out from this same wing, I'd wondered how to perform at all on such a broken night. I didn't know how to address the crowd. I remembered every single song I'd played that evening, every word I'd said. That audience and I, we'd needed each other.

The room had looked empty with so few seats filled that night; I'd called them all forward. Now it was far emptier. Two people sat in metal folding chairs near the room's center. The rest—eighteen of them, I presumed—had scattered in pairs in such a way that they were near the barrier but nowhere near each other. A phalanx of cameras filled the space between the barrier and the stage.

"How are we supposed to play to that?" I asked. "They won't even come near the front."

"They're fans, Luce," Marcia said. "Even if they only know the one song. Even if they've never been to a show. Don't judge them."

She was right.

"Here we go," said the Director's voice in my in-ear monitors.

The house lights dimmed. Three spotlights waited for us, ringed by cameras. When we walked out, they shifted to make a path for us, then shifted again to close the route behind us.

We were greeted with a scattering of applause from the scattered audience.

The Director spoke in my ears. "Don't worry, we're beefing up the crowd noise for the simulcast."

I hoped we weren't going to have to listen to him through the whole show.

"The second you step to the mic, you're on," the Director said. He'd told me twice earlier. I wanted to tell him to shut up and leave me alone in my head.

I lingered outside the light. I couldn't see the empty room, but there was no mistaking the silence; a full house could never be this quiet. I had to pretend. Pretend this was a 2020 show, or one of the dozens of tiny spaces I'd played alone or with the new band. Those places were sometimes empty, too. It wasn't lack of audience wigging me out; it was lack of response. The moment I started playing, we'd be beamed to millions of Hoodies expecting me to pretend I was playing directly to them. I needed to feel them, and there was no way to do that.

The techs had taped a square where they wanted me to stand except for the times they'd scheduled movement. Taped down my set list. Taped exact channels where I was allowed to roam to interact with Marcia and Silva at the specified moments. Lots of shows were choreographed, I reminded myself, even if mine never had been. I'd agreed to all of this. Why?

Without triggering the cameras, I called to the room off mic. "Come closer. Please."

Nobody moved. I gave Silva and Marcia a panicked look over my shoulder, which they didn't return.

"Treat it as a practice," Silva said. "We can just have fun."

"Luuuuuuuuuuuuce!" came a ragged shout from nearby. I shielded my eyes and spotted Rosemary standing front and center. Play to Rosemary. She had to be the one person in the room who was there to hear me, rather than the ghost of who I used to be. Play to Rosemary. Play.

I stepped forward.

The first song on the set list was "172 Ways," which I'd written specifically for this new trio. Before I could think myself into another corner, I kicked into the opening riff. The band joined me after four repetitions, Silva matching my guitar two octaves lower. We ripped through the song. I relaxed a little. The sound boomed through the room, but it didn't sound awful. Play it to Rosemary; maybe she'd be excited to hear something she hadn't heard before.

We let the last chord ring, and Marcia drummed through the transition between songs, as planned, seamlessly switching beats. No surprises. She counted off, and we moved from "172 Ways" into "Don't Even Think About It." A 2020 audience would have screamed at that point, but I didn't hear anybody, even Rosemary. No applause in the transition, either. In a real live show, we might throw a few extra bars in here to build, but we'd been warned not to do that. Stick to the plan.

I tried to force myself into the moment. The second song was always the one that mattered. First song, some people still aren't paying attention, and you're still feeling out the room and getting comfortable. The second song is where you win them over.

A light appeared in the back of the house, a single bright spot in the darkness. Interesting, but playing to a guide took concentration, so I put it out of my mind. Another change in the darkness halfway down the room, on my left. We kept going. The chorus came around, and this time I heard a couple of voices singing along. Rosemary, maybe, and maybe one of the contest winners had actually seen me play before? This song had been around a long time. It was possible.

The edges of the dark changed. Something was happening just beyond my vision. I wanted to know what it was, but there was no good way to find out. People were coming closer; that was it. Bodies filled the space beyond the barrier.

The song ended with a build and a sudden drop-off, stopping on the IV chord, no resolution. This time, the applause was far more robust than it had been when we walked out; much louder than I'd expected twenty people could be, but maybe their clapping carried in the empty space. Maybe they'd reached some kind of acoustic sweet spot.

Except that wasn't it, because they kept cheering, and it was more noise than twenty people could make.

"Next song needs to start," said the voice in my ears.

Next song was "Look, a Gift Horse," four to the floor, pulsing like a disco. It had a long enough intro for me to look around, long enough to take a few permitted steps toward Silva. I was supposed to stay with the spotlight, or move slowly enough for it to stay with me, but I deliberately zagged forward before turning, so I could see into the house.

"You're off track," said the voice in my ears.

I crossed the stage to Silva, as I was supposed to. Leaned over to play guitar to guitar, and whispered to him, "There are people out there."

Lots of them. From the stage's edge, where really, I should be allowed to play, I'd seen them. Two doors were open, one at the back and one on the side, and a steady stream of people poured in.

I made my way back to my mic, mind buzzing. What was going on? The Director in-ear hadn't said anything yet, but his focus was probably on what his monitors showed, not the actual theater. We were part of a fiction he was creating, which didn't have any room in it for the reality of the situation.

Whoever they were, I felt their presence. The room's sound changed, and so did the energy, which was to say energy existed now that hadn't minutes before. Shapes writhed, shifted, danced. Silva and Marcia felt it, too, or else they felt the change in me and responded. I hadn't realized how lackluster the beginning must have been.

I'd approached this show as an obligation, something I'd promised without fully committing myself. Body, but not heart, the concert an orchestrated necessity leading up to an orchestrated action. Not once had I considered it to be a real show, of the kind I gave night after night for audiences small and smaller, even though I'd picked the venue deliberately.

I'd lied to myself about not wanting a conjuring. Somewhere out there, in their Hoodies, thousands watched and listened. Some of them because of StageHoloLive and "Blood and Diamonds" and this silly comeback feature, but some because they'd seen a video that made them think I might have something worthwhile to say. Why did I have to keep learning that there was never a moment to phone it in?

I turned my brain off, then. Turned off the part of me that debated where I should be on the stage, and what I should say next, and what song came next, and who was out there listening, remotely or in person. Play for all of them. Play to reach just one of them. Play.

When the song ended, the cheers were definitely louder than they'd been at the beginning. I still couldn't tell how many people were out there, but they were into it. I wanted to greet them, but we'd been given no permission to talk until the second-to-last song. We launched "Ricochet," then "Noise on Noise," then "Light Me Up." Brought it down for "Leaving Town"; I couldn't see Rosemary anymore, but she was there in the song. Then "A Minor Second," and everyone was there in my head, and I sang to April and my family and Alice and the 2020 and all the people who'd passed through my life, or who'd let me pass through theirs. With no filler, we sped forward through the set, barreling toward the one moment I'd truly been waiting for, until we were there.

The space we'd left for "sixteen-bar band introduction" came just before the song. They wouldn't cut me off at this point, not when we hadn't played "Blood and Diamonds" yet.

I turned to Marcia and Silva. "Watch me for the changes," I said, though we'd discussed it already and it didn't need to be said. They rolled into the groove we'd chosen, ready to follow. The underpinning to disguise my intent, to make it harder for editors to clip any of this out for their on-demand video after the fact.

I shielded my eyes with my hand to see beyond the spotlight. In a normal show, I'd ask to turn the house lights up, but I knew that wasn't allowed in this in-between space. Still, I could tell they were out there.

"Hi," I said. "I suppose you're all wondering why I gathered you here today."

Don't be silly, I told myself. You have sixteen bars to do this. You know what you want to say.

I told them about the last show here and why we'd played that night. I told them about the parking lot the night before. And the nights after, waiting to be told we could tour again. About April getting sick, the fear, the protests, the list on my collective's wall of all the things we lost.

The Director's voice hit my ears. "That's sixteen bars. Launch the song."

I pulled the monitors from my ears and kept going. "I used to own this club called the 2020. Not Before; up until pretty recently. I tried my best to make it a home base for every musical weirdo looking for community outside of hoodspace, and we made some pretty good music there. It isn't that hard to carve a space like that if you're willing to break the law, but there's no reason for it to be illegal anymore. We need to take community back ourselves—nobody's going to give it to us."

I told them about the 2020, and how they could do the same or similar for art or storytelling or theater if music wasn't their thing. Hoping this wasn't the moment they cut us off, I told them what StageHolo did to venues, and what I thought they needed to do, the little actions and the big ones.

"I think enough time has passed. It's okay to be afraid, but we don't have to let it rule us. We're all afraid; it's what we do when we're afraid that matters. People are a risk worth taking. Let's create something new together."

That was the cue Silva and Marcia and I had worked out to kick the song for real. Without monitors, I didn't know if we were still on the air, if the Director was shouting at me or had given up on us entirely, but I didn't care anymore.

"Manifest Independence." The glowing lyrics hidden behind a

dresser in a hotel in this very town. The second draft, played years later to a bunch of drones at Graceland. Revised again until it became actual song, rather than screed, then revised again, until it said everything I needed it to say. An instruction manual, a guide, a call to action.

Without monitors, I couldn't hear my guitar or my vocals, but I had the beat behind me, the anchor of Silva's bass. I bashed at my guitar. My cuticles split and bled. My voice was full, guitar strong: we were all one living organism. "Manifest Independence" was a seismic shimmer, a drumbassguitar wall of noise; sound made physical, tangible, breathable. A benediction. All my hopes for a new After to strive for together, a new and better Now, however long it took to build. Everything that mattered in the moment.

I broke a string, then another. Pulled a third off to get it out of the way. Silva and Marcia were right there with me, following as I repeated the chorus, echoed it with the strings I had left, the voice I had left, the last of my energy. I didn't want it to end. We finally brought it to a clattering stop, but it was hard to tell, because the room was just as loud when we hit the last chord, full and screaming. I didn't know where this audience had come from, if I had drawn them from my mind, but I was willing to believe in them for as long as they believed in me, as long as they spread the good contagion, the one that answered our song in one voice, saying we're with you, we're here, we did this thing together.

"Blood and Diamonds" was an afterthought. I switched to my acoustic because the electric was out of strings, and stuck the monitors back in my ears. How did StageHoloLive bands handle broken strings, given their strict timing? A question for another time.

"This is for the contest winners," I said in the smallest act of appeasement ever. I didn't hate the contest winners. I hoped they weren't too put out by the mystery crowd, if the mystery crowd was even real.

I didn't hate "Blood and Diamonds," either. Wouldn't have played it given the choice, but I didn't hate it. I knew it had gotten me here. It wasn't the song I needed anymore for me; if it still spoke to others, reminded them of a place or time where it mattered to them, that was okay, too. I played it like it mattered, like my nineteen-year-old self had meant it.

The song ended, met with extended applause. I wiped my sweaty face with my equally sweaty arm. "Thank you," I said, meaning it.

"Hold still for three . . . two . . . one," the Director counted down, "and we're clear."

The house lights came on. The space was full of people, still cheering, even as they edged toward the doors.

"What the fuck?" asked the Director. As if they'd heard, the crowd emptied out. Not frantically, not crushing each other, just a steady stream toward the exits. A moment later, twenty confused contest winners stood scattered around an otherwise empty room.

38

ROSEMARY

Coda

Rosemary's instructions to the people she'd invited were clear. One thing she'd learned in her diversion shows: give everyone a way to get in and out safely—don't withhold any information. Some had already been through this with her a couple of times and knew how it went. Some of the audience had been through real raids, like everyone she'd convinced to come from Baltimore. The riskiest were the ones she'd reached out to in hoodspace and invited to experience the real thing after they'd raved about the Graceland video.

It had gone as well as she'd hoped. She'd unlocked all the doors before the show started, and they waited until after the first song to start slipping in. StageHolo hadn't bothered with security for twenty contest winners. Any managers or executives who were watching watched remotely, and the cameras were all pointed at the stage, not the audience. The camera operators and sound engineers all had jobs to do and singular focus. The company would hesitate to risk calling the cops and interrupting the show for all the SHL viewers. Ironic that this might prove to be the safest gig of all.

Luce's energy changed as the space filled. She needed that audience. Once she could feel them in the room with her, she relaxed and played like she had at the 2020. The kind of show you had to be there to experience fully.

The 2020 people were used to proximity and crowded close, as did the others Rosemary had met at shows. They led the way for those who had ventured out of hoodspace for the first time at her invitation, people who hadn't gone looking for secret venues, or hadn't known they were out there to seek, like Rosemary in her own personal Before. Their body language interested her: the ones who had done this long ago and let memory dictate their behavior; the ones who were clearly trying to conjure their own invisible bubbles of space. She wanted to tell them all they would be okay, that this was a first step, that it would get easier. A few had Hoodies up. Recording, she hoped, so there would be a second record of this show, one that included the full audience, and couldn't be edited by the company.

She entered hoodspace once herself, partway through the set, to see what the SHL viewers saw. She could've spawned directly into the show, but she chose to enter from outside. They'd rendered the marquee as it was meant to be, all letters whole and lit. Inside, a vast, crowded space, made to look like the Peach but more generic. She found a path through and approached the front. Luce's eyes were open, roving the crowd she couldn't see, an act of faith Rosemary had never credited before. She looked worn but happy. Her angles were sharper than Rosemary remembered, her arms ropy and muscular and bone thin.

Leaving the concert playing in the background, she opened a staff chat to see what the techs were saying; they were frantic and overwhelmed. They'd had to mirror the show dozens more times than they'd expected to accommodate for all the extra traffic. She wasn't really supposed to be there, but it had been easy enough to get access to their channels.

Almost as easy as the other tiny tweak she'd made: the one where she'd sneaked into the back end of the SHL site and created a free guest code for the show, a code which she'd distributed far and wide through an anonymous account. SHL would still make bank. If a few thousand people had happened upon a discount code, well, that was nobody's fault. A glitch in the system.

When Rosemary dropped her Hoodie again, she felt a momentary dislocation; her actual position was ten feet left of where she'd been standing in the virtual space. Luce was a smaller figure onstage than in hood, but the music hit in a different way. It surrounded Rosemary fully, emanating from the amplifiers, pulsing from the speakers, and up from the floor, and from the people around her, dancing and singing along. She joined them.

Luce had told her she'd be using the penultimate song to talk to the audience, wherever they were, and when the time came, Rosemary listened along with them. She was them. It was everything she'd thought it could be: a call to action, short term and long term. If it spoke to the rest of them the way it spoke to her, it would work.

"Let's create something new together," Luce said, and then, by some invisible cue, the song that had been building behind her exploded. Rosemary could go to shows every night for the rest of her life and she'd never cease to be amazed at the way musicians spoke to each other onstage without speaking. Rosemary shot a grin at Sadie and Nolan, standing a few feet to her right, and they both returned her smile. This was what she had promised them. The same band from the barn show, but not the same performance, not the same songs.

This was the song from the Graceland gates, the song she'd been sent at the beach, but bigger, more fully realized. As big as the ocean. She dropped any thoughts of the company, the job, the people she'd brought in, the trouble, the room, her body, the bodies around her. Luce was a giant, she was the whole room as she attacked her guitar, but Luce didn't matter anymore, either. Only the song, the moment, the song, the moment, the moment, the moment she was in and already past, looking past, saying I am here, I am here, I will always have been here, everyone here is marked by their presence.

And then it ended. Luce stood onstage again, a human-sized person above them, staring out as if she couldn't quite see them but she knew they were there. Strings dangled from her guitar in all directions. One of the strings must have sliced her when it snapped: a thin line of blood trickled down her forehead, which she wiped away as if it were sweat.

Rosemary had told people to leave during "Blood and Diamonds" or right after, before SHL could figure out what to do about them. She knew she should be helping clear the room, but she couldn't resist stopping to listen to "Blood and Diamonds." No matter how many times she saw Luce in the future, she knew she'd never hear her play that song again.

It sounded different with this trio, different with the years on Luce's voice. Not in a bad way, but in the way of something welcome and familiar and changed. She wasn't a kid in a hospital anymore, either; she could hold on to the memory of the song's reassurance without being called back there. She clapped and cheered as hard as she could to make up for the dwindling crowd.

The lights came on, leaving Luce and her band looking mystified. Her bassist whispered in her ear, and she handed him her guitar and climbed down to chat with the contest winners, who looked equally confused, but satisfied.

Rosemary took a moment to pop back into hoodspace to see whether people were talking about the show. When she ventured into the discussion forums, they were full of people trying to figure out what to do to answer Luce's call. A law student offering to start a group to take on congregation laws, someone else saying they wanted to host a show in their basement, someone else talking about running for office on a pro-congregation platform. Good.

Luce was chatting with a contest winner. An artist liaison should probably check if the artist needed anything, but Rosemary was suddenly afraid to approach; afraid she hadn't done enough, or that she'd gone over the top, that she still might not be forgiven.

Then Luce spotted her, and she smiled, and Rosemary knew that her terrible past actions might not entirely be past, but she'd been given another chance.

Rosemary tried to make herself unobtrusive, hoping the SHL employees who had seen the crowd wouldn't associate it with her. They all seemed to be pretending it hadn't happened, since they couldn't explain it. A few contest winners stood chatting with each other, still energized, buzzing with excitement. They hadn't left yet even though the concert had been over long enough for the equipment to all be packed away. Canned music played over the loudspeakers, and two women danced by the exit.

"Thank you." Luce appeared beside Rosemary, holding out her arms. Her back was soaked with sweat, her forehead smeared with blood, but it didn't matter. When they hugged, it felt familiar. "Do you want to take a walk? I wouldn't mind a walk."

Rosemary recognized Luce's mood, the way she'd always surrounded herself with people after a show. She nodded. They exited through the front doors, still unlocked. Across the street, past the parked cars, there was an overgrown path down into a small park, broken-branched trees lining either side. The path led them to a tiny footbridge, where they leaned on their elbows and looked down at a stream, shallow but fast moving.

"I thought that went really well," Rosemary said.

"Great, really. Sound could've been better, but we couldn't have asked for a more perfect evening." Her eyes shone, the same postshow glow Rosemary remembered. She'd seen it in other performers, too, but few fed on live music the way Luce did.

"You were amazing."

"Thanks. Uh, was I hallucinating, or were there a few more people in there for part of the show? Or is that part of the StageHolo experience? I could've sworn . . ."

"I might've invited a few people. I'd heard you wanted an audience."

"Nice, kid. Was that company-approved?"

Rosemary shook her head, trying to underplay her pride. "Not approved. We'll see whether I get in trouble, or if they're still happy with me for bringing you in."

"So you're going to keep working for them?"

"I don't know what to do anymore. You're right that I'm perpetuating the system, not changing it, but I keep feeling like if I stayed long enough, maybe I could get them to see these are stupid policies."

"Maybe," Luce said. "I guess there's something in helping them see there's room for us to exist."

They both grew quiet, watching the stream run beneath the bridge. There was movement in the trees, and an owl darted out of the darkness to skim the water. It came away with a small silver fish writhing in its talons, then disappeared back into the woods.

"Huh." The look on Luce's face was pure amazement.

Rosemary was surprised, too. "I've seen hawks attack package drones. And mice in the fields. I don't think I've ever seen an owl hunt before."

"I grew up in Brooklyn. Pigeons and parrots."

Rosemary had never seen a single interview where Luce mentioned Brooklyn or her childhood. She decided not to call attention to it. "Hey, Luce, do you know if Joni is playing somewhere else now? I got her to talk to me once, but then she wouldn't respond after that."

"I think she's involved with a warehouse series. Outsider art and music and theater, all interwoven. Don't send your goons, please."

"I wouldn't! I'm trying to stop them from doing that, I really am. It's just going to take time." If she stayed, people she liked would always be saying that. That was her choice: stay and try to change things from the inside, or find another path. She was surer that other paths existed now than she had been.

Luce shrugged. "I should probably get back. We're driving tonight."

"You're still my favorite performer." Rosemary hadn't meant to say that out loud; it hung in the air.

"You need to get out more."

"Ha. Well, have a safe drive. See you down the road."

"Coming soon to a town near you. Look, if you ever want another option, maybe we could use you as a tour manager for a little while. Or booking agent. Or both. It would be way easier to arrange shows if we had someone more . . . plugged in . . . on our team. The money would be crap, and you'd have to get used to sleeping in very tight quarters, but it's an alternative."

"For real?"

"For real. Find me when you're ready." Luce turned to walk away.

"So you're just going to keep doing those little shows?" Rosemary called after her.

Luce stopped and looked back. "It's a decent way to spend forever."

Rosemary recognized the lyric from "These Turning Hands," but she didn't doubt that was exactly what would happen if Luce wanted it. She had a way of making things turn out. She was a small figure walking back toward the Peach now, shoulders uneven, gait hitched like someone balancing on a boat deck. She rounded a curve in the path and vanished from sight.

There were other things Rosemary would have liked to say to her. How she had learned to stand her ground in a crowd, as Luce had taught her; how the idea of a crowd had gradually become less terrifying. How the job she had invented for herself, her secret subversion, had brought SHL inches closer to what she had originally believed it to be. How she thought she might build a career trying to right her biggest wrong, and she still wasn't sure it would be enough.

Luce had once told Rosemary how you grabbed on to a single note and, if it sounded good, you played it until you were ready to pick a new one. And the thing she hadn't said, but Rosemary had learned from her, later: that in any given moment, there's no such thing as a wrong note. Any note can be played over any chord, and any chord can be played over any single note. That it's possible to be a note nestled into a chord, off but right, in the moment before the song moves on around you.

ACKNOWLEDGMENTS

The funny thing about having my first novel arrive on the heels of my first collection is that I got to do a lifetime's worth of thanking six months ago, and I'll probably have amassed another lifetime's worth in this chaotic year, but I'm writing this in the limbo in between. Even so, it's inevitable that I'm going to forget someone. This is an apology in advance, and an acknowledgment that it's absolutely impossible to thank by name everyone who had a hand in making this book happen. That said, here goes:

Thank you first and foremost to Zu for understanding why I need to do this and for making it easier, and for being the best person I know.

My agent, Kim-Mei Kirtland, is smart and wise and willing to answer even my most ridiculous questions. My hugest thanks to her and Megan Gelement and everyone else at HMLA.

I want to thank my editor, Rebecca Brewer, for believing in this book, and for having a clear vision of how to make it better. Also huge thanks to Megha Jain, Alexis Nixon, Tara O'Connor, Jessica Plummer, Sheila Moody, Miranda Hill, Jason Booher for the cool cover, and the rest of the team at Ace and Berkley.

Thank you to LJ Cohen, Donna Buckles, Kelly Robson, Amira Pinsker, Ellie Pinsker, and Marlee Pinsker for reading the first draft and giving excellent feedback, and then sometimes later drafts and random panicked questions along the way, and to Rep Pickard and Sherry Audette Morrow for reading various chapters at various times. Thanks to my writing buddy Kellan Szpara for not only keeping me company, but also for reading at least two drafts and helping me wrap my head around edits.

I want to thank Sheila Williams (and Emily Hockaday!) at *Asimov's* for buying and editing my novelette *Our Lady of the Open Road*, which features Luce at another point in her life. This novel wouldn't exist without that story, and that story always wanted to be an *Asimov's* story.

Thank you to the Red Canoe (Josie, Tina, Matt, and everyone else) for letting me write the entire first draft at their family table. Actually, I wrote the original story there, too.

Thank you to my father, to Esther, to Milton, to the Tudhopes, to the Verskins, to my mother and sisters and cousins and aunts and uncles and siblings-in-law and nieces and nephew, for your unwavering support and enthusiasm. I love you all very much.

Thank you again to my critique partners and workshop buddies and retreat hosts and Slacks and SFWA, and all the blurbers and everyone else in this amazing community. I absolutely adore the writing community I've found, both locally in Baltimore and around the world. Thank you all, individually and as a group, for your friendship and support. You inspire me.

Lastly, stories and music work on similar magic. This book wouldn't exist without music and the music community, even though I've been neglecting that side of things of late. Thank you to SONiA for being the first person to take me out on the road and show me how to live a principled life in music, and to her band disappear fear for teaching me how to always have a clean towel on the road. Thank you to John Seay and to my band-brothers in the Stalking Horses, Jes Welter, Chris Plummer, and Tony Calato, for every wonderful show. Thank you to every band I ever shared a stage or a circle with, and to every musician who ever stepped onstage and mesmerized me, some of whom have tributes hidden in this book. (Apologies to Rahne Alexander & the Degenerettes for titling a chapter after the song "Baltimore" and thus ensuring they have no idea it was meant for them.) I know this might seem like it belongs in my album liner notes instead of my novel, but not a single word of this book would have been possible without all those people and the songs they set loose in the world.

ABOUT THE AUTHOR

Sarah Pinsker is a singer, songwriter and author. Her short stories have won the Nebula, Sturgeon and Philip K. Dick Awards. Currently finishing her second novel and fourth album, she lives with her wife in Baltimore, Maryland and can be found online at sarahpinsker.com and twitter.com/sarahpinsker.